Folly

ALAN TITCHMARSH

Folly

HODDER &
STOUGHTON

First published in Great Britain in 2008 by Hodder & Stoughton
An Hachette Livre UK Company

1

A CIP catalogue record for this title is
available from the British Library

Hardback ISBN 978 0 340 93685 6
Trade Paperback ISBN 978 0 340 93686 3

Typeset in Plantin Light by
Palimpsest Book Production Limited, Grangemouth, Stirlingshire

Printed and bound in the UK by CPI Mackays, Chatham ME5 8TD

Hodder & Stoughton policy is to use papers that are natural,
renewable and recyclable products and made from wood grown
in sustainable forests. The logging and manufacturing processes
are expected to conform to the environmental regulations
of the country of origin

Hodder & Stoughton Ltd
338 Euston Road
London NW1 3BH

www.hodder.co.uk

For Annie Darling, with love and thanks

Contents

Acknowledgements

All novels nowadays seem to carry that disclaimer 'Any resemblance to actual people living or dead, events or locales is entirely coincidental,' so writing a novel in which a real character appears is rather a tricky undertaking. I have loved paintings of horses in general, and those of Sir Alfred Munnings in particular, for as long as I can remember, and can only hope that I will be forgiven for including him as a character in *Folly*. There is absolutely no evidence that he met any of the other characters, who live only in my imagination, but my portrayal of Munnings himself, along with his thoughts, opinions and manner of speaking is, I hope, accurate. I have gleaned much from his three volumes of autobiography – *An Artist's Life*, *Second Burst* and *The Finish* – and from Jean Goodman's *AJ: The Life of Alfred Munnings* and Reginald Pound's *The Englishman*.

Mary Ann Wingfield's *A Dictionary of Sporting Artists* and Sally Mitchell's *The Dictionary of British Equestrian Artists* have both been useful, though I have to confess that the latter contains no reference to John Macready and I hope the author does not mind me implying that it does. As an inveterate reader of auction and art catalogues, I must record my gratitude to Christie's, Sotheby's and Richard Green, and also to Paul Cresswell for his engaging book *Bath in Quotes*.

I am lucky enough to have friends who do not seem to mind being rung up at all times of the day to answer questions. I am enormously grateful to Steven Alais, who has advised on legal matters, to Luigi Bonomi for his own particular brand of enthusiasm and encouragement, and to Victoria Law, Bendor

Grosvenor and Philip Mould, who have given me valuable insights into the art world, which continues to be fascinating, rewarding and scary in equal measure. All of which is in danger of making this book sound like a learned treatise. The very idea! It is, as ever, a romantic adventure, and any mistakes – either factual or emotional – are no one's but my own.

I

Bath
November 2007

'Well, 'tis a curious place, to say the least,' observed Moon;
'and it must be a curious people that live therein.'
Far From the Madding Crowd (1874), Thomas Hardy

'Any more bids?'

In most salerooms this is not an anxious request. Brisk,
yes, at times chivvying, but not anxious. It can even be
delivered carelessly. But then the auctioneer on this occasion was not typical of his breed. Not the sort most usually
found in a provincial saleroom – the tweedy sort with florid
cheeks, a pair of half-moon spectacles to peer over and a
voice owing its resonance to Taylor's Vintage Port. No. He
was in his thirties. Just. Slim. Quite good-looking. And at
the moment he seemed a little uneasy. His name was James
Ballantyne, which made him sound rather more confident
and considerably more literary than he really was, and he
was the last in line (presently, at any rate) of a firm of
auctioneers who had been established in Bath for three
generations.

'Going once . . . going twice . . .' He scanned the room again.
'I'll have to let it go, then . . .' Those in the front row would
have detected the merest hint of a wince in that muscle just
above the top lip where involuntary reactions can often give
the wearer away.

And then, just as he was lifting his hammer, an arm was
raised towards the back of the saleroom. That was all he could
see – just an arm. He leaned sideways. The figure was partially

obscured by a pillar. He could make out the slender frame of a fair-haired woman in a red jacket. She moved into his eye line and smiled at him.

Those who noticed the earlier flicker of the facial muscle would now have detected a movement in the jaw, which, but for the summoning of an iron will, would have dropped open. Instead it was turned rather neatly into a breath, and followed by a question: 'Was that a bid, madam?' he asked, and then closed his mouth again, doing his best to look natural.

The woman nodded and raised her numbered paddle in confirmation. Number one.

It was a muscle in his cheek now that twitched involuntarily.

'With you at seven and a half thousand pounds, then . . . and against you, sir.' He paused and looked in the direction of the fat dealer on the front row who had made the previous bid. The dealer pointedly stared at the floor.

James Ballantyne cleared his throat. 'This really is a nice little Herring; I don't want to have to let it go at this price, but I am selling . . .' He cast his eye once more in the direction of the long-legged thoroughbred – the one in the painting – a dark animal with wild eyes, set against a stable wall and a manger full of hay. A horse blanket lay folded over the feeding trough. All things considered, it didn't exactly light his fire. He looked back at the young woman who had raised her arm. She fixed him with an unblinking stare, defying him to offer the painting to anyone else.

His loyalties were split now, between the bidder and his professional pride. John Frederick Herring was a respected artist, and the work was a good one; his mother would be disappointed it had not fared better. The woman was still staring at him, and now he could see the corners of her mouth breaking into a grin.

'The Herring's going, then . . .'

'Junior,' the dealer on the front row muttered to himself. 'Not worth it.'

'Selling, then, at seven and a half thousand pounds . . . All done?' He brought down the hammer and the customary soft murmur drifted around the saleroom. The blonde in the red jacket looked down. He could not see her expression now, as she recorded the price in her catalogue. He noted her name in his ledger. The dealer on the front row shot James a withering look and shook his head.

But James did not see. His head was filled with questions that he tried to put aside. Why was she here? Where had she been? But there was no time to dwell on them. He checked his notes. 'And so to lot two hundred and thirty-four – our final lot today. The Munnings.'

A man in a navy blue overall manoeuvred the painting in its gilded frame on to an easel to the right of the auctioneer's desk.

James soldiered on. 'The highlight of today's sale. A lot of interest here . . .'

It was a simple painting of a woman on horseback, set against a leaden sky. It measured twenty inches by twenty-four inches. The horse was a grey, and the woman was seated side-saddle in a riding habit and a wide-brimmed brown hat. The horse was arching its neck forward to graze. The woman held the reins with her left hand. In her right hand rested a riding crop, and she gazed directly out of the picture towards the artist with an expression on her face that seemed startlingly familiar.

The next few minutes he found hard to recall in detail later that evening. The bidding had been brisk and competitive. Within what seemed like the blinking of an eye the picture had sold for seven hundred and fifty thousand pounds, and the name he had written in his ledger was the same as for the previous lot. Both had been sold to the woman in the red jacket with the short blonde hair; the woman he had grown up with but had not set eyes on for the past five years. Her name had always had a magical ring to it. Artemis King. She hated it herself. Said it made her sound like a character from an action movie. As a consequence she had been known from childhood as Missy.

Like James – known to *his* intimates as Jamie – she had been born into this world of artistic expression and high finance. Her grandfather had founded King's Fine Art fifty years ago, while Jamie's had established Ballantyne's, the auction house. Both old men were pillars of Bath society now. But it had not always been so. Once, they were simply grammar-school boys with grand ideas. How life had changed. How well they had done for themselves.

2

Oxford
April 1949

Thou hast most traitorously corrupted the youth of the realm
in erecting a grammar school.

Henry VI, Part 2 (1592), William Shakespeare

It was the most perfect April day. The sort of day that makes
you forget things. Like the future. And exams. And earning a
living. The long trails of willow wands were still unblemished
by summer breezes and they sketched evanescent patterns on
the water as the freshly varnished rowing boat nudged its way
forward beneath them. The sky had been painted by Titian.
At least, that's what Leo Bedlington claimed. The rest of them
just laughed. Three of them, anyway. The other simply curled
his lip. Leo was reclining at the sharp end of the boat, trailing
his hand over the side. He was wearing cricket flannels (not
that he ever played), and the sleeves of a thick milk-white
jersey were draped over his shoulders. His fair hair, parted at
the side, flopped over his eyes and he would throw it back
from time to time and breathe deeply, murmuring, 'Bliss, just
bliss,' to no one in particular.

Alongside him, leaning forward with his elbows on his
knees, John Macready was having none of it. 'Bloody
Brideshead. What do you know about Titian?' The Glaswegian working-class tones sounded especially discordant on
such a day. And then he stopped himself. 'Oh. But I suppose
you've got a few?'

Leo's eyes were closed. 'Just the one.'

Their finals looming, the five students were out for an

afternoon on the river, putting aside books and papers, forsaking the Bodleian Library and the Radcliffe and making the most of the unseasonable weather.

'You see, Mac, you just walk into it, don't you?' Harry Ballantyne was on the starboard oar. In between the concentration needed to maintain his stroke, he grinned and looked over his shoulder at the two men lounging in the bows of the boat.

Tall and dark, he cut an unlikely figure alongside the stocky, sandy-haired youth who sat beside him and encouraged him to keep up. Richard King bit his bottom lip and pulled harder, the beads of sweat glinting on his reddening brow. 'When are you going to do some work, Leo? It must be your turn.'

'Tomorrow.'

'And tomorrow and tomorrow,' muttered Richard, as he pulled again on his oar.

'Does it matter? On a day like today does it matter?'

The four men looked in the direction of the voice. It belonged to the woman sitting in the back of the boat. Her long and slender legs were neatly folded underneath her on the varnished wooden seat. She wore cream slacks and a crisp white blouse with the two top buttons undone – enough to arouse curiosity, but not sufficient to encourage disparaging comment. Her feet, now hidden from view, were bare. On her head was a broad-brimmed straw hat, round which daisies were threaded, and in her expressive hands lay the ropes that moved the rudder to right and left. She wore a reproachful frown, and her pale features were set off by the bob of dark shiny hair that framed them. She was every undergraduate's dream of a girl. Well, almost every undergraduate's.

'You're so right,' murmured Leo. 'No point in falling out.' He closed his eyes once more and leaned back towards the water.

Richard and Harry glanced sideways at each other and,

with a brief nod, changed the direction of their stroke. The boat stopped abruptly, and with the deftness of a seal slipping from a rock into the waiting sea, the Honourable Leo Bedlington disappeared over the side with hardly a splash.

Seconds later his head emerged from the ripples – 'Bastards!' – and then he coughed up more river water before repeating the sentiment.

Mac leaned over the side and grabbed Leo's arm as the two oarsmen, now laughing uncontrollably, pulled in towards the bank and allowed him to clamber up on to the grass, the muddied cricket whites dripping with water from the Cherwell.

'You are mean,' scolded the girl. 'Leo did bring the hamper.'

The oarsmen showed no sign of contrition, but busied themselves with the unpacking of the wicker basket and the unstoppering of the bottled beer.

'Beats me how he manages to get hold of all this,' muttered Mac. 'I mean, how many ration books does he have?'

'Probably comes from the family estate,' confided Harry, holding up to the light a clear glass jar filled with asparagus spears.

'Not unless the estate is called Fortnum and Mason,' said Richard, scrutinising the label on a tin of olives.

'Let's just be grateful, shall we?' whispered the girl, anxious that the provider of the luncheon should not overhear their ingratitude.

'You'll find a bottle of Pol Roger in there somewhere,' instructed Leo, from under the towel that the girl was using to dry his hair.

Eleanor Faraday had more than a little sympathy for Leo. The others might take the mickey out of him thanks to his life of privilege, but she had a gentler approach. Not that it would ever lead to anything. Leo was interested in women only as confidantes, not as companions. The environs of

Lady Margaret Hall held little fascination for him. He didn't seem to have very much interest in men either. His eyes might alight on them from time to time. Occasionally he would even take a fresher under his wing, but it would be the briefest of encounters. There never seemed to be 'a relationship'. He lived, apparently, entirely for art. But he was always good company, enjoying the social attention of both sexes, if not the intimacy of either, and was always ready to burst Eleanor's bubble when she became too intense or, in his eyes, too grand.

She looked across at the other three, now intent on discovering what was for lunch. Mac, the Glaswegian, was the quietest of the trio. A grammar-school boy like the other two, he was the son of a postal worker and had managed to win a scholarship to Christ Church. Thanks to his artistic talents, he had become something of a local hero. Not that the role suited him. He rarely let his emotions show, could hardly ever be accused of being verbose and of the five of them was the one who was the hardest to read. She knew he liked her – or else why would he seek her company? – but of more than that she could not be sure. Perhaps she and the others just amused him. Or irritated him. Or both. He was constantly getting at Leo, but that had become a habit rather than a calculated strategy. His tirades, while delivered with conviction, never degenerated into abuse. An enigma, that's what Mac was, she decided, for want of a more reasoned explanation. An enigma with a bit of a chip on his shoulder.

Richard King, on the other hand, was much easier to understand. Good-looking and athletic, he had the typical build of an Oxford blue if, at five feet nine inches, not quite the typical height. She admired his muscular frame, the pale green eyes and the way he had of making her feel that she mattered. There was no doubt that he was keen on her, but she wished sometimes that he were not quite so intense. He did have a sense of humour, but it surfaced only rarely. It was not that he was humourless, rather that there seemed to be other things more important to him, further up his list of priorities. He liked fine art, fine wine and fine women, and had a will as strong as an ox. Compared with Richard, the most implacable mule would appear biddable.

And Harry? Well, Harry was just . . . Harry. Tall and gangly with dark hair and deep blue eyes and a vague, faraway look. There was an otherworldliness about Harry. His thoughts often seemed to be elsewhere. When questioned about it, he just shrugged and smiled that disingenuous smile of his. There were times when he seemed preoccupied, and then he would disappear for days on end before emerging once more into the daylight and asking brightly, 'Have I missed anything?' Harry could melt her heart with a single sideways look. Not that he seemed remotely aware of it. What was he thinking? Probably nothing to do with her at all. Why were men so difficult to read? Except for Richard, of course, and even he had his moments . . .

Where Richard was intense, Harry was flippant. But some-times, when he had had a glass or two of beer in the evening, she thought he looked at her in a way that meant something more than simple friendship. And then there was that one evening when they had kissed. She smiled to herself, then shook her head as if to clear it and asked, 'Is anybody going to bring me a drink?'

She knew who would be first off the mark. 'Beer or fizz?' asked Richard.

'Beer, I think. I'm thirsty.'

'Bottle or glass?'

'Oh, bottle. It's a picnic.'

Before Richard had a chance to act, Harry flipped the stopper off a bottle and bent down to where Eleanor lay on the grass, dangling it in front of her.

'Thank you.' She took it and put it to her lips, slaking her thirst with the golden liquid.

'Good?' asked Harry.

Eleanor nodded, her mouth still filled with the frothing beer. She giggled and tried to swallow quickly. Then she lay on her side in the long grass, propping up her head on her elbow and nestling the bottle of beer in a patch of clover by the now discarded straw hat.

The only sounds on that still spring afternoon were the distant shouts of students punting on the river, the honk of alarmed geese fleeing for their lives and the gentle rustle of the willow leaves above the glassy water. For a moment the world seemed perfectly content to stand still, and their lives to hang in the balance. Eleanor looked wistfully at the chequered flowers of the snakesheads pushing up their shepherd's crooks through the first flush of young grass. She stroked their broad-shouldered bells with her index finger and let her dreams run free.

Leo looked at the backs of his eyelids, his knees crooked in front of him as he reclined on the riverbank. Mac looked across at Richard and Harry, and saw both of them gazing at Eleanor – Richard as though he were examining a fine painting and Harry as though he were regarding a cherished retriever.

While the others lost themselves in spring reverie, Mac pulled a drawing pad from a canvas bag stuffed under the seat of the boat. With a soft pencil he began to sketch out the scene in front of him. Deftly he traced the outline of Eleanor lying in the grass, and to her right the muscular frame of Richard rising like a sideways 'Z' from the lush grass of the riverbank. He took his time sketching out Richard's face with a soft pencil: the short, fair hair, the prominent brow and the chiselled features. He framed the scene with a curtain of willow wands and, beyond them, with a single stroke, the undulating skyline of Oxford, shimmering in the April afternoon.

Their collective mood was one of quiet thoughtfulness, but there was, seething beneath it, a hint of apprehension. It would not be long now before they would split up and go their separate ways, but relationships had been forged, or at least part-forged, and a vague question mark hung over the way in which matters would proceed. With the end of term looming, it was time for them all to take stock, to plan ahead, as far as they might, and to find some sense of direction, however vague. But that seemed so final, so decisive. It was easier for now to put off the evil moment.

Mac closed the cover of his sketch pad and turned to look at the river. It seemed unnaturally smooth. He felt down among the grass for a pebble, located one and tossed it into the water. The plangent 'gloop' woke them from their separate reveries. Unlike the other four, his pragmatic approach to life could not be subdued for long. 'So what's next?' he asked of no one in particular.

'Today, tomorrow or in life?' responded Leo absently, as though talking in his sleep. His eyes were still closed.

'Considering that the next few days are spoken for, let's go for the big one.'

'Do you mean what do we want of it or what is it likely to bring?' asked Eleanor.

Mac fixed her with a cynical eye. 'Do you think the two can ever be the same?'

Eleanor took evasive action. She rolled on to her stomach and propped up her head in her hands, then looked at the two men before her – Harry and Richard, now sitting back to back with their legs out in front of them. They were watching her as she spoke, so she turned her head away again and looked towards the river. 'I don't know,' she murmured. 'But it would be nice if they could be.'

'I think I'm expected to go and work for my uncle,' offered Richard.

'Doing what?' asked Eleanor.

'He's an estate agent. Says that when the boom comes, now that the war's over, he'll need a junior partner.'

'I didn't think that estate agents had "junior partners",' offered Harry.

'Family firm,' muttered Mac. 'They can use any title they want.'

'I have other plans,' said Richard. 'For a gallery. One day . . .' He turned to Mac and asked, 'What about you, then?'

Mac shrugged. 'I'll go back to say goodbye, but I'm not staying up there. Don't want to get stuck.'

'Stuck where?' asked Eleanor.

'In some dead-end job just to earn money. Rather keep my independence.'

'Doing what?'

'Painting.'

'You think you can earn a living?' asked Harry with a note of doubt in his voice.

'I can bloody well try. Anything has to be better than going into the shipyard.'

Richard asked, 'You're not serious? They don't expect you to go into the shipyard now that you've been to Oxford?'

Mac looked gloomy. 'They expect me to go back with my tail between my legs. Told me I wouldn't be able to stay the course. I'm buggered if I'm going to give them the satisfaction.'

'So where will you go?' asked Eleanor. 'Where will you live?'

Mac smiled. 'I haven't a clue. Anyway, I'm not the only one, am I, Harry?'

'Mmm?' As usual, Harry had been lost in his own world. Or so it appeared.

'What are you going to do when you leave?'

'Travel.'

Eleanor looked anxious. 'What, for ever?'

'No. Just for a while.'

'Where will you go?' she asked, trying to sound detached. 'Venice? Rome? Florence?'

'Ah, the Grand Tour,' pronounced Leo. 'Following in the footsteps of my ancestors.'

'Hardly. I was thinking of Cheltenham, York or Exeter. Somewhere like that.'

Richard grinned. 'You know how to live. What do you want to go there for?'

'To get a feel for the market.'

'What sort of market?'

'The auction market. I thought I might open a saleroom. Plenty of people looking for furniture now, and the market has to pick up soon.'

'That's my feeling, too,' said Richard. 'But I don't want to have to sell chests of drawers. The art market is poised for a revival, I'm sure of it.'

'So you're not going to be an estate agent, then?' asked Mac.

Richard shook his head. 'No. I know exactly where I'm going, and I think I'll get there.'

The others sat in silence for a moment. Of them all, Richard was always the confident, self-assured one. The one who seemed to have his life mapped out. Where they dithered and considered, Richard stormed ahead, fearless and forward-looking.

'I wish I was as sure,' murmured Eleanor.

Leo opened his eyes and sat up. 'Do you want Gypsy Rose Bedlington's prediction?'

Eleanor laughed. 'Yes. Go on, tell us what you think will become of us.'

Leo placed his champagne glass on the ground, pulled his

jersey around his shoulders like a shawl and began making circular motions over the glass with his hands as though it were a crystal ball.

'Hang on a minute,' said Harry, getting to his feet and reaching into his pocket for a large red-and-white spotted handkerchief. He flapped it open, then tied it round Leo's head to complete the image of the fortune-telling gypsy.

'Oh, it's all too cloudy,' intoned Leo in the voice of the soothsayer. 'But it is clearing. Yes, it is clearing . . .'

'Probably because you've drunk it all,' muttered Mac.

'Please, please, don't break the spell.'

Eleanor laughed again, then asked 'What can you see?'

'I see a woman.'

'Well, that's a first,' said Harry under his breath.

Leo came out of character. 'Are you going to take this seriously or not?'

'Oh, yes, of course,' said Harry, with assumed gravitas. 'Do carry on, ma'am.'

Leo frowned and stretched his arms out once more over the glass. 'I see a woman with a man.'

Harry drew breath to speak again, but a sharp glance from Leo made him keep silent.

'They are in an art gallery. Looking at a picture.'

'What sort of picture?' asked Eleanor.

Leo spoke more softly now and they had to lean forward to catch his words. His voice sounded strangely disembodied, and his face took on a look of intense concentration. 'A picture of a woman with an Arab.'

'Anyone we know?' asked Mac.

'Oh, yes,' breathed Leo.

'The woman, or the Arab?' asked Mac under his breath.

Leo seemed not to hear him. 'And there is another man looking at the picture, but they are unaware of him. Another man who wants the picture. He wants it very badly. But it is wrong. He says it is wrong. Says it is not what it is meant to be . . . not *who* it is meant to be.'

Harry glanced at Richard, then asked, 'What do you mean?'

Leo looked distressed. 'The people are all muddled up. The man and the woman...'

Eleanor noticed the colour draining from Leo's cheeks, and that he was beginning to sway from side to side. The sun was high in the sky. It was mid-afternoon and unseasonably warm.

'Harry, I think he's going to—' Before she could finish her sentence Leo's eyes had rolled in their sockets and he had slumped forwards, upsetting what was left of the champagne and sprawling in front of them on the grass.

All four of them darted over and helped him to a sitting position. Eleanor removed the handkerchief and brushed the long hank of fair hair back from Leo's brow. She was relieved to see the colour returning to his cheeks. He opened his eyes and seemed dazed.

'A cold river and hot sunshine,' scolded Eleanor. 'No wonder you passed out.'

'Did I?' asked Leo.

'No,' said Richard. 'I reckon you were probably possessed.'

Harry grinned. 'Pissed more like.' Then he noticed Eleanor frowning at him and corrected himself. 'Possessed by spirits.'

'Never touch them,' murmured Leo. And then, partially recovering himself, he asked, 'What were we doing?'

'Finding out what you thought the future would hold for us,' said Mac matter-of-factly. 'Through your crystal ball.' He gestured to the glass, which now had a broken stem.

'Oh. And did I know?'

Harry looked sceptical. 'Can't you remember?'

Leo shook his head. 'Not a bloody thing. I remember falling in the water . . .'

Eleanor handed the handkerchief back to Harry. 'You must

just have been a bit delirious. Cold water and hot sun and alcohol – fatal mixture.'

Leo brightened. 'Oh, I've always rather enjoyed the combination.'

Eleanor sat back on the grass. 'Strange what you were saying, though. Have you ever done that sort of thing before?'

'Never, no. I say, was I rather good at it? Shall I do it again?'

'I wouldn't bother,' muttered Mac. 'At least, not without an interpreter.'

Harry looked thoughtful. 'There is that rather sweet French girl – the one who keeps asking me to help her with her verbs.' His eyes brightened, and then he was suddenly aware of a tingling sensation down his spine. For a moment he wondered what it was, and then he looked up to see Eleanor pouring a bottle of beer down his neck.

3

Bath
November 2007

Dear Bath, nowhere so much scandal; nowhere so little sin.
Water Poetry (1729), Lady Wortley Montagu

The saleroom began to clear, but at first he could not see her. The grumpy dealer, whose only successful bid had been for a pair of Edgar Hunt paintings of 'domestic fowl' was shuffling towards the back of the pillared room, still grumbling. And then he heard her voice.

'Jamie!'

He turned. She was walking towards him, her eyes bright and her hands thrust deep into her jacket pockets, the catalogue under her arm. He looked down at her, rather as an indulgent father might at a favoured daughter, even though she was his exact contemporary. The brilliance of her eyes almost dazzled him. The thrill of the chase, clearly. For a picture. He didn't want to kid himself that it was the thrill of seeing him again.

'Well, to what do we owe . . . ?'

'The pleasure?' she asked mischievously.

He did not answer, but instead bent to kiss her on the cheek, then asked as levelly as he could, 'How long are you here for?'

Missy shrugged. 'Who knows? A while, I guess.'

Jamie chuckled.

'What?' she asked. 'What's the matter?'

'"I guess" . . .'

She looked at him quizzically.

'"I guess", rather than "I suppose". It shows where you've been.'

'Oh, I see.' Then she looked concerned. 'It's not that bad, is it?'

'Well, I've only heard half a dozen words so far. Five years across the pond. You could have turned into Dolly Parton.'

She hit him on the arm with her rolled-up catalogue. 'I might be blonde, but there the resemblance ends.'

Jamie looked her up and down. 'Oh, I don't know . . .'

Missy's eyes widened. 'You cheeky bugger!'

'Oh, no. Still very Anglo-Saxon. What a relief.'

'Look, are you pleased to see me or not?'

'Of course I am. It's just that you might have told me you were coming back. I could have prepared myself.'

'How would you have done that?'

'No, I suppose a surprise is better, all things considered. Come on, I'd better buy you a coffee, seeing as how you must be spent up.'

'Not my money.'

'No, of course not.'

'Grandpa's. Fun, isn't it . . . spending other people's?'

With a note of scorn he countered, 'I wouldn't know. I only sell the stuff.'

'Oh, poor you.' She looked at him with mock sympathy and put her arm through his.

'Do you mind not doing that here?' He extricated his arm.

'Oh. Too embarrassed to be seen fraternising with the enemy?'

He walked her towards the back of the room, past the cash desk, where half a dozen successful bidders were waiting to pay for their lots. The grumpy dealer, last in the queue, opened his mouth to speak, but Missy beat him to it.

'Sorry I pipped you. Nice chickens, though.'

Jamie took her arm now and wheeled her past. 'Do you mind not upsetting the other clients? I'm hoping they'll come back.'

'Lovely word, "clients". Always sounds slightly suspicious.'

'Probably the company you keep.'

He held open the door to the small café at the back of the saleroom. The atmosphere here was more intimate, though the elegant white Corinthian columns were still in evidence, holding up the cast-iron Victorian framework of the glazed roof.

Jamie asked the waitress for two coffees and sat down opposite Missy at a small table in the corner. He was beginning to relax now.

'Quite a morning that.'

'Yes. Better than your auctions used to be.'

'Hey! Just be careful. I am standing you a coffee.'

Missy frowned. 'After spending three quarters of a million I should think you are. I'd have hoped for at least a table at the Ivy.'

'If I'd known you were coming, I'd have booked.' He leaned back in his chair and breathed deeply. 'Anyway, I'm glad that's over.'

Missy smiled. 'You did well. You got a good price for the Munnings.'

'Yes. It made up for the Herring. *You* did rather well there.'

She did her best to look guilty, but failed. 'The old guy wasn't too pleased. Having to settle for a couple of hens.'

'He never is. Poor Mr Blunt. A life of disappointment. But then, he could have kept on bidding.'

'He doesn't think the Herring is a Senior.'

Jamie looked concerned. 'No. And I have an uneasy feeling that we didn't either. That might be why there was a low reserve. What do you think?'

'Oh, it's genuine all right. J. F. Herring Junior's stuff is much more fiddly.' She paused, then added pointedly, 'To the trained eye. The father's work is stronger. The son used to copy him. There was a great family row back in eighteen something or other.'

'Sounds familiar,' murmured Jamie.

She ignored him, warming to her subject. 'Beeswing took the Ascot Gold Cup in 1842. She was nine years old by then. Amazing horse. Won fifty-one out of her sixty-three starts between 1835 and 1842, and Herring Senior painted her for her owner. A man called William Orde, who lived in Northumberland. You can see his initials on the rug in the stable.'

The waitress arrived with their coffees and the conversation was temporarily halted. Jamie noticed the fire that shone in Missy's eyes when she got on to her pet subject. He felt a little disappointed; he had hoped that a little of her excitement was due to them meeting again, and not solely the result of a passion for sporting paintings that she had inherited from her grandfather. He made an effort to sound more interested. 'So it couldn't just be a copy? The father copying the son?'

'Unlikely. It's just too . . . well . . . elegant.'

'Mmm. It looked a bit stuffed to me. So if it is a Herring Senior, what is your seven-and-a-half-thousand-pound painting worth?'

'In a London gallery, around a hundred thousand.'

'Bloody hell!'

Missy stirred her coffee; there was an expression of satisfaction on her face, but she was conscious of not wanting to appear too smug. 'Don't worry; we can't get those sorts of prices in Bath. We'll probably ask around seventy-five thousand and see how we do.'

Jamie looked dejected, and then concerned.

'I'm surprised you're not more across it,' said Missy. 'And that there wasn't a higher reserve put on it.'

'I wasn't responsible for that. Not my bag, sporting paintings. I wasn't meant to be doing this auction. A bit embarrassing, really. Peter Cathcart called in sick this morning. I had to step in at the last moment. I did as much homework as I could – checked all the reserves. The Herring went through bang on the nose.'

'Maybe the owner suspected that it wasn't the real thing. Or Peter Cathcart did.'

'Maybe.' Jamie continued to look thoughtful. 'I knew that the Munnings was high end, but I'm not right across the sporting market. Ben Nicholson's more in my line, if you remember.'

'Oh, please! Squares and circles stuck on to plywood and painted grey? No, thank you. Give me a Stubbs any day. Or a Munnings.'

'Oh, come on – we'd never get a Stubbs in here. They go to Christie's and Sotheby's. Pretty unusual to have a Munnings. A decent one, anyway. We've had a few of his gorse bushes on Exmoor – that sort of thing – but never one as good as this. Still, at least I made you pay for it.'

'Bargain,' murmured Missy, doing nothing to disguise her relish.

'At seven hundred and fifty thousand, plus buyer's premium of twenty per cent and then the VAT, that's not much short of a million.'

'I know. But Munnings is top dollar now.'

'So what would you pay for him in one of your London galleries, then?'

She knew the reaction she would get, and proceeded to play Jamie like a trout on the end of a line. She milked the moment by pausing to consider. 'One and a half million. Two and a half for a larger one.'

Jamie grimaced. 'We had a reserve of half a million on it and I thought that was a bit high.'

'Not any more. Cheaper in the States, with the exchange rate so favourable. But over here the demand is still high.' Then she said brightly, 'That's why I'm back.'

'Maybe Peter Cathcart is losing his grip,' offered Jamie.

'I'm surprised he didn't get more dealers in.'

'There were enough of you. You did get a run for your money.'

'Yes. There were a couple of hair-raising moments, but . . .' She shrugged.

Jamie leaned forward in his chair. 'OK, then, so what would you have gone to?'

Missy smiled mysteriously. 'Ah, that's for me to know and you to wonder.'

'And you think you can make a decent profit on it?'

'Grandpa reckons he already has done. He's got a client lined up.'

'Lucky him. I just hope *my* grandfather doesn't get wind of me selling him such a bargain. Mind you, it'll be all over the local paper tomorrow – we don't flog a decent Munnings every day.'

'Oh, I should think three quarters of a million will keep him happy, don't you? Especially when it's coming out of the pocket of *my* grandfather.'

'I hope so.' He brightened. 'So your grandfather has called you back, then?'

Missy nodded. 'More trade over here.'

'And you just came running?'

'That's a bit unkind. I go where the work is.'

'And there was nothing to keep you over there?'

She cocked her head on one side. 'Are you fishing?'

'Just catching up.'

Missy looked away. 'No. Nothing. Not now.'

Jamie felt guilty at having asked the question. Her grandfather had always been her guiding light. He was aware that more than a little jealousy had prompted him to ask the question. He offered an olive branch. 'I just wish the two of them could bury the hatchet. It's all so long ago now. I mean, they'll be eighty next year.'

Missy drained her cup. 'Yes.' She gazed into the middle distance. 'It would be good if they could get along a bit better. After all these years.'

They sat in silence for a few minutes, and then Missy said, 'Why don't we make them?'

'What?'

'Make them get on. Well, at least *encourage* them to speak to one another.'

'And how do you think we're going to do that? They've been daggers drawn for around sixty years; it's going to take more than you and me encouraging them to get them to kiss and make up.'

'We could rope in your mum and my dad,' she offered.

'Well, *they* barely tolerate one another.'

'Yes, but if we worked on them a bit, made them see sense, maybe we could effect some kind of transformation.'

'You always were the optimist.'

'And you the realist?'

'Sometimes.'

Jamie knew Missy's terrier-like instincts. Once she had an idea in her head there was little point in trying to dislodge it. You might, with great cunning and not a little guile, try to redirect her intentions, but it needed considerable skill, and he was rarely up to it. The fact that they had managed to stay friends throughout the years was down to Missy's iron will and Jamie's loyalty, though there were times when even he might have buckled under family pressure had it not been for Missy's tenacity and bloody-mindedness.

It was only during the last five years that their contact had been more sporadic. Immediately before that, it had seemed that their friendship might develop into something more. Jamie had been on the brink of taking it a step further when she had been sent to the States by her grandfather to run his gallery in New York. He had felt hurt at her apparent willingness to leave the country, but for the other members of both families, it had been something of a relief, a temptation out of the way.

And now here they were. A latter-day Romeo and Juliet, *sans* the romance. Together again in the same city. For better or worse. A circumstance that would doubtless ignite the families' antipathy once more.

Jamie had finished his coffee and was getting up from the table. Missy, whose thoughts had been elsewhere, came to and looked up at him. 'Going so soon?'

He was pleased to see that she seemed genuinely disappointed. He glanced at his watch. 'I must. Sorry. I'll have to do a de-brief. You know, chew the fat. Explain myself.'

She saw the look of resignation on his face, then said, with a hint of mischief, 'Well, I hope I don't get you into any trouble.'

He looked at her with a curious expression. 'Since when did you ever do anything else?'

4

Oxford
June 1949

To-day girls and young men share in university life, in amusements as well as studies.

Oxford (1951), D. Erskine Muir

April's weather continued through May with a heatwave, until June brought its usual capricious mixture of sunshine and showers, thunder and rain, and skies that had every art student in Oxford reaching for Payne's grey and Prussian blue, cadmium yellow and rose madder. While Leo and Eleanor turned to watercolours, Mac let rip with oils – filling canvas after canvas with rolling hills and angry skies, dramatic seas and vertiginous mountains.

But their life together was coming to an end. Already each of them was spending several days away at a time, some seeing family once more, others avoiding them, all intent on making a fresh start in some way. For Eleanor there was another problem, one that concerned both Richard and Harry. She could not let matters rumble on. She had to decide between the eager, attentive Richard and the engaging if unpredictable Harry. It did occur to her that she might be being presumptuous. Certainly in Harry's case. Over the next few weeks she would have to make serious decisions about her future, whether it lay with one of them or neither.

She felt foolish even contemplating the subject. She should be concentrating on getting a job – in a London auction house, or an art gallery, or in that dreadful thing called 'education'. That was what her degree – if she achieved it –

would fit her for. There were many women who would kill to be in her position, making their mark in a man's world.

When she had arrived at Oxford she had seen herself as the archetypal bluestocking – keen to work, to be independent, to prove herself – but now that early fire had abated. Somehow it did not seem as important as it had done then. Eleanor was naturally sociable. Always had been. She was not what her mother would have called 'a floozy', but she was a girl who felt more at ease in the company of men than women. She worked hard; played hard, too, but carefully, thought-fully. Having finished her course, Eleanor knew that she had no intention of becoming a career girl. Her degree was to prove something – to her family and her peers, yes, but also to herself. She had done that now, made her point, and somehow her single-mindedness had evaporated. It made her feel slightly ashamed, but she had enough sense to be realistic. Yes, she would look for a job, but it was no longer the focus of her life. What she wanted more than anything was the company of someone else of like mind, which would bring a different kind of freedom and a longed-for close-ness. And a family. She wanted a family more than anything. The war had left her unsettled. It had also left her father-less. A childhood of loss, of coming home and wondering if your house – let alone your family – would still be there, had left its mark. A house, a home, a family, these were her priorities. And yet she felt guilty at wasting such an education, at giving others a chance to think that her scholarship would have been better gifted to someone able to make more use of it.

She was sitting in the window seat of Leo Bedlington's room, hunched up with her head on her knees, looking out over the city. The setting sun glinted on spire and dome, weathervane and cupola, and the scene seemed to match the wistful mood of her dreams. Leo was packing, in a desultory sort of way. He was used to having it done for him and seemed unable to fold the simplest garment into something that would fit into a bag or a trunk, of which there were several scattered about the room. He was muttering to himself. 'Why do I need this? I mean, what is the point in collecting all this stuff? And I haven't even started on the books yet. Why Osborne couldn't come and do my packing for me I don't know.'

Eleanor didn't answer.

Leo looked across at her, silhouetted against the pale-pink early-evening sky. 'Oh goodness,' he said.

'Mmm?' she responded absently, still gazing into the distance.

'You know, if I were that sort of man, I'd sweep you off your feet right now.'

She looked round. 'What?'

'You. There you sit in your shorts and plimsolls and your neat little blouse, with your hair tied back. You look like something out of a Hollywood movie.'

'Don't be ridiculous, Leo.'

'I'm not being ridiculous.' He walked over to where she sat, then lifted a finger and lightly stroked her hair. 'You really are quite beautiful, you know.'

'No I'm not. My nose turns up too much, my eyes are too big, and—'

'And you have every student in Christ Church running after you.'

'No I don't. Only one.'

'Why so sad, then?'

Eleanor looked up at Leo and he noticed the start of a tear in her eye. 'I don't know,' she said softly. 'Wrong one, perhaps.'

'Oh, I see.'

'I'm not sure that you do.'

Leo eased in beside her on the window seat and put his

arm round her shoulder. 'You mustn't think that I haven't noticed, you know.'

'Noticed what?'

'The fact that someone wants you more than you want him, and that the one you really want doesn't seem to notice.'

Eleanor nodded resignedly.

'Maybe he just needs a push,' said Leo.

Eleanor sat up. 'I can't do that!'

'No, I don't suppose you can. But I could.'

She turned to face him. 'Leo, you mustn't.'

'Why not? He thinks the world of you. He just needs a bit of encouragement.'

'You are not to do anything. Or say anything. And anyway, how do you know?'

'I do have eyes.'

Eleanor turned away. 'You must think I'm such a fool.'

'No, not a fool. Or foolish. Just unlucky.'

'You don't think I'd be throwing it all away?'

'That rather depends what "it" is. I think you're being very honest with yourself, but I do think you need to think it through a bit.'

'Oh, I have. I've been through it so many times. I've imagined what *might* happen. What *could* happen. I know what I want, just not how to *make* it happen.'

Leo began to hum to himself, and then to sing very softly, 'See how the fates their gifts allot, for "A" is happy, "B" is not. Yet "B" is worthy, I dare say, of more prosperity than "A".'

'I never did like Gilbert and Sullivan,' said Eleanor.

'No, but they have a point.'

Now it was Eleanor's turn. 'You never talk about it yourself.'

Leo shrugged. 'Nothing to talk about.'

'Out of choice?'

He smiled weakly. 'Not entirely. But it's difficult when . . .' He trailed off, then, seeing she was waiting for more, said 'When it's not quite as straightforward as it should be. It means you can't ever . . . well . . . relax.'

It was the first time he had ever admitted as much. Eleanor sat quietly, not wanting to interrupt.

'So there you are. I do know how it feels. I've been there. Once.'

'Recently?'

'Recently enough. But the one I want doesn't want me, so . . . better to concentrate on other things. Don't want the family reading about me in the papers. And with father being ill, it probably won't be long before I'm Lord Bedlington.'

'Don't say that.'

'Well, it's true, I'm afraid. He's not got long. Bloody war.'

'Mmm.'

He noticed that she was looking out of the window again. 'I'm sorry. At least I still have mine. Just.'

'Yes.'

He laid his hand on her shoulder. 'Do you miss him?'

Eleanor nodded, and he saw that her eyes were full of tears.

'What a war. What a waste of lives. But then . . . at least we had a chance to come here. That wouldn't have happened if we'd lost, would it? I mean the freedom.' He stroked her hair and looped it behind her ear. 'I don't think you want a job, do you?'

She shook her head but did not speak.

'Just a man to look after you. And your babies.'

'Oh, Leo! Am I being really stupid?'

'No. I don't think so.'

'But all this . . .' She waved her arms around her and gestured out of the window. 'Such a waste if I only want to have a family.'

'It's never wasted,' said Leo. 'It helps make you who you

are, fits you for life. Education isn't only useful in a job, you know. I mean, look at me. I'll never have a job, not a proper one. Does that mean I don't deserve an education?'

She looked up at him and wiped away a tear.

'No. Don't answer that. As far as the rest of them are concerned, I'm a Hooray Henry. But I'll go back to Bedlington Park and it won't be long before I have to take charge of the place, and the staff. Worry about their housing and their wages. There are fifty of them, you know. We're the largest local employer. Well, we were before the war. I'll have to try to build it up again. Get some flowers back. It's all bloody vegetables at the moment. Allotments on the front lawn. That's what I'm destined for – social work.' He smiled ruefully.

Eleanor waited, but nothing more was forthcoming. After a few moments she broke the silence. 'Anyway, we all go our separate ways soon.'

Leo brightened. 'Out into the wide blue yonder. And you don't know if you'll see either of them again?'

'Oh, Richard wants to see me. He's got all sorts of ideas.'

'And you? You do like him, don't you?'

'Richard? Of course.'

'More than like?'

'Yes. I suppose. He's very sweet, very attentive, hugely attractive . . .'

'I sense a "but" coming.'

'Yes.' Eleanor looked embarrassed.

'And Harry? Hasn't he said anything?'

'Not really, no.'

Leo stood up and threw a pile of clothing into a large leather-bound trunk. 'Look, tell me to mind my own business – I mean, I haven't exactly poured *my* heart out to you when it comes to relationships – but have you ever, with either of them . . . ? I mean . . .'

Eleanor spoke calmly. 'No. Almost, with Richard. One evening, down by the river. And then we were interrupted by a man walking a dog.' She smiled at the memory and looked at Leo. 'It was a Bedlington terrier.'

'Well, I apologise on behalf of the family.' He looked suitably contrite. 'And Harry? Nothing's happened there?'

'He's put his arms round me a few times, and we did kiss once – after a party on the way home. That was all.'

'But enough to know?'

Eleanor nodded. 'Oh, yes.' Then she added, anxiously, 'I wouldn't want you to think . . .'

'I don't think anything. I just want you to be happy.'

'Unlikely, the way things are going.'

Leo flipped the lid of the trunk and it slammed shut with a thud that startled Eleanor.

'Right!' he said.

'What?'

'Time we took your mind off things, gave you a good day out.'

'Where?'

'At the races.' He walked over to the battered mahogany desk, which was pushed against the wall. Above it hung a large picture of a madonna and child, and alongside it a smaller frame containing a brightly painted icon. He lifted the latter from the wall and handed it to Eleanor. 'There you are – you hold on to that while I find the *Racing Post.*'

Eleanor took the icon and asked, 'Why the *Racing Post?*'

'Because we're going to the races. Unless I'm very much mistaken . . .' He riffled through the pages until he found what he was looking for. 'Yes. Here we are. Newmarket, tomorrow.'

'What about it?'

'Black Tarquin.'

'Who's Black Tarquin?'

'My uncle's horse. He's running tomorrow in the Princess of Wales's Stakes. Up against Lord Derby's horse – Dogger Bank. That should be worth seeing. Uncle Freddie can't stand Lord Derby. Looks likely to be a close-run thing. I think we should go and give him our support, especially as he's carrying rather a lot of weight.'

Eleanor was staring at him with her mouth open.

'Close it, dear; you'll catch flies.'

Eleanor composed herself once more. 'Er . . . we?'

'The five of us. I'll round up the boys and we'll make a day of it – you, me, Mac, Harry and Richard.'

'Oh, but—'

'Now don't go all wobbly on me.'

'But I don't know if—'

'It will just be a bit of fun.'

'But I don't want you meddling . . .'

Leo held her by the shoulders. 'I'm not meddling, I promise. I just think that we could all do with a day out. It will get me away from this ghastly packing and it will take you out of yourself. It might also wake some people up to the fact that we won't always be together . . . unless we do something about it.'

'But . . .'

'I really don't think you can have any more "buts".' He pointed to the icon. 'You just hang on to that for a bit.'

'Who is it?'

'St Anthony of Padua.'

'Oh?'

'Yes. Being a good Catholic boy, I have him hanging by my desk, along with the BVM.' He nodded in the direction of the madonna and child.

'Why him?'

Leo shook his head. 'Didn't they teach you anything in your lessons about Fra Angelico or Titian?'

'I didn't do them, and the Impressionists weren't big on icons.'

'St Anthony is the patron saint of lost things.'

'Oh,' said Eleanor, 'I see.' She slipped the tiny icon into the pocket of her shorts, gave Leo a gentle kiss on the cheek and walked silently out of the room.

5

Bath

December 2007

Where all drink the Waters to recover Health,
And some sort of Fools there throw off their Wealth,
And now and then Kissing, and that's done by stealth,
There's rare doings at Bath.
Wit and Mirth: or Pills to Purge Melancholy (1719),
Thomas d'Urfey

It was the day of the furniture sale, three days after the sale
of the paintings. Lunchtime. Jamie did not want to be too
obvious about it, too quick off the mark, but at the same
time he did not want Missy to think that he was completely
uninterested, or that her return had gone uncelebrated. It
would need to be handled carefully, and circumspectly, and
the family, if possible, kept in the dark.

He would keep his tone even on the phone. He would
suggest a drink – safer than supper, which might seem more
formal. After all, if the drink went well, they could go on for
a meal afterwards. If it didn't, well, then they were both off
the hook.

'Lovely. When?'

Her brightness took him by surprise. 'Er . . . tonight?' It
was a stupid suggestion. She was bound to be busy. He would
have been better asking *her* to suggest a date.

'Lovely.' Again, lovely.

'Right. Well, shall I meet you outside the Pump Room at
about eight?'

'Perfect. See you then.'

And that was it. He put the phone down almost as if it were radioactive. He had asked her and she had said yes. They would be meeting again in – he looked at his watch – six hours. Right. He felt rather pleased with himself and there was a spring in his step as he walked into the saleroom and mounted the dais.

'Welcome back, ladies and gentlemen. We start the afternoon session with lot two hundred and fifty, the Queen Anne mahogany four-poster bed.'

Richard King held the painting in both hands and walked over to the window, manoeuvring it to catch the light. At first he looked troubled and she worried that he was not pleased with it, but then his anxiety seemed to evaporate. He looked almost relieved. 'Well done,' he said softly. 'Very well done.'

'So you're happy with it?' Missy was leaning on the back of the Louis Quinze chair, anxious to see if her grandfather approved. He had been away on business the day before and it was only now that she could show him the painting. It had spent the previous evening propped up on the bookshelf in her flat on the top floor of the Royal Crescent gallery.

He lowered the painting and turned round. 'Perfectly.'

She had hoped he might smile, but instead his face bore a look of concern and preoccupation. But then, she told herself, he has just spent a lot of money. Maybe that still worried him, even after all these years.

'Such a clever man,' he murmured, almost to himself.

'The best,' agreed Missy. Then she asked, 'Is it true that Augustus John used to criticise him? Said that if a horse was brown, then why not paint it brown instead of green?'

'Sorry?' Her grandfather's response was muted. He was still gazing intently at the painting.

Missy persisted. 'Munnings, the way he used reflected light. You know – when a horse was standing on grass, it would pick up something of the colour. Or of the sky.'

Richard replied without looking up. 'Yes. Yes, he was very good. Almost unique.'

Missy detected that something was troubling him. 'What is it?'

Her grandfather came out of his reverie. 'Nothing. Nothing at all. I was just remembering things.' He lowered the painting now and walked over to a corner of the room, where he leaned it face against the wall.

Missy was rather surprised that he did not want to hang it immediately and gaze at it, which was his usual *modus operandi* with a newly acquired painting. 'So where's it going off to?' asked Missy.

'Nowhere.'

'Oh, I thought you had a buyer.'

'I would have, ordinarily, but this one's different. I don't want it going off to the Emerald Isle.'

'Ah, I see. The racing man?'

Her grandfather nodded.

'He must have quite a collection now. I just don't know how people can afford so much – I mean, so many of them.'

'Oh, there's still a great appetite for them.'

'More money than taste?'

Richard frowned. 'Never insult the client.'

'No, not in this case, but . . . well . . . some of them seem more interested in a painting matching their curtains than being a work of art. Still, this one's mainly grey, so it's unlikely that would be the case.'

'No.'

There was a momentary lull in the conversation, then Missy nodded in the direction of the painting, now hidden from view, and asked, 'What's special about it?'

Richard shrugged. 'Just . . . sentimentality, really.'

'You know it, then? I mean, you've seen it before.'

'Yes. A long time ago.'

'It's funny,' said Missy.

Her grandfather looked at her enquiringly.

'Her face – the lady in the painting – it seems familiar somehow.'

Her grandfather removed his spectacles, folded them and slipped them into the breast pocket of his jacket. Then he fixed her with the look she knew so well. He was a dapper man. Not tall, admittedly, but well dressed in grey trousers and a navy blazer, blue shirt and pale yellow tie. A silk hand-kerchief peeped out of the pocket into which he had just slipped his glasses. His hair was white now and his com-plexion that of a well-scrubbed schoolboy – as pink as a rose and always clean-shaven. Ever since she could remember he had always smelled of a particular brand of aftershave – Trumper's West Indian Limes. She used to think, when she was little, that he smelled like a box of oranges. She found it comforting.

They stood together in the first-floor drawing room of the gallery in the Royal Crescent. He had always been anxious that clients should feel as though they were entering a well-furnished house rather than a purpose-built art gallery. The view from the tall sash windows was of the City of Bath spread out in the valley before them like a theatre set. Below them the abbey nestled among Georgian terraces, and beyond, on the rising hills, were more modern houses, crafted in local stone but somehow lacking the grace and character of their predecessors.

Missy had been spoiled as a child. Not in the sense that she had been given everything she wanted, but in that she had lived in a beautiful house, among beautiful things.

Richard King had done well for himself. He had started

with a small gallery in Bristol, struggling to pay the rent, but that was a long time ago now. By the time Missy was born he lived outside the city of Bath in Peel Place – a rambling Georgian rectory set in ten acres – and ran King's Fine Art from the house in the centre of the Royal Crescent. In his eightieth year he might be, but he still spent a part of every day there. His wayward son, Patrick, had returned to the fold, but he seemed happiest spending most of his time wining and dining prospective clients, so it was helpful having Missy back. He could see she was more than capable. Her stint in New York had given her a new-found confidence, but he still kept a fatherly eye on things and a fifty-one per cent share in the business. He found it hard to admit that he trusted his granddaughter more than his son – both in terms of judgement and reliability – but that was the way it was. He had always been a realist, sharp at character assessment.

Missy waited for a response about the lady in the painting, but her grandfather said nothing. He seemed lost in thought once more. Then he asked absently, 'So what are you doing today?'

'Oh, some cataloguing, for the fifty-year exhibition.'

He brightened now. 'And then? What are you doing this evening? I thought we might . . .'

Missy hesitated. 'Ah. Well, I'm going out.'

Her grandfather was walking to the desk in the corner of the room. 'Anyone we know?' He asked the question carelessly, more out of politeness than curiosity.

'Jamie Ballantyne.'

During the ensuing silence Missy thought that she could hear her ears ringing.

He did not turn to face her, but carried on shuffling the papers on his desk. 'I see.'

She attempted to reassure him: 'He's very nice, you know,

and I haven't seen him for years. We just thought it would be good to catch up.'

'We?'

'I met him at the auction. He sold me the picture.'

She could see the displeasure on her grandfather's face. 'Jamie Ballantyne,' he murmured to himself.

'Oh, Grandpa, you can't still be cross. Not after all these years.'

'Cross? Do I look cross?'

'You know what I mean. Come and sit down.' She gestured to an ornate sofa pushed against the wall, then sat down on it and gently patted the seat next to her, as if coaxing a favourite pet to join her. Richard did as he was bid. Missy took his hand in hers. 'You can't go on like this for ever, you know, bearing a grudge. It's not worth—'

Her grandfather interrupted. 'Just because it was a long time ago—'

'Too long ago. Let it go.'

'—doesn't mean it's easy to forget.'

She kissed him lightly on the cheek. 'Look, I know that you and Harry Ballantyne fell out at university, but what is it about the rest of the family? Surely you can't have anything against them?'

Richard turned to her. 'Jamie's mother wasn't sorry to see you go to America.'

'No.'

'Dreadful woman.'

'Well, I know she didn't like me, and that she's a bit scary, but I wouldn't call her dreadful.'

'Well, she saw him off – her husband. After she'd made him change his name.'

'What do you mean?'

'Why do you think she's called Ballantyne?'

'I imagined she'd reverted to her maiden name . . .'

'No. Married Frank Bottomley on the rebound and made him change his name to hers because she didn't like the sound of it. Ridiculous. Then when Frank pushed off with another woman, she got even more bossy.'

'Poor Jamie.'

'Oh, he'll be all right. He's a bright lad.' He looked worried again.

'She never found another man, then? Jamie's mum, I mean.'

'No time. Devoted herself to the business when Harry started to take a back seat and the baby started to grow up. Business and baby, that's what she concentrated on. No time for a man.'

'But just because you don't like her—'

'It's a family thing,' Richard interrupted again. 'Been going on too long to do anything about it now.' He pushed himself up from the sofa. 'Just don't get involved, that's all.'

'But you can't—'

'I can't make you do anything. I know that. I'd just be grateful if you kept your distance.'

Her grandfather began looking at his papers, and Missy gazed out of the window across the Bath skyline, now framed by ominous-looking clouds. Then she looked back at the painting leaning against the wall. What a shame that her grandfather did not seem to want to hang it. The woman on the horse was really quite beautiful.

'Well, I can't say I'm pleased when I'm not.'

Jamie regretted telling his mother the moment he had done so. It was as if he were still tied to her apron strings and he could not help but feel resentful.

'You know my feelings,' she continued.

'I am thirty, Mum. Old enough to—'

'Old enough to know better.'

'Know better than what?'

'To get involved with the Kings.'

'You make it sound like a criminal offence, or something out of a soap opera.'

'Don't be ridiculous.' Emma Ballantyne was sitting at her desk in the office at the back of the saleroom. It was difficult to avoid her eye when his own desk faced hers.

'I'm only going out for a drink, not proposing.'

'Don't even joke about it!'

It was at times like this when he could see how easily people could be intimidated by her. There she sat in her large chair, determination seeping out of every pore from the velvet Alice band at the top of her head to the black patent shoes on her feet. Her perfectly manicured hands, with their deep-red nail varnish, tapped with the Cartier pen on the blotter in front of her as if to make her point. Even her pearls seemed to be defying him.

'Well, don't be so bossy!' he scolded. 'Don't make so much of it.'

His mother made a disapproving 'Hurrumph' and put on her reading glasses, pretending to scrutinise some catalogue in front of her. She began muttering. He could not hear what she said but grasped the general tenor.

He was determined that she would not win this one. 'And it's no use chuntering away. I shall do what I want. Anyway, you were happy enough to take their money yesterday.'

'That's quite different. That's business.' Emma Ballantyne looked up from her catalogue – she had not absorbed any-thing of its content – and took off her spectacles. Time to try another tack. 'Oh, Jamie, you know I don't want to interfere . . .'

'Ha!'

'Well, I don't. It's just that there are far more suitable girls . . .'

'Suitable? Excuse me, it's nothing to do with you, as far as I'm aware.'

His mother looked chastened. 'No. Of course not. It's just that—'

'No. I've heard enough. There's absolutely nothing wrong with Artemis King. She's great fun and good company, and if she hadn't gone off to the States when she did . . .' He stopped himself from going on.

'Exactly. But then she did go off to the States, didn't she? Thanks to her grandfather. At least we both shared the same sentiments there.'

'You think he sent her there to keep her away from me?' Jamie almost laughed.

'Probably.'

'Oh, I think his reasons were purely commercial.'

'Don't you be so sure. I think he was every bit as put out as I was.'

'Oh. Put out, eh?' Then his tone changed. 'I mean, it's not as if anything happened, not as if we had a chance.'

'No.'

'Don't tell me you're still harbouring a grudge.'

His mother leaned back in her chair. 'It's not a grudge, it's . . .'

'A way of life?'

Emma sighed. 'I suppose so, if I'm honest.'

'But why keep it going?' asked Jamie, with a note of desperation in his voice.

'Because your grandfather would be upset if we started . . . well . . .'

'Fraternising with the enemy?'

Emma considered. 'Yes, I suppose so.'

Jamie came and perched on the corner of her desk. 'Don't you ever bump into Patrick King?'

'Whenever he sees me he crosses the road to avoid me. I see no point in talking to him.'

'But don't you ever want to ask him why you both continue the feud?'

'I'm not sure that he'd know, to be honest.'

'There, then. Isn't that a reason to bury the hatchet?'

Emma looked stern again. 'I don't think I could ever strike up a conversation with a man who treated his own daughter as he did. I know that what happened was tragic, but there was really no excuse to abandon her. If it hadn't been for her grandfather . . .'

Jamie seized his opportunity. 'There you are, you see, there is something good about him.'

Emma realised she was cornered. 'Yes, well . . .'

'Did you ever know Missy's mother?'

'Briefly. Before she was married, not after. Charlotte was a lovely girl.'

'But Patrick didn't appreciate her?'

'Quite the reverse. Apparently he doted on her.' There was a different note in her voice now. If Jamie didn't know better, he would have said it was wistful. He kept silent and let her continue.

'They married the same year as I did. Occasionally I'd notice them at parties – you could see the look in her eyes when he brought her a drink or helped her on with her coat. He would check every now and then to see where she was, like a devoted spaniel.'

Jamie murmured, 'Hard to believe now.'

'Yes. He and that friend of his Charlie Dunblane were the two men all the girls round here ran after. I rather fancied Charlie Dunblane myself. Very dashing.' She had a faraway look in her eyes, then came back to earth. 'Anyway, then he was killed in a car smash – driving his MG too fast through the village lanes. Hit a tree and died instantly. That really shook Patrick. Two weeks later Charlotte died having Missy and he just sort of flipped. Couldn't bear to look at the child who'd caused the mother's death. Wouldn't have anything to do with her.'

'Poor Missy.'

'Yes. I did feel sorry for her. But then her grandfather took charge.'

'And Patrick went away?'

'It was years before we found out what had happened to him. Some people thought he might have run off with another woman; well, he and Charlie were both a bit fast and loose. I just thought it was all too much for him – losing his best friend and his wife in the space of a month. It turned out he was living in Italy – Umbria I think – on his own. In some old farmhouse. Left his daughter behind like a piece of luggage "not wanted on voyage".'

'And her grandfather just let him?'

'Oh, I think he would have had something to say about it, knowing Richard King. In the end, though, when he saw it wasn't having any effect, he just brought Artemis up as his own.'

'Did he give her the name?' asked Jamie.

'Yes. I ask you. Poor little thing.'

'And then Patrick came back?'

'Eventually – after twenty years or so. A different woman on his arm every few weeks. But he's back in the firm, so his father must have forgiven him.'

'And they get on now, then – Artemis and her dad?'

Emma got up from her chair and walked to the door. 'You'll have to ask her that won't you? Tonight, when you have your drink.' As she left the room, she turned to deliver her valediction. 'But don't raise your hopes too high. You do know your Greek mythology, don't you?'

'What do you mean?'

Emma could not resist throwing a pitying look at her son. 'Artemis, daughter of Zeus and sister of Apollo.'

'I know,' said Jamie. 'You've told me before. She was a huntress.'

'Yes,' said his mother, with a bright smile. 'But she was also the goddess of chastity.'

6

Newmarket
June 1949

> . . . the place for the rich, the young, the inexperienced and the daring . . .
>
> Ben Marshall (1833)

The open-topped Talbot Ten bounced along the uneven turf, jolting the occupants to left and right and resulting in spilled beer and cries of disapproval directed at the driver.

'Don't blame me. I've never driven the bloody thing before,' cried Harry. 'And seeing as I'm the only one who can . . .' He braced himself for another bump. It came and Leo, Mac, Richard and Eleanor momentarily left their seats again, to be suspended in mid-air until the car caught them on the way down. 'Aaaaargh!' came the collective cry.

'Can't you get a decent car?' asked Mac of Leo.

'This *is* a decent car. It's only twelve years old.'

'Thought you'd have had a Rolls,' complained Mac.

'Don't be ridiculous. Far too showy. The Talbot has never let me down. Well, it's never let Osborne down.'

'Never driven yourself, then?'

'No need,' said Leo matter-of-factly. 'But there's no room for Osborne today, so . . .'

'So it's a good job that at least one of us can drive, isn't it?' There was a touch of irritation in Harry's voice.

'Three cheers for Harry!' cried Eleanor, at which the others grudgingly raised their beer bottles and aimed for their respective lips. They missed, on account of the fact that the Talbot found another rut in the grass.

Leo reluctantly swapped seats with Harry and on they motored, past the grandstand, slowing down as they came to an area of paddock reserved for the cars of those punters fortunate enough to be motorised. As Harry steered the Talbot into a generous-sized gap between a Daimler and a Wolseley, gently ground to a halt and turned off the engine, the trio gave a resounding cheer.

'What an ungrateful lot you are,' murmured Leo.

Eleanor reached over from the back seat, where she had been seated between Mac and Richard. She put her arms round Leo's shoulders and gave him a peck on the cheek. 'Not really. We're grateful to be out. Grateful to be away from Oxford. Aren't we, boys?'

'A bit too near Cambridge for my liking,' muttered Mac. 'Funny lot around here.'

'Any more beer?' asked Richard, grinning.

'I should bloody well hope so,' said Harry. 'The driver's gasping.'

Leo slapped him on the back. 'Well done. Your reward will come in heaven.'

Harry looked disappointed. 'I was hoping not to have to wait quite that long.' Eleanor ruffled his hair and dropped a bottle of beer into his lap. He turned to look at her. 'Thank you. At least someone cares.' He shot her a smile.

Eleanor, caught unawares by the compliment, felt her face colouring and said, 'Right, come on. Which way do we go?' She turned away from Harry so that he could not see her face and busied herself with getting out of the car and brushing down her floral skirt. Then she looked up and was suddenly captivated by what she saw.

Around them were cars disgorging their passengers – smart couples from the town in racy MGs and lumbering Humbers, small groups of friends who had crammed into Morrises and Austins, assorted family saloons and occasional vans, a motley collection of dark grey and black, burgundy and bottle green. The June sunshine glinted on chrome headlamps and radiator grilles, freshly polished paintwork and newly washed glass. Among the sprinkling of Rolls Royces on the rough green turf was one in black and yellow, in the back of which an old dowager was draining her glass of champagne, while her gaitered butler was packing up the hamper.

The quintet of Oxford students had arrived later than expected, due to their getting lost on the way. They did not need a map, insisted Leo. He knew the way, having been there so many times before. It was not long before they realised that he was familiar with the route only when he had a chauffeur. Now they were here, it didn't seem to matter any more.

It was exactly as Eleanor had hoped it would be. In the distance she could hear the rallying cry of the loudspeaker, could see the fluttering bunting laced between the tall white posts. She could make out the top of the white-painted grandstand and was now desperate to see more.

Harry was draining his bottle of beer, and Mac, Leo and Richard were grouped around the back of the car, stretching their legs. They wore white flannels and striped blazers. The blazers were not their own, but brought by Leo. Striped blazers were not Mac, Richard or Harry's idea of racing apparel, but they went along with it and entered into the spirit.

'Everybody else is in tweed,' grumbled Mac, 'or normal jackets and trousers.'

'Yes, and look at them, they're all cooking,' said Leo. 'Time we had a bit of colour. The war's over now, and we're not at Royal Ascot so there's no need for morning dress.'

'Come on, then!' pleaded Eleanor. 'I want to see what's going on.'

'But we haven't eaten yet,' wailed Richard, his eyes betraying the fact that although he might not have eaten, he had certainly drunk.

'Oh!' Eleanor went to the hamper that lay in the now open boot of the Talbot. She undid the leather straps and removed the chequered tablecloth to reveal an assortment of comestibles that reminded her of the picnic scene in *The Wind in the Willows*. If nothing else, Leo was as brilliant at picnics as the Water Rat, and jars of pickled onions and pickled walnuts, pots of pâté and cheeses, an assortment of pies and loaves, pasties and sausage rolls lay there like some Elysian feast.

'Why don't you just grab something and bring it with you? Then we can go and explore.'

'Walk around eating?' asked Leo incredulously.

Eleanor looked at him appealingly.

Leo shook his head. 'What would the family say?' He picked up a meat pie and bit into it. Then he smiled. 'Bugger the family; come on!' He held out his arm and Eleanor took it and walked with him towards the grandstand. Mac and Richard followed his lead, grabbing a chunk of bread and a piece of cheese, or a pie and a pickled onion, and sauntered off in the direction of the activity.

Harry, last to broach the hamper, asked, 'Do I lock the car or what?' but by then the others were out of earshot. He shook his head, closed the boot and locked the doors, which seemed rather futile bearing in mind that the hood was down. Then he looked up at the sky and smiled. It would not rain. Not today.

Eleanor somehow felt that the day would turn out to be special. She didn't know why. She just felt some inner surge of happiness that swept away her worries. Right now the future didn't seem to matter. Good-humoured racegoers were all around, and the four men she liked most in the world were close by. Richard put his arm round her shoulder as they stood by the rails watching the gleaming horses flash by on their way to the start, the jockeys' silks in pink and lime green, lemon yellow and scarlet dazzling in the afternoon sunshine.

Her eyes were regularly drawn to Harry, carrying his blazer over his shoulder, his sleeves rolled up and his brown arms and face soaking up the sun. Richard was taking less kindly to the heat. His face was pink now, and his freckles were becoming more noticeable. 'Why don't you take your blazer off?' she asked, and he did so without demur, pushing his hands in his pockets and carrying it over his arm.

'We'd better get a bet on,' said Leo, 'or we're going to miss this race.' What do you fancy?' He pulled a race card from his back pocket and ran his finger down the list of runners.

Eleanor leaned on his shoulder and looked at the list. 'That one.' She pointed to the fourth horse on the card, not bothering to look any further down.

'Yes. I don't know why I asked, really,' said Leo softly. 'Come on, then, let's find a bookie. You coming, chaps?' He turned to the other three, who were hunched over the *Racing Post.*

'You go on – we haven't looked yet,' said Mac, who was already sketching a horse and jockey on his race card with a stubby pencil.

Leo took Eleanor by the hand and led her along the rails to where a row of bookies were standing under makeshift stands. 'Which one do you fancy?' he asked her.

Eleanor ran her eyes along the row, past Honest John and Billy Bingham to one she felt they should do business with. 'That one,' she said, pointing to a tall man in a grey check suit. 'He has a happy face.'

'You'd have a happy face if you'd won as much as he has,' grumbled Leo, but then he brightened and walked with Eleanor towards the board that said, 'Taffy O'Shea.'

'Oh, but what do we put on?' she asked.

'How flush are you feeling?'

She looked embarrassed. 'Not terribly,' and she began to reach into the pocket of her floral skirt.

Leo patted her hand. 'You keep your money in your purse. Uncle Leo's treat.'

'Oh, but I couldn't possibly . . .'

Leo waved away her objections and hailed the bookmaker. 'A shilling each way on Tall Dark Stranger, please.' He looked at Eleanor, who smiled ruefully.

'A good choice, ma'am,' confirmed the bookie. 'You'll have me bankrupted for sure.'

Eleanor glanced at the Gladstone bag open on the small table to his side and realised that it was unlikely, but the bookie flashed a warm smile at her and she felt glad she had chosen Taffy O'Shea.

'Let's go and see how he does.' They walked back to where they had left the others, but there was no sign of them now. 'Don't worry,' said Leo. 'They'll be back when they've placed their bets.'

But the other three did not return before the race had started, so Eleanor could cheer as loudly as she wanted at Tall Dark Stranger without fear of any sideways glances or suggestive remarks.

She cheered at the start, when her horse got away well, and cheered at the corner, where he seemed to be holding the lead, his blue-silked jockey driving him on, but then as the finish approached, he could not quite maintain momentum and despite the encouragement of both Eleanor and the jockey, Tall Dark Stranger came in second.

'Oh dear,' she said, as she looked up at Leo.

'Not to worry,' he said brightly. 'You had an each-way bet. Time to collect your winnings.'

Leo escorted her back to Taffy O'Shea, who handed her three shillings and sixpence.

'And there was me thinking you were going to ruin me,' he said. 'Three shillings and sixpence. There you go.' He handed Eleanor a half-crown and a shilling, which she attempted to give to Leo.

'No, no, no, your winnings. And there are more races. Come on.'

Eleanor looked across toward the winners' enclosure and saw number four placed second on the towering board above their heads. First was number seven. 'Who was number seven?' she asked Leo.

'I didn't catch the name.'

'Let me look at your race card.'

'No point. Time to sort out the next one and to find the boys.' She was easily distracted and Leo was rather glad. It didn't do to set too much store on superstition when it came to the races.

It was easy to spot Mac, Richard and Harry thanks to their blazers, now back on since the sun had gone behind a cloud, but also because they seemed to be in high spirits.

'Hello, you two!' shouted Richard, his eyes bright and his cheeks even redder than before. 'Ready to celebrate?'

'I suppose so,' said Eleanor brightly. 'We came second. What about you?'

'We won!' said Mac, with a look of incredulity on his face. 'We bloody well won, and I'm surprised you didn't, too.'

'You mean you didn't back it?' asked Richard, looking disappointed.

'Back what?' asked Eleanor.

'The winner, King Dick.'

She felt a sinking feeling in the pit of her stomach, a feeling compounded partly of guilt and partly of disappointment. She did not see Harry glancing down at the *Racing Post* to check the name of the horse that had come second. Neither did she see him look up again, nor the quizzical look on his face.

'The only thing that I ask in this next race is that we have solidarity,' said Leo. 'It's Uncle Freddie's horse and we should stick by him, especially as he paid for our tickets.'

'Shouldn't we go and see him?' asked Eleanor.

'Good God, no! He'll be plastered by now and I don't want to embarrass you.'

'I won't be embarrassed,' said Eleanor.

'No, but I will,' replied Leo. 'We'll do our bit by backing Black Tarquin and leave it at that. Anyway, he'll be in the owners' enclosure and we haven't got passes.'

'Mr O'Shea again?' asked Eleanor.

'If you like. Right, gentlemen, let me have your money and I'll put it on with the jolly Irishman,' said Leo.

But Mr O'Shea had even better luck in the Princess of Wales's Stakes, when Black Tarquin came in fourth to Lord Derby's Dogger Bank.

'We should have known by the weight,' complained Mac. 'Black Tarquin was carrying two stone more than Dogger Bank.'

'And Dogger Bank was number thirteen,' said Harry.

'Are you superstitious, then?' asked Mac.

'Not any more,' said Harry.

Leo felt it was time to change the subject. 'Anyone fancy a drive?'

'Are we leaving already?' asked Eleanor.

'No, not leaving. I just think we ought to drive along to the other end of the course – by Devil's Dyke. You get a different view from there.'

And so, accompanied by assorted murmurings, they made their way back to the car and followed Leo's directions, which were more accurate this time, to the part of the heath known as Devil's Dyke – an ancient earthwork twenty feet high that stretched away across the county. There were fewer people here, and the landscape was open to the skies. Skylarks sang above them, and Eleanor sat on the running board of the Talbot, parked in the rough grass, and strained her eyes to see tiny specks of birds singing their hearts out, while the men made inroads into the picnic, soaking up the beer they had drunk earlier with pies and pasties, bread and fruit cake. The sun had come out again, and they lay back on the grass, eating and drinking and swapping silly remarks. From time to time small aeroplanes would sweep in across the sky and land on the heath down by the stand.

'I don't know how they can do it,' said Leo.

'Fly a plane?' asked Harry.

'No. Find the petrol. They must need fifty gallons or more.'

'Maybe *they're* not rationed,' mused Eleanor.

'Some folk always find a way round these things,' grumbled Mac. 'I mean, look at all those cars down there. There must be two hundred of them. Where do *they* get their petrol from?'

'It's a mystery to me,' murmured Harry. 'But hey, it's a lovely day.' He moved over to the car and sat down next to Eleanor on the running board. 'Hello.'

'Hello,' she answered back, not looking at him, but gazing out over the heath.

There was a different atmosphere here – less frantic than where they were before. She could see haycocks in the large field on the other side of the racecourse, and smell the wild thyme and herbs beneath her feet, mingled with the sweet-smelling grass.

'Isn't it lovely?' she said.

'Yes.'

They sat silently, side by side for several minutes, neither of them wanting to break the mood. Then Mac, who was sitting on the back seat of the Talbot, asked, 'Who's that over there?'

'Where?' asked Leo.

'On the end of the dyke. There's a man painting.'

They looked in the direction of his gaze and saw the distant figure, standing at an easel. He wore a nondescript jacket and trousers and a panama hat on his head, and he was painting the scene in front of him – the rolling heath, the horses and riders, the cars and the distant white-painted stand. Not that they could catch any details on the canvas from where they stood.

'Let's go and look,' offered Eleanor.

'And make ourselves really popular?' countered Mac. 'You know what it's like being watched while you paint . . .'

'Oh, I don't want to interrupt him' said Eleanor, who had got to her feet and was rearranging her skirt. 'Just to have a glance at what he's doing.' And before any of them could argue she was walking down the heath towards the man with the easel.

Mac glanced at Harry, who shrugged and got to his feet to follow her. The others did the same and within a few minutes were quietly advancing on the artist from behind, so as not to distract him. They had got to within a few yards of where he stood when he said, without looking up, 'Lovely day!'

Eleanor, who was still ahead of the others, was taken by surprise and jumped a little before agreeing, 'Yes, lovely.'

The man turned to face her now and raised his hat politely. Eleanor nodded in acknowledgement as the others caught her up.

The man took in the party and asked, 'Having a good day?'

Leo responded on their behalf. 'Yes. Mixed fortunes, though.'

'Ah, 'twas ever thus. You'll find it's calmer up here.' He seemed to be examining a particular part of the landscape.

Eleanor felt emboldened to enquire, 'Do you come up here a lot?'

The man nodded. 'Several times a year. Best place of all. More my bag than Ascot.'

'Always to paint?'

The man smiled. 'Yes, always.' He turned back to his canvas and made several sweeping strokes with his brush. Eleanor gasped at what she saw. This was clearly no amateur. The man looked up again. 'Was there something . . . ?'

The group looked embarrassed now. 'Sorry,' blurted out Mac. 'I said we shouldn't have come. We're disturbing you . . . Only . . . we're art students.'

'Ah, I see.' The man laughed. 'Well, it's no use looking at what I do. Not everyone approves.'

Mac had edged closer now, riveted by the canvas. 'Oh my God!'

'Was that incredulity, young man, or just disbelief?'

'Er . . . I . . .'

'You don't have to like it.'

'No. I mean, it's amazing.'

The man smiled again and said softly, 'Thank you.'

It was Richard who spoke next. 'You are, aren't you?' he asked.

'Now what am I meant to reply to that? I am or I am not what?'

'Munnings,' whispered Harry softly, almost under his breath, and then, having cleared his throat, 'Mr Munnings. I mean . . . Sir . . .'

'Yes,' said the man, and carried on painting.

Eleanor looked shocked. 'We must go,' she said.

'Oh, don't worry,' said the artist. He was wiping his brushes on an old rag now. 'I'm all but finished for today.' Carelessly he tossed the brushes into a paint-spattered wooden box and wiped his hands on a large spotted handkerchief that he had pulled from his pocket.

Another handkerchief was tied round his neck, and as he turned to face them, Eleanor could see take in his appearance more fully. He was a tallish man with fine yet craggy features and a face that lit up when he smiled. He had a faintly patrician air and looked as though his mood could change in the twinkling of an eye. He pushed the panama to the back of his head and wiped his brow with the handkerchief.

'So you're art students. And whereabouts do you study your art?'

'Oxford,' blurted out Richard.

'Oh, goodness me, you're a long way from home. It's usually the other lot who drift around here.'

Eleanor was warming to him. She found him a little intimidating, but at the same time quite compelling. He directed his next question at her. 'And these four young men are squiring you for the afternoon, are they? Lucky chaps!'

Eleanor giggled. 'I don't know about that,' she murmured.

'So are you all painters?'

The other four turned in the direction of Mac and said, almost as one, 'He is.'

Mac looked distinctly uncomfortable. Eleanor could not remember seeing him colour up before. That was usually Richard's province.

'Well, I . . .'

'Oil, or watercolour?' asked the artist.

'Both,' Mac stammered. 'But mainly oils.'

'Brave man.' He turned once more to Eleanor. 'So you don't paint?'

'A little. Watercolours. But I'm not that good.'

'Oh, we all think that.'

'Even you?' she asked.

'I don't know any artists worthy of the name who are satisfied with what they do. And I know a good many who shouldn't even call themselves artists.'

'Like Stanley Spencer?' offered Mac.

There was a brief silence. Mac wondered if he had gone too far. He had not meant to be rude, just to show that he knew to whom he was talking, and that he sympathised. But perhaps it had not come out right. He shifted his weight from one foot to the other. Then the artist's face broke into a grin. 'Have you been reading the papers?'

Mac nodded, relieved that his remark had not offended.

'Bloody modernists. Absolute junk. No time for 'em, and people pay fortunes for 'em. Fools.' His eyes were blazing now.

None of the five felt they should risk further comment. But Munnings's mood changed once more. 'So who do you admire, young man? I didn't catch your name . . .'

'John Macready, but everyone calls me Mac.'

'Well, who are your heroes, John Macready?'

'Turner.'

'Oh, he's everyone's hero.'

'And Reynolds. And Lawrence.'

'Portraitists, then?'

'Not always.' Mac looked embarrassed again. 'I like your work.'

'Thank you.' Munnings raised his panama in appreciation.

'Particularly your horses.'

'Ah, yes. Not the landscapes.'

'No . . . I mean . . . I like the horses especially.'

Munnings was beginning to pack away his paints. 'Do you ever paint them?'

'I try. Bloody difficult.'

'Read your Stubbs?' asked the artist.

'*Anatomy of the Horse*? Yes. I've done lots of drawings.'

The other four were grouped together, watching the two artists converse rather as if they were spectators at a tennis match – first looking towards one player, then the other.

'Bought my copy for fifty bob when I was in my twenties. You've got to know what goes on *inside* to be able to paint the *outside*. Don't you think? Amazing man Stubbs.'

'Yes.'

The artist had taken down the painting from the easel and handed it to Eleanor. 'Can you hold this for me a moment?'

Eleanor took the painting from him without speaking and held it out before her like some valuable religious artefact. The others fixed their gaze upon the still-wet landscape of Newmarket Racecourse as if they were in a trance. None of them had ever been this close to a Munnings, and certainly not to one that was so freshly painted.

Munnings began to fold up his easel. 'So how long have you left at university?' he asked.

It was Harry who replied. 'We go down this summer.'

'And if the rest of you don't paint, what will you do?'

Harry continued, 'I want to run an auction house, Richard wants his own gallery, Mac wants to paint, and Eleanor . . .' He paused, unsure of what to say.

The artist helped him out. 'What does Eleanor want?' he asked.

'Eleanor's not sure yet,' interrupted Leo.

'Oh. And your name is . . . ?' There was the slightest note of irritation in Munnings's voice.

'Leo. Leo Bedlington.'

Mac stepped in. 'With any luck Leo will just buy my paintings.'

Munnings's expression altered to one of recognition. 'Ah, Bedlington. Would that be Bedlington Park?'

Leo nodded.

'In which case I shall be very nice to you. The current

Lord Bedlington has helped swell the coffers. Which only
leaves Eleanor, who isn't sure.' He lowered his head and
looked in Eleanor's direction. Eleanor tried to avoid his eyes.
Then Munnings laughed. 'Not to worry. You're young. Plenty
of time. And you have four young men to choose from.'

At which point none of the quintet felt able to say anything.

'Right, well, if I might have my painting back . . .'

Eleanor came back to earth. 'Yes. Of course.' She handed
over the canvas, somehow sorry to be parted from it. Her
eyes followed it as she handed it back to its creator.

Mac, too, was riveted by the image, which did not go
unnoticed.

'So what will you do in the summer?' Munnings asked of
Mac.

'Paint. I'm not sure where.'

'You should come and see me. Come and watch if you
like. Not for the entire summer – I can't offer you that.
Anyway, we'd probably get on each other's nerves. But you
could come down for a day or so, if you like.'

'But you don't . . . I mean, I might not . . .'

'No, I don't. And you might not. But you won't know until
you've tried, will you?'

'Well, if you're sure . . .'

'Oh, I'm sure. I might send you packing when I see what
your painting's like, but if you're prepared to take the risk . . .'

'Yes. Well, yes . . . thank you . . .'

The artist fished in his pocket and pulled out a small white
card. 'Here you are. Get in touch with me in a couple of
weeks. I'll see what I can do.'

Mac held the card in both hands as though it were a fine
jewel, and his face had upon it an expression that could have
signified the completion of five rounds with a prize fighter
without disgracing himself. 'Thank you very much,' he
murmured.

Munnings turned away from them now, lifted his panama to bid them farewell, then picked up the painting and paraphernalia and began to walk back down the slope. 'And you can bring Eleanor with you, if you like. Perhaps by then she'll have worked out what she's doing.'

7

Bath

December 2007

It is lucky for us that Bath is so evidently entering another
of its optimistic periods . . . Wherever you look, there seems
to be initiative or restoration, and even on one of those des-
pondent mornings when Pope's pit seems more than usually
pit-like . . . somehow you feel the old place stirring with new
life and bounciness.

Jan Morris (1982), *New York Times*

Jamie deliberately put on the first clothes that came to hand,
as if to convince himself that the evening would probably
turn out to be nothing special and also that nothing was
expected of it. Nothing serious, anyway. He had high
hopes that she would still be as much fun as she was, would
still make him laugh, but beyond that . . . Well, time
would tell.

He had known her now for longer than he had known
anyone except the members of his immediate family. They
had been together at nursery school, through some oversight
on their parents' and grandparents' part. When, at the age of
eleven, they were sent their separate ways – young James to
the local grammar and Artemis to boarding school in Surrey
– they had kept in touch through occasional letters and more
frequent phone calls.

Eventually they both gravitated to their home territory of
Bath, happily for the most part, though to Missy the words
of Dr Johnson, learned in her Eng. Lit. lessons, would for
ever eecho. It was, he said, 'a city with small ideas'. Never-

theless she found in her grandfather's art gallery a larger world into which she could escape. She had flirted with the Impressionists and the Pre-Raphaelites, with the Scottish colourists and the 'Glasgow Boys', but found her métier in the world of sporting art – an unlikely choice for a girl who had been steadfastly unsporting at school, but maybe that was why; it was a world slightly removed from her own. She could look at horses with an artist's eye rather than an equestrian's. Where dogs craved affection and cats demanded respect, horses inspired admiration and awe, and any artist who could catch their spirit seemed to her to be peerless.

Jamie, on the other hand, was a modernist with a liking for William Scott and Ivon Hitchens. He liked the way they made him feel – exhilarated and slightly uneasy. Rather like Missy. Going into dealership was not, for him, an option. The family had assumed he would come into the auction house as a junior partner and he had put up little resistance. The chance to avoid a gigantic overdraft had played its part. For most of the time it was an enjoyable job, though there were still occasional tensions. It was ironic to think that Jamie's impatience with his mother was due to her continuous close proximity, while Missy's discomfort was down to her father's earlier absence. One parent too near and the other too far away.

Jamie had showered and shaved, dressed in a brown leather jacket and chinos – liberated from the navy blue Paul Smith suit he had worn during the day – and splashed on some aftershave, taking care not to overdo it. He was not, as a rule, an aftershave man, but he thought a dab of something from Hackett might build his confidence without overpowering his date. There. He had used the word. Why was he so busy trying to convince himself that this was not 'a date' when it so clearly was? Whatever. He lost patience with himself and picked up his car keys. As he did so, the phone rang. He murmured, 'Damn,' to himself and went to pick it up. It occurred to him that it might be Artemis about to cancel, but then he heard his grandfather's voice at the other end. As ever he had to strain to hear the softly spoken voice of Harry Ballantyne.

'Jamie?'

'Granddad, how are you?' He glanced at his watch, hoping that his grandfather's call would not last as long as it usually did.

'Oh, you know. Buggering on.'

'Good for you. And Gran?'

'She's fine. Went to the quack today. Fingers are a bit stiff, but he seems to think she's all right. Expected at her age, he said. Gives her trouble with the Chopin, but then I suppose she'll have to get used to it now.'

Jamie glanced at his watch again. 'Granddad, could I give you a ring in the morning? Only I'm just on my way out . . .' He hoped his grandfather would not ask where he was going.

'Oh, sorry. Yes. I just wondered if you could pop in tomorrow.'

'Of course. Everything's all right, isn't it?'

'Yes, yes, everything's fine. It's just that I want to talk something over with you, a sort of proposition. It shouldn't take long.'

'Fine. Yes. Look, I'll come over at about ten, if that's OK. We've no auction tomorrow. Two in one week is quite enough. It's clearing day, so I'll have plenty of time.'

'Right. We'll see you at about ten, then. I'll have the coffee on. Look after yourself.'

'And you. Love to Gran.' He put the phone down and stood for a moment, wondering what it was that his grandfather wanted to talk about. It would not, he hoped, be another lecture.

★　★　★

He parked his car opposite the Theatre Royal and walked
along Upper Borough Wall before turning down Union Street
towards the Pump Room. The shops were shut now, but
there were still enough folk about to give the city a sense of
bustle, dressed for early autumn rather than winter, scurry-
ing about on their way for a drink or a meal, a trip to the
cinema or the theatre. There were chattering girls in skirts
of ill-advised brevity, well-to-do couples smartly turned out
and arms linked, men in suits with an attaché case in one
hand and a mobile phone in the other into which they were
making excuses. It was early December and unseasonably
mild – little danger this year of a white Christmas, the
weathermen said. In a week or two's time the shops would
stay open later and the streets would be seething as people
shopped for Christmas with greater intent. But the decora-
tions had been up for a month or more now and the citizens
of Bath had learned to pace themselves. In Bath Abbey
churchyard there were men at work erecting the small wooden
chalets that would become the Christmas market, turning
the precincts of the Anglican abbey into something
reminiscent of Bayern Munich.

Jamie sighed at the thought of it all. Christmas. He could
not say that he was looking forward to it – flitting between
his mother's cottage in a village just outside the city, where
she would entertain a never-ending stream of county types
for lunchtime drinks and evening meals, and his grandparents'
house in the Circus, where things were much quieter. Feast
or famine, it seemed there was nothing in between. He put
the thought from his mind, turned the corner and walked
towards the Pump Room. He was embarrassed to find that
she was already waiting at the entrance.

He looked at his watch. 'Am I late?'

'No. It's me. I'm always early. Sorry.'

'Oh, yes. I'd forgotten.' He leaned forward to kiss her on

the cheek. Then he stepped back and stared at her. 'You look . . .'

'Different?' she asked, with a concerned expression.

'No, not different. Just . . . well . . . gorgeous.'

She smiled and looked relieved. 'Oh. That's nice.'

In that one moment he was aware of a complete change in his mood. He had been working so hard at convincing himself of the unimportance of the evening that it came as a shock to discover a feeling that he had not experienced since she had left and gone to America. It was a sense of total relaxation. Of complete ease in the company of another person. However many years it was since she had been removed from his life, it did not seem to matter. He looked at her now and experienced once more the deep delight in her closeness to him. It made him laugh – an exclamation of a laugh – brief and quite involuntary.

'What is it?' she asked.

'It's just that . . . I mean . . . it doesn't seem . . . well . . .'

'As if we've ever been apart?' she asked, suddenly afraid that she had imputed too much into his hesitant attempt at an explanation.

'No.'

There was a brief silence now. It was not uncomfortable. It seemed like a moment in which they could tacitly acknowledge each other's presence. A welcoming silence of mutual recognition. Then Jamie said 'Shall we go and eat?'

'Yes, please,' said Missy. 'I'm starving.'

They found a corner table at Loch Fyne where they could see everything going on around them. Not that they appeared to notice. For most of the time they leaned in across the table and swapped stories about the intervening years – of Jamie's gradual taking on of more responsibility at Ballantyne's and Missy's exploits in the States.

'So did you like it there?' he asked.

'Some things, yes – the buzz, the art world, the shopping.'

'But not everything?'

She looked reflective. 'I missed the greenness, the country-side. And the architecture.' Then, brightening, 'How sad is that?'

'Not sad at all. I know what you mean. I was watching the Christmas stalls going up and wondering what Beau Nash would have made of it all. And then I thought I ought to get a life.'

She reached across the table and put her hand on his. 'I'm glad you're still you.'

'Sad old me?'

'No. Just thoughtful old you.'

'Too thoughtful for my own good.'

She squeezed his hand and then let it go. 'Shall we order?'

Over a bottle of Sancerre and plates of fish they talked about the city and how it had changed – or not changed – since they had grown up.

'I mean, most people move away, don't they?' said Jamie.

'Why do you think?' asked Missy.

'Too expensive?'

'I guess so. We're lucky. Or spoiled.'

'Speak for yourself.'

'Ah. Sorry. You pay for yours, then?'

'You bet I do. Still, I can just about manage.'

'Where are you?'

'Batheaston.'

'Not too far out, then.'

'No. But I'd quite like to be in town. More buzz.'

Missy grinned.

'What is it?' he asked.

'Nothing. It's just that coming from New York, it seems funny to think of Bath as having a buzz.'

Jamie saw the funny side. 'I told you. I'm just sad. I ought to get out more.'

'Have you never wanted to?' asked Missy.

'Oh I did a few years ago. I even applied for a job in London – with Christie's. Got it, actually.'

'What happened then?'

'I stayed for about six months. Couldn't stand it.'

'The job?'

'No. The place. Too big, too . . . unhappy. I knew I should have stuck at it. The job was interesting but I just couldn't hack the place. Then Mum and Granddad made me an offer I couldn't refuse.'

'A partnership?'

'Yes. So here I am.'

'Happily?'

'Ish. Yes. Yes, I am happy. Work-wise.'

'I sense a "but" coming on . . .'

Jamie took a deep breath. 'I am very happy in my job, and I am very happy in Bath. As for the future . . . we'll see.'

Missy fixed his eye. 'Exciting prospects, then?'

Jamie tried hard to suppress a grin. 'That depends.'

'Eat your fish,' said Missy. And then, raising her glass, 'Here's to—'

At which point Jamie cut in. 'Here's to us,' he said. 'Whatever happens.'

'Yes,' she agreed. 'Here's to us.'

They chinked glasses and took a sip of wine. Then, as Missy lowered hers to the table, she said, 'By the way, the Munnings you sold me . . .'

'Yes?' Jamie put his glass down and looked concerned.

'Oh, don't worry, it's fine. It's just that . . . Do you know anything about it? Its provenance?'

'No. Not really. It came from a private collection.' Jamie

looked thoughtful. 'If I remember rightly . . . Oh, but then I have to retain client confidentiality.'

Missy gave him her best 'oh, go on' look.

Jamie had always found her difficult to refuse. 'It was someone called Stephens or Stephenson or something. Not a name I recognised. And I couldn't possibly tell you where they came from. Anyway, why do you want to know?'

'Oh, nothing. It's just that Grandpa has a particularly soft spot for it. Seemed very pleased to have it, and yet he didn't hang it on the wall.'

'Is that a problem?'

'Not exactly. It's just that he has a sort of routine when he gets a new picture. He always takes another one off the wall – the wall by the window, where there's really good light – and then hangs up the new one and looks at it straight away. A bit like a child with a new toy – you know, wanting to play with it immediately.' She looked reflective. 'Like me when I get a new top or a skirt – I like to put it on and see how it looks.'

'And he didn't? See how it looked, I mean.'

'Well, he did briefly. He held it in his hands, examined it and seemed quite satisfied with it in a preoccupied sort of way. Then he put it down and stood it with its face to the wall, and I can't understand why.'

'Is that all?'

'No. It's the picture itself. The lady on the grey horse. Did she remind you of anybody?'

Jamie rested his knife and fork on his plate. 'That's funny.'

'What do you mean?'

'I glanced at the picture when the guys in the saleroom put it on the easel. It was a bit of a shock.'

'Why?'

'Oh, probably just my imagination, or a trick of the light.

And the fact that you were bidding for it and I haven't set eyes on you for however many years.'

'But . . . ?'

'The lady in the picture looked just like you.'

8

Dedham
July 1949

I feel very lazy and loose,
For pictures don't seem any use,
But days that are sunny
Are better than money,
So working may go to the deuce.
An Artist's Life (1950), A. J. Munnings

They were not at all sure that it was a good idea. He had given Mac his card, but it was on the spur of the moment and it was well known that he was a temperamental old stick and just as likely to claim that he had done nothing of the sort.

There were only three of them in the Talbot this time. Leo had insisted they take it, in spite of the fact that his father had taken a turn for the worse the night before and he had had to stay behind at Bedlington Park. Richard was, to his great irritation, confined to bed in his lodgings with a heavy cold. With only a week to go before they left Oxford, he was reluctant to let Eleanor go without him, but she insisted that she would be well looked after by Mac and Harry, who was driving. It crossed Richard's mind that she would be all too well looked after, but he was powerless to win this particular argument, and with an elaborate sequence of coughs and sneezes that sounded like a wind band warming up for an especially energetic work by John Philip Sousa, he sloped off to bed.

It had been a long drive to Dedham on the Essex–Suffolk border, and the clock on the tower of St Mary's Church struck one as they motored slowly down the High Street in search of Castle House.

'Oh! How pretty it is!' exclaimed Eleanor.

Harry grinned.

'Well, it is!'

'Stop the car!' instructed Mac suddenly.

Harry pulled in beside the kerb. 'What's wrong?'

'Nothing,' said Mac. He was looking up at the elegantly pinnacled tower of the church. 'Just the same.'

'The same as what?' asked Harry.

'The same as when Constable painted it.'

The trio gazed up at the church in front of them, solid and impressive on a warm afternoon in early July, its warm buff stone almost glowing in the sunshine.

'Friendly,' offered Eleanor.

'Yes. Unthreatening. Very . . . friendly,' confirmed Mac.

'Let's hope your artist is the same,' muttered Harry, as he eased the Talbot forward down the High Street, past the rows of higgledy-piggledy Georgian houses – some pink, some white and some the colour of Jersey cream.

'Where do you suppose it is?' asked Eleanor.

'Not a bloody clue,' confessed Mac. 'We'll just have to carry on looking. I think it's a big house. At least it looks like it in the painting.'

'Which painting's that?' asked Harry, glancing to left and right in the hope of spotting something that resembled the house of a successful artist, whatever that might be.

'The one of him and his missus out the back. Painted about fifteen years ago. She's on a horse – a bay – wearing a black riding habit and a silk top hat. He's standing next to her with the painting itself and a palette, and there's a sort of bow window, but I shouldn't think you can see that from the street.'

'He *is* expecting us, isn't he?' asked Harry.

'Well, I've had a postcard saying he is,' confirmed Mac. 'I just hope he remembers.'

'I think I'll stay in the car,' said Harry.

'You will not!' scolded Eleanor. 'I've come to give Mac moral support and you're here to give it to *me*.'

Harry smiled. 'Oh, that's nice, considering I'm only the driver.'

Eleanor flushed. 'You know what I mean.'

The village was long and winding, and the dwellings were more scattered now. After a mile or so, just as they were about to give up and turn round, they spotted a likely house on the left-hand side of the road. A lane ran down one side of it and behind were paddocks where horses were grazing. The house was painted a warm shade of cream, and attached to it was an assortment of buildings, at least one of which could pass as a studio.

'Stop, stop!' exclaimed Mac. 'I think this is it.'

Harry pulled up the Talbot at the entrance to a short gravel drive. Mac leaped out and walked round the side of the house. They watched as he craned to see through the bushes and over the fence. He turned to them and nodded, then walked back to the car. 'I can see the bow window. This is it.'

The three of them looked at one another. 'Good luck,' murmured Harry as he manoeuvred the car into the short drive of Castle House.

Mac grabbed a large folio cover from the back seat. They walked up to the front door and Harry motioned to Mac to ring the bell. Mac took a deep breath and did so. Nothing happened. Then they heard a booming voice from above. 'If you're a bloody tradesman, use the tradesman's entrance.'

They looked first at one another and then for an alternative door. They found it round the back of the house. By the time they got there, Sir Alfred James Munnings, KCVO, PRA, was standing in it with his hands on his hips. His cheeks were highly coloured, and he wore a yellow riding stock at his neck and a rough check tweed jacket over grey flannel trousers. There was a rose in his buttonhole. It matched the colour of his cheeks. His eyes shone, and he drew breath and let out a stream of invective. 'Can't a fella have a quiet bloody hour after his lunch on a summer's afternoon?'

None of them spoke. Instead they stared as if hypnotised at the man berating them for interrupting his afternoon nap.

Only Mac was brave enough to offer, 'Well, you did tell us to come, sir. I'm sorry we're a bit late.'

'You cheeky young sod. What do you mean . . . ?' and then he caught sight of Eleanor hiding behind the two men.

'Ah! Oh, yes. Bugger me, so I did. It's you, is it?' And then, directed at Eleanor, 'You must forgive a crotchety old man. Bad day. Glorious light, but bad day. Gout.' He waved his hand as if to illustrate the problem. 'And an invisible sitter.' And then, recovering himself, 'Well, don't stand there like statues, come on.'

He led them outside, past lawns and brilliantly planted flower beds that the three visitors barely had time to take in. Then they crossed a paddock. Horses looked up to see what was disturbing their quiet afternoon, and eventually the party arrived at the building the artist used as his studio. 'In you go.' He motioned them inside. All three were amazed by what they saw. From the ceiling hung an assortment of racing silks in rainbow colours – yellow and violet, scarlet and blue, pink and orange. There were easels supporting half a dozen partly completed canvases, and pots stuffed full of brushes were scattered like shuttlecocks among paint-daubed palettes and pieces of board. Odd items of furniture – spattered stools and an assortment of tables – filled the rest of the space, along with riding crops and boots, a hunting horn, bridles and horse collars.

'Gosh!' exclaimed Eleanor.

'Yes. Sorry it's such a mess. In the middle of something, I'm afraid. No time to be tidy.'

'No,' murmured Mac, entranced by the scene in front of him. This is what he had spent his life dreaming about – becoming a real artist, painting real pictures, in a place like this. His eye ran along the canvases stacked against the wall, and those propped up on the easels. Most of them were of horses – with and without riders; others were landscapes, of Munnings's beloved Exmoor, and of the Essex–Suffolk border country he now called home.

The artist saw they were entranced. It rather pleased him. 'Had it since 1906 – the studio. The original, anyway. At Swainsthorpe where I used to be. Had it moved here lock, stock and barrel when I came to Dedham after the war in 1919. It's twice as big now, but it's still the same place.'

Mac was examining a picture of a horse race – the brightly caparisoned jockeys vying for position on their bays and greys against a background of bright green turf.

'Always the start, never the finish,' said Munnings. 'Impossible to capture the finish with any reality. The start is always a better bet.'

'How long . . . ?' asked Eleanor.

'To finish one? They all ask that,' snorted the artist. And then, seeing that she was embarrassed by the dullness of her question, he answered in kindlier tones, 'It varies. Three or four days mostly. Longer if they are more complicated. Usually three days for a horse and three for a rider, plus any extra time to work it up.'

'You paint them separately?' asked Mac.

'Usually. I use that.' Munnings pointed to a sort of giant trestle on which was placed a saddle. 'I can do the horse and then put the rider in place in the picture afterwards without making the poor animal stand there for days on end. They deserve better than that.' Then he noticed Mac's folio, tucked under his arm. 'Come on, then. You've seen mine; let's have a look at yours.'

Mac demurred, 'Oh, I'm not sure it's really worth it.'

'Nonsense. That's what you came for, isn't it? Let's be having a look. I'll tell you what I think, mind. It's a tough world, the art world; there's no point in me being kind if you haven't any talent. Let me look on that proviso and I'll give you an honest opinion.'

Mac hesitated, then eased the folio from under his arm and handed it to the master, who walked over to a table and undid the ribbon ties that held it together. He pulled out three paintings. There was a study of the Norfolk Broads – all water and sky – another of the Cherwell with a punt going by and a third of a horse grazing in a paddock. Munnings scrutinised them silently. Mac began to wish they had not come. The silence was deafening.

Having pored over each of them in turn, without saying a word, Munnings put the painting of the Norfolk Broads on a vacant easel. 'Right,' he said. 'This one – good sky, very good sky, but the water needs more work. You have to study it more carefully, day after day. See how the light plays; give your water depth *and* movement.' He took the painting down. 'Next, the river. The water here is better. You've taken more trouble. You know it better, yes?'

Mac nodded.

'And then the horse.'

All three of them waited for the expected criticism. Munnings turned and looked directly at Mac. 'You have a talent. You've caught the muscle and the anatomy well, plus the light. It can do with even more mastery, but your horse is alive. That's rare. Keep at it and at it and at it until you think you know the beast inside out and you'll be a fine painter. And believe me, I don't say that to just anyone.'

Mac hardly knew where to put himself.

'And now I've embarrassed you.'

'No, it's just . . .'

'Oh, I'm not an easy man to please, but you should be even harder on yourself. One day, when you're accepted into the Royal Academy . . .'

Mac shook his head.

'Oh, you will be, if you keep at it. On that day walk right in there with your ticket and don't faint when you see how awful your picture looks. These are your youthful years, when the brain absorbs easily and learns quickly. Begin to be a serious student and let all business of young Macready and young genius go and during years to come you'll possibly make a hit. But go and do some real study – outdoors. That's where your talent lies. And look at other artists' work – the good stuff, the stuff that leaves you breathless with admiration – and ask yourself, How did he do that? I do. Still.' The artist stopped.

The three students stood silently, and then Mac said simply, 'Thank you.'

'Not at all. Now, then, how about you doing me a favour?'

The three looked at each other: then Mac said, 'Yes, anything.'

'You see this painting?' He walked them over to an easel on which stood a partially completed painting of a grey, leaning forward and browsing. 'It needs a rider. It doesn't matter who it is, so long as it's a woman. I'm painting it for an exhibition, not on commission. My sitter failed to turn up this morning. A woman in the village. Her mother's gone down with influenza or something and she cried off.' He turned to Eleanor. 'Have you ever ridden a horse?'

'Well, yes, but . . .'

'Recently?'

'Until a few years ago I rode every week. Now it's every few months.'

'So you'll know how to sit. Perfect.'

'Oh, but . . .'

'No "buts". You hop up there into that saddle' – he gestured at the saddle wedged on top of the trestle – 'and I'll use you as the model. There's a riding habit and boots behind that screen. Go and see if they fit.'

'A habit?' enquired Eleanor.

'Yes. So much more ladylike than jodhpurs and a hacking jacket. A good figure in a well-cut habit is the essence of grace and beauty.'

It seemed futile to argue. Munnings turned to Mac and the hitherto silent Harry and said, 'Go back to the house and find the kitchen. Ask the housekeeper for a beer apiece and go and have a look at the horses if you want.'

Both Harry and Mac stared at him blankly. 'Go on. She's safe with me. You can come back in an hour when I've got started and see how it's going, but I don't want you peering over my shoulder for a while, is that understood?'

The two men nodded and walked quietly from the studio, allowing the former president of the Royal Academy to make the acquaintance of his new sitter and to immortalise her on canvas. As they disappeared across the paddock, they could hear his voice ringing out behind them. 'What a go!' he said. 'What a go!'

9

Bath
December 2007

Let us not speak, for the love we bear for one another –
Let us hold hands and look.

'In a Bath Tea Shop' (1945), Sir John Betjeman

'Maybe that's why he bought the painting,' offered Jamie. 'Because he thought it looked like you.'

'Oh, I don't think Grandpa's that sentimental. Not to the tune of three quarters of a million, anyway. No, it would have been a business deal, nothing more.' She looked a little disappointed.

'Hey!' He tried to pull her out of her reverie. 'Don't let it spoil your evening.'

'No, it won't.' She smiled wistfully. 'It would have been a nice thought, though, wouldn't it? That somebody loved you so much they had to buy a painting that looked like you?' She took another sip of her wine.

'Mmm,' said Jamie teasingly, 'I never thought of you as particularly high maintenance.'

'What, then?'

'I think the word they use is "feisty".'

'Oh, I hate that. It sounds so . . . tough . . . without being sensitive.'

'And you're not?'

'I'd like to think I'm both. How about you?'

'Oh, I don't think feisty is a word that's applied to men very often.'

'No, silly, I mean tough.'

Jamie frowned. 'When I need to be. But sensitive, too.'

'Oversensitive?' She was pushing him gently.

'Sometimes. But then it's difficult to get it right, especially where women are concerned. There seems to be a fine line between being a pushover and a chauvinist. I'm never quite sure I've cracked it.'

'As long as you err on the side of the pushover, I wouldn't worry too much.'

Jamie laughed. 'That sounds like an invitation.'

'Well, it's not. Just an observation. You've always been sensitive, and that doesn't mean weak.' She lowered her voice conspiratorially. 'Except where your mother is concerned.'

'Hey, that's not fair! If you knew what I had to go through to come here with you tonight, you wouldn't say that.'

'Oh, not you as well.'

'You mean you had the same?'

Missy nodded. 'From Grandpa. Not exactly the third degree, but pretty disapproving.'

'If it weren't so depressing, I'd feel flattered that he thought I was dangerous.'

Missy raised her eyebrows and leaned back in her chair. 'Oh, you mean you're not?'

Jamie paused and leaned forward on the table. He tried to suppress a grin, and almost succeeded. 'Do you want me to be?'

Now Missy leaned forward so that she was closer to him. 'Just a bit.'

Jamie sat up. 'You're such a tease. Always were.'

She looked resigned now. 'I know. It's a good safety valve.'

They were interrupted by the waiter. 'Would you like coffee, madam? Sir?'

Jamie looked across at Missy enquiringly.

'No, thanks.'

'Just the bill, then, please,' confirmed Jamie.

Missy said matter-of-factly, 'I thought you might like to come back to my place for a coffee. Unless you think that's too forward?'

'Well, it has taken you about twenty-five years to ask me, so at that rate we should be able to sleep together in 2109.'

'Oh,' she said. 'That soon.'

'Bloody hell,' exclaimed Jamie. 'You don't mean to tell me you live in the Royal Crescent!'

They were walking along Brock Street towards the city's most prestigious address.

'Only a part of it,' replied Missy. 'A very little part of it.'

Jamie looked at the discreet brass plaque beside the door of the lofty Georgian terrace house near the centre of the graceful arc of Bath stone. 'King's Fine Art,' it said, the black lettering partially eroded by daily applications of Brasso and elbow grease.

Jamie cleared his throat and announced, 'The Royal Crescent is Bath's finest terrace. Begun in 1767 by John Wood the Younger, it was the first terrace of its kind to be built anywhere in the world. It faces due south, catching the best of the sunlight.' Then he added, as an aside, 'Which means that your grandfather must have invested heavily in opaque blinds for all the windows.' He saw Missy's look of surprise, but refused to be deflected from his pronouncement. 'It impresses even the most hardened of architectural critics. The one hundred and fourteen Ionic columns support a Palladian cornice. The four-storey houses – plus basement – many of them now divided into apartments, continue to be much sought after.'

'What was all that about?' asked Missy.

'I used to do a bit of tour-guiding in the school holidays, remember, and now I'm doing my best not to turn green with envy.'

Missy laughed. 'Come on,' she said, turning her key in the lock and opening the front door. Before Jamie could say anything, he was pulled by the arm into the egg-yolk-coloured, white-pillared Georgian hallway, to the accompaniment of a beeping alarm. Missy closed the door and punched a series of numbers into a small panel concealed behind a column that supported a white marble bust of Sir Joshua Reynolds. She apologised as a matter of habit when she withdrew her hand from between his shoulder blades.

Jamie was standing in the hallway open-mouthed. He had been in some of these houses before, to value furniture and paintings, so he knew what to expect, but the fact that Missy should live in one came as a complete surprise.

'I thought you just had an ordinary flat,' he murmured.

'It is an ordinary flat. It's just in an extraordinary house.'

It then occurred to Jamie that there would be hell to pay if he were seen here. 'Look, don't you think I should go before your grandfather . . . ?'

'No need to worry. He doesn't live here. He goes back to Peel Place every night now. That's why I can live here, in Grandpa's old flat. I have the place to myself. Come on.'

She began to climb the majestic staircase with its ornate, white-painted balustrade. To Jamie, the sensation was of walking in wonderland. To right and left of the staircase hung paintings of superb quality. Even he could see that. He read the names on the gilded labels at the base of each frame. Here a Seymour, there a Wootton. To the left a Barraud, and to the right a Munnings. At the top of the first staircase was a large landscape with horses – a grey and a bay – and the label beneath it confirmed his suspicions. It was a Stubbs.

'Even you must like that,' remarked Missy as they passed.

'Oh, yes. Bloody hell, it must be worth . . .'

'Don't go there. Anyway, it's not ours. We're trying to sell it for a client. Just enjoy it while you can.' He had stopped in front of the painting and was staring at it intently. 'And you'd rather have a Ben Nicholson, would you?' she asked accusingly.

He sighed. 'That's not a fair comparison.'

'No, I don't suppose it is. Not with the finest horse painter who ever lived.'

'I'll give you that,' conceded Jamie. 'It's beautiful. Far better than your little Herring,' he added disparagingly.

'Come on.' Missy slipped off her shoes now and padded further up the stairs until they reached a glazed door on the third floor. She slipped another key into the lock and pushed it open. What met Jamie's eyes then caused his jaw to drop once more.

The apartment was entirely white – the carpet, the curtains, the soft furnishings and the walls. The only colour to be seen was that from one enormous painting on the far wall. It was of three men on three horses. They looked for all the world as though they were riding rocking horses – three burly farmers intent on chasing a hare.

After the initial shock, Jamie's face broke into a grin. 'Nice,' he said. 'Very nice.'

'Not the best painting, I'm afraid, but I've always liked it. Thomas Weaver. About 1818. Three stout yeomen on three stout horses. The hare gets away, so it's OK.'

'So I see.'

'It used to belong to the Marquis of Bute.'

'Well, it's found a good home, and so have you.'

She moved from the main sitting room through an archway. Jamie followed her and found that it led to a kitchen. She punched some numbers into another keypad on the wall and the sound of soft chamber music filled the air.

'You really have got this sorted, haven't you?' conceded Jamie.

'I'm very lucky,' Missy admitted. 'But I don't take it for granted, and none of it really belongs to me.'

'You are a part of the firm now, though, aren't you?' he asked.

'Yes, but only a relatively small part. There's Grandpa, Patrick – my dad – and me.'

'Enough, then.'

She nodded and smiled. 'Enough.'

He watched her as she moved about the place, easy and relaxed in his company.

'You can take your jacket off, you know.'

He did so, and then watched as she made coffee, before following her back to the sitting room, where the various lamps – on low tables and white-painted columns – were now dimmed. There was a vase of white lilies in one corner and their perfume filled the air.

Missy put down the tray on a low table and walked towards the window. 'Come and look,' she said. She pressed another button, which caused the white cotton blinds of the tall sash windows to lift and reveal the sparkling lights of the City of Bath below them. 'Isn't it beautiful?'

'Yes, it is,' he admitted, but he was not looking at the view.

Over coffee they chatted about his own place in Batheaston and how it would have to do 'for now', however long that might be. Then she asked him quite directly, 'So what about your love life?'

'Ah, yes, well . . . that will require a short answer.'

'You mean there isn't one?'

'Yes and no.'

'On and off, then?'

'Well, more off than on. Or to be honest, totally off.'

Missy curled her feet up underneath her as she sat on the white sofa, losing herself partially in the soft, deep cushions. Her legs were encased in black trousers, her body in a cream woollen sweater that showed off her figure. She pushed her blonde bob behind her ears and took a sip of coffee.

Jamie sat on the sofa opposite, trying to look relaxed yet upright and in control. 'We met at Christie's. Quite a big thing for a while, but when I said I wanted to come back to Bath, she wasn't too pleased. Said that if I was serious I'd stay in town with her.'

'Well, she did have a point,' said Missy.

'She could have come with me.'

'You could have stayed with her.' She realised that she was beginning to sound judgemental and so asked gently, 'What's the situation now?'

Jamie smiled ruefully. 'There isn't one. She's found another guy, in China.'

'China?' asked Missy incredulously.

'Ceramics. It's a department at Christie's.'

Missy erupted in a burst of laughter. Then Jamie laughed, too. 'I suppose if I had really been serious, I would have stayed there, but if I'm honest with myself, she wasn't the one for me.'

'Oh, come over here.' Missy patted the sofa beside her. Jamie rose from the opposite sofa and walked round to sit beside her. She squeezed his hand. 'Still the same old Jamie. Still a bit of an Eeyore.'

'Me? Nah. It's all a front designed to get sympathy from the opposite sex.' Then he looked at her enquiringly and asked, 'Do you think so?'

'Just a bit. But I wouldn't have you any other way.'

She leaned forward and kissed him very gently on the forehead. Then he put his arm around her shoulders and rested his head against hers.

'I'm glad you're back,' he said.

'So am I,' replied Missy. 'So am I.'

They sat silently for a while, he gently stroking her hair,

she resting her hand on his arm. Then he asked, 'What about you? You said there was someone in the States. Has he gone away, too?'

''Fraid so.'

'And you don't mind?'

'I did at the time. I found out he was seeing someone else as well as me. When I said it was her or me, he decided it was her. Simple as that.'

'So here you are, on the rebound.'

She pulled away from him. 'No!'

'Only teasing,' he said softly. 'Sorry. Unkind.'

He put his arm round her once more. 'And there's nobody else?' he asked.

'Well, yes.' Missy paused and waited for the reaction. 'There is, actually.'

Jamie withdrew his arm. 'Oh.' He did his best to sound unaffected. 'I see.'

'I don't know how to say this.'

'No, go on, please. It really doesn't matter.'

'It's been going on a long time now.'

'I see.'

'I thought that when I went to the States, it would all blow over, thought that if I put all those miles between us, it would make a difference. I'd meet new people in a new world and all those thoughts I had about him would disappear. I'd get over him.'

'And you didn't?'

Missy shook her head.

'I see.' Jamie did his best not to sound disappointed. 'So what's the situation now? Does he know?'

'I'm not sure.'

'Does he know you're back?'

'Oh, yes.'

'And has he made contact?'

'Yes. I've been out to dinner with him.'

'God! You didn't waste any time, did you?'

'No.' She looked down and he read her embarrassment.

'I'm sorry,' said Jamie. 'I should be happy for you.'

'I do hope so.'

'It's just that . . .'

Missy said nothing, but waited until he spoke again.

'It's just that . . . well . . . if ever you're let down again, would you . . . ? I mean . . . just give me a call. I'm always here for you, you know.'

She reached out and took his hand. 'I know.'

Jamie looked wistful. 'And I thought you'd come back because your grandfather summoned you.'

'Not really. I came back because of this someone else. I've known him a long time. I never really considered him as anything other than a friend because we were always around one another. We got on so well. We'd finish each other's sentences, laugh at the same things, shared the same values, but I was very young. I didn't realise how rare it was. So when my grandfather suggested I go to the States, I jumped at the chance. I went off to see the world and met lots of people. Lots of men. And the bottom line is that none of them matched up to him.'

'I see.'

'I wouldn't want you to think that I put myself about. I wasn't a tart.' She patted his knee to make her point.

'No,' he said.

She saw the look of abject disappointment on his face. 'Anyway, here I am. Back in Bath.'

'And what does this guy think?'

'He's told me he's pleased I'm back.'

'I see. And you think there's a future in it?'

'I hope so. I really do hope so.'

'Good.' Jamie stayed quite still for a moment. Then he got

to his feet. 'Well, I think I'd better be going.' He glanced at his watch. 'Busy day tomorrow, and my grandfather's summoned me. Don't know what all that's about.'

Missy remained seated, then looked up at him. 'You don't know who it is, do you?'

Jamie hesitated. 'No. No, I don't. But it doesn't matter. I think it's lovely that you've—'

'You silly man.'

Jamie looked at her and saw that her eyes were beginning to fill with tears.

'I came back because of you. Because however hard I try, I simply can't get you out of my head. You're so much a part of me that it hurts when I'm not near you. Wherever I am and whoever I'm with there is hardly a thought in my head that doesn't involve you.' She brushed away the tears that ran down her cheeks. 'And now I've probably made a complete fool of myself and all you'll want to do is get out of here and go home.'

Jamie stood motionless. The words echoed around his head for what seemed like an age. 'Me?'

Missy nodded.

'I don't know what to say.'

Missy tried to make light of it. 'That's all right. You don't have to say anything.'

'Come here,' he said softly.

Missy rose to her feet and went to where he stood. He put his arms round her and held her so close she felt she might melt into him.

'If you only knew how many times I've hoped you'd say something like that.'

'Really?' She half laughed through the tears.

'Dreamed about it. But I was never sure you felt the same as me. I didn't dare risk asking you, and then you went away and I thought that was it. I'd blown it, missed my chance. Then the letters stopped.'

'Not because I wanted to. Just because I had to find out if it would go away, that was all.'

'But it didn't.'

'No.'

'And now here we are.'

She nestled her head deep into his shoulder. Then she said, 'It's funny, isn't it?'

'What?'

'That feeling.'

'What feeling?'

'The ease of it all.'

He made no reply, but stroked her hair.

She asked, 'Why is it, do you suppose?'

'Because we know each other so well?' he offered.

'But that could make it boring, couldn't it? Predictable, over-familiar. It doesn't feel like that at all. It just feels . . .'

'Right,' he said softly.

'Yes.'

They stood in each other's arms for a few minutes more, and then Missy asked quite softly, 'Would you come to bed with me?'

10

Dedham
July 1949

Long shadows stretch across the lawn,
Where dew lies undisturbed since dawn
Before the footsteps pass.
They take their colour from the sky,
So peacefully they seem to lie,
The shadows on the grass.
'The Shadows on the Grass', Sir Alfred Munnings

Just across from the house, Harry and Mac sat on a grassy knoll in the shade of a monkey-puzzle tree, slaking their thirst with a mug of beer each.

'So what do you make of him?' asked Harry.

'Rum bugger but a brilliant painter,' confessed Mac.

'What a place, though,' mused Harry, looking around him at the softly rolling landscape. The land behind Castle House was divided up into lush paddocks studded with oaks and elms. Six or seven horses grazed contentedly, looking up occasionally as some movement or sound caught their eye. After a few seconds of intently staring in the direction of the temporary disturbance, quietly chewing all the while, they would stoop once more to tear at the fresh green grass, which was just beginning to lose its early summer lustre. The house nestled easily into its surroundings, almost as though the hills and valleys had grown up around it over the centuries. In the distance they could hear the sound of farm workers cutting an early crop of hay. An occasional shout would echo across the still afternoon, and from time to time the sound of horses' hooves pulling a farm cart would echo up the lane.

'How long do you think we ought to leave them?' asked Harry.

Mac glanced at his wristwatch. 'Another half-hour. Daren't risk upsetting him again.'

Harry planted his half-empty beer mug in the grass and leaned back on his hands, the better to take in the view. 'He seemed to like your painting, though.'

'Yes. Bloody surprise that. I thought he'd send me packing.'

Harry laughed.

'What?' asked Mac.

'You've no idea, have you?'

'About what?'

'About just how good you are.'

Mac shrugged.

Harry turned towards him. 'You've just been appraised by the country's finest equestrian painter, the finest painter of horses since George Stubbs, who's told you that you have a great talent and you're still not convinced.'

'Maybe it's my Glaswegian bloody-mindedness.'

Harry was determined to make his point. 'Look, Mac, whatever else I know about you, the one thing I'm certain of is that you're the finest artist at Oxford.'

'Bollocks.'

Harry shook his head. 'Well, you think what you want, but just promise me that you'll do what the old master said and give it a go. Work at it. Work bloody hard – that's one thing you can do – and just see what happens.'

'Oh, I'll do that all right. I can't do anything else. Sometimes I think I'll go mad if I don't paint.'

'Madder than you are already?'

'Probably. I mean, what makes me want to do it? What makes me want to hold a brush every hour of every day?'

'Don't analyse it, just be grateful for it. I'd kill for your amount of drive, and your talent.' He reached down for his beer and took a long gulp. 'That and the power to see into the future.'

Mac turned from gazing out across the valley to look at Harry leaning back in the grass. 'You're not serious? Look where it got Leo.' He grinned.

'No, not really. I just feel a bit rudderless sometimes.'

'You're tired, that's all. Tired after three long years.'

'But look at Richard. He must be tired as well, and yet he's got it all sewn up, hasn't he? He'll have his own gallery in no time, just you wait and see. He'll be selling your paintings before you can say "Alfred Munnings".'

'Funny you should say that.'

Harry looked more serious. 'He's asked you already, hasn't he?'

'Well, he's sort of hinted at it. Asked me if he could have first refusal if I put together an exhibition.'

'Wily bugger.'

Mac watched as Harry ran his long fingers through a clump of meadow buttercups, lost in his thoughts. A large cloud drifted over the sun and the long, purple shadows on the grass slowly disappeared. The scene had a flatness about it now.

'It's not a problem,' offered Mac. 'Richard can sell them at low prices when they're still wet, and you can flog them in your saleroom as Old Masters when I'm long gone. That way you get to make all the money.'

Harry smiled at the thought. 'Thank you, but I think those days are a long way off yet – certainly as far as the saleroom is concerned.'

'No money?' asked Mac.

'A bit put by. I'll have to rent to start with.' He slapped the ground with the flat of his hand. 'Oh, I'll manage somehow.'

'It's not that, though, is it?'

'Mmm?'

'The thing that's really worrying you. It's not the saleroom.'

Harry said nothing for a moment. Then he said, quite softly, 'No.'

'She's quite keen, you know,' said Mac.

Harry shook his head. 'Oh, I don't think so.'

'She is, I tell you. She's not going to make the first move, though, and if you don't get your bloody act together, you'll lose her. She'll go off with Richard and that will be that.'

'I think she's already there, isn't she?'

'Only because she thinks you're not interested, not seriously.'

'Hah!'

'Well, come on, you've not exactly given her much to go on, have you?'

'I wish . . . I wish I could . . .'

'What? You wish you could what?'

'Well, tell her, I suppose. But tell her what? That I think she's the best thing that's ever happened to me. Or never happened to me. We've never talked deeply about anything.' Harry sighed and tapped at the side of his mug of beer impatiently. 'The thing is, have you ever felt so terrified of life that you want the earth to open up and swallow you? I mean, have you?'

Mac nodded. 'Most days.' He took a deep gulp of beer. 'This helps,' he said, holding up the mug.

'Well, you know, then. It's absolutely bloody hopeless. I'm a grown-up. I should be able to say things, take risks. Sometimes I can, but not with her. As long as I put off asking her, there's a chance she might one day say yes. But if I do ask her and she says no, then it's all over. And I can't stand the thought of that. So there you are. I'm travelling hopefully and never arriving.'

'Travelling hopelessly more like. Look, take a tip from me.

I'm not exactly experienced in these matters, but I can read folk pretty well. I think your fears are groundless. She really is waiting for you to make the first move.'

'I wish I shared your confidence. Anyway, why are you on my side and not Richard's?'

Mac stood up and thrust his hands into his pockets. 'Oh, all sorts of reasons. Let's just say that I'm very fond of Richard, but I don't necessarily think that Eleanor is the girl for him, or that he's the man for her.'

'It's not like you to interfere.'

Mac looked uneasy. 'No, and I don't know that I should, but I do think that at least you should find out how she feels about you so that you can clear the air. Make it a level playing field. Resolve things one way or the other, that's all.'

Harry shook his head, but Mac persisted. 'All right, so let's do a bit of analysis, shall we? Plan A: you don't ask her during the next few days. That way, you're not disappointed in her answer. Result? She goes off with Richard. And she will, you mark my words. She may not love him as deeply as she should, but she probably loves him just enough to take the plunge. Especially if the man she really fancies is showing no interest. Eleanor's had it with education. She wants a man and a home life. It's written all over her. She needs a replacement for her father.'

Harry demurred, 'Oh, no, surely—'

'No, I don't mean that unkindly. It just that losing him hasn't helped. She needs a man in her life. Eleanor's a man's woman. Anyway, back to you. We've established that Plan A won't get you anywhere, so we move on to Plan B: you do ask her and she says no and goes off with Richard. That will prove that I've been wrong all along and she really does think he's the bee's knees. But at least then you know the lie of the land and you can get on with your life. But if you adopt Plan B and she says yes, then I was right and you both live happily ever after, which is something that is never going to happen if you stick to Plan A.'

'Simple as that?'

'Absolutely. So, apart from the girl, what have you got to lose?'

Harry sighed again. 'Well, Richard as a friend, but apart from that . . . Oh, I don't know. We'll see. But I can't see me getting the opportunity now. We'll be heading off back to Oxford and to Richard this afternoon and then she'll be out of my life for ever. I should have made a move when I had the chance.' He tossed a buttercup flower into the long grass, and the sun came out once more, bathing the fields in a warm, golden glow.

'Oh, something will turn up, Harry. Come on, let's risk going back to the studio to see how they're getting on. There's a chance I might be able to watch him paint.'

'You go back,' said Harry. 'I'll stay out here and look at the horses. Give myself time to think. I'll join you later, after I've finished my beer.'

'If that's what you want. Anyway, she's probably run off with Munnings now – talk of the village and all that.'

Harry shot him a withering glance.

'Sorry. Only joking.'

Mac slipped into the studio as quietly as he could and stood in the shadow of a large canvas propped on an easel.

'It's no use standing behind that,' boomed the artist. 'You won't see anything from there. Come over here and watch, but just be quiet.'

Mac did as he was bid and stood within a yard of the old man's shoulder, watching closely as he mixed his paints and applied them to the canvas. His deftness was astonishing, and his ability to create form out of a simple stroke or two left Mac in awe of the painter's talent. He checked the colours that Munnings was using – raw sienna, French blue, cadmium yellow, vermilion, yellow ochre and flake white – watched as he mixed them with turpentine and studied his technique of applying them in generous measure to the canvas. He looked across at Eleanor, sitting side-saddle on the trestle. She smiled back at him nervously, hardly daring to move or say a word.

'Are you all right?' barked Munnings. 'Not too stiff?'

'No, I'm fine, really,' replied Eleanor.

'Another half-hour and that should do it for today. My bloody hand's playing me up. Damned gout. I can hardly feel my left thumb in this palette. I'll need you again tomorrow to finish it off.'

Eleanor looked troubled. 'Oh, but we have to get back to Oxford tonight.'

'What? No, no, no. We'll have a word with the Sun Hotel. They'll have rooms. They'll be able to put you up.'

'But—' Eleanor tried again.

'No "buts". It's a waste of a painting if I don't get you finished, and if we make an early start tomorrow, I should be able to get you away by mid-afternoon.'

Eleanor looked pleadingly at Mac, but he seemed unconcerned. 'It's not a problem. We've nothing important to do tomorrow.'

'That's settled, then.' The artist noticed the worried look on Eleanor's face. 'If it's the bill you're worried about, don't even think of it. I'll take care of that. Only fair when you've sat for me so beautifully.'

It was not the bill that Eleanor was thinking about. It was Richard, back in Oxford, confined to bed with a cold and wondering why she had not returned. Then again, how would he know she was not back? She would probably not be seeing him for a day or so anyway, until his cold was better, so perhaps it wouldn't matter if she were out for the night with Harry and Mac. She brightened a little.

'That's better,' said Munnings. 'A much happier expression.'

Eleanor's face broke into a smile.

And so did Mac's.

Bath
December 2007

Like a queen enchanted who may not laugh, or weep,
Glad at heart and guarded from change and care like ours,
Girt about with beauty by days and nights that creep
Soft as breathless ripples that softly shoreward sweep.
'A Ballad of Bath' (1901), Algernon Swinburne

All thoughts of restraint, or of the inadvisability of their liaison, or of their being together at the top of her grandfather's gallery were absent from Missy's mind as she and Jamie made love in her bed. She experienced a tenderness that she had never felt before, an outpouring of years of affection concentrated in this one moment.

For the most part, she was bathed in tears. Tears of relief. Tears of joy. Tears of love. She had hardly dared to hope that he would share her feelings, certainly not after their years apart. She had convinced herself that she would come home to find that he was married, maybe even that he had children. The temptation to call him up while she was in New York had been overwhelming, but she had fought the urge to make contact, had battled with herself to make the effort to go out into the world, to be independent, to see if that life she had had in the small, intimate City of Bath really was the world that she was destined to be a part of. When the man she had been seeing in New York had rejected her, she knew that it was partly her fault, knew that she had never been capable of giving herself to him wholeheartedly. He had said as much when they parted, told her that he wanted someone who made him feel that he was the only one. In spite of her trying to reassure him that there was the case, she knew that there was a hollowness to her protestations, and though she felt that she should be heartbroken at his leaving, it came, if she were honest, as something of a relief. It freed her emotions to dwell on the man she had always loved. She could see it now, quite clearly, and with the realisation came a growing panic that she had left it too late.

Her grandfather's call to come home had filled her with hope but also with fear. What would be his attitude towards her? Would he still care? Would he remember what they had shared, or had it all been magnified by her imagination? Supposing it was simply a friendship from his point of view, not love at all; supposing she had completely misread the situation, what then?

When she had seen him in the saleroom sitting atop the dais, gazing out across the rows of heads, it seemed as though her heart would thump its way out of her chest. She had had to stand behind a pillar to block him from her view, just so that she could stay in control.

Then, when they had met, the relief at discovering he was still unattached had made her heart leap. That he still seemed fond of her raised her hopes even higher, and then when he had asked her out, there was simply no way that she could sound indifferent, or play hard to get. She had waited five long years for that moment. She had put down the phone and shouted, 'Yes!' punching the air with joy.

Yet she knew she must not take anything for granted, knew that there was a chance he was just being polite. Only when she looked at him across the table at dinner did she think that it might be possible that he still felt something for her, something deeper than mere friendship.

Now she lay in his arms, knowing that this was where she really wanted to be. It did not matter what her family thought.

Some pointless feud, caked in the dust of time, was not going to stop her from being with the man that she had yearned for.

He was sleeping now, as dawn broke over the city. She looked at the clock. It was seven minutes to eight. Her arm was across his chest. She lifted it and ran her fingers lightly over his skin, as if to prove to herself that this was no dream, that he really was there, in her arms, in her bed. He was so beautiful. The tight, dark curls on his head were matched now by the gentle growth of early-morning stubble. It struck her that she had never seen him unshaven. Here he was, waking up with her. She had never felt so deliciously happy, and once more the tears, unprompted, began to flow down her cheeks, landing on his olive-coloured skin and causing him to stir. She wondered what his reaction would be on waking. Once more she worried that he might regret having stayed, that he would tell her it had all been very nice but that it really could not continue.

Instead, he opened his eyes, squinted at the light, saw her and smiled. His face showed no signs of regret or alarm. There was no suggestion of anything but contentment. 'Hello,' he murmured.

'Hello.'

He kissed her softly on the lips and they made the gentlest love once more.

Jamie left the Royal Crescent at a quarter past nine, forty-five minutes before the expected arrival of Missy's grandfather. He could not remember ever feeling happier. Happy that she felt the same, happy that they had finally got together. There would be, he knew, certain difficulties ahead as far as the families were concerned, but they would have to be over-come. He had never felt more certain of anything in his life. His only surprise had been that Missy had been unaware of the depth of his feelings towards her. Well, that and the strength of her own feelings towards him, which he had never dared hope for.

The weather was in tune with his thoughts. The early December morning was bright and crisp, and a fine skein of mist wove through the city below, hovering over the Avon like a ribbon of fine muslin. Soon it would dissolve into another unseasonably warm day.

The Circus was just round the corner from the Royal Crescent. He had arranged to call on his grandfather at ten. He glanced at his watch. Too early yet. He would go and get a paper.

The man in the paper shop in Queen Square picked up on his mood. 'You're cheery this morning, Mr Ballantyne.'

'No reason not to be, George. Lovely day.'

'Is it? Oh. I've been folding papers since five; I haven't really noticed.'

'Anything worth reading?' asked Jamie casually.

'No idea, sir. Never get a chance to read them until I puts me feet up at the end of the day, and then it's usually the local paper, not the national stuff. Not interested in that. Doesn't seem to affect me, what I read in them. Took me twenty years to work that out, you know. Now I contents myself with the *Bath Chronicle* of an evening.'

Jamie smiled and folded *The Times* under his arm, placing a pound coin on the papers in front of him on the counter.

'Change in the charity box, sir?'

'Yes, that's fine.'

'We like to support the local guide dogs. Every little helps at local level, doesn't it?'

Jamie smiled again and left the shop. Ordinarily at this time he would be dressed in a suit and tie, clean-shaven and sitting at his desk in the auction house, but there seemed little point in going back to Batheaston to change and then coming all the way into town again. He had showered, and Missy had a spare toothbrush that he had used. He was quite sure his grandfather wouldn't even noticed he hadn't shaved. He couldn't think why he would want to see him so urgently. He was normally much more vague about meeting and seemed happy for his grandson to just drop in from time to time.

Jamie sat on a bench in the sunshine and riffled through the paper. It was one of those days when he felt forced to agree with the newspaper vendor. It might be that his mind was temporarily filled with other things, but there was simply nothing in it to interest or affect him at all, except for one of the obituaries. It concerned a man that he had heard his grandfather mention from time to time. Someone called Lord Bedlington.

'Leo Ravenswing Malahide Bedlington, who has died aged 81, was an aesthete, socialite and seventh heir to the earldom of Bedlington, which was established in 1738 when Thomas Malahide Bedlington was rewarded for his landscaping services to King George II. A sometime associate of William Kent, the two fell out spectacularly over Kent's friendship with Lord Burlington, which Bedlington considered ill advised. It was later suggested that Bedlington and Kent were more than just good friends, though this fact cannot be established with any certainty. A popular rhyme of the day ran; 'Will Kent, when all is done and said, stuck to the Bur and spurned the Bed.' The First Earl failed to see the joke. He spent his remaining years improving the family estate, where the maintenance of his elaborate water features was to become a heavy burden on his successive heirs. The family fortunes went through many vicissitudes, not least during the Seventh Earl's own lifetime, when death duties of eighty per cent almost bankrupted him. His father, an inveterate collector – from whom he inherited his love of art and of the high life – achieved the rank of brigadier and fought with General Montgomery in the Battle of El Alamein. Hector Malahide Bedlington died of his wounds some six years later, nursed at the end by his only son (his wife, Caroline, née Ravenswing, having

died in childbirth). Only by selling most of the family's art treasures and the country seat of Bedlington Park in Shropshire did
Leo Bedlington manage to stave off total penury and settle instead
for financial ruin. Having been brought up by a series of his
father's mistresses in lavish surroundings, his own taste for the
high life never deserted him. He studied art history at Christ
Church, Oxford, just after the war and dabbled in the art world,
but seldom effectively. He spent his latter years in the Villa Fabrice,
near Menton on the Côte d'Azur, where he entertained in rather
more straitened circumstances than he had been used to, though
still with a devoted skeleton staff.

He is fondly remembered by those who knew him as sociable and
good-humoured, despite his dwindling fortune. He was unmarried
and, at the end, alone; his companion of many years, the artist John
Macready, having predeceased him in 1995 in a swimming accident.
Their relationship was one of mutual tolerance, the Scottish artist
having declared once that they were 'the unhappiest unmarried couple
in France.'

Jamie folded up the paper and placed it on his lap. He had
no idea his grandfather had known a character who had led
such a colourful life. He must ask him about those early days,
the days at Oxford when he had clearly been part of the
Bedlington set. He had never thought of his grandfather as
having enjoyed a youth that smacked of *Brideshead Revisited*.
What a time he must have had.

12

Dedham
July 1949

To be a painter you mustn't be pious but rather a little wicked and entirely a man of the world.

John Ruskin

There were three of them round the table in the low-beamed back room of the Sun Hotel – Eleanor, Mac and Harry.

'Shouldn't we really have gone back to Oxford?' asked Eleanor. The worried look had returned to her face.

'What for?' asked Mac. 'So that we could all have caught Richard's cold?'

Eleanor sighed. 'No, I suppose not.'

Harry gazed gloomily into his beer.

'Well, you two are a bundle of laughs, aren't you?' said Mac. 'Here we are, spending a couple of days in the company of the best equestrian artist in the country – in the world probably – you're even being painted by him, and all you can think of is King Dick curled up in bed with the flu.'

Eleanor looked embarrassed. 'Yes. I'm sorry. Stupid really.'

'So how did it feel?' asked Harry, brightening. 'Being immortalised by the master?'

'A bit strange, to be honest,' confessed Eleanor. Her face broke into a smile. 'And a bit silly – sitting sideways on top of that trestle thing and trying to pretend it was a horse.'

'Well, you looked fine,' said Harry, having a stab at a compliment. After finishing his beer, he had rejoined the others in the studio just before Munnings had called it a day. 'I could actually see the horse you were sitting on.'

'Oh, yes?' said Mac teasingly. 'What was it, then?'

'Well, as you saw in the painting, it was a grey, with a thick black mane.' Harry was warming to his subject. 'And it was nibbling grass. What I bet you didn't notice, though, was that when that other horse walked past – the mare – the grey began to look really interested. I thought for a moment that he might bolt.'

Eleanor threw back her head and laughed.

'That's more like it,' said Mac. 'Come on, drink up, they'll be here with our supper in a minute and I've ordered a bottle of claret to go with it.'

'Claret! Bloody hell, you're pushing the boat out!' exclaimed Harry.

'Nothing to do with me. The barmaid said that "'Im down the road 'ad said as we 'ad to 'ave a couple of bottles of the best wine in the 'ouse" and so the claret's warming up as we speak.'

'Red wine makes me tipsy,' said Eleanor with a worried frown.

'Oh, good,' retorted Mac. 'It's time you relaxed a bit after all that riding.'

'The clothes were a bit strange' she offered. 'Not sure about the riding habit.'

'Oh, I don't know,' said Harry absently. 'I've always found riding gear rather sexy.'

Eleanor blushed and Harry tried to make light of his comment, noticing the broad grin on Mac's face. 'Well, I have! I just think it's . . . well . . . flattering on a woman. Shows off her shape well.'

'You're getting in deeper,' murmured Mac, before draining his glass of beer.

Harry's further embarrassment was saved by the waitress, who arrived to show them to their table. 'Would you like to follow me?' she asked. 'I'm afraid it's a bit of a limited menu tonight. Pea and ham soup for those as wants it, followed by rabbit pie, then orange jelly with real mandarins. But the claret's good,' she added as a placatory measure.

She showed the three of them to a corner table in the low-ceilinged bar that doubled as a dining room. The dark oak beams were hung with horse-brasses and harnesses, and the large inglenook was piled with logs, rather than the roaring fire that burned there when there was an 'r' in the month.

'Pea and ham soup in July,' muttered Harry.

'And what's wrong with that?' asked Mac accusingly. 'If you came from as far north as I do, you'd be grateful for a drop of warming broth at any time of year.'

'We're in Essex,' said Harry, 'not the frozen north.'

'Why don't we go straight on to the rabbit pie, then?' Eleanor suggested.

Her diplomacy was cut short by the arrival of the claret, a dusty bottle from which the cork had already been extracted. Mac tasted it and pronounced it the best claret he had ever drunk. The glasses were filled and the three set to for an evening of rabbit pie and orange jelly with real mandarins.

Over the next hour and a half the wine flowed freely, thanks to the generosity of their host. The three of them began to relax. They talked not so much of the future, but of the past: of punting on the Cherwell, of picnics in meadows, of the dances and the long evenings in student rooms overlooking grassy quads and dreaming spires.

Eleanor watched as Harry and Mac sparred with one another. She was sorry that Leo was not here to enjoy the fun. Then she felt a pricking of conscience about Richard, who, while they were laughing and enjoying themselves, was probably sitting with his head over a bowl of Friar's Balsam inhaling the curative fumes. She put such thoughts out of her head. She had considered him enough. The wine was good and she felt more relaxed than when they had arrived.

She was still in control of herself, but the evening now had a velvety texture that made worry seem unnecessary. And what had she to worry about? It was not as if she were committed to Richard. He had not claimed her as his own. He did, when she thought about it, take her rather for granted. Expected her to be there when he called round.

Well, she was still free, still unattached, and in the company of two good friends, to one of whom she was especially attracted. She watched as Harry chatted relaxedly to Mac, noticed the tilt of his head, the furrowing of his brow, the expressive hands when he was making a point and the thick, dark hair that curled gently round the back of his ears.

Those who met him for the first time might think him rather aloof, but there was nothing grand about his manner. He was just reserved, careful about letting himself go. So careful. Now, though, he was more relaxed than she had ever seen him. He leaned back in his chair and she noticed the sparkle in his eye. Occasionally he would glance at her and her cheeks seemed to burn under his gaze. How she enjoyed simply being there with him. In the same room. At the same table.

At half past ten Mac pushed back his chair and stood up. 'I'm done in. I'll leave you two to wash up.'

For a moment Eleanor took him seriously. 'Oh, do you think . . . ?' Then she saw the expression on his face. 'You're a dreadful man, John Macready, and one day you'll get your comeuppance.'

'Goodnight, both,' he said. 'Sleep well.' As he turned, he prodded Harry on the shoulder, unseen by Eleanor, who was reaching down for her cardigan, which had slipped to the floor.

Harry was about to speak when the waitress came into the room once more. 'Oh, one of you's gone, and I was going to ask if you wanted coffee in the snug.'

Eleanor and Harry glanced at each other, questioning whether the other would like to stay. For a moment it seemed uncertain what the outcome would be. And then, in perfect unison, they said, 'Yes, please.'

To begin with, Harry sat opposite her in a chintz-covered armchair, while Eleanor, in her customary fashion, had slipped off her shoes and tucked her feet underneath her on the sofa.

The snug was a small, low-beamed room with a grand-father clock in the corner, its dial decorated with the face of an impassive moon with rosy cheeks and rosebud lips. The low, sonorous beat marked the slow passage of time in this particularly picturesque patch of East Anglian countryside known as 'Constable country'.

In the small inglenook here there was a fire – three logs gently glowing to take away the chill of the summer evening. The sweet smoke of apple wood filled the air, but the Camp coffee was not to Eleanor's taste and she left it, untouched, on the round, brass Indian table.

Harry tasted his and winced. 'Not good, is it?' he whispered.

Eleanor shook her head. 'It doesn't matter.' She was smiling.

'Would you like something else instead? A nightcap?'

'Not for me. I've had enough wine. It was lovely.' She snug-gled down into the sofa, gazing at the lazy flames that licked the logs in the grate.

Harry looked around. They were the only people left now, the locals having sloped off to their beds before another heavy day of haymaking. Tomorrow they would hear again the distant shouts of the farm labourers as they pitchforked the hay into stooks and then into the perfectly formed haycocks that studded the fields of Dedham Vale. For now, though, time seemed to have stood still, despite the steady beat of the grandfather clock that argued to the contrary, and the occasional spit of the apple logs on their way to becoming dying embers.

'What a day,' murmured Harry softly.

'Yes.' That was all Eleanor could manage. She could not recall the last time they had been alone. It seemed that she only ever met Harry in company – with Richard, with Mac or with Leo. Leo. She remembered his words that afternoon two weeks ago in his room. 'Maybe he just needs a push.' But she could not do it. How could she 'give him a push' without appearing to be the sort of woman that Harry would not look twice at?

He seemed to be reading her thoughts, or at least one of them. 'I wonder how Leo's father is.'

'Not very good, I think.'

'Poor Leo. Just when he wanted a bit of freedom, it looks as though he's going to be saddled with everything, as well as losing his pa. Were they very close?'

'I don't think so. He was away fighting most of the time. In Africa, I believe.'

'Same as mine,' said Harry. 'But mine got off more lightly. He's back selling insurance now. Not very glamorous, but at least he survived.' Then he realised his unintentional lack of tact. 'Do you miss yours?' he asked gently.

Eleanor nodded. 'Some days more than others.' She had not intended to cry. She had been feeling particularly happy, but at the mention of her father the tears welled up and she felt them tumbling down her cheeks.

Harry got up and crossed to where she sat. 'I'm so sorry. I didn't mean to . . .'

Eleanor smiled through the tears. 'No. So silly, I don't know why that happened. Oh dear.' She reached into the pocket of her cardigan, which lay on the sofa, pulled out a small lace-edged handkerchief and dabbed at her eyes. 'You must think I'm very feeble,' she said.

'No, not feeble. Just . . . sensitive.'

'And feeble.' She laughed and dabbed again at the remaining tears.

'And beautiful.'

She was not at all sure that she had heard correctly and found herself saying, 'What do you mean?'

'I mean that you are the most beautiful girl I've ever met,' said Harry, reassured by the fact that she had neither got up and walked away nor slapped his face. He pushed back a stray wisp of hair that had fallen across her face.

It struck her that since that single kiss they had shared all those months ago, when they had both had too much to drink, it was the first time he had ever touched her. She searched for a reply but could only manage, 'Really?'

Harry leaned over towards her and kissed her very gently on the lips. Then he moved his head away slightly and laid his hand on her shoulder. At first she did not know quite what to do. She looked into his eyes, as if searching for something. Then, at exactly the same moment, they both leaned forward and kissed again, more passionately this time. When their lips parted, she drew away briefly before twisting her body so that her head lay on his chest. He put his arm round her and they sat together on the sofa for several minutes before she said, 'This is nice.'

'Yes.'

Then they heard the iron sneck lift on the door behind them and the waitress came into the room. 'I'm locking up now, so . . .'

They both sprang to their feet. 'Yes, of course,' said Eleanor. 'We'll be going up.'

The waitress nodded and held the door open. The two walked through it like a pair of schoolchildren being called to the headmaster's study, and climbed the dark wooden stairs that led to the bedrooms above. On the landing, they found themselves alone beside a large oak dresser on which the amber glow of a small lamp provided what was considered sufficient light to show the guests the way to their rooms and to the facilities at the end of the passage, should they wish to avail themselves during the course of the night.

Their rooms were adjacent to one another. For a moment they both hesitated. 'I'd better say goodnight, then,' said Harry.

'Yes. Yes, I suppose so.' Eleanor tried not to sound disappointed. She did not want either to pressurise him or to give the impression that she was too willing. At the same time she could not bear to let him go.

He seemed to read her confusion. 'Such a shame. We wait all this time and now . . . I've left it too late.'

Eleanor could feel her heart beating in her chest. She found it difficult to speak, aware that the next words she said would probably affect her whole future. What should she say? How could she explain her own feelings without appearing too eager? And yet if she did not speak now, she might never have another chance.

'You don't have to go,' she whispered softly.

Harry looked deep into her eyes. 'Are you sure?' he asked.

13

Bath
December 2007

Bath is not fit for a young man to begin life in: it is too confined to females and invalids.

Fanny Burney

Jamie rang the bell of his grandfather's house in the Circus, looking up as he always did to take in the carved stone frieze above the door with its serpents and its nautical emblems. He loved the Circus even more than the Royal Crescent. Begun in 1754, thirteen years earlier than the Crescent, and completed after John Wood's death by his son, it is a perfect circle composed of three arcs, each comprising eleven five-storey houses. William Pitt the Elder had lived at numbers 7 and 8, number 17 had played host to both Thomas Gainsborough and William Makepeace Thackeray, and Harry Ballantyne and his wife had moved to what was then a dilapidated terrace house in the late 1960s. The fact the auction house was doing well for itself meant that they could afford to do it up.

The symmetry of the Circus had always appealed to Jamie, and its honey-coloured stone seemed warm and welcoming. Today it was dappled with sunshine and shadows cast by the bare branches of the tall plane trees in the centre of the circle.

Coming to see his grandparents had always been a treat. As a child, he would be allowed to run up the staircases inside with his younger sister and would try to understand why so many of the walls were strangely angled, unlike those of their mother's house, which were straight and whose rooms were square. The Circus was a place of dreams, as exciting and magical as *The Lion, the Witch and the Wardrobe* – the book that his grandfather had given him for his seventh birthday.

The door was opened by Tilly, his grandfather's daily. 'Hello, Master Jamie.'

He had always been 'Master Jamie' to Tilly, though he often thought he could detect a hint of irony in her voice when she said it nowadays. A smile was never far from her lips, though, and that made any teasing easier to forgive.

'Mr Ballantyne's in the drawing room.' Tilly tilted her head towards the curving staircase behind her. His grandfather would be sitting in his usual chair by the window, probably reading Patrick O'Brian. Like the newspaper vendor, Harry Ballantyne had little time for the dailies, gleaning what news he needed from the local evening paper and spending his spare time in the Napoleonic wars with Jack Aubrey and Stephen Maturin aboard a square rigger. The paintings on the wall of the staircase reflected his taste – a Thomas Whitcombe of two barques in a squall off Gibraltar, a Samuel Scott of the Thames and two smaller paintings of the Siege of Algiers and the Battle of the Nile by an unknown artist. He would probably have acquired them through his own auction rooms in the way that he always did – by making his wife sit among the other bidders and raise her paddle to show that everything was above board. The pictures were now as familiar to Jamie as the pattern of the stair carpet, though these days it was more threadbare than it had been in his youth.

His grandparents had decorated the house when they took it on, but had done little since, believing that a job done well would see them out. Thanks to Tilly's ministrations, the house was always clean and tidy, and the furniture gleaming and smelling of lavender polish, even if the carpets were verging on the embarrassing.

He pushed open the drawing-room door and saw his grandfather, not sitting but standing looking out of the window across the Circus. He was wearing a lemon-yellow sweater and an open-necked shirt. He hated ties, always had done. He had his back to Jamie. It was not quite as ramrod straight as it had been in his youth; now he stooped a little, but the hair was still thick, even if it were iron grey rather than the black it had been forty or so years ago. Jamie was grateful for the fact that baldness would be unlikely to afflict him.

He turned on hearing Jamie enter. 'Ah, Master Jamie,' his grandfather teased.

'Hello, Granddad.' Jamie walked over to where the old man stood and gave him a hug. 'Lovely day.'

His grandfather looked out of the window again. 'Yes. It won't last, though. The wireless said it will be raining by lunchtime. Shame. Still, it is December.' He looked thoughtful for a moment, and then took in his grandson's mode of dress. 'You not working this morning?'

'I thought you wouldn't notice.' Jamie looked at his reflection in the gilt-framed overmantel. He did look more dishevelled than he would have liked. He spoke briskly, hoping that he would not be quizzed about why he should be unshaven and crumpled at ten in the morning. 'I'm on my way to change.' He hesitated and then said, 'I had to see someone early about . . . something . . . and so I . . . Anyway, how are you?'

'As well as can be expected.' His grandfather flashed him a brave smile. 'Amid the trials and tribulations of old age. Bloody leg doesn't get any better, but then I suppose I'm beginning to wear out.'

'And Gran?'

'Oh, she's fine. Nothing seems to bother her, except her fingers. She's nipped down to the supermarket for something or other. Don't know what. Lunch, I suppose.' He looked pensive again.

Jamie was used to these spells of reverie on the part of his grandfather. He had learned not to interrupt. It was best just to let him drift for a moment or two. He would quickly come back to the matter in hand, having allowed his thoughts to play on whatever had distracted or diverted them.

Harry Ballantyne soon recovered himself. 'Tilly's on the way up with coffee. At least, I hope she is.' He motioned Jamie to sit down in an easy chair and lowered himself carefully on to the edge of the leather-covered club fender that surrounded the fireplace. 'Easier to get up from here when she arrives,' he muttered by way of an excuse. 'How's your mother?'

They chatted about Emma Ballantyne – Jamie taking care to mention nothing about her disapproval of the liaison with Artemis King – until the door was pushed open by Tilly, who entered with a tray bearing coffee and biscuits.

'I should pour it pretty quickly, Mr Ballantyne – it's been standing for a few minutes so it should be strong enough, and I don't want it to go cold on you.'

Jamie's grandfather mumbled his appreciation and Tilly left the room with a knowing wink at her boss's grandson. Strong and hot was how Harry liked his coffee. Tilly did her best to oblige, though in a five-storey house without a service lift, it was sometimes a tall order. Quite literally.

'Coffee for you?'

Jamie nodded. 'So what did you want to see me about?'

His grandfather did not speak but concentrated on pouring the coffee into two china cups. Jamie could not work out whether the silence was due to Harry's preoccupation with decanting from the cafetière or because he was considering what to say. It turned out to be the latter.

Harry handed Jamie a coffee, took his own across to the

other side of the fireplace and lowered himself carefully into the facing armchair. He took a sip of coffee and put down the cup on the fender at his elbow. 'I've been thinking . . .' he said.

Jamie resisted the temptation to tease, as he would usually have done. Instead, he let his grandfather pause and then pick up his train of thought.

'Your grandmother and I have lived here for more than forty years now. It's a lovely house. Big, but lovely. It's been a good place to bring up a family, even if it was a small one, and . . .' he searched for the words '. . . rather fragmented.'

The reference to Jamie's absent father did not go unnoticed, but Jamie was used to such comments. He realised that his grandfather needed to let off steam occasionally, and it was usually Jamie who was on the receiving end. There was little bitterness in these outbursts. It was more regret at Jamie's mother and father not having tried harder. Harry did not blame Frank Bottomley for pushing off. He would probably have done so himself, he reflected, had he been on the receiving end of his daughter's tongue, but she was still his daughter and he still loved her, even if she had driven him to distraction over the years.

'I've talked to your mother and asked her if she wants to take it on.'

'Oh?' The subject of his grandparents moving out had never come up before. If he had thought about it, he would have realised that the five floors of the Crescent must have presented a challenge to two septuagenarians on the cusp of becoming octogenarians, but since they had always lived there in his lifetime, he had idly assumed that things would remain that way.

'Your mother seems happy where she is in the country – with her country friends and her little dinners. Doesn't want to move into town.'

It began to dawn on Jamie that a part of his life was about to be dismantled. He felt unsettled. 'But you've always lived here . . .'

'In your lifetime, yes, but we lived in more modest surroundings before you were born. In Gay Street. We couldn't always afford something like this.'

'No, but . . . well . . . I suppose I've always taken it for granted. I just don't like the thought of the place not being a part of the family.'

'Nor I. That's why I'd like you to have it.'

For a moment Jamie thought he had misheard. He must have done. Maybe his grandfather meant that he wanted him to have a room here, but then the situation was clarified.

'There's no one else to leave this place to. Your sister doesn't want it . . .'

Jamie was suddenly aware that arrangements had been made of which he was totally unaware. 'You mean you've asked her? Fran knows about this?'

His grandfather detected a little anger in his voice. 'Now don't go off at the deep end. I wanted to make sure that she didn't have a problem with it before I approached you. It wouldn't have been very fair on her to tell her that I'd offered it to you without consulting her, now would it?'

'Well, no, I suppose not. But . . .'

'Fran will get her share. She wants to stay where she is – working with the horses. She doesn't want to come back to Bath. Though why she needs to be in Argentina beats me. Plenty of horses in Newmarket, or Lambourne or somewhere. Darned sight nearer. It's beyond me why she has to be with the Argies.' Harry noticed Jamie's admonitory frown. He cleared his throat. 'And anyway, you're the elder.'

'Oh, Granddad: you don't still believe in that, do you? What's it called . . . primogeniture?'

'No, of course not, but I was just making a point.'

Jamie scratched his head. He had begun the day in a complete daze thanks to the events of the night before. Now here he was being offered a house of his own. Two out-of-body experiences within twenty-four hours. 'But how will you . . . I mean . . . when . . . ?'

'As soon as you like. Your grandmother and I have found a serviced flat on the other side of town. Better for us than all these stairs.'

Jamie sat in silence for a moment. Then he said, 'I don't know what to say. I mean, I'm not sure I can afford—'

'Don't worry about that. You won't have to pay us anything. Well, you'll have to fund your own council tax and water rates, that sort of thing. But it would have come to you anyway on our . . . when we . . . you know . . . so we'd rather you had it now.'

Jamie pulled himself together. 'Granddad, are you sure? I mean, are Fran and Mum both happy with that? It's a heck of a lot of money . . . I mean, its value.'

'Most houses of any size cost more than their aged owners paid for them. The grandchildren might as well enjoy the investment sooner rather than later.' He looked across at Jamie with a mock-serious frown. 'As long as you don't let it go to your head.'

'No, of course not. But it's a big house for one person.'

'Well, you won't always be on your own, will you?'

The events of the previous night ricocheted around Jamie's head. 'Er, no. Well, I hope not.' Worried he sounded evasive, he quickly tried to change the subject. 'It'll be nice to have a bit of space, actually. I'm beginning to burst out of Batheaston. Mind you, it'll take me a while to get this place sorted.' Then he realised he might have sounded rude. 'Oh, I mean . . . decorating and . . .'

'Don't worry. We'll give you a spot of cash to help you do it up. It needs a lick of paint. Well, to be honest, it needs a bit of plumbing and rewiring, too, but we'll help to cover that. I don't want to bankrupt you at the outset.' He paused. 'You are pleased, aren't you? I mean, you would like to take on the place?'

Jamie shook his head and at first his grandfather thought he was refusing. 'I can't think of anything I'd rather do, anywhere I'd rather live. I just . . . I'm not sure that I deserve it.'

'Rubbish. You've worked hard. Taken on the lion's share of Ballantyne's over the past few years, and you'll need to keep working hard. They take a bit of upkeep, these old houses, but there should be enough left to avoid you going under when we've gone.'

'I do wish you wouldn't say that.'

'Well, I'm not going to be around for ever, and it's nice to know that the place will be in good hands. I'm glad it'll stay in the family.' His face suddenly brightened. 'Oh, and you did rather well the other day.'

Jamie looked puzzled. 'Sorry?'

Harry picked up the *Bath Chronicle* and pointed to a column at the top of page five. 'With the Munnings.'

Jamie noticed that the column was headed 'Top price paid for sporting picture.'

'Oh, yes. I was quite pleased with that, and a bit surprised.'

His grandfather looked him in the eye. 'But not with who bought it?'

'You know, then.'

'I guessed.'

'Do you mind?'

'Not any more.'

'It was a lovely painting,' Jamie offered.

'Yes, I know.'

'Not really my bag,' confessed Jamie, 'but there was good competition for it. Do you like his stuff?'

'Oh, I'm more of a seascape man myself, but I have a soft spot for Munnings.' The old man looked reflective.

Jamie thought he detected a hint of sadness on his grand-father's face. Perhaps the thought of losing his house was affecting him more than he cared to admit.

'Never wanted to own one, then?' he asked, as much to bring the old man out of his reverie as anything.

'Only one,' he murmured. 'Only one.'

Jamie watched as his grandfather seemed to lose himself completely in his thoughts. He seemed so very far away that Jamie felt unable to intrude, but then he remembered the morning paper. He had quite forgotten in the excitement of the past few minutes. 'Oh, did you see the obituaries today?'

'Mmm?'

'The obituaries, in this morning's *Times*.'

'No. You know I've stopped taking the morning paper. Too depressing. Too many people of my age dying.'

'Oh. Perhaps I'd better not say, then.'

Harry Ballantyne brightened. 'Oh, don't worry. It's some-thing of a relief to read the obituaries and find I'm not there. It means I can get on with my day.'

'Well, I'm sorry to be the bearer of bad news, but some-body you were at university with is in there today.'

'Who? Obviously not Richard King?' he asked with a wry grin.

'No. Lord Bedlington.'

'Good God! Has he died? Old Leo.'

'At his place in France, apparently.'

Harry Ballantyne looked out of the window again. 'Well, well, well.' Then his facial expression changed and he said very softly, 'That'll put the cat among the pigeons.'

14

Dedham
July 1949

The artist brings something into the world that didn't exist before, and . . . he does it without destroying something else.
Writers at Work (1977), John Updike

Harry woke up alone in his room at the Sun Hotel, stirred into consciousness by a coloratura blackbird performing in the elder tree outside his window. The events of the night before replayed in his mind. Had she planned to invite him to her room? Had Mac conspired with her to effect their meeting alone after supper? He did not know. He certainly could not ask her, and he knew that Mac would deny all knowledge. Eleanor had seemed happy to be with him, appeared finally to have put Richard from her mind and concentrated wholeheartedly on him. It was a strange and novel sensation, and one that here, alone in his bed, he was happy to savour. Then he thought further. What now? Where would it lead? And then, as happens on occasions like these, he fell to wondering if it had been nothing but an impulsive moment that would not be repeated. Surely it was more than that? Eleanor was not that sort of person. Was she?

He rose and washed at the basin in the corner of the room, then looked at himself in the mirror. The image reflected was not a pretty sight – half shaven and tousled. He splashed water on his hair to try to flatten it, with only partial success. He glanced at his watch – a quarter past eight – then dressed quickly, slipped quietly out of his bedroom door and went downstairs to the room where they had dined last night. No longer was it warmly lit by candles and the soft glow of a standard lamp; instead it was flooded with the bright white light of a summer morning. It all felt quite different.

He squinted as the sun's rays caught him smack in the eye, and then heard a broad Glaswegian accent commenting, 'Ah, you're up! I was going to send a search party.' He turned to discover Mac sitting at the table in the corner, a freshly cleared plate, still stained with egg yolk, lying in front of him. He was breaking off the crust of half a loaf and mopping up the remains of his breakfast.

Harry wondered for a moment if he knew, but decided to play safe and say nothing. He sat down opposite Mac. The third chair at their table was still empty. He considered asking if Eleanor had come down, but was not confident that it was something he could achieve without looking either sheepish or falsely unconcerned.

Mac appeared not to notice and clarified matters by saying, through a mouthful of bread, coffee and the remains of his egg, that Eleanor had not appeared yet. There was nothing at all suggestive in his comment, so Harry decided not to tempt fate. He was happy instead to give his order to the waitress, even if it did comprise only three words. He gestured towards Mac and said, 'The same, please.'

No sooner had the waitress taken his order than Eleanor appeared in the doorway. The two men stood up on seeing her. Not for her the appearance of the morning after the night before; instead she stood there looking fresh and radiant, her neatly brushed hair shimmering in shafts of sunlight that streamed in through the window. It was one of those occasions when Mac would have instantly reached for his brushes and paints, but then the feeling of egg yolk running down his chin reminded him that this was probably neither the time nor the place. He dabbed at the misplaced trickle of breakfast with his chequered napkin as Eleanor approached. Her cardigan was draped round her shoulders, and she seemed to glide towards the table before sitting down between them.

Harry gazed at her and she smiled at him. There was no embarrassment, no acknowledgement of what had gone before, and he wondered, for a moment, if it had all been a dream.

'What time are we expected?' Eleanor asked Mac.

'Half past nine. Are you all right with that?' he asked.

Eleanor nodded and turned to Harry. 'Are you?'

Harry hesitated. 'Er . . . yes. Yes, of course. I mean, I'm only . . .'

'The driver, I know.' Eleanor completed the sentence for him. 'But I just wanted to check, that was all.' She smiled at him kindly.

He thought he detected a faint flushing to her cheeks, but he couldn't be certain. He wanted to ask her if she was all right, if she had slept well, but in the presence of Mac such an enquiry would be unwise. He would be anxious to know if Harry had taken advantage of his retiring early the night before, and Harry was in too much confusion to want to talk about it.

Eleanor ordered coffee and toast, and the conversation turned to the weather, to what time Munnings would be finished with them and when they thought they might get back to Oxford. There was a note of sadness in the air. The two-day trip had come as a surprise to all three of them. For Mac, it was an unexpected opportunity to watch the master at work in greater detail than he could have imagined. For Eleanor, it was her first experience of being an artist's model. And for Harry? For Harry, it might have been an evening that would change the course of the rest of his life. He only hoped that Eleanor felt the same way. Right now there was no way of knowing.

The more he analysed the events of the night before, the

more he realised that he had done all the running. She had not exactly admitted anything, had not expressed any feelings towards him. It was he who had done all the talking, and now it was the following morning and they were not alone. How could he manage to find out if she did feel anything, or if she was just being kind, just being friendly? He hoped that having finished his breakfast Mac would leave them, even if just for a few moments, but he did not. He sat and waited for them to finish theirs, and then it was time to go back to Castle House for another tantalising day in her company. A day when he knew they would not have a single moment alone together.

At first Harry thought that Munnings would send them off again and that Mac might begin to question him about the night before, but today he operated rather differently. For a start, he greeted them warmly and was ready to start work almost immediately, having summoned the housekeeper to bring coffee for his guests. This was real coffee, unlike the chicory-based brew they had tasted the night before. Harry wondered how long it would be before rationing was abolished and they could choose to eat and drink whatever they wanted. It had been four years now since the war had ended, and there were still times when certain things were in short supply, or priced beyond the reach of mere mortals.

Munnings must have seen the look on his face. 'An appreciative client in South America,' he explained, holding up his beaker of coffee.

Harry nodded his appreciation.

'I never asked your name,' ventured the artist.

'Harry. Harry Ballantyne.'

'And what do you want to do when you grow up, Harry Ballantyne?' he asked with a sardonic grin.

Harry smiled. 'I want to become an auctioneer.'

'Ah!' exclaimed Munnings. 'You want to make money off the back of the likes of me, eh?'

Harry stood his ground. 'Oh, I don't think I'll be there for a while yet, sir. More like bedroom furniture, chests of drawers, that sort of thing.'

'But eventually?'

Harry nodded thoughtfully. 'With any luck, yes.'

Munnings put down his beaker and reached for his palette and paints. 'Well, just make sure you deal with real artists. None of these Picasso fellas and Stanley Spencer – that sort of rubbish. Indecent, that's what they are. Indecent con artists.'

Eleanor slipped behind the screen to change into the riding habit, while Munnings warmed to his subject. 'They've fooled the nation. People pay thousands for those daubs, but where's the talent, eh? Compare them with Stubbs – no contest.' Then, seeing that both Harry and Mac had fallen silent, he confided, 'Of course, the Academy think I'm wrong, think I can't spot talent when I see it, can't see "the way forward", as Rothenstein and his cronies like to call it.' Then he spoke directly to Mac. 'Don't be fooled. You work at your art. Paint what you see, and don't expect anyone to pay a fortune for the convolutions of the inner recesses of your mind. Art is certainly about representation of mood and atmosphere and spirit, but it's about beauty and truth, too.'

The pair of them had fallen silent. Munnings noticed the look in their eyes, a cross between fear and awe. He threw back his head and laughed. 'Come on, let's get started. You, John Macready, you stand over here and watch. We shouldn't be too long now. And, Mr Auctioneer, you can sit quietly on that chair and muse on the day when you'll be able to sell my paintings for far more than I ever will in my lifetime.'

Eleanor walked out from behind the screen and eased herself up on to the trestle. Munnings stepped forward to arrange the folds of her riding habit and to position her arms where they had been the day before. When he was satisfied that all was as it should be, he stepped back to his easel and disappeared once more into his own world, softly murmuring, 'What a go, eh? What a go!'

Harry watched from the chair across the studio, and Mac got as close as he dared to study the master and his brush-work. At seventeen minutes to two the artist threw down his brushes, laid his palette on a paint-spattered table and declared, 'There we are. That'll do. Enough.' The painting was finished.

He turned to look at Harry, who had sat silently against the far wall. 'Come on, Mr Auctioneer, come and have a look at the lady.'

Harry got up and walked across the studio to where Munnings and Mac were standing.

'What do you think?' asked the artist.

Harry examined the still-wet painting and marvelled at the brushwork, which had created, seemingly from a few spare strokes, an image so full of life and vitality that it took his breath away. There were highlights of brilliant yellow and rich cream, shadows of green and grey and lavender blue, colours that he would not have expected to see in a painting of a horse and rider, all applied with a virility and freshness that made him gasp. And there, atop the grey horse, sat Eleanor in her elegant riding habit, with that look in her eyes that seemed to see right through him. Munnings had caught it perfectly.

'Can I have a look?' she asked tentatively, from her seat atop the trestle.

'Of course. How rude of me.' Munnings helped her down and she came round to look at herself and the horse. She let out a little gasp. 'Oh, goodness!'

Munnings smiled. 'You sat very well. You're very patient.' Then his face contorted into a frown and he began to rub his left thumb. 'Enough, I think. Bloody gout! It'll be the end of me as an artist.' He turned to Mac. 'Just pray it doesn't affect you, John Macready.'

Mac did not really hear. The tough Glaswegian was staring intently at the painting of the girl on the horse, and Harry noticed that there were tears in his eyes.

Mac sat next to Harry in the front of the Talbot and Eleanor sat in the back. It took them some time to get out of Dedham. The main street was milling with tall-wheeled carts piled high with hay – one or two of them pulled by growling tractors belching out blue smoke, but the majority being towed by carthorses. Slowly but steadily they clattered their way down the High Street and through farm gates. Harry was unwilling to sound the horn and speed up progress – it seemed dis-respectful – and in the distance large grey thunderclouds were building. The carters and the haymakers would be anxious to get their harvest under cover or stacked into weatherproof haycocks before the onset of the downpour, which now seemed inevitable.

Harry pulled into the side of the road on the outskirts of the village and called to Mac to help him with the hood. No sooner had they hauled it into place than large spots of rain began to fall, spattering loudly on the black fabric that was the only thing that stood between them and a soaking. It was a long, plodding journey back to Oxford, with labouring windscreen wipers that seemed to go more slowly still when the car made its way uphill.

The sky began to clear as they approached the city, and the spires and domes were illuminated by the soft light of evening, which had a freshness and clarity not experienced of late. The summer dust was laid, and cupolas and turrets were polished by the welcome downpour.

Harry wound down the window as they motored down The

High and inhaled the astringent scent of rain-washed pavements. His mind, too, was awash with thoughts – of the immediate past and the near future. What now? Where did they go from here? He wondered what to do next when a voice from the back seat said, 'Here's fine.'

Harry came to. 'What? Sorry?'

'You can drop me here,' said Eleanor.

Harry had not noticed that they were alongside her hall of residence. It had caught him unawares. Suddenly he felt a rising sense of panic. There were things to say, things he wanted to clarify, not least the time when he would see her again.

He pulled in at the side of the road, and before he could do anything Mac had leaped out and was tipping his seat forward so that Eleanor could get out of the back. Harry opened his own door and walked round to where she stood. She was kissing Mac on the cheek. She turned to find him next to her. She said nothing for a moment, just looked up at him. Then she laid her hand on his arm and reached up to kiss him. He wondered at first whether she would kiss him on the lips. She did not. She kissed him as she had done Mac, on the cheek, but she squeezed his arm and said softly, 'Thank you.'

Harry took a deep breath and asked, 'When—'

That was the only word he managed to get out. The blaring of a horn and the raised voice behind him curtailed any further conversation. 'Move yer bloody motor, will you, mate? I'm trying to get this bloody street clean. 'Ow can I do that if you're parked 'ere?'

Harry looked up at the towering green lorry behind the Talbot, its stiff, circular brushes whirring in the gutter and the hose squirting water on to the road.

He looked pleadingly at Eleanor, then back at the now cursing road sweeper. Quickly he darted forward and kissed her on the cheek, then offered her a look that he hoped said everything he wanted it to. He ran round the car, slipped back into the driver's seat and, with a brief wave, drove off into the rain-soaked evening.

'Oh,' said Mac, almost to himself, 'well, I suppose I'll have to walk from here, too.' At that moment a sudden shower broke, splashing on the pavement and drumming on the roof of the road sweeper's lorry. Mac lifted his folio above his head and, calling goodbye to Eleanor, who was now sheltering in the doorway, ran off briskly in the direction of his lodgings.

He did not notice the look of bewilderment on her face, or the fact that it was a few minutes before she moved from where she stood, having watched the Talbot make its way down the glistening street until it disappeared from view round a corner. It had all happened so fast. She had no time to think, no time to say the things she wanted to say. No time, really, to work out the significance of the past two days. But one thing she did know: she would have to go and talk to Richard. It was only fair that he knew. It was just a shame that he was stuck in bed with that stupid cold. But then, if he hadn't been, the previous two days would have turned out quite differently.

She looked up at the sky. The fleeting shower had subsided, but it was growing dark. It would be too late to go and see Richard now. She would leave it until tomorrow. Apart from anything else, it would give her more time to work out what she wanted to say.

15

Villa Fabrice, Menton, Côte d'Azur
December 2007

Lay not up for yourselves treasures upon earth, where moth and rust doth corrupt, and where thieves break through and steal.

Matthew 6:19

'I really don't know anything about art,' said the American lady in the long camel coat. 'Or furniture, really.'

'Well, if you just decide which pieces you want to keep, madam, you can leave the rest to us,' said the man in the dark suit with the wire-rimmed glasses. 'We can have an inventory made and get in touch with the auction house to arrange disposal.'

'Would that be the best way, do you think?' asked the woman.

'That's what's stipulated in Lord Bedlington's will – that you should be able to retain any items you want to keep, but that the rest should be sold at auction and the proceeds split between yourself, as his sole surviving relative, and another beneficiary, whose name we were asked to keep confidential – it's something called a secret trust.'

'Is that legal?'

'It is indeed, madam.'

The woman looked puzzled. 'Intriguing. But then I suppose I should go along with his wishes and be grateful that he thought of me at all.' She ran a finger along the front of a tall, glass-fronted armoire. 'So all this will be sold off?'

'Unless you want to take possession of any of it yourself,'

said the suit. 'In which case you'll have to arrange shipping and export licences and—'

'Oh, no. I don't think so. But I'm not sure it should be sold here in France. Could it be sold in England? I think Uncle Leo would have preferred that.'

'The will stipulates exactly that, madam. And fortuitously, I do think the market might be more favourable there. Apart from a few pieces of French furniture, the majority of the contents are English.'

She ambled up to the French windows, framed by silk curtains that were now showing their age. Great gashes interrupted the smoothness of the fabric, and the once-rich crimson, still visible in the folds, had faded in most places to a dusky rose pink. Beyond the rampant wisteria that engulfed the balustrade of the veranda, cracking at least one of its pillars, was the overgrown garden. Most of the leaves had fallen from its trees and shrubs now, but it was still possible to make out that this had once been a well-tended, if vaguely Arcadian landscape, something the fallen leaves, swirling crisply in little eddies, could not disguise. In the far distance, she could see the narrow ribbon of the sea – a thin sliver of *eau de Nil* beneath the pale sky. She shivered involuntarily, then turned back to face the man. 'Such a sad life,' she murmured, looking around her at the faded grandeur.

The man in the suit made an effort at conversation. 'Did you know Lord Bedlington well, madam?'

'No, not at all. I'd heard of him as a child, but we were only distantly related. I feel rather guilty inheriting this. Not that there's much to inherit. A few paintings and a few sticks of furniture, hardly a life-changing legacy, and not the sort of stuff that's at home in the Hamptons.' Her face bore an expression that was a mixture of sympathy and disappointment. 'Not really worth coming all this way to see. Still, it had to be done.' She was suddenly aware that she might be sounding like an ungrateful American and so made a stab at showing she was not a total stranger to social graces. 'Did *you* know Lord Bedlington?' she asked.

'Alas, no. We just happen to be his solicitors. A long association going back two generations. The Bedlingtons have been coming to Gray's Inn Square for a long time.' And then, realising that what he had said was not strictly accurate, 'Well, dealing with us, anyway. To be honest, we seldom saw them in person.'

'I see,' she said, but her interest was waning. She walked over to the wall at the back of the faded salon, where a picture of a horse hung above a lumpy *fauteuil* whose stuffing was doing its best to escape the confines of the upholstery. 'Not my thing at all, but one or two of these pictures do look quite good, don't they?'

The solicitor nodded. 'I think madam might be rather surprised at what they fetch.'

'Do you?' She looked startled. 'Well, let's hope you're right. Poor Uncle Leo could have done with a cash injection in his own lifetime, I guess, looking at the state of this place. Why didn't he sell them and do the house up, or move into a more easily managed condo down in Cannes?'

The man smiled weakly.

She walked around the room, looking to right and left. 'Who will you sell the stuff with?' she asked casually. 'Christie's or Sotheby's?'

'Neither, madam. Lord Bedlington stipulated the name of the auction house in his will, so that decision is made for us.'

'I see.' She looked around her once more, trying to find at least something that she could take with her from the un-exciting miscellany of furniture and paintings that surrounded her. Her eyes lighted on another object. A smaller one this time. 'Would you look at that!'

The suit glanced in her direction and saw that the woman was advancing on a small painting that stood on the battered ormolu desk.

'An icon.'

'Yes, madam.'

'I wonder who it is.' She looked thoughtfully at the small image of the saint in her kid-gloved hand, examining it carefully. 'So delicate. Would it be all right if I took this with me?'

'Alas, madam, that is the one item that was a specific bequest.'

'Oh.' She looked crestfallen. 'What a disappointment.' She put down the icon and dusted her hands together. 'Well, I guess that's it, then. Better be making tracks. I'll leave you to arrange for the disposal of the rest of the contents with . . . Who did you say would be selling this stuff?'

'A small auction house in Bath, madam. Ballantyne's.'

'Never heard of them.'

As she walked to the door, her eye lighted on a small book-case. It was empty except for one small volume lying flat on the top shelf. She glanced at it and picked it up. '*An Artist's Life* by A. J. Munnings,' she read. 'Wasn't he the guy who painted the horses?'

'Yes, madam, I believe he was.'

She opened the cover. 'Hey, it's signed. "To John Macready, with high hopes from A. J. Munnings.' Could I take this? I could read it on the plane. Horse paintings are not really my bag, but it'll help pass the time.'

'If you wish, madam.'

'Who was John Macready when he was at home, then?'

The solicitor fished in his pocket for the house key. He had tired of the banality of her questions now. 'I have no idea, madam. Perhaps he was a guest of Lord Bedlington's and left it behind.'

'What a pity. I'd rather hoped you would have said he was a great artist.'

16

Bedlington Park
July 1949

And though if the Van Dycks have to go
And we pawn the Bechstein grand,
We'll stand by the stately homes of England.
'The Stately Homes of England,' (1937), Sir Noël Coward

Harry did not know what had kept him driving. The only difficult point had come when he had realised he needed more petrol. He had managed to find enough money to put in a few gallons and had got as far as the bottom of the drive at Bedlington Park before the Talbot finally conked out. He had driven through the night and, fearful of waking up the entire Bedlington household, had bedded down in the back of the car under a plaid rug until he was woken by the early morning light. He glanced in the rear-view mirror and was not heartened by the vision that gazed back. He now sported three days' stubble and was in need of a bath. If the local bobby came along on his bike and stopped to investigate, thought Harry, he would be sure to slap handcuffs on him and take him into custody. Even the most gullible member of His Majesty's Constabulary would be likely to question the veracity of an unshaven tramp claiming that he had been loaned a glistening Talbot Ten and was returning it to its owner.

He glanced at the clock in the walnut dashboard. The hands showed that it was a quarter past seven. What time did earls get up? Then he remembered that Leo was nursing his father, and that the hours of the day would probably be meaningless. Would he just have fallen into bed having sat through the night with him, or would he have retired early and risen with the dawn? Perhaps the staff were actually doing the nursing and Leo was simply in attendance. The inconclusiveness of his thoughts irritated him. He had driven through the night partly to get the car back, but also partly because it gave him something to do other than simply think.

Right now the thinking was all that was left. Irritably he eased himself from the back seat and opened the door. He stumbled out on to the tree-lined drive and looked out at the view across the park. A herd of fallow deer grazed beneath the ancient oaks. One or two of them look up and stared disdainfully in his direction through the early-morning mist, then returned their attentions to the more interesting subject of breakfast.

Harry stretched, shut the car door and began the long walk up the drive of Bedlington Park to seek assistance. A spot of breakfast would suit him, too. Then he fell once more to thinking about the previous day, and that it had now been more than twenty-four hours since they had breakfasted together. He wondered if they would ever do so again.

'What timing,' said Leo. He was standing in the doorway of Bedlington Park. He looked, if anything, even more dishevelled than Harry.

'I'm sorry. Have I woken you?' Harry asked.

Leo shook his head. 'No. I've been up all night.'

'How is he?'

Leo spoke evenly. 'He died at half past five this morning.'

'Oh, I'm so sorry.' Harry's own worries were, for the moment, put aside.

'No. It's a release, really. He's been ill for a long time. First they thought they could save the leg and then they couldn't. Then they thought he was making a good recovery and his heart started playing up. Poor old stick has really been through it. In the end I think it just wore him out.' Then Leo realised that his friend was still standing on the doorstep. 'Oh, I'm sorry, come in.'

Harry walked through the large pair of glazed doors in the centre of the Palladian portico and into the hall of Bedlington Park. The floor was of parchment-coloured limestone: the walls were painted creamy grey and hung with hunting trophies. The whole effect was rather oppressive. Leo led the way through a doorway to the left of the hall, which was flanked by two blackamoor gondoliers who carried their oars like halberds. As they passed through it, Harry glanced up and noticed the head of an impala, clearly caught in mid-flight by its pursuer. He ducked involuntarily.

'Make yourself comfortable,' instructed Leo. 'I'll go and organise some coffee.'

Harry perched on the arm of an easy chair and looked around. The drawing room was much less intimidating than the hall. A collection of English-country-house furniture and chintz-covered chairs and sofas were dotted around the room, whose egg-yolk-yellow walls were decorated with a rich mixture of pictures, from the expected Georgian ancestors and a rather grubby Van Dyck to more modern works by Nash and Nicholson. There were pictures of horses, too. A large Herring of two racehorses approaching the finishing post, a stable scene by John Ferneley and a collection of hounds in a kennel by John Emms. Harry was quietly pleased that he could identify most of the artists without having to go close enough to read the signatures. At least something must have rubbed off over the last three years.

By the fireplace were two small paintings of Bedlington terriers. They made Harry smile. Then he fell to wondering what would happen to all this now that it had been left to Leo. Would he happily turn into the lord of the manor, the local squire, or would he sell up and move on? Unlikely, thought Harry. Leo had never had a close relationship with his father, but he did have a sense of duty and an awareness of the need for continuity. In that moment of seeing Leo in the doorway he could understand acutely the responsibility lying upon his shoulders. A few days ago he had been a scion of the aristocracy, the Hooray Henry who had nothing to do but enjoy himself. Within the week the carefree young blade had been transformed into a man of property and a landowner with obligations. Harry felt sorry for him. The trappings were one thing, the responsibilities were quite another.

And then he saw the Munnings. It was hanging in an alcove. It was of a woman on a horse and not dissimilar in composition to the one that the artist had painted of Eleanor riding side-saddle. His thoughts returned to her. Maybe he should have been more positive. He should have run after her and asked when he could see her again, but the intervention of the road sweeper had thrown him and in the second or two it took to consider what he should do he had missed his opportunity.

His reverie was interrupted by the opening of the large mahogany door. Leo came into the room, followed by a butler, stooping under the weight of a tray laden with tea and coffee, milk and sugar. The butler needed no instruction. He put down the tray on the large padded stool in front of one of the sofas, bowed respectfully from the neck, fixed Harry with rheumy eyes for as long as it took to register his presence and then turned and exited without a word.

'I don't think Sands will ever get over it,' said Leo dejectedly. 'He's been here for thirty-odd years. Not that Pa was home very much, but he always relied on Sands to keep things going.' He leaned forward and began to pour coffee, motioning Harry to help himself to milk and sugar. 'Pa came and went, but Sands was always here, year after year. "The Sands of time" Pa used to call him. Not very funny, really, but I think they had an understanding. Pa would do his own things, and Sands would keep the place going.' Leo looked around him. 'Trouble is, I don't think he'll have the energy to carry on now.'

'So what will you do?' asked Harry.

'Stay and sort things out. This is where I'm at now, like it or not. There'll be lawyers to see – all that sort of thing – and until I've met with them, I don't really know what will happen. In the lap of the gods, I suppose.'

Leo got up from the sofa and walked over to one of the long windows that looked over the park. He sipped his coffee thoughtfully and then said, 'Look at all that. Two hundred years of history. It would be a tragedy if I were to lose it all now – even the bloody fountain. It's never worked properly.'

Harry stood up and walked to the window, standing beside Leo and looking out over the park. There were handsome clumps of oak, scattered seemingly at random, and great sweeps of grass, dotted with deer. Right in front of the window, at a distance of a hundred yards or so, was a large fountain of Neptune sitting atop a trio of dolphins and raising his trident in the air. Water spurted from every orifice, engulfing the entire work of art in a welter of spume and mist.

'Quite appalling,' murmured Leo, 'but I do so love it.' He turned to face into the room once more, and Harry could see that his eyes were filled with tears.

'Perhaps I should be going,' said Harry, draining his cup.

'You'll do no such thing,' insisted Leo. 'You've driven all this way. It was really good of you. If I'd thought about it, I could have sent Osborne to pick the car up, but I was a bit preoccupied . . .'

'No. It was fine,' said Harry reassuringly.

'Anyway, there's no way I'm letting you leave this house looking like that. The locals would think standards have really slipped.' Leo glanced across at a large, ornate looking-glass on the wall of the drawing room. 'Mind you, I'm one to talk. Come on, I'll get Sands to send someone up to run us baths and then we can catch up over breakfast. I want to know exactly what happened with that wicked old horse painter. Take my mind off things.'

It might take your mind off things, thought Harry, but it won't help me much.

They breakfasted in a small summer house to one side of the mansion. It was surrounded by roses, thickly planted, their fragrance lying heavily on the early-morning air.

'Better in here at this time of year,' confided Leo. 'The dining room's far too lofty and dark.'

Harry was about to ask if Leo would keep on all the staff when they were interrupted by the sight of a woman walking briskly across the far side of the lawn in the direction of the stables, which lay to the east of the house. She carried a coat over one arm, and her free hand held a smart vanity case. She was being followed, rather less briskly, by Sands, who was weighed down by two large suitcases.

'Ah,' murmured Leo, 'that didn't take long.' He saw Harry's quizzical look. 'That's Isabella, the last in the line.' And then, seeing that he was still not carrying Harry with him, 'Pa's latest – well, last – mistress. Never liked her. Gold-digger. Unlike most of the others.'

Harry raised an eyebrow.

'Regular stream, I'm afraid. Several of them became surrogate mothers when I was young, but they gradually fell by the wayside.'

'And she's going already?' asked Harry.

'The old man told her last night that she wouldn't get a bean. He did it very nicely – said he hoped she'd had a nice time but that he'd be leaving everything to me. That went down well, as you can imagine. So off she pops.'

'I see.' Harry tried to get a handle on this world, which was so very different from his own.

'But enough of my local difficulties. What about yours? How did the visit go?'

Harry told Leo of Munnings's hospitality, of his unexpectedly helpful attitude towards Mac and of his painting Eleanor sitting on the horse.

'You've seen the one of Mama, of course?' asked Leo.

'In the drawing room?'

'Yes.'

'I didn't know who it was.'

'Painted the year before I was born,' confided Leo. 'But then it would have been, wouldn't it . . . ?' He checked himself. 'Died having me, I'm afraid. Not a nice thing to have to live with, but to be honest I couldn't do much about it.' Harry saw in Leo's face a mixture of sadness and stoicism, an acquired ability to shrug off the most dreadful circumstances with a mixture of irony and grit. His face betrayed a deep sadness, but then he said brightly, 'So how is Miss Faraday? Has being an artist's model gone to her head?'

'Oh, I shouldn't think so. You know Eleanor.'

'Yes,' said Leo. 'But do you?'

Harry looked surprised. 'What do you mean?'

'Well, you've been at university with her for three years, but how well do you know her?'

'I'm not sure.'

'She's quite soft on you, you know.' Leo's tone was casual.

'You think so?'

'I know so.'

'That's what Mac said, but I'm not so sure.'

Harry did not want to give away details of their evening together, not simply for fear of revealing his own hand, but also to avoid embarrassing Eleanor.

'Why is it that some chaps can't see what's staring them in the face?' asked Leo.

'Not you as well.'

Leo looked at him questioningly.

'Mac gave me the third degree, too.'

'Well, there you are,' said Leo. 'Two of us can't be wrong.' He popped a piece of toast and marmalade into his mouth and asked, 'So what are you going to do about it?'

Harry stood up and walked to the open door of the summer house. 'Go and see her before she leaves. Ask her ...' His words trailed off as he gazed out over the green lawns of Bedlington Park.

'Ask her what?'

'If she'll marry me.'

17

Bath

December 2007

In certain circumstances, Sotheby's may print in the catalogue the history of ownership of a work of art if such information contributes to scholarship or is otherwise well known and assists in distinguishing the work of art. However, the identity of the seller or previous owners may not be disclosed for a variety of reasons. For example, such information may be excluded to accommodate a seller's requests for confidentiality or because the identity of prior owners is unknown given the age of the work of art.

Sotheby's 'Guide for Prospective Buyers'

The letter came as a complete surprise. Jamie was sitting at his desk at Ballantyne's reading it through for the second time when his mother came into the office.

'You look worried. What's the matter?' she asked, bustling her way to her own desk and throwing off her cashmere cape.

'Not worried, just surprised. Did you see the paper this morning? The obituaries? One of Granddad's old university friends has died.'

'Which one?' Emma Ballantyne was busying herself with her shopping bag now, taking out of it an assortment of files and papers.

'Lord Bedlington.'

She carried on emptying her bag. 'Oh dear. Still, he must have been a good age, I suppose.'

'Eighty-one.'

'Does your grandfather know?' she asked.

'Yes. I was with him this morning.'

His mother stopped what she was doing. 'Oh.'

'He asked to see me.'

'He said he was going to.'

'And you know what about?' asked Jamie.

'Yes,' answered his mother as evenly as she could. She looked slightly guilty, as if she were expecting her son to sound off at her. He did not.

'So what did you say?' she asked cautiously.

'What could I say?' said Jamie. 'I told him I'd be delighted to move into the Circus, it's just that I can't really take it in. I'll be sorry to see him and Gran move out, and I've no idea how I'm going to fill it, or what it will cost me to keep up, but I just know it's the right thing.' And then, almost to himself, 'I think I must be bonkers.'

His mother looked relieved. 'I think your grandfather is just pleased that it will stay in the family.'

'But why don't you want it? I thought it would have suited you for your entertaining and everything.'

'Me? Oh, I've done my stint in the town. I'm happy where I am. If he'd have offered it to me ten years ago, I might have jumped at it, but not now. Too late. It's better that you have it. You'll fill it one day.' She sat down at her desk and murmured under her breath, 'I just hope that it's with the right person.'

'Mother!'

'What?' She looked at him innocently.

'Anyway, there's something else. This letter came this morning.' Jamie walked over to her desk and dropped the letter in front of her on her blotter.

Emma reached for her glasses and held the letter at a suitable distance, reading out loud:

Dear Sirs,

<u>Re: the late Lord Bedlington</u>

In the terms of the will of our client Leo, the late Lord
Bedlington, the deceased requested that his goods and
chattels, such as were not claimed directly by the two
parties named therein, should be disposed of through the
offices of Ballantyne's of Bath and the proceeds thereof
distributed to the named beneficiaries of his will.

Such goods and chattels are, at present, contained within
the property known as Villa Fabrice, Menton, Côte d'Azur.

I would be grateful if you would be so good as to
contact me at the address above so that our former client's
wishes may be expedited.

Yours faithfully,

Edward Chesterman

for Chesterman, Chesterman and Paine, solicitors

Emma took off her glasses and looked up at her son. 'Well,
I never. Why do you suppose he wanted *us* to sell it?'

'Maybe for old times' sake. But when I told Granddad that
Lord Bedlington had died, he said, "That'll put the cat among
the pigeons." Why do you think?'

Emma looked blank. 'I've absolutely no idea. But you'd better
get on to' – she checked the letterhead again – 'Chesterman,
Chesterman and Paine and find out what they want us to
do. As I recall, Leo Bedlington was all but penniless at the
end, so I can't think that there will be much of interest. The
majority of his inheritance would have gone in death duties.'

'That's what the paper said, in the obituary. Eighty per
cent, apparently.'

'Ah, well. I suppose we can do our bit for the old boy.'

'Did Granddad talk about him at all?' asked Jamie.

'Not much. But whenever he did it was always quite
affectionately. I don't think they saw a lot of each other after
their university days.'

'What about Richard King? Did he know him better?'

'Oh, as far as I'm aware, Leo Bedlington's relationship with Richard King was even less cordial than your grandfather's.'

'Why?'

His mother sighed deeply and pushed back her chair. 'Relationships in those days were not quite as simple as they are today, if you know what I mean.'

Jamie looked puzzled.

'Oh, Jamie! Your grandfather and Richard King are both red-blooded males, but that doesn't necessarily mean that everyone they knew at university was of exactly the same persuasion. Is that clear enough?'

'Well, yes, but . . .'

'There were jealousies.'

Jamie perched on the edge of his mother's desk. 'Good God! I never imagined Granddad being involved in all that sort of thing.'

'He wasn't involved in "all that sort of thing", as you call it. Far from it. But that's not to say others weren't. Your grandfather was a very good-looking young man, and so was Richard King.'

'Meaning?'

'Meaning that young men in their late teens and early twenties are still finding out about life and about themselves.' She saw Jamie's eyebrows raise but continued with her explanation. 'I'm quite sure your grandfather and Richard were completely certain about their own sexuality, but they would have had friends who might not have been.'

'Like Leo Bedlington?'

'Yes.'

'And what about his friend?' Jamie scanned the obituary column lying on his desk. 'John Macready – described as his "companion of many years". He died in a swimming accident.'

'I think your grandfather was rather surprised by that.'

'His death, or the fact that they lived together?'

'Both.' Emma tapped her fingers on the desk impatiently. 'Why don't you ask him yourself? I'm sure he'd tell you about it.' She put down the letter and reached for the phone. 'Well, if you're not going to ring Chesterman, Chesterman and whoever, then I suppose I'd better.'

'I'll do it, I'll do it. I'm just a bit surprised, that's all. It's been a bit of a morning, all things considered.' Then it occurred to him that he could not remember being happier in his entire life. He reached for the telephone, but paused before dialling and wondered what she might be doing now, up at the top end of town.

Missy was working her way through the new exhibition catalogue, writing descriptions of paintings, indicating their provenance and working out in her head exactly what would be hung where. The show would mark fifty years of King's Fine Art and would also be something of a personal celebration for Richard King at eighty. At the core of the exhibition would be the major equestrian artists of the eighteenth, nineteenth and early twentieth centuries, with a few modern pieces thrown in to offer broader appeal.

She straightened her back and looked up and directly ahead of her. Her grandfather had now hung the Munnings of the woman on the horse on the far wall. It stood alone. She must remember to ask him if he wanted it included in the exhibition. It would make a good counterpoint to the Stubbs that she planned to hang on the opposite side of the room.

She looked back at her laptop and tried hard to concentrate on the description of a Ben Marshall painting showing Mr Henry Vansittart's chestnut colt Burleigh with Sam Chifney by the rubbing-down house at Newmarket. It was an odd painting, when she came to look at it. The rubbing-down house looked a bit like a brick privy, and Sam Chifney, in his pink silks, did seem to be holding the reins as if he were pushing a baby in a pram. Prams ... babies ... marriage ... her train of thought took her to the night before and she felt little inclination to continue with the cataloguing. He had not said anything before he left, but she did not feel anxious, as she would previously have done in such circumstances. Instead she felt a kind of inner calm – an echo of the sensation she had experienced the night before, lying there in his arms.

Her reverie was interrupted by her grandfather. He pushed open the door with more force than was necessary and stood in front of her at the desk. Missy looked up. There was something odd about him. He was not his usual calm self. Instead, his cheeks were flushed and he drummed his fingers on the edge of the desk.

'What on earth's the matter?' she asked.

'Oh, nothing, really. Just had a bit of a shock. Old university chum died. Read it in the paper.'

'Oh, I'm sorry.' Missy got up. 'Let me make you a cup of coffee.'

'No, no, it's all right.' Richard King turned away from the desk and walked over to the window. It was raining steadily now, more like December than it had been of late. More in tune with his mood.

'Did you know him very well?' Missy asked.

'Once.'

'But not recently?'

'No, we hadn't met for years.'

'But he would have been about your age, though?'

Her grandfather smiled ruefully. 'Old enough for it not to come as a shock?' he remarked.

'Oh, no ... I didn't mean ...' Missy was aware that she was on sensitive ground.

Her grandfather moved to placate her. 'Oh, don't worry.

Everyone of my age realises we're on borrowed time, it's just that we don't need to be reminded.'

'No.' Missy looked suitably contrite.

'Look, I will have that coffee. And a biscuit, too, I think. Would that be all right?'

'Of course.' Missy got up and walked through the gallery to a small door at the end, which led to a tiny kitchen. She made coffee and arranged a small plate of biscuits for him, then took them back through to the gallery on a small marquetry tray. Everything in the Royal Crescent gallery was of top quality, even the tea tray: it was something Richard King prided himself on – attention to detail.

Her grandfather was once more looking out of the window when she came back.

'Here we are. One sugar?'

'Please.'

Missy handed him the china cup and saucer, and slipped a fig roll into the saucer. He loved fig rolls.

'So will there be a funeral?' she asked.

'Oh, I don't know. Probably over in France, I should think. That's where he lived at the end. Mind you, he was so very English, maybe they'll bring him back over here and bury him in the family vault. I should think there is one.'

'Who was he?' asked Missy.

'Leo, Lord Bedlington. He was a friend at Christ Church back in the forties. He was just "the Honourable" back then, of course. A long time ago. A lot's happened since then.'

'And you lost touch?'

'Yes.'

Missy was flipping through the pages of *The Times*. 'Here it is . . . the Earl of Bedlington.'

Richard King moved towards her. 'Oh, you've got the paper.'

'Yes . . . a landscape gardener, the original earl. His father was a collector ... Death duties ...' Missy was speed-reading the obituary. 'He "dabbled in the art world, but seldom effectively".'

'Yes, well, it's probably all very boring to you.' Richard made to move the conversation on, but Missy was now intent on finishing the obituary.

'"His companion of many years, the artist John Macready."' Missy lowered the paper. 'I didn't know that John Macready lived with him.'

'Well, there you are.'

'Did you know him as well, Grandpa?'

Richard King hesitated. 'Vaguely.'

'But didn't he study art at Christ Church, too?'

'Oh, probably. A lot of people studied art at Christ Church. I didn't know them all.'

Missy was surprised at her grandfather's impatience. He was normally composed, calm and imperturbable, but he seemed distinctly vexed now. Perhaps it was just the shock of his old friend dying. And the weather.

'We've sold his pictures here – not recently, but over the years. I just thought you might have encountered him.'

'Well, of course I encountered him, but that doesn't mean I knew him.'

'No, of course not. Sorry.' She felt unnerved by his irrita-tion and began to wish that she had not asked about his past, but he had never seemed particularly sensitive about it before. Why should he be so nettled now?

Her grandfather drained his cup and put it back on the tray. He had not touched the fig roll. 'Well, if you'll excuse me, I've things to do. I'll probably be back late afternoon if anyone asks for me.'

'Fine. OK.' She could not let it rest there and did not want to spend the rest of the day worrying about him. 'Grandpa, everything is all right, isn't it?'

He realised he had acted out of character, that his behaviour had alarmed her. 'Yes, of course. I'm sorry. Just a bit of a shock, that's all.' He bent forward and kissed the top of her head. 'Just a bit of a shock.' Then he smiled at her and left the room.

Missy folded up the paper and lay it in her in-tray. She looked up at the wall, which for some reason now looked quite different. Then she realised why. The picture of the lady on the horse – the Munnings – was no longer there.

18

Oxford
July 1949

Deep in my soul that tender secret dwells,
Lonely and lost to light for evermore,
Save when to thine my heart responsive swells,
Then trembles into silence as before.

'The Corsair' (1814), Lord Byron

Richard was feeling very sorry for himself. He had contemplated not getting out of bed, but truth to tell, he was bored of lying there. If he was honest with himself, his bones did not ache as much as they had done, and his nose was no longer a streaming torrent. He reasoned with himself that if he washed and shaved, he would feel even better. That, and the prospect of leaving Oxford the following day, galvanised him into action.

Towelling his hair dry, he looked around the room at the scene of devastation – the clothes lying everywhere, albeit in orderly heaps, and the piles of books sorted into categories ready for packing. Richard enjoyed order – if it wasn't a right angle, it was a wrong angle – but he tried to be reasonable and realistic when it came to inflicting his precision on others. Around the room, trunks and cases were open to accept their load, and by tomorrow he would be packed and ready to go.

The knock at his door came as no surprise. A steady stream of students – some of whom he knew well, others only slightly – had come to say their farewells over the past twenty-four hours. He had peered over the bedclothes and been as cheery as he could, and received an ample amount of sympathy for his trouble. He was waiting for Eleanor to return. He had expected her the previous day, but she had clearly left him to stew with his cold. He was a bit miffed by that, but then it was understandable – why should she have to risk catching it as well?

'Come in if you're healthy!' he yelled in the direction of the door.

The door opened and Mac put his head round. 'Any better?'

'A bit, thanks. Well, quite a lot, actually. It was a real bugger. Don't know where I picked it up.'

'Ah, well, you know colleges – always something doing the rounds.' Mac looked at the open suitcases and trunks. 'You ready for the off, then?'

'Just about.'

'I've done mine. A life packed into suitcases.' He looked pensive for a moment, then said, 'Thought I'd go for a pint down by the river. Do you fancy one?'

Richard was not sure that drinking was a good idea after being confined to bed for two days with sinuses that felt like blocked drains, but the moment had come where he needed to take some kind of drastic action to rid himself of the last vestiges of his ailment, and drowning it in beer might be as good a way as any.

They sat at a table beside the river, and the pint glasses began to pile up. Two, then three. They were on their fourth now. Richard had thought – at around two and a half pints – that his head was beginning to clear. Now the fog was descending again, but at least he minded less. 'So when do you leave?' he asked Mac.

'Tomorrow morning. The early train.'

'To Glasgow?'

'To start with. Better see the folks and break it to them that I'm not staying.'

'What then?'

Mac shrugged. 'That depends.'

'On what?'

'On all kinds of things, I suppose. I just want time to think, time to get myself sorted out.'

Richard took another gulp and lowered his glass to the table, where it landed with more of a thump than he had intended. 'That sounds a bit serious.'

Mac turned to look in the direction of a passing punt. 'I suppose so.'

There was a wistfulness in Mac's tone Richard had not noticed before. Maybe it was just the beer. 'Are you all right?' he asked. 'I mean, it's nothing serious, is it?'

Mac laughed, but his laughter had a hollow ring to it. 'No, it's not serious. Not serious at all, more's the pity.'

Richard grinned. 'It's not a woman, is it? You haven't gone and found yourself a woman? Not after keeping yourself pure for the last three years . . .'

Mac shook his head, and then wished he hadn't. He held his head in his hands for a moment. 'No, I haven't gone and found myself a woman.'

'Too tied up in your painting, that's your trouble,' muttered Richard, reaching for his glass once more.

'That's me. Always tied up in my bloody painting. Too concerned with Prussian blue and Hooker's green deep, the only hooker I'm ever likely to meet.'

'Oh, now don't say that. You don't want to meet a hooker. You want a nice girl, a girl like Eleanor. Except not Eleanor. Another nice girl.'

'You reckon?'

'Yup. That's what you need.' Richard was studying the remaining contents of his glass with the concentration of a biologist examining the contents of a Petri dish.

Mac's eyes were on the river, and his mind was elsewhere as he murmured, 'I wish it were that simple.'

'Whaddya mean?'

'As simple as finding the right girl.'

Richard looked up from his glass now and put his hands flat on the table, the better to steady himself. 'You see, all the years we've been here, you've never bothered, have you? You've never gone and found a girl. Or several girls, even. You could have had lots of them. You're not bad-looking. Not as good-looking as some of us, granted, but you're not bad. You just never got off your arse and tried, and now you're going back to Glasgow on your own and—'

'I'm not going back to bloody Glasgow. Well . . . I am going back there . . . but only for a few days. I'm not staying.'

'But you're on your own.'

'I wish you'd stop saying that as though it were some kind of disease.'

'Now there's no need to be rattled. I didn't mean it was some kind of disease, just that . . . well . . . you know . . . it's a bit of a shame, that's all.' Richard tried to look sympathetic, but his eyes were red and watery.

Mac drained his glass. 'Another one?'

Richard looked at his watch and tried to read the time from the fuzzy-edged hands.

'No. No, I'd better not. Better get back and pinish my facking.' He grinned. 'That didn't come out right, did it?'

'No, but sometimes things don't come out right, do they?'

'I suppose not.'

Mac sighed. 'Are you happy?' he asked.

'I wish I hadn't got this bloody cold. And that I hadn't had so many pints.'

'No, but are you happy generally, with the way things have turned out?'

'Ha! Well, they haven't turned out, have they? Not yet.'

'No.'

'And I don't know where she is. She said she'd come and

see me, but she hasn't shown up yet and it's . . . it's . . .' he was screwing up his eyes and looking at his watch '. . . later than it should be.'

'Are you sure she's the one for you?' asked Mac, trying to sound as level as he could.

'Yup. The only one. Stands to reason. I think she thinks so, too. Got to sort things out today. Set the record straight.' Richard's brow was furrowed with the effort of concentrating, then he gave up and asked, 'What about you? Are you happy? With your painting?'

Mac looked irritated. 'I wish you wouldn't keep going on as though my painting were the only thing worth living for.'

'Well, it is, isn't it? I mean, that's what you do. We all know that. You're far more dedicated than we are – and the best artist of the lot of us.'

'And that should be enough?'

Richard shrugged. 'I don't know. You tell me.'

'I wish I could,' murmured Mac.

'And what's that supposed to mean?'

'Nothing. Nothing at all.'

A hint of aggression began to bubble up inside Richard, the emboldening effect of alcohol. 'No, come on, you said you wished you could tell me, so tell me.'

'It doesn't matter.'

'Yes it does. It does matter.'

'It's pointless.'

'Nothing's pointless. Tell me. Go on, tell me what you wished you could tell me.'

Mac shook his head. 'You've no idea, have you?'

'About what? I don't understand . . .'

'No, you wouldn't. I mean, why should you?'

Richard looked enquiringly at Mac, who was staring out across the river. In spite of the fact that Richard had had too much to drink, and was having difficulty focusing, he could see that Mac's eyes were full of tears. Well, there was a turn-up for the books. Mac, the tough one, the one who never showed emotion.

Mac spoke softly. 'If ever there's anything I can do, to help you, you will let me know, won't you?'

Richard smiled. 'You mean, when you're a successful painter, you'll let me sell your work for inflated prices and take a massive commission?'

'That's not what I mean.'

'What, then?'

'You've never noticed, have you?'

'Noticed what?'

Mac turned to face him. 'About the girl thing?'

Richard was puzzled. 'What about it?'

'It was never an option.'

'What do you mean?'

'It was never . . . an interest.'

'I know. Too dedicated to your work.'

Mac shook his head. 'Not just that.'

The slow dawning of reality broke over Richard's face. 'You mean . . . not girls . . . but—'

Mac cut in gently, ''Fraid so.'

'Christ! And have you . . . ?'

'God, no, never. Promiscuity never appealed. There was only one, you see. And I knew that was pointless. You've never given me any reason to believe that you felt the same way.'

He smiled, and the colour, so recently returned to Richard's cheeks, drained from them once more. He stared at Mac, unable to believe what he had heard, and then said, very softly, 'Oh, shit.'

'I'm sorry. I knew it would shock you. That's why I had to get pissed to tell you. I knew there was no chance you felt the same way as me, but I couldn't leave without letting you know. It's . . . important somehow that I told you.'

Never had so few words had such a sobering effect on Richard. 'I see,' he said softly.

'Well, there we are. Stupid, really.'

Richard interrupted, 'What made you . . . ?'

'Oh, who knows? It wasn't as if you gave me any encouragement. Any hope, even. It's just the unfairness of life, I suppose. I can't say I wanted it to happen, can't say I ever realised quite what was going on in my head. Until it was too late.'

'No.'

Mac looked suddenly worried. 'There's no reason why it should alter anything. I don't want you thinking I'd do anything stupid or . . . I mean, just forget it. Forget I ever said anything. Put it down to being pissed or something.'

Richard's mind was whirring. It was not a situation in which he had ever found himself before. He neither knew what to say nor how to behave. He was torn between wanting to hit Mac for daring to say such a thing and wanting to apologise to a man who had been a good friend, a staunch friend, for being unable to return his feelings. The events of the past three years swirled around in his head. He searched in vain for things he might have said or done that could possibly have given Mac any reason to believe that there was the remotest chance that his feelings could be or would be reciprocated. He found none. Mac had been a friend, just a really good friend. There was nothing remotely fey or effeminate about him. Quite the reverse; if anything, he was the most resolutely masculine of the four of them. Did Harry know? he wondered. That particular question was answered immediately.

'There's no need for anybody else to know, is there?' asked Mac.

Richard detected a note of fear in his voice – fear of being found out, fear of being spurned by the people he had been closest to over the past three years.

Richard shook his head. 'No, of course not,' he said.

'I'd better go,' said Mac. He stood up and swayed a little. Then he laid his hand on Richard's shoulder, partly to steady himself and partly as a gesture of fondness. 'Don't lose touch,' he said.

Richard could say nothing. He stared at the table for a few moments, and when he looked up to speak, Mac had gone. It may have been the note of despair in Mac's voice, or it may have been his own acute discomfort at the unexpected revelation, but somehow, deep inside, he knew that they would never meet again.

Eleanor was resolutely determined. She had put off the evil moment long enough. She could delay no more. She would be leaving the following day and needed to square things up before then. It was unfair to leave things as they were, from everybody's point of view.

She took the long route to Richard's lodgings, the better to square in her mind what she wanted to say. Along the banks of the Cherwell she walked, past swathes of hemp agrimony and meadowsweet. She watched as the last few students remaining in the city punted noisily up and down the river, remembering the times she had sat in the back of rowing boats and skiffs as attentive students vied for her attention. She knew now that there was only one of them she really wanted to be a part of her life.

For three years she had lived here, loved here and discovered more to herself than she had thought existed. It was time to move on. There was a hint of wistfulness to her mood, but mainly a sense of purpose, a sense of resolve.

She passed Mac's digs on her way to see Richard. She would go and and say her goodbyes there, too. Might even tell him what she was going to do. She climbed the stairs. The door swung open as she knocked, but there was no sign of Mac, or of his luggage. He must have packed and gone. But how could he, without saying goodbye? He had been booked on to the Glasgow train for the following morning. Had his plans changed? Where was he? Baffled by the unexpected turn of events, she retraced her steps and walked out into the street again, looking up at his window and half expecting him to wave back at her and say that he had just popped out for a few moments, but he did not appear.

She walked on down the street, preoccupied, trying to make sense of so many things. As she rounded the corner by Richard's lodgings, in the next street to Mac's, she did not see the lone figure in the distance, laden with suitcases, crossing the road and then disappearing in the direction of the station. If she had done, she would have run after him, but she didn't. In that moment he faded out of her life. Just as he had faded out of Richard's.

Harry hoped that she would be in her room, but when he got there, the cleaner said that she had left half an hour ago. 'Where was she going?' he had asked. 'How should I know?' retorted the cleaner. 'I just clean, I don't baby-mind. And anyway, she's not a baby.'

It was not a good start. He would just have to do the rounds of the various digs and lodgings and hope that somewhere along the way he would bump into her. He set off in the direction of Mac's, but when he found his rooms empty, he realised that she must instead be with Richard. That could be tricky, though he could at least go there and somehow get her away. It was his only hope. Why had he left it until now? Why had he not told her earlier? Three long years he had shilly-shallied. How on earth could he have allowed himself to get into this ridiculous situation? Nobody else would leave it this late, would they?

★   ★   ★

Mac's revelation had had a sobering effect on Richard. He played over and over in his mind the conversation that had just taken place, and mingled the emotions they had stirred with the events of the past three years, still at a loss to understand how such a situation could have arisen.

Had Leo approached him, he could have understood. They all knew where Leo's predilections lay, but the law being what it was, he had always been circumspect about things, had never openly discussed it with any of them, at least not to Richard's knowledge. The situation had been tacitly understood and, as such, none of them had felt uncomfortable with it or inclined to dwell on it. And anyway, nothing had ever happened, not even between Leo and Mac, at least not to his knowledge. Quite the reverse, in fact. Mac had always seemed to be impatient with Leo, intolerant of his sensitivity and his harmless posturings, almost as though they embarrassed him.

Richard knew that he should appreciate the amount of courage it must have taken Mac to express his feelings towards him, but instead of feeling sympathetic, the very thought made him shudder. There was never any chance of Mac's sentiments being reciprocated; how could he possibly have imagined there would be? It was obvious he was a red-blooded male, and his fondness for Eleanor should have proved that. While he chided himself for not being able to look Mac properly in the eye, he wished with all his heart that he had kept his feelings to himself. However hard he tried, he could feel nothing except revulsion and embarrassment for a man who, for the last three years, he had thought of as his friend.

So deep was his preoccupation with these thoughts that at first he did not register when Eleanor put her head round his door.

'Hello?' she said questioningly, aware that his mind was somewhere else.

He looked up and stared at her blankly.

'You look as though you've seen a ghost. Are you all right?'

Richard pulled himself together. He had promised Mac that he would say nothing. It was a promise he would have no problem whatsoever in keeping. And anyway, how would it reflect on himself if he were to explain it even to Eleanor?

'I'm fine.' He gestured about the room. 'Just packing. Like everyone else.'

'Mac's gone,' she said.

'I know.' He saw the troubled look on her face.

'But he never came to say goodbye.'

Richard thought quickly. 'He had to catch an earlier train and asked me to say goodbye for him.'

'Oh.' Eleanor looked crestfallen. 'That's not like him.'

'No. He really was sorry.' He tried to change the subject. 'I'm glad you came. I wanted to see you.'

'Yes. Me too.'

It pleased him that she needed to see him. It came as a relief after the events of the last hour, but it puzzled him that she seemed distracted, distant.

'I need to talk to you,' Eleanor said.

'Yes.' Richard walked over to the chest of drawers that stood next to the window. 'I need to talk to you, too.' He thought it best to get in first, do the right thing, override the last conversation he had had with one that was more suitable. One that was the right way of doing things. He slid open the top drawer, which was now empty, except for a small box. He withdrew it and turned to face her. 'I have to ask you something.'

Eleanor looked uneasy.

Richard walked towards her with the small box concealed in his hand. 'I wanted to do it earlier, but then I got that rotten cold and you were away for a couple of days.'

Suddenly she felt she knew what was coming and she began to panic. 'I think you need to . . .'

He opened the box and held it towards her. It contained a small diamond-clustered ring. 'Will you marry me?'

'Oh, Richard!' she said.

Those were the only words that Harry heard. He was standing outside the door, choosing his moment to interrupt them. He was, he realised in that instant, the complete master of mistiming. He had, indeed, left it too late. She was Richard's. She was not his. He turned away quietly and retraced his steps back down the stairs.

It was not easy letting Richard down. She had done it as lightly as she could, but he had not taken it well. She had sat with him for a while, explaining that while she was very fond of him, she did not think she could marry him. She did not mention Harry, feeling that it would be more than Richard could bear. Eventually she left him, sitting alone on the bed gazing at the wall.

She went at once to look for Harry, but he was nowhere to be found. His room was tidied up, and his cases were on the bed, already packed and waiting to go. She waited for half an hour, hoping he would return, but there was no sign of him. She rummaged in her bag for the stub of a pencil and a piece of paper. She wrote the briefest of notes, but hoped that it would have the desired effect.

> Dear Harry,
> I came looking for you and waited for half an hour, but you are obviously busy. I need to see you. Please get in touch at my hall. I'll wait there until I hear from you. It's very important.
>   Love,
>   Eleanor x

Harry returned from his walk by the river in a trancelike state. There was no point in waiting. He would simply leave.

Better that way. He lifted his cases off the bed and saw, out of the corner of his eye, something flutter to the ground. He stooped and picked it up. It was a note. He read the brief message and then sat down on the bed. 'Please get in touch ... It's very important.'

She clearly needed to tell him herself, to break it to him that she was going to marry Richard. How could he listen while she let him down as gently as possible in that wonderfully sympathetic way she had? How could he bear to look at her? The sight of her and even the sound of her voice would be more than he could endure. To lose her was bad enough; to have to hear her say the words and sit through a rejection of the greatest love he had ever felt was impossible. No. He could not do it. He would not get in touch with her. He would just go. He would walk out of her life, as she had just walked out of his.

Eleanor's cleaner did not think to tell her that Harry had been looking for her. Why should she? She was having a rotten day – all these students going and new ones coming to take their place. What did she care? They were all as bad as one another.

It was early evening when Eleanor went once more to Harry's digs. The room was bare now. The cases had gone and so had Harry. All that remained was the bed, the chest of drawers, a table and a chair. Beside the chair was a waste-paper bin; it was empty, she noticed, except for one scrap of screwed-up paper.

19

Bath

December 2007

He who does not bellow the truth when he knows the truth makes himself the accomplice of liars and forgers.

Lettre du Provincial (1899), Charles Péguy

Missy was glad of the diversion, and particularly glad of the direction from which it had come. He had no time for a leisurely lunch, he had said, but if she was free, they could meet for a quick bite at a sandwich bar round the back of the abbey at around 2 p.m.

They sat side by side on stools at a shelf that ran round the window, and if, as they say, we are what we eat, he was a double espresso and a BLT, and she was a hot chocolate and a tuna salad on foccacia. For a while neither said anything much of consequence.

'Funny, isn't it?' she said after a few minutes.

'What?'

'How easy it is.'

Jamie grinned. 'I'm glad I'm an easy lay.'

She dug him in the ribs. 'That's not what I meant.'

'No, I know. Do you think we're being complacent?'

She looked anxious. 'No. Is that what you think? Are you just taking me for granted?'

'Don't be silly. Sometimes there are things you just know, you don't actually have to express them.'

'That sounds a bit like an excuse . . .'

Jamie frowned. 'I'm agreeing with you. We've known each

other long enough to trust each other's intentions. Haven't we?'

Missy nodded and laid her hand on Jamie's knee. 'I hope so. Sorry.'

'What is it?' he asked.

'Nothing.'

'No, there is. You're worrying about something. Us?'

'No. Not us.'

'What, then?'

'Oh, just Grandpa. He's been a bit funny of late, uneasy. As if he's not totally in control.'

'Could just be his age. He is getting on a bit. They all are – the grandparents, I mean.'

'But Grandpa always seems to have been at ease with himself, well, confident, you know, self-assured.'

'Yes, you could say that.'

'Oh, I know some people interpret that as arrogance . . .'

Jamie raised an eyebrow.

'Yes, all right, then, sometimes he is a bit arrogant, but he deserves to be – he's done really well for himself over the years.'

'Mmm,' murmured Jamie.

Missy realised what he was driving at. 'And I know your grandfather has, too. It's just that I've never got to know him. Doesn't he worry you, too, sometimes?'

'Not really, no. I suppose he's always kept himself to himself. No, that's not true. Self-contained would be better.'

'But you seem to know him well, to get on with him . . .'

'Yes, I do. Funny, really. I'd like to think I was like him, I suppose. Nothing much rattles him. He always seems to be calm. Mixes easily with everybody – well, with the odd exception.' He shot Missy a knowing glance, which was immediately acknowledged. 'It's as if he's been through so much that nothing surprises him any more.'

'Oh. That sounds rather sad.'

'I don't think he's sad.'

'Content, then?'

'I always thought so.'

Missy furrowed her brow and asked, 'Past tense? What's changed your mind?'

'Oh, I suppose he's reached that age, too, where he's wondering how it's all going to end. I mean, he's not maudlin – far from it – but there is a sort of resignation about him now that didn't used to be there, a kind of acceptance of whatever the world might throw at him.'

'Maybe that's what happens.'

'Anyway, today he dropped a real bombshell. Told me he and Gran were moving into a serviced flat and asked me if I'd like the house in the Circus.'

Missy's eyes widened. 'What did you say?'

'Well, I couldn't say anything at first, but then . . . well . . . I accepted.'

'Bloody hell!'

'Yes. Bloody hell indeed.'

'And yesterday you were so impressed with my little flat in the Royal Crescent. Now I feel like a poor relation.'

Jamie looked at her anxiously. 'Do you think we're both spoiled? Too much too soon?'

'Oh, yes. But the important thing is that we don't let it go to our heads like some.'

'And you haven't?'

'Do I look like Paris Hilton?'

Jamie considered for a moment. 'Well, you know, now that you mention it, there is a certain resemblance . . .'

Missy pushed his arm away.

'I think it's the hair.'

'God, I hope not. Dreadful thought.'

'Oh, I just hope I can make it work.'

'A house in the Circus?' asked Missy, her voice shot through with irony. 'You'll make it work.'

'Well, it worked for Granddad all those years, so I hope so.'

Missy was stirring her hot chocolate and scooping up the frothy top with a long-handled spoon. 'Do you think he is happily married?'

'Yes. Well, I suppose so. I've never really thought about it. Nobody's ever suggested otherwise – Mum or Gran or . . . anybody.' He looked thoughtful. 'Why do you ask?'

'Oh, I don't know. It's just that I wonder sometimes if my grandma and grandpa are really happy. He always seems to make the running. Asks her if she's got what she wants, makes her tea every morning, always checks to see where she is and how she's getting on.'

'Isn't that just normal married life?'

'I suppose.'

'Do you mean she doesn't seem happy to be fussed over?'

'No, it's not that. She's never unpleasant or ungrateful or anything; it's just that there's a certain sort of understanding between them.'

Missy saw the puzzled look on Jamie's face. 'I don't mean like our understanding. It's different.'

'Different how?'

'I can't really put my finger on it, but . . . there's not that real ease that you find between people who really, really love one another. I mean, I suppose they are quite comfortable together, but . . .'

'No spark?'

'No.'

'Maybe it disappears after fifty years of marriage.'

Missy looked disappointed. 'Do you think so?'

Jamie shrugged. 'Who knows?' Then he smiled. 'A bit early to worry about that.'

Missy blushed.

'Good Lord, the lady blushes.'

'You really are a dreadful man.' She took the spoon out of her chocolate and laid it on the saucer.

Jamie glanced at his watch. 'Look, I'll have to be going. I've a client to see about a sale of contents at three o'clock in Melksham, so I'll need to get my skates on.'

'Oh. That was a short lunch.'

'Well, I did warn you.'

'I suppose.' Missy reached for her bag and stepped down from her stool.

'But I never told you . . .' he said.

'Told me what?'

'That you look lovely.' He kissed her on both cheeks.

'That was very chaste,' she said.

'I'll be better tonight,' he promised.

She cocked her head on one side. 'Oh, there'll be a tonight, will there?'

'Unless you're busy,' he said, making for the door.

'I'll try and fit you in,' she said. 'My place at eight?'

'Perfect.'

'Oh, just one thing . . .' she added, following close behind him.

He looked at her questioningly.

'Don't lose the spark.' She beamed at him and walked off across the abbey green.

By the time Missy got back to the gallery her grandfather had still not reappeared. She returned to her cataloguing of the paintings for the forthcoming exhibition, working her way methodically through the list. At four o'clock she still had half a dozen pictures to write up when the doorbell rang and the voice of a parcel courier came through on the intercom.

'I'll be right down.'

She opened the door to an overalled youth with spiky fair hair who had a flat parcel in one hand and an electronic touchpad in the other. He handed her the parcel and tapped in a seemingly endless stream of digits before asking Missy to sign the screen and confirm receipt and acceptance.

'I'm sorry I'm late. I'd have delivered it this morning only the van broke down.'

'No problem. I'm still here.'

'Lucky,' said the youth, giving her a smile and a wink.

'Yes,' replied Missy with a sardonic frown.

'Enjoy your evening, then,' said the youth, with yet another wink, as he pulled himself up into the cab of his van and revved it up as though he hoped it might turn into a Ferrari. 'You're my last drop. Out clubbing tonight.'

Missy watched as he flung the van round the corner, clearly trying to impress. She found it hard not to smile. Then she looked at the package. It was clearly a picture, though it was rather late for a delivery. Parcels normally came late morning, when her grandfather would be around to open them and confirm their origins.

She closed and locked the front door behind her and took the parcel upstairs. She wondered if it was another one that she was expected to catalogue. There was no label showing where it had come from, just a clearly printed address in broad felt-tip pen and some labels printed in French. The package was addressed to her grandfather at King's Fine Art. She had better open it, just to make sure it was in one piece. It looked tired somehow. As if it had had a long journey.

She tore away the brown paper and a good deal of bubble wrap, slicing through the parcel tape with a Stanley knife. Finally the gilt frame came into view and the last layer of bubble wrap drifted to the floor. She turned it to face her.

It was another Munnings. The label on the stretcher described it as *Gypsies in Hampshire*. The picture showed a group of colourfully caparisoned Romanies around their green-painted caravan, with a grey horse tethered to one side and a smoking campfire at the other. There was a white envelope slipped under the stretcher. Missy pulled it out, slit it open with a paper knife and removed the sheet of paper it contained. It bore no address and said, quite simply, 'For you. With apologies, M.'

She stood the painting on the easel in front of the desk and examined it closely. It measured twenty inches by twenty-four inches. She knew that Munnings had painted hop-pickers in Hampshire between the wars, but there was something about the painting that intrigued her. She had been a part of the art world for over ten years now. She had learned much, but she had also discovered a certain aptitude that is inbred rather than acquired a sort of intuition that told her when something was 'not quite right'. Very occasionally that intuition would prove to be misguided, or misplaced. If an artist was having an off day, it was sometimes all too easy to assume that the painting was not genuine. The odd thing about this painting, though, was that it seemed, if anything, to be 'too Munnings', rather than the reverse.

She sat down in her chair and stared at it, willing the painting to give up its secrets.

It had the life, the vitality and the easy, almost slap-dash paint application of Munnings, and yet, she just felt . . . doubtful.

Missy got up from her chair and walked round the desk to look more closely at the painting. The signature seemed genuine enough, with that looping sweep under the tail of the final 's'. But signatures were easy to forge. No, it was more than that. What was it that made her suspicious? Perhaps it was the fact that the picture had arrived with no provenance, no indication of any part of its life to date. Somehow she felt she had seen it before.

She looked closely at the brushwork. It gave her every bit as much pleasure as the brushwork of the master always did – so assured, so bold, so individual. The reflected colours on the coat of the horse could only be achieved by Sir Alfred Munnings. She shook her head. It was probably her imagination.

She left the painting on the easel and concentrated on cataloguing a John Ferneley, then a Benjamin Herring and a John Wootton of the Duke of Devonshire's horse Flying Childers, which made her smile. The horse, painted in the early eighteenth century, was shown as Wootton showed most of his horses – standing four square with a groom holding the bridle, its tail docked, its nostrils flared and its eyes staring as if it were in the middle of a cataleptic fit.

Two small paintings by Francis Sartorius followed, and a James Seymour, before she came to more modern works – a Henry Koehler of a saddle and a polo mallet and helmet, and a John Skeaping pastel of three horses taking a fence.

She glanced at the clock. It was a quarter to six. Time she packed up for the day. There was still no sign of her grandfather; he had clearly thought better of returning to the office and gone home to Peel Place. She was glad of that. Maybe tomorrow he would be his usual self again, and hopefully he would be able to shed some light on the Munnings that had just arrived.

She got up from the desk and stood the paintings she had catalogued in a row against the wall, to remind herself how far she had got. The next one in the ordered stack had its back to her, and on the stretcher she could see the name of the artist. Normally she would have left it that way until the following day, but the artist's name compelled her to pick up the painting and turn it round.

She studied it carefully. It was a portrait of a single bay horse, its bridle held by a groom wearing jodhpurs, a hacking jacket and a flat cap. She removed the Munnings, placed the new painting on the easel and stood back a little. The sky was a refreshing confection of forget-me-not blue and creamy white – huge cumulus clouds building above the flowering elder trees that provided a background to the horse. It was an accomplished piece of work. It stopped short of greatness, perhaps, but was still a fine painting of the sort that any collector of equine art would be pleased to have in their collection. The artist's signature, in the bottom right-hand corner of the painting, was clearly visible: J. Macready.

She wondered if her grandfather knew that he had a Macready in the fifty-year exhibition. He still kept a close eye on their stock, but her father, too, bought paintings and did not always share the news of his own purchases with his father and daughter. Maybe the Macready was one of Patrick's acquisitions.

Missy looked more closely at the work and admired the artist's dexterity. Then, not really knowing why, she picked up the Munnings and slid it into place above the Macready on the easel, so that one painting lay above the other.

For several minutes she stared at the two paintings, then went to the bookshelves behind her desk and pulled out *The Dictionary of British Equestrian Artists* by Sally Mitchell and looked up John Macready. The entry was brief:

MACREADY, John Kelvin 1928–95
Glasgow-born artist who studied art history at Christ Church, Oxford, just after the Second World War. Spurning any practical training, he became a self-taught painter of landscapes and occasionally equestrian subjects. He was an artist of considerable ability, a fact recognised by Sir Alfred Munnings, whom Macready had met while at Oxford. He seemed to spend the rest of his life emulating the master until he died, tragically, in a swimming accident in the south of France.

Missy closed the book. Not much to go on. She looked again at the two paintings, and the words 'emulating the master' echoed in her head.

What if? No. Not possible. A coincidence, nothing more.

She rubbed her eyes and stretched. It had been a long day, and at eight Jamie would be here. Time to change. She glanced in the mirror and noticed that she had smudged her mascara. What a sight. She flicked at her hair to give it some semblance of order, and behind her, in the reflection in the mirror, she saw the two paintings once more. The Munnings of the caravan and the gypsies suddenly looked more familiar. She *had* seen it before? But where?

Impatiently she tapped her fingers on the corner of the desk. 'Come on, come on,' she murmured aloud. 'Where? Where?' She ran her fingers along the shelf, past the books and to the auction catalogues that sat there from sales going back over the years. It was not that long ago. It was in New York, when she was there. Backwards and forwards her eye ran over the catalogues, then, lighting on one from 2001, she pulled it out and flipped through the pages.

No. No. No . . . Then . . . yes! There it was. A painting of gypsies in Hampshire. A green caravan, a grey horse, a campfire gently smoking. A mirror image of the painting on the easel.

She steadied herself. This was not necessarily unusual. Artists often repeated a particular scene. Munnings was no exception. He had reproduced the famous portrait of himself painting, with his palette, and of his wife on her horse outside their house at Dedham several times – each one almost an exact copy of the first. *Almost* an exact copy.

She held the catalogue in front of her, while looking at the reflection of the Munnings in the mirror. It was identical, except that it was a mirror image. Why would Munnings have done that? Surely if he were repeating the picture – as requested by a client or a gallery – he would have painted it the same way round as the original, wouldn't he? But if one of the two paintings was a forgery, which one was it? And who had painted it?

Missy lay the open catalogue on her desk and thought for a moment. The conclusion she felt bound to come to was not one that she really wanted to believe. She could only hope that she was wrong. If she were not, the consequences did not bear thinking about.

20

Chawton, Hampshire
November 1949

Chumps always make the best husbands . . . All the unhappy
marriages come from husbands having brains.
                    The Adventures of Sally (1920), P.G. Wodehouse

The Church of St Nicholas at Chawton stands close to the
impressive house that Jane Austen's brother inherited upon
agreeing to change his name to Knight. Richard King's
mother had always loved it and, had she married a Knight,
which had been her fervent hope, she might just have lived
there, too. She did not marry a Knight, however; she married
a King, who was, perversely, not quite so well off. As a more
achievable option, she arranged for her son to be married
in the church next door. It made her feel that she had not
totally failed in her aspirations, even though the couple had
insisted that only immediate family and close friends be
invited.

Richard's father was one of those easy-going men who find
it more congenial to toe the marital line than to make ripples
and so the wedding was arranged for the last day of November.
At least with so few guests the wedding breakfast would be
unlikely to break the bank.

It was not the happiest of days for any of the parties
concerned. Richard's mother would rather he had found a
better catch, someone with a title, perhaps. Richard's father
had had to forego a trip to Cheltenham to the National Hunt
meeting. Richard himself had hoped that his bride would be
by his side because she knew that there was no one else in

the world who meant so much to her, rather than because she had always been 'fond of him'. At least she was marrying him. That was the main thing. That was what he really wanted. For Eleanor, it was the saddest day of her life. She put a brave face on it; after all, she was grateful to Richard for being so persistent. Having turned him down the first time, she had no right to expect that he would ever ask her again, but he did, only two months later.

She accepted and asked if they might be married as soon as possible. Richard had agreed. They slept together almost from that moment onwards. Richard was surprised when she agreed, and equally surprised and not a little embarrassed when she very quickly fell pregnant, but then he knew she had been desperate for a family. Maybe this was her way of making sure she got one.

Eleanor would never understand what had happened to Harry. Why, after that wonderful night together, had he never spoken to her again? Why had he gone away without responding to her note? Where had he gone? What had she done to so turn round his feelings towards her? Perhaps they were not genuine feelings after all. Maybe he was just charming her into his bed. She did not want to believe it possible that she could have been so deceived, but she had to consider that he might have intended it to be nothing more than a one-night stand. The very thought of it left her heartbroken.

Eleanor's mother watched the ceremony through a haze of tears, a nurse on either arm. After it was over, they would take her back to the hospital and she would not remember much at all. Eleanor glanced at her and wondered how it was possible for one person to bear so much grief.

Leo, who had given the bride away, watched the ceremony from the front pew with an aching heart. How could the girl who just a few months ago seemed to be on the way to eternal happiness now be condemned to a life of ordinariness? Why had she changed her mind? Where was Harry? He had not seen him since that day at Bedlington Park when he had vowed that he was going back to Oxford to ask her to marry him. What had gone so terribly wrong? Why had he not contacted Leo to explain?

At first he had thought the worst; thought that Harry must have been knocked down and killed on the way back to Oxford, or had suddenly collapsed and died. It seemed that only something so dramatic could have stopped him from proposing to the girl he was determined to marry. Then he had heard, a few weeks later, that Harry had been seen in York, in an auction room. So what had happened to change his mind?

In each and every one of those present at the wedding there were unanswered questions.

The reception at a local hotel had been a low-key affair. In the absence of Eleanor's father, Leo made a brief speech. He was not at his sparkling best. How could he be? He knew this was not a marriage made in heaven, whatever the parson might have said, but he did his best and managed at one point to make Eleanor smile with a comment about seeing into the future. Oh, how it tore at his heart when he thought how different the day would have been had another groom been standing there.

They parted with promises to keep in touch, though as Leo was driven away by Osborne in the Talbot, he saw her through the back window and knew that further contact was unlikely. Why? Maybe it was something Richard had said at the wedding breakfast: that the rest of their life was in front of them now and it was time to move on. It seemed to Leo to be directed at him. With a heavy heart he journeyed back to Bedlington Park, to face the solicitors who were to tell him that in a matter of months his home, his fortune and those who had surrounded him for the first twenty years of his life would be taken from him. His life was about to be dismantled. The prospect for all of them, except Richard, seemed little short of bleak.

21

York

November 1949

Swift moons make good their losses in the sky.

Odes, Book 4 (*c*. 13BC), Horace

'You'll have to be prepared to take the rough with the smooth and muck in, you know. I can't 'ave a fancy Oxford type thinking 'e's above the rest of us. There'll be smelly 'ouse clearances as well as Chippendale commodes to dispose of.' The full-bellied, tweed-suited partner of Fidler, Son and Bowker was sitting behind a large mahogany partners' desk with his arms folded, as best they could be, over the vast acreage of his burgundy waistcoat.

Harry was perched on the stool that had been pulled up in front of the desk, doing his best to look relaxed and comfortable. It seemed that his inquisitor was in danger, at any moment, of bursting out of his clothes and sending buttons flying to the four corners of the book-lined room. All three chins wobbled as he made his point, and his cheeks were the colour and shape of Worcester Pearmain apples. A fountain pen was clenched between pork-sausage fingers, and so fat were his thighs that he had trouble getting them into the kneehole under the desk. It might have been a partners' desk, but fortunately for Ernie Bowker, he was the only working partner left, Fidler having retired and the son of Fidler, after deciding that the family business was not for him, having become a sleeping partner.

'I'm very happy to ... er ... muck in,' confirmed Harry. 'That's what I'm here for – to get a handle on the business and work hard.'

'With a view to?' asked Ernie Bowker.

'Well, with a view to becoming a good auctioneer and valuer.'

'Right answer!' He banged his hands on the desk and Harry steadied himself to avoid falling off the stool during the subsequent earth tremor. 'Too many smart alecs come in 'ere thinking they can do it like falling off a log, and when I ask 'em what sort of job they want, they say, "Yours." I think they think they're being funny. They're not. Mind you, there's nothing mysterious about auctioneering. It's a straightforward job. If an item's going to sell, it's going to sell.'

Harry raised an eyebrow.

'Oh, you can create a bit of an atmosphere, jolly folk along, but you'll not get 'em to pay a penny more than they want to, not up 'ere at any rate.'

Harry nodded to imply that he understood the northern way of things.

Ernie was getting into his stride now. 'Eyes and ears, those are your best assets. Do you wear glasses?'

'No.'

'Oh, pity. If you can look over 'em, it sometimes chivvies folk into speeding up a bit. Had your ears syringed lately?'

'No.'

'I recommend it. Means you can pick up the rustle of fabric when they raise an arm. Mind you, there's Ted and Wally to keep an eye out for any bids you miss. They'll shout soon enough if you don't spot 'em.'

'So do you think . . . ?'

'Aye, you'll do. If you've got stamina, I'll give you a go. Why don't you come and work for a week for nowt just to see if you like it? If you do, I'll take you on. I can't say fairer than that. 'Ave you got any digs?'

'I'm lodging with Mrs Fairbrother in Coppergate.'

'Oh, well, watch 'er daughter – she's a man-eater – and

the old lady'll fleece you every Friday so you'd better 'ave ten bob on account.' He reached into the inside pocket of his jacket with some difficulty and pulled out a battered black wallet from which he withdrew a ten-shilling note. Having flicked it a few times to make sure it was not adhering to any of its friends, he handed it over and slipped the wallet back into its snug resting place. 'Are you courtin'?'

'No.'

'Just as well on what I'll be paying you. Now, then, you can make a start by sorting out them catalogues over there.' Ernie pointed to a slithering pile of auction catalogues, those of Fidler, Son and Bowker as well as London and other provincial auction houses. 'Ours go over that side' – he pointed to the wall to the right of the window – 'and the others go over there' – he pointed to the left – 'Christie's on top, Sotheby's underneath, Phillips below them, and . . . Well . . . you'll get the hang of it. They're useful for working out values. Look at what things go for in London, divide by two and you'll get a rough idea of what your estimate should be up 'ere. Don't worry too much if it's on the low side – that encourages 'em to come and bid, and once you've a couple of keen bidders, they'll jack it up for you. With me so far?'

Harry nodded.

'Now, then, I've said it's straightforward, but there are a couple of things you can do to help the party along. Bids off the wall.' Harry looked suddenly anxious and Ernie noticed his change of expression. 'Oh, now don't go all holy on me. Everybody does it and there's nothing wrong with it in moderation. We're here to get the best price for the vendor and it's our duty to find out what the maximum is that a bidder will pay. If you find that something's moving a bit slowly, you can help it along by spotting a bidder at the back of the room. It's as well not to take more than a single bid from 'im in case you get rumbled. If you want to play safe, then look down at your book and suggest that you might have a commission bid of a certain amount. But be careful. I don't mind you coming a cropper and buying the odd item yourself because you miscalculated, but more than once in an auction and I'll start charging you for it. Is that clear?'

Harry nodded again.

'That's for the good stuff. When it comes to the rubbish, try and embellish its 'istory a bit and you might get a few bob more, but not very often.' He leaned on the desk and pushed himself upright. 'I'm goin' for a spot of dinner down the Red Lion. I'll be back about one o'clock. You can go then, but you only get 'alf an hour. All right?'

'Yes. Fine. Thank you.'

They were interrupted by a gentle tapping at the door.

'Ah, that'll be my dinner date.' Ernie Bowker grasped the brass knob, which almost came off in his Samsonic grip, and opened the door of the office to reveal the figure of a dark-haired young woman in a headscarf and a mackintosh. She smiled at them both and walked in through the door, slipping off her headscarf as she did so and letting her dark, shiny hair tumble over her shoulders.

'It's bitter outside, Dad. You'll need a coat.'

'Not in this tweed I won't, and not with my lagging.' Ernie winked at Harry and then affected the introduction. 'This is Harry Ballantyne. He's coming to work with me. Well, 'e's givin' it a try at any rate, to see if we get on.'

The girl nodded in understanding.

'Harry, this is my daughter. My youngest unmarried. The rest have families now, but she's more into improving 'erself.'

Harry held out his hand.

'Sally Bowker,' she said, and Harry noticed that her eyes were almost as dark as her hair, and that her smile, flashed at him again, lit up the room. She reminded him of someone else, someone he was trying to forget.

'Hello,' he managed.

'Are you coming to lunch?' she asked.

'It's dinner up 'ere,' corrected her father.

'Well, whatever it is, are you coming?'

'I . . . er . . . don't think . . .'

'E's got work to do,' insisted her father. 'Catalogues to sort out . . .'

'Oh, Dad, don't be such a meanie. If it's Harry's first day, you should at least take him out for lunch . . . dinner . . . whatever.'

Her father was clearly putty in her hands. 'Well, I suppose to seal the deal, though it's a bit premature . . .'

'Oh, I don't think so,' she said.

That night Harry sat in his small back bedroom in Coppergate, listening to Mrs Fairbrother remonstrating with her daughter before she went out for yet another night on the tiles. Here he was, two hundred miles away from where Eleanor would be now. He wondered what she would be doing, but knew that whatever it was, she would be doing it with Richard and not him. He felt suddenly foolish, for pinning all his hopes on one woman, for assuming that after that one night they had together she might feel the same way as him. It was four months ago now and there was still barely a moment when she was not in his thoughts. Such a waste. It was time to move on. Oh, how easy to say and how hard to make reality. A part of him would be for ever hers. The raw truth of that particular sentiment he would never fully comprehend.

He lay on top of the pink candlewick bedspread and gazed at the suitcase on top of the wardrobe while he relived the events of the day. Old man Bowker was not a bad sort – a likeable rogue whose bark was probably worse than his bite.

And his daughter? Yes, very nice. Well, more than nice, to be honest.

The first week went well. The customers seemed to like him – 'Clients lad, not customers' – and he was even let loose for half an hour on an auction, which feat he accomplished without too many sniggers on the part of Ted and Wally. He confused a chiffonier with a commode, and a lowboy with a washstand, but these were minor misdemeanours that his employer seemed willing to overlook. The fact that his daughter had taken a shine to her father's prospective employee might have had something to do with it.

At the end of the week he was called into the office once more. Ernie Bowker looked at him over the top of his horn-rimmed half-moons, in the manner that had been used to pressurise many a bidder over the years, and told him to sit down. A walnut dining chair had replaced the stool this week. Things were looking up.

'Well, 'ow was your first week, then?' he asked.

'All right, I think.' Harry looked anxiously at his potential employer, waiting for reassurance.

His luck was in. 'Aye, you've not done bad. A couple of cock-ups, but nothing too serious. So if you still fancy it, I'll be 'appy to take you on.'

Harry smiled. 'Thank you.'

'But you're not there yet, mind. There's a lot to learn.'

'Yes, of course.'

'But if you frame yourself, I think we might make an auctioneer out of you yet.'

'I hope so.'

Ernie leaned back in his chair and looked expansive. With his shape it was difficult to look anything else. 'You've enjoyed your first week, then?'

'Yes, very much.'

'Aye, well, you've caught Sally's eye, I'll say that for you. But just be careful.'

Harry wondered where the conversation was leading.

'I'm not much of a one for mixing business with pleasure, and I've seen lads before trying it on with yon.' He nodded in the direction of the door, implying the direction in which Sally had last been seen.

Harry was anxious to pre-empt any misgivings the father might have. 'Oh, please, I—'

'Nay, lad, don't worry. I've seen enough over the last week to know that you're a decent sort. I'll not be interfering. Your life's your own. Just don't break her heart, that's all. She's been to university like you – music she studied, in Manchester – seen a bit of the world. She doesn't need me watching over her like an 'awk. But you know what fathers are like with their daughters.'

Harry nodded. 'Of course.'

'Well, there we are, then. I'll be off for my dinner.'

Ernie squeezed past him and then turned before he walked through the door. He held out the sausage-like fingers. 'Welcome to Fidler, Son and Bowker. Play your cards right and you could become a partner one day.'

And that, in the fullness of time, is exactly what happened. Harry became a partner in Fidler, Son and Bowker. He also married the boss's daughter.

22

Bath
December 2007

And the best plan is, as the popular saying was, to profit by
the folly of others.

Naturalis Historia (*c.* AD 77), Pliny the Elder

It took some time to track her father down. Patrick King had
always been elusive, but Missy had become accustomed to
his habits. Tonight, with any luck, he would be in the Boater
in Argyle Street. She found him at one end of the bar.

'To what do I owe the pleasure?' he asked with a grin,
which quickly turned into a worried look. 'Everything all
right?'

'I'm not sure. Can you spare me a few minutes?'

'Course. Pull up a stool.'

'No, not here – back at the gallery.'

Patrick King looked at his watch. 'Well . . . I'm a bit
pushed . . .'

'It's really important, Dad.'

He noticed the worried look on his daughter's face and
drained what remained of his glass of red wine. 'See you
tomorrow, Taffy; I'm dining at the Hole in the Wall tonight
so I won't be back.' He got down from the stool and slipped
his arm through Missy's as they walked out into the street.

They were an unlikely couple. Missy in her smart red jacket
and black trousers, he in a baggy tweed jacket and corduroys,
a bright pink shirt open at the collar and his unruly hair
rather longer than suited a man of his age. 'So what's the
problem? Man trouble?'

'No,' she said scoldingly. 'Well, not in the way you think.'

'Oh. That's me put in my place, then.'

She could tell from his delivery that the glass of wine he had drained was not his first.

'What do you know about John Macready?' she asked.

'I don't think there *is* much to know, is there?'

'How well did Grandpa know him?'

'Blowed if I know. He's never talked about him. Not that I can remember, anyway.'

'But he must have said something over the years. I mean, they were at university together.'

'Were they? He never said.'

They were walking over Pulteney Bridge now and her father glanced down at the water as the street lights caught the shimmering surface. 'God! That looks cold tonight.'

She knew that his mind was elsewhere – probably with the woman he would be meeting at the Hole in the Wall. For someone who put in so few hours at work, he certainly knew how to live. Missy sighed and tried to get back to the point. 'Has the gallery handled many of his paintings?'

'A few, over the years. He died, didn't he? Back in the nineties. Some kind of accident.'

'Swimming.'

Her father glanced once more at the water. 'Poor bugger. Rotten way to go. Though they do say, don't they, that death by drowning is quite easy? Especially if the water's cold. It sort of anaesthetises you and you drift gently away.' He shuddered involuntarily and clasped her arm tighter. 'Yeughh! Not for me. I'd rather take to the bottle.' He noticed her withering glance. 'Yes, all right, I know you think I have already, but you're wrong. I don't knock it back *every* night.'

They walked up Gay Street and across the Circus. Missy glanced at the houses, trying to remember which one Jamie was about to inherit, but then her thoughts returned to the matter in hand. She decided to wait until they arrived at the gallery before she broached the topic again.

As they walked along Brock Street, her father asked, 'How *is* your love life, then?'

'Fine, thank you.' She tried not to be rattled.

'Anyone we know?'

'That's none of your business.' She put the key in the lock and he walked in after her.

'Only taking an interest.' Again he saw the look she gave him. 'Yes, I know. Better late than never.'

Missy led the way to her office and flicked on the lights. The paintings were still on the easel in front of her desk. Her father walked over to them. 'Ah, Mr Munnings.' He leaned forward to look at the lower of the two paintings, then raised his eyes to the one above. 'Who's this one by?'

'John Macready.'

'Really? Bloody good, wasn't he? What a waste of a talent, dying in an accident. How old would he have been? In his sixties? Well, that's not old nowadays is it?'

Missy walked to his side. 'Notice anything familiar about them?'

'I haven't seen them before, if that's what you mean.'

'Neither of them?'

Her father considered further and screwed up his eyes in concentration. 'Mmm. Well, we might have had this one a while.' He tapped the frame of the Macready with his finger. 'But I can't recall coming across the Munnings before.' He straightened up. 'Did you really bring me all the way up here just to see if I can remember a couple of paintings? Is it some kind of intelligence test?'

'No, not exactly. The Munnings arrived today, parcel post, addressed to Grandpa. But look at this.' She showed him the catalogue and the mirror-image painting.

For a few moments he said nothing, but read the catalogue description and the provenance thoroughly before straightening up and saying, in a tone more serious than before, 'I see.'

Missy looked at him enquiringly. 'What do you think?'

Her father thrust his hands into his pockets and walked over to the window. 'I think we've got a problem.'

Missy waited for more information.

Slowly her father turned to face her. 'What's your take on it?' he asked.

Missy sat down on the chair behind her desk and folded her arms. 'Well, there are several options. The first is that Munnings painted another copy of the gypsy painting in mirror image, but that would be unusual. He would have been more likely to have painted the same composition as before, which we know he did with certain paintings.'

'The second option?'

'The second option is that it's a forgery by a hand unknown and we're in possession of a fake, which is bloody annoying, very costly and more than a little embarrassing if Grandpa has just bought it.'

'And the third?'

'Well, I think you know what the third option is, but like me, you probably don't want to believe it.'

'Go on.'

'The third option is that it was painted by John Macready to be sold as a Munnings.'

'Not impossible, but why should that be any worse than option two?'

'Because Grandpa went to university with him and people are bound to make connections. Added to which, the note that came with it' – she handed her father the piece of paper – 'was signed "M".'

Patrick King examined the piece of paper and the few

words written on it. 'Mmm. Not much to go on. But do you really think Dad would be doing something like that?' he asked incredulously. 'Richard King, the pillar of the world of fine art? And anyway, John Macready's dead.'

'Yes.' Missy paused, then said, 'Oh, I don't know. Maybe it's just my overactive imagination. But look at the brush-work on the two paintings. It's so similar. John Macready was inspired by Munnings. He even met him, apparently, and was known to emulate him. Supposing he and Grandpa . . . oh, I hardly want to say it . . .'

'There's a world of difference between emulating some-body and forging his work.'

'I know, I know. But I just have this feeling. I can't really put my finger on it.'

'Instinct?'

'Yes.'

Her father smiled sympathetically. 'You'll need a little more than that if you want to be certain.'

'I know.'

'And you haven't told Dad?'

'Heavens, no. And that's the other thing – when I was asking him if he knew John Macready, he got really shirty with me, said that he might have been at Christ Church at the same time but that he only knew him vaguely. I'd have expected him to have been interested at least, but he just sort of brushed it off and got very irritated.'

'So what are you going to do?'

'What do you think I should do?'

'I think you should put the so-called Munnings into the storeroom under lock and key and say nothing.'

'But he'll be expecting it to arrive.'

'Well, wait until he asks about it before you give it to him. There's probably a perfectly rational explanation.' Patrick put his arm round his daughter's shoulders. 'Look,

congratulate yourself on a bit of detective work, and be
pleased that you spotted it before anyone else did. It happens
every now and again. It won't be the first time we've had
our fingers burned. We're pretty sharp nowadays, but every
now and again even King's Fine Art can come a cropper,
even your grandpa. That's probably what it is, a silly – if
very expensive – mistake.'

'I guess.' Missy looked downcast.

'Perk up, old girl! Worse things have happened.' Patrick
glanced at his watch. 'Oh, bloody hell, I'll have to dash.
Business meeting at the Hole in the Wall.'

'Business?'

'Well, sort of.' Her father gave her one of his 'you know
me' apologetic looks and made for the door. As he reached
it, he pointed at the painting. 'Brown paper and string, back
of the storeroom with some sort of label to warn anyone off
opening it. Something on the lines of "Artemis King school
art project". That ought to do it. At least until the old man
asks. But he might not. Cheer up, chicken!'

And with a cheery smile he was gone and Missy was alone
again with the two paintings.

'What on earth's the matter with you?' asked Jamie.

Missy was holding the door open as he walked through.
'Oh, just a long day, that's all.'

'Are you sure?'

She reached up and planted a gentle kiss on his lips.

'Mmm, that's nice.'

She rested her head on his chest. 'Bit of a day,' she
murmured.

'You could tell me about it.'

'Oh, maybe later. Come on, let's have a glass of wine.' She
led the way to the flat at the top of the house and once again
he was enveloped in its cool comfort.

Missy went to the kitchen and returned bearing a bottle of wine and two glasses.

'I hope I can make my place as nice as yours,' he said as he sat at one end of the sofa.

Missy finished pouring her own glass of wine and asked, 'When do you think you'll move in?'

'Before Christmas.'

'What?'

Jamie grinned. 'I know. It's a bit sudden. A serviced flat has come up and Granddad wants to be in it as soon as possible. He rang this afternoon to say they're moving out next week and I can have the Circus when I want.'

'But what about decorating and everything?'

'Well, I can move into the top floor, like you, while the plumber and the electrician do their stuff in the rest of the house and then I thought I could do the painting and papering myself, sort of work my way up from the ground floor.'

'But it'll take ages.'

Jamie shrugged. 'I'm in no rush.'

'No, I suppose not.'

He looked at her, standing in the archway that led to the kitchen. She seemed dazed.

'Are you going to come and sit down?' he asked.

She came to. 'Yes. Sorry. It's just that . . .'

'It's all a bit sudden?'

'Yes.'

'Lucky me, eh?'

'Yes, lucky you.' She dropped on to the sofa beside him, slipped off her shoes and tucked her feet underneath her. Then she raised her glass. 'Here's to you and the Circus.'

'You still haven't told me what's the matter,' said Jamie.

'Probably just me making a mountain out of a molehill.'

Jamie looked at her enquiringly.

'I came across a picture that I think is a forgery.'

'Oh dear. An expensive mistake?'

'Looks like it.'

'And you have to foot the bill?'

'Not me personally, but the gallery.'

'Embarrassing?'

'Very. But . . .'

'But that isn't all?'

Missy sighed deeply, then asked, 'If you thought that a member of your family was being less than open with you, how would you handle it? I mean, would you pursue it like a terrier, or would you let it go?'

'Plump for the quiet life, you mean? Don't rock the boat?'

Missy nodded.

Jamie thought for a moment, then said, 'It depends on the seriousness of it, doesn't it? I mean, whether you *can* let it go or whether you feel you really do need to get to the bottom of it.'

'I suppose so.'

'So who's being "less than open"?'

'I'm not sure. Grandpa, I think. Maybe Dad as well.'

'Are we talking about something that has legal implications? Maybe even . . .' he hesitated for a moment '. . . criminal ones?'

Missy looked worried. 'I don't know.'

'But it's possible?'

'It's possible.'

'But not probable?'

She turned to him. 'Oh, I do hope not. Maybe it's just my vivid imagination . . .'

'You can tell me, you know – in spite of the fact that I'm the enemy.'

'You're not the enemy. Don't you ever say that. You're the only one I can talk to – certainly about this.'

'So?'

'Oh, let me brood on it for a while. I'll probably turn up something that will prove that there's a perfectly straight-forward explanation.'

'For a forgery?'

'Well, maybe just a copy.'

'There's a difference?'

'You know there is.'

'Only if it's indicated as such.'

'Yes, well, maybe it was once and the paperwork has just gone missing.'

'Oh dear . . .'

Missy asked with feeling, 'I'm not sounding very convincing, am I?'

'Nope.'

Missy took a deep breath and explained to Jamie all of the possibilities surrounding the provenance of the painting: the fact that it could have been painted by an unknown artist, or by Munnings himself, unlikely as it seemed or, even more unlikely but just possible, she thought, that it had been painted by John Macready.

'And you think your grandfather might have colluded with him?'

'Oh, I don't know. I feel dreadful even thinking about the possibility. I really don't want to believe it. I mean, why would he do that?'

'Well, I hate to say it, but there really is only one reason, isn't there? For financial gain.'

'But why should he need to? I mean, Grandpa isn't without money and he's always been scrupulously honest in his dealings.'

'So far as you know.'

'Yes, so far as I know. But I know him so well. It's just that when I asked him about John Macready, he went all funny on me. I've never known him like that before.'

'It seems a lot to surmise just from the fact that your grand-father went "all funny" on you.'

I suppose.'

'And you've been through all this with your father?'

'Yes. He told me to pack the painting up, stick it at the back of the storeroom and say nothing.'

'And you don't know if that's what you should do?'

'No.'

'How old is the painting?'

'Well, Munnings died in 1959.'

'But if it was a fake, then it could have been painted after his death.'

'Yes.'

'And when did John Macready die?'

'In 1995.'

'So if you could date it accurately—'

Missy interrupted. 'But I'm not sure I want to date it. Do I want to prove to myself that it's a fake and open up that can of worms?'

'That's what you have to decide, isn't it?'

Missy nodded. 'You see why I've had a bit of a day?'

'I do. Time you unwound, I think.' Jamie took her glass of wine from her and put it beside his on the low table in front of the sofa. Then he took her head in his hands and kissed her tenderly on the lips.

'Oh, that's better,' she said softly. 'That's so much better.'

At Peel Place, on the outskirts of Bath, Richard King had shut himself in his study. It was unlike him. Normally when he returned from town he poured himself a large Scotch and sat down in the drawing room to talk over the events of the day with his wife. Today was different. She noted his absence and poured herself a gin and tonic before walking to the desk that sat in the bay window and looked out over the rolling lawn towards the cedar tree.

On the blotter lay the day's post. She had been out since mid-morning and so had missed its arrival. First there had been the hairdresser's, then lunch with a couple of friends from the bridge club, followed by an afternoon's shopping for a new hat for the Christmas carol service. She sifted through the envelopes – some buff, some white – nothing of particular interest. At the very bottom lay a small padded envelope. It had been sent by recorded delivery and signed for by the daily help. It had a French postmark. She took the paperknife and slit open the envelope, withdrawing a small object, which was further protected by a layer of bubble wrap. She pulled at the sticky tape that held it fast and then withdrew a small frame and picture that she had not seen for nearly sixty years. St Anthony of Padua gazed up at her with his wide, blue eyes, causing her heart to miss a beat. She sat down, then noticed the white envelope that had tumbled from the bubble wrap. She picked up her reading glasses, muttering as she always did about the perils of old age and the irritation of losing one's sight.

The envelope was addressed in her maiden name: 'Eleanor Faraday', in neat typescript. She took up the paperknife once more and slit open the second envelope, withdrawing the two sheets of paper that it contained. Unfolding them, she sat at the chair and read the message:

Villa Fabrice, Menton, Côte d'Azur

My dear Eleanor,
You will receive this after my death. I wanted you to have it – there is precious little else left of my fabulous legacy! We had such happy times together at Oxford, and I think of you with nothing but fondness. By now you will be as old as me (well, almost) and it is time to set the record straight. You might

call me a meddlesome old fool, and you might even think that I have no right to send a message from beyond the grave (how ghastly that sounds!), but I would hate to think that you, too, will pass away (dreadful euphemism) without knowing the truth.

It can change nothing now, of course, but you should hear it nevertheless. I know you believed that Harry Ballantyne deserted you for no apparent reason. I was puzzled myself at the time, but have since come to understand much that was unknown to me.

I am now convinced that he thought you had set your sights on Richard rather than him (even though it was clear to those of us close to you that the reverse was true) and that he went away because he believed (wrongly) that you intended to accept Richard's proposal of marriage. His leaving was, in his eyes, I am sure, simply to spare you any pain. It is tragic that in reality it had the opposite effect.

To see you on your wedding day, and to give you away to a man I know you did not love, was the most heart-rending thing I have ever had to do – and that includes having to wind up my father's estate. The loss of goods and chattels is as nought compared with the loss of true love. Believe me, I know.

Oh, it is too late for us all now, but try to find a little understanding in your heart for a man who clearly adored you and who, for whatever reason, made a hash of things. In our short lives we all make many mistakes. Mine has been full of them, not least those involving matters of the heart. Mac was a great companion, even if some of his actions were not always easy to understand. There may have been times when he persuaded me to do things against my better judgement, and I fear I was not always as appreciative as I should have been, but I know that without his companionship my life would have been the poorer, in more ways than one.

Forgive my ramblings. I lack the ability to be as concise and to the point as I once was. What has not changed, however, is my love for you. Not, alas, the sort of love that a man can feel for a woman (ah, how I would have cherished you!), but the sort of love good friends can share.

After my death you will no doubt hear stories. Treat them with a degree of scepticism and a touch of compassion.

Of what remains of my estate I have bequeathed one half to my only living relative – someone in America I have never met – and the other half to your granddaughter, Artemis. I never met her, but I know that in two respects we are alike. First there is our love and respect for you, and second the fact that we both had the misfortune to lose our mothers in childbirth. In spite of the fact that you and I have not kept up, I have managed to keep an ear to the ground and to hear of your progress. I wanted to make sure that your descendants benefited from your earlier kindnesses to me.

I thought it fitting that Ballantyne's should handle the sale of my effects. It seems a perfect way to end things and Harry's family should make a tidy commission. Neat, don't you think? And a good way of saying thank you to two people I have been so fond of.

Do not be angry with me for telling you all this. It is done with the best intentions by a man who would have fought tooth and nail for your hand had life turned out rather differently.

I remain, my dear Eleanor, your affectionate friend,
Leo Bedlington

Eleanor folded up the letter and returned it to the envelope, sliding it underneath the paper of the blotting pad and out of sight. She picked up the icon of St Anthony and stood it on the desk in front of her. Then she leaned forward on to the blotting pad, rested her head on her arms and wept.

23

York
March 1958

The toad beneath the harrow knows
Exactly where each tooth-point goes;
The butterfly upon the road
Preaches contentment to that toad.
         'Pagett, MP' (1886), Rudyard Kipling

'But I thought he was a sleeping partner,' said Harry.

'He *is* a sleeping partner,' confirmed Ernie Bowker, 'but he has just woken up. He's had better things to do for the last ten years, but now he's decided that he'd like to be part of the firm.'

The two men were sitting at either side of the partners' desk in the office above the saleroom at Fidler, Son and Bowker. Harry, who had been made a partner five years ago, was surprised and unnerved to discover that the 'Son' of Fidler, Son and Bowker, having wanted out for so many years, now wanted in. 'But what will he do?' he asked his father-in-law.

'Pretty much what he wants,' muttered Ernie bitterly.

'Has he any experience?'

'Not so's you'd notice. He's never wielded the 'ammer.'

Harry leaned back in his chair. 'I don't know what to say.'

'Not much you can say, really. 'E starts tomorrow.'

'What?'

Ernie shook his head. 'I know, I know. But I think there's a desk in the sale today – we'll need another one, else 'e'll 'ave nowhere to sit.'

'So how do you see it affecting us?' asked Harry cautiously.

'You mean, 'ow do I see it affecting you?'

He looked suitably abashed. 'Well, yes, I suppose so.'

Ernie took a deep breath. ''Ard to say. But young Arnold Fidler is not what you'd call easy-going. You know the sort. You can't tell 'im anything. If you say it's Queen Anne, 'e'll tell you it's William an' Mary. You say it's a cabriole leg and 'e'll tell you it's a sabre.'

'I thought you said he had no experience?'

''E 'asn't, but 'e collects. The worst sort – a dabbler. They think they know everything when really they know bugger all.'

'That sounds ominous.'

Ernie hauled himself up from behind the desk. 'I'm not a natural pessimist, as you know, 'Arry, but I can't say I'm looking forward to this association one bit.'

'Then why didn't you put your foot down?'

'Because Tom Fidler gave me a start in the business, just like I gave you a start. I can't tell 'im that I don't want 'is son just because I don't like 'im.'

'But doesn't Tom Fidler know you don't like him?'

'Oh, that 'e does. But 'e's never been able to say no to that lad of 'is. I reckon that's why 'e's turned out the way 'e 'as. A right jumped-up little—'

They were interrupted by a knock at the door. The caller did not wait for the invitation to enter. Instead he walked straight in and marched up to Harry. 'Hello. You must be Harry Ballantyne. The son-in-law.'

Ernie's eyebrows were somewhere near the picture rail that ran round the office wall. For a moment he was lost for words; then he recovered himself. ''Arry, this is Arnold Fidler.'

Harry regarded with curiosity the man who had entered like a whirlwind. He was short and wiry – the exact physical opposite to Ernie – with wire-rimmed spectacles and a green tweed jacket, from the pocket of which dangled rather too much of a pale lemon silk handkerchief. His shiny brown shoes glowed with ox-blood polish, and the burgundy tie at his neck was tied with a knot so small that it could probably only be undone with the aid of a marlinspike. The thick brown hair – with a sheen that owed its existence to something out of a bottle – was parted on one side, but kept sliding over his left eye. His look was hawklike, which matched the shape of his nose.

'Coming tomorrow, but thought I'd say hello today,' he said, the brief introduction having already been effected by Ernie.

'Yes, hello,' said Harry, finding himself temporarily bereft of more intelligent conversation.

'I say, where am I going to sit?' asked Arnold, glancing around the office. 'Not really room for three, is there?'

'We've another desk coming,' confirmed Ernie, anxious to smooth over the already rippling waters.

'Oh, I see.' There was a note of disdain in Arnold's voice now, and having briefly acknowledged the presence of Harry, he did not give him another glance or, to judge by his single-minded examination of the office, another thought. Instead he scrutinised the room as a prospective buyer might survey a house. 'Do with a lick of paint, Ernie.'

Ernie said nothing, but Harry noticed his face had turned a deeper shade of beetroot than normal.

'Still, there'll be time to sort that out when I've got my feet under the table.' He looked again at the partner's desk, and Harry saw in his hawklike eye the unmistakable look of a predator.

The liaison lasted six weeks, at the end of which time Harry knew that one of them would have to go. It was clearly not going to be Arnold Fidler, who was determined to claim his birthright.

'You've only given it six weeks,' said Sally. 'Can't you try a bit harder?'

They were sitting side by side on the sofa of the little house off Micklegate. 'I can't try harder than I am,' complained Harry. 'He's a sly bugger and I wouldn't trust him as far as I could throw him.'

'But aren't you being just a bit feeble?' She stroked his arm to show some degree of sympathy in the light of such a critical comment.

'I don't think so. I'm not hugely ambitious, you know, Sal. I just want to rub along. I enjoy the job, and I'd like to expand the firm, but only gently. With Arnold there, I seem to have lost my appetite for it.'

'I could talk to Dad,' she offered.

'I don't want you fighting my battles for me. Besides, I don't think there's any point. Ernie's over a barrel. Tom Fidler sees this as his son's right, and so does his son. As far as they're both concerned, I'm an interloper.'

Sally sat quietly for a moment, then she asked, 'So what do you want to do?'

'I think I'll have to look for another job.'

'But where? Who with? There's nothing round here.'

'I know.' He turned to face her. Her wide eyes were looking up at him, and every time she looked that way it reminded him of another time, another place, another woman. He had long since given up trying to erase the memory from his mind. Instead he had learned to live with it, told himself that it was a part of his life now. Eleanor would always be there, in his head, and sometimes the boundaries between the way he felt for her and the way he felt about Sally became blurred.

He and Sally would leave York early on Sunday mornings, in the tiny Wolseley, and travel up to the Dales. Wharfedale was Harry's favourite. He liked the terrain there more than the Vale of York. The moors were powerful, brooding even, but the River Wharfe that flowed through the bottom of the dale calmed his soul. They would paddle in the river at Burnsall, and then go for lunch at Grassington or Bolton Abbey – maybe have afternoon tea in the Cavendish Pavilion before coming home and falling into bed exhausted but happy.

Sally was a good woman, and though there were moments when he hated himself for thinking that, for settling for what some would call second best, he knew that life did not always turn out perfectly, that sometimes you had to make compromises. Over the past few years he had learned the difference between idealism and reality, and that reality was not so bad when you came down to it. And anyway, there were other reasons why he had cause to be grateful. One of them was sleeping upstairs in the tiny back bedroom. Emma was four years old now. A bit of a character, her own person, spirited. Wilful, yes, but his own. Cherished. Loved. Like her mother. He did love Sally.

He looked at her now, her dark hair tied back in a ponytail, sitting at the small upright piano with its brass candlesticks that he had bought from the saleroom for her last birthday, and playing a Mozart sonata of which she knew he was especially fond. It brought tears to his eyes, partly because of its beauty, partly because Sally was playing it for him, but also because it awoke within him those memories it was so uncomfortable to recall. It was only in those rare moments – which he tried to avoid – when he probed deep down into his innermost self that he could differentiate between loving someone and being 'in love'. It did not do to go there, though. Being 'in love' was for the young, for students at university, for dreamers. Contentment was more lasting. But now even that seemed to have been taken away. What could he do except grit his teeth, take the bull by the horns and move on? But where?

Sally had found the advertisement in *Country Life*. It was for a small saleroom in Bath. The old proprietor was retiring and the business 'with goodwill' was being sold.

At first Harry was dead against the idea. He knew little about Somerset and the West Country. Why could they not go up to the Dales? To Skipton, perhaps? But then he told himself that he was being churlish and too set in his ways. There was nothing on offer in Skipton. You had to take opportunities when they presented themselves. They would go and look around. He knew Bath was supposed to be beautiful, but would that mean they could not afford to live there? And yet it would be a good place to have a saleroom, surely? All those artistic types. It might even mean that he could sell better furniture than the run-of-the-mill stuff that came his way at Fidler, Son and Bowker. He had been rather hoping that one day his name might make it on to the letterhead and the sign above the saleroom – Fidler, Son, Bowker and Ballantyne – but it was not to be. Ernie had said that it would be best not to change a winning formula. Well, it was a good job that the name had not been changed. It would save them having to change it back again.

The auction house in Bath was simply called 'the Saleroom'. No ego of any kind there. High time, then, to go it alone, to take the risk, to sell his share in Fidler, Son and Bowker, and open Ballantyne's of Bath. The thought of it, the euphony and the alliteration, gave him a greater thrill than he would have imagined.

He watched Sally's eyes glow as he explained what they could do. She was crouching in front of the fire, her freshly washed hair tumbling in dark tresses around her shoulders as she dried it in front of the glowing coals, and for a moment he forgot the past and looked to the future.

'Ballantyne's of Bath,' she murmured softly. 'It does have a nice ring to it, doesn't it? Sort of classy.'

He saw the reflection of the flickering flames in her eyes and it seemed to offer promise of a bright future. Of course it was the right thing to do.

On 31 May 1958 Harry, Sally and Emma Ballantyne moved into a terraced house in Gay Street, Bath. Ernie had been more than generous to his youngest daughter and given her husband a payment that was rather over the odds for his brief partnership in the firm, but, he said, what was money for if not to look after your nearest and dearest?

He came to Bath just the once, to check it over and see that it came up to his expectations. He found the hills rather steep, after the flatness of the Vale of York, but he admired the architecture and approved of the move. He also enjoyed the local brew and told Harry that he would have plenty of places to go for his dinner. They took him to the Pump Room and gave him afternoon tea – as many scones and sandwiches as he could eat. He left them with a wink and a merry wave, but Harry knew that life with Arnold was taking its toll. Ernie had lost his sparkle. Sally had always been her father's favourite, and now they were so far away she did not get to see him as often as she would like. They had a modest Morris Eight, but the journey from Bath to York was not an easy one, especially with a small child and the paraphernalia of pushchair and high chair and goodness knows what. As a result they managed it only rarely.

Six months after Harry and Sally moved to Bath, Ernie retired from the business. Arnold had said that if the business were to survive it would need to change. 'Aye,' said Ernie. 'Well, there's one change that I can make. I'm buggering off, so you can run the bloody business yerself, and good luck to you, you little shit.'

Sally's worry that her father would now have nothing to occupy him was justified. He got up late most mornings and had his 'dinner' down at the Red Lion. In the evenings he sat and looked at the small television he had bought – the first one in the street. He proudly pointed out the H-shaped aerial on the roof to any passers-by and explained that the television had a lovely walnut cabinet – floor-standing, mind – and that the screen was ten inches across. There wasn't much on the one channel, though, and the broadcasting hours were brief.

On Christmas Day 1958, after watching the Queen's Christmas Message to the Commonwealth, Ernie died of a heart attack while sitting in his armchair.

He did have a telephone – again the first in his street – but he didn't like using it and would shout into it as though his voice had to carry all the way down the wire from York to Bath. It was when there was no reply on Christmas afternoon that Sally became concerned. Harry explained that he had probably gone out to see friends, but Sally knew when he had not returned by nine o'clock that something was wrong. She hardly slept that night, and first thing on Boxing Day morning they left Emma with a neighbour and motored up to York. They found him in his armchair. The television was still on. Sylvia Peters was presenting a review of the year and explaining that in June the Queen had opened Gatwick Airport, that in November Donald Campbell had set a new water speed record of 248.62 miles per hour on Coniston Water and that an American rocket carrying a monkey had recently been lost in space over the Atlantic. And still, thought Sally, we could not get to my dad before he died.

She blamed herself for not having had her father with them in Bath, but what was the point, asked Harry, when you knew he wouldn't come because of the hills?

It was not a promising start to their new life, but as the months passed, they came to look upon the West Country as home, and the visits to Harry's beloved Dales became less frequent due to the pressure of work. Ballantyne's of Bath grew slowly but steadily from a saleroom that dealt in everyday household goods to one that had occasional sales of finer furniture. These became more common and, to Harry's relief, more profitable.

By the mid-1960s the firm was on a high. It seemed that everything was rosy in Harry Ballantyne's garden – he owned a successful and expanding business, his wife ran the concert club, and his daughter was doing well at school. And then a new art gallery opened in the Royal Crescent. Richard King moved his business to Bath, and with him came his wife.

24

Glasgow
July 1959

Long ago, acorns were planted along hedgerows. Nothing of
the kind happens now, and when all the oaks and elms and
woodlands are gone, ours will be a base scene indeed.

Letter to the *Daily Telegraph* from
Sir Alfred Munnings (1958)

In his later years Sir Alfred Munnings was bedevilled by gout,
his hands and feet distorted by the complaint, the pain of
them a numbing, stultifying force. He found painting difficult. In 1956, grumbling all the while, he was admitted to
East Suffolk Hospital, where he was treated for cardiac
asthma. He was not an easy patient. His language was
colourful, he was prone to outbursts of violent temper, he
refused any special diet that was recommended, and he made
it clear that he wanted to go home at the earliest opportunity.
In spite of all this, the nurses remained fond of him, but then,
he was fond of almost all of them.

On his release he involved himself with a one-man retro-
spective of his work to be held at the Royal Academy – only
the third man to be so honoured in his lifetime. It gave him
satisfaction to see how far he had come from those early
days, and it helped, in its own way, to ease the pain a little.

He still ranted and railed about the perils of modern art,
the fire still burned within him, and he forced himself to
continue painting both indoors and out – in all weathers. He
wrote letters to *The Times* and the *Daily Telegraph*, complaining
that scientific progress and technology were ruining the

countryside he so loved – a tirade directed particularly at the jet aircraft that ripped apart the skies above his Suffolk home and destroyed the peace and quiet of beautiful Dedham Vale. Here, in his youth and childhood, the horse and cart – whose source of power had played such an important part in his life – had been the only form of transport, the clip-clop of hooves and the cries of the drover the only sounds that were carried abroad on the air.

As the weeks and months wore on, he became weaker. In early June 1959 he spoke on the telephone to a would-be visitor and told him, 'I'm not fit to see a dog. I've done with this world.' He entered Essex County Hospital in Colchester in July 1959, and a week after he returned home, on 17 July 1959, Sir Alfred James Munnings, KCVO, PRA, RWS, RP, the finest painter of horses since George Stubbs, died in his sleep at Castle House. A private cremation took place at Colchester, and the following week a memorial service was held at St James's Church, Piccadilly. The congregation was so large that it spilled outside into the summer sunshine. Among the mourners was Augustus John, who, after the service, pronounced that 'Munnings was greater than Stubbs. He made it move, had greater narrative quality, and his groupings are better.'

All of which was read in the newspaper later that week by Mac. He folded up *The Times* and lay it down by the side of his chair on top of the pile of yellowing *Glasgow Herald*s. In that moment the years fell away. He saw, in his mind's eye, the studio at Dedham, Eleanor sitting atop the wooden horse, felt the warm, sweet grass beneath him and heard Harry's voice asking about Eleanor's feelings for him. He thought about Richard, but then he had often thought about Richard, about how he had made a fool of himself, about the stupidity of his pointless admission. How he had come here and shut himself away, not wanting to see anybody, not wanting to have to talk or explain or justify himself.

Then he thought about Leo and the catastrophe that had befallen him. How he used to tease that scion of the British aristocracy born with the silver-gilt spoon in his mouth, and how now they were brought low by fate. Well, fate in Leo's case, bloody-mindedness in his own. Oh, how much had happened since those days ten years ago. Then they were eager if apprehensive, with an unknown future ahead of them, but it was a future filled with hope and anticipation. On their part, at least. For some of them, perhaps that future had been fulfilled. But how could he know? He had lost contact with all of them. All except Leo, that is, who had sent him a note from somewhere in France.

And what about Mac himself? What had he achieved in the intervening years? He looked around the untidy attic room, rented for one pound ten shillings a week. He saw the canvases stacked against the grimy walls, many of them unfinished and all of them, to his eye, third rate, unsatisfactory.

It would not do. Something better must come of life than this, surely? He pulled at the grizzled beard that now covered his chin and ran his hands through the tangled but thinning hair on his head. Time to make amends. Now that the man who had so inspired him had gone, wasn't it time to fulfil the expectations of his mentor? He half laughed at the thought – not only at the scant regard he had for his own talent, but also that a man he had known for just two days of his life could be rightfully regarded as a mentor. What did it matter? The important thing was to be fired up, and in recent months the fire had left him, except for the fire he found in the bottle. He had no one, except the stray tabby cat that turned up each morning on the steps of the seething Glasgow tenement. Glasgow, the city that he had been determined to leave. What had happened to the determination? Gone the way of the ambition – washed away by the waters of the Clyde and the contents of a bottle of Scotch whisky.

He pushed himself up from the chair and went to the sink in the corner of the room. He turned on the tap and stuck his head under the stream of cold water that gushed from it, then glanced up and looked at himself in the broken shard of mirror that hung on the wall above. There was nothing reassuring about the image that stared back. He slammed his hand on to the draining board with such force that the dirty dishes rattled and the cat, curled up in the corner of a filthy chair, shot out of the door and down the fire escape.

Enough. It was time to move on, time to do something different. He picked up the bottle of Bell's and put it to his lips. Then he stopped. He did not throw back the liquid as he normally did, waiting for the welcome fire to burn the back of his throat and the comforting haze to blur his senses, but slowly and deliberately eased the neck away from his mouth. For a moment he considered. Then with great care, precision and determination, he tipped the contents down the sink and very gently placed the empty bottle upright on the drainer. He looked at it steadily, examining its shape. Then he lifted it up and held it under the tap, rinsing it out so that no vestige of the contents remained. He put the plug in the sink and filled it with water. There was nothing resembling detergent anywhere in the place, but with an old paint-spattered rag he washed and wiped at the dishes, the knives and forks until they were spotless, then stacked them neatly on the draining board.

Next he began to take off his clothes. He washed himself from top to toe in the chilly water, rubbing away the grime until his skin tingled. He caught a glimpse of his body in the glass and winced. He did not want to see. More and more he rubbed until his skin was pink with the abrasion. Naked and cleansed as best as cold water would allow, he walked to the battered chest of drawers at one end of the room and searched within them for a selection of clothing that, while not exactly clean, was less acrid-smelling than the garments he had removed.

He dressed, found a sheet of brown paper and some rough string, and tied into a bundle the clothes he had been wearing. He put down a saucer of food for the cat, then took a tin from the mantelpiece. It had once held toffee. Now it held an old letter and his savings. He laughed at the total. He put two one-pound notes under the empty whisky bottle, pushed the letter into the pocket of his trousers and set about gathering together his brushes and paints, stuffing them into a threadbare canvas holdall.

When he was satisfied that he had all he needed, he picked up the bag and the bundle and walked to the door. He turned for a moment to take in the scene one last time. A book lying on the bottom shelf where he stacked his paints caught his eye. He hesitated for a moment, made to leave, then thought again and turned to stare at the solitary volume. For several minutes he gazed at it transfixed, before slowly crossing the room to where it lay. He picked it up and wiped from it the accretion of dust. Then he slid it into the bundle and retraced his steps. He would leave the paintings for the landlord, who would curse him for running out, but then the canvases and the couple of pounds under the bottle should more than pay his dues.

As he walked down the metal fire escape, the cat passed him on the way up. He put out his hand to stroke it. The cat did not notice. It was too intent on seeking food. Mac stopped and watched as the cat climbed the rest of the stairs and disappeared inside the door of the garret. An artist's garret. All he had dreamed of once. Some dream.

25

Bath
June 1964

O! beware, my lord, of jealousy;
It is the green-eyed monster which doth mock
The meat it feeds on.
Othello (1602–04), William Shakespeare

It came as a shock to both parties to discover their close proximity. Richard King had set up business in Bristol in 1958 and, once things were doing well, had decided that a move to Bath would make great sense. The Georgian city was more like a town and seemed more suited to the world of fine art – good for the image of the firm and a better place in which to live. He had failed to notice that Ballantyne's of Bath was the main local auction house because of one simple fact. He had congratulated himself on being up-to-the-minute in using a firm of business analysts to report on the potential there, and their report had confirmed the presence of smaller galleries, which fed a healthy and expanding market, and a thriving saleroom that was a cut above the norm. What they had omitted to mention was the name of the firm. It was as simple as that.

Eleanor could remember the exact moment that she discovered she was living in the same city as Harry Ballantyne. She was leafing through the *Bath Chronicle* in search of a bicycle for Patrick, who had outgrown his existing machine and was desperate for a racing bike. She had spotted the advertisement for the sale of household goods at Ballantyne's of Bath. At first she had thought it must be a coincidence, but then, when she had steeled herself to go to the saleroom and look, she had seen him in the office on the other side of the glass partition at the back of the main hall. The moment she saw him she had dodged behind a pillar, thinking perhaps that she could escape without being seen. Her heart was thumping. It surprised her that nobody could hear it, but the people around her continued to open drawers and look under chairs as though nothing untoward had happened.

She looked towards the exit. It was at the opposite side of the saleroom. She could not escape without coming into full view of the office window. In vain she scanned the room for tall furniture behind which she could make her escape unnoticed, but to no avail. Linen presses and wardrobes, dressers and screens were arranged against the back wall. There was no cover.

'Are you all right?' asked a piercing voice.

Eleanor glanced to her left. The enquiry came from a woman in a floral dress with blue hair and white-framed spectacles that looked as though they had sprouted wings and were about to lift their wearer clear of the ground. She regarded Eleanor with a gimlet eye.

'I'm with St John Ambulance. I can offer first aid if you need it.'

Eleanor was aware that standing, as she was, hard against a pillar and holding her chest, she must have looked in need of medical assistance. 'No, really, I'm fine, thank you.'

'You look very pale.' The sharp-nosed woman was now closer than was customarily polite and Eleanor began to feel overwhelmed by her proximity.

'Really, I'm fine. Just a little warm.' She backed away from the pillar and into full view of the glass-walled office.

'Well, if you're sure.' The woman began to rummage in her large, white plastic handbag. 'I have some smelling salts in here somewhere . . .'

'Please . . .'

The woman shrugged. 'Well, if you say so, but my training leads me to believe that there's a strong possibility you might pass out. I should sit down for a few minutes.'

'Yes. Yes, I will. Thank you.' Eleanor flopped down on to a striped Regency sofa and did her best to become invisible. It was not easy, especially with St John Ambulance's finest trilling over her and willing her to collapse so that she could bring her expertise to bear.

The would-be nurse snapped shut her bag and reassured Eleanor, 'I'll be keeping an eye on you,' before she moved off to examine a glass dome filled with stuffed birds.

Eleanor felt like a stuffed bird herself, or a butterfly pinned to a board in the centre of the saleroom. The woman gradually made her way across the room and left Eleanor to contemplate her means of escape, but she was too late. Harry had come out of the office and was walking across the saleroom directly towards her. Feverishly she began to examine the fabric on the sofa, running her hands over it and looking deeply into the recesses beneath the arms.

'That's rather a good one, isn't it?' he asked.

She could not help but look up, and as her eyes met his, there was on his face a sudden look of recognition that would live with her for the rest of her life. It might have been her imagination, it might have been all manner of things from wishful thinking to self-delusion, but she thought that in that split second when he saw her he looked at her in exactly the same way as he had in Dedham that evening fifteen years ago.

For a moment he could not speak. Then he said, quite straightforwardly, 'Oh, hello.'

Eleanor was surprised by the evenness of his tone. She expected him to be as overwhelmed as she was – as over-whelmed with joy, with emotion, with confusion – but he was not, or did not appear to be. Her feelings were suddenly shot through with anger. How dare he be so unaffected at the sight of her, so equable in temperament? Why was *his* heart not beating faster as hers was? Why did *he* not have to sit down as she did?

He held out his hand to shake hers. She did so without thinking. She was still sitting down.

His expression was one of polite interest. 'What are you doing here?' he asked.

'Looking for a bicycle,' was all she could reply.

He seemed taken aback for a moment, then pointed to the back of the room. 'We leave them at the bottom of the stairs, so they don't put oil on the furniture.'

Fifteen years of wondering what he would say if they ever met again and never once did her thoughts ever come close to 'We leave them at the bottom of the stairs, so they don't put oil on the furniture.'

'Of course,' she murmured. 'Oil on the furniture.'

'But . . . what are you doing in Bath?'

'We've moved here, moved the business here. We're opening the gallery in a couple of weeks. In the Royal Crescent.'

At least he had the good grace to look bemused, she thought.

'I see. You must have done well.'

'We have. Well, Richard has. I just . . .'

He looked at her questioningly.

Oh, how she wanted to ask him where he had been, what he had been doing, but more than anything why he had gone and left her that day, the day after they had made love so tenderly in the hotel room at Dedham.

Suddenly she felt an enormous welling of emotion and it took all of her strength to push herself up from the Regency sofa and stand beside him. She took a deep breath, the better to speak steadily, and said, 'Well, I must go and look at bicycles.'

'Yes, of course.'

Eleanor could manage no more conversation. She bit her lip until it hurt and tried to smile as she brushed past him.

Harry watched her go. She had lost none of her beauty; if anything, she was even more devastating in womanhood than she had been when she was a girl. He felt weak at the knees and slid gently down until he was sitting on the Regency sofa.

'Are you all right,' asked a shrill voice. 'I'm a trained St John Ambulance first-aider.'

But Harry did not hear. His mind was back in Dedham, reflecting on what had gone wrong fifteen years ago. Then he fell to wondering how on earth he was going to carry on living in the same place as the woman he loved when she was married to someone else.

Richard sat quite still when she told him. He said nothing, just gazed out of the window and over the city.

'It doesn't make any difference,' she said, though she did not for one minute believe the sentiment she was expressing.

'No. No difference at all,' he murmured, without turning round. Then he said, 'I shan't meet him if you don't mind.'

'Of course not,' said Eleanor, and as she watched Richard staring out of the window, she could not recall ever feeling so empty, not since the day she had married.

26

Bath
December 2007

A secret in the Oxford sense; you may tell it to only one
person at a time.

Lord Franks (1977), *Sunday Telegraph*

They were surprisingly large crates of personal effects for
someone who had supposedly died in penury, but then, thought
Jamie, everything was relative. Penury to him would mean
living in rented accommodation that he could barely afford,
whereas penury to Lord Bedlington would mean not being
able to live in a stately pile and cutting your staff by half.

He watched as Ballantyne's saleroom stewards – Frank and
Len, 'the removal men' – methodically emptied the wooden
creates of their contents, unwrapping the brown-paper cover-
ings so carefully put in place by the house-movers to the
upper classes, Cadogan Tate. A mahogany bureau appeared
like Venus rising from the scallop shell, then a Wellington
chest. There were several *fauteuils* with threadbare seats, side
tables and chests, dining chairs and a *lit bateau* that Jamie
thought looked a romantic but fiendishly uncomfortable way
of spending a night. At six foot two his feet would have
dangled over the end.

As the floor of the empty storeroom beneath the saleroom
began to fill, Jamie wandered back upstairs to the office,
where his mother was standing behind her desk and filling
her capacious handbag with the day's necessities.

'Any good?' she asked.

'Oh, nothing special. Some elegant pieces, but I guess not

especially good. There's quite a lot of it, though. I thought there would be less, somehow, seeing as he lost most of his money.'

Emma Ballantyne shot him a wry smile. 'Ah, well, that's the aristocracy for you. Always have a bit put by.'

'That's a surprisingly left-wing comment for you.'

'Not really. Just the voice of experience.' Emma snapped her bag shut. 'The older I get, the more I realise that other people's values are not necessarily your own. You might think they are PLU, but they often turn out to be NOS.'

Jamie smiled indulgently. They were two of his mother's favourite expressions. Those of whom she approved were PLU – People Like Us; the rest were NOS – Not Our Sort. 'So Lord Bedlington was NOS, then?'

'Not really. I think your father was rather fond of him in a sneaky sort of way. Not that he'd ever admit it. A bit too shocking.'

'What, because Leo Bedlington was gay?'

'You must remember that it was different in those days. Society wasn't nearly so tolerant. It was illegal, for a start, which meant that those of that persuasion who had any sense kept very quiet about it.'

'Yes, but Granddad isn't . . . I mean . . . he's not exactly homophobic, is he?'

'He's always been very open-minded, if that's what you mean, but he did grow up in an era when men of that persuasion were called "queers" and "pansies". He's definitely a man's man – always has been – but I think he's made a real effort to avoid being anti-gay.'

'What about Richard King?'

His mother shrugged. 'Who knows what goes on in that strange man's mind?' She looked thoughtful and then asked, 'Are you still seeing his granddaughter?'

'Does it matter?'

'It probably does to him.' She picked up her bag and made for the door.

'But not to you?'

Emma paused in the doorway. 'I don't think that whatever I say will make any difference to what you do.'

'But?'

'I can't approve, Jamie, but then I have no right to disapprove, either. I've been thinking about all this – this feud that's been going on for so many years. To be perfectly honest, I've lost my appetite for it. Its origins are lost in the mists of time and I think everyone would be better diverting their energies into today, rather than yesterday.'

'Oh.' Her reply rather took him aback.

'So there you are. You do what you want. You'll have no more trouble from me, but I wouldn't expect a smooth ride from those at the top of the hill.' She nodded her head in the direction of the Royal Crescent, then shot him a pitying look and said, 'I won't be back again today – lunch out, then I'm away home. I'll see you tomorrow.'

'Yes. Right. Tomorrow.' Jamie looked puzzled and distracted. What had made her change her mind? Then he shook his head, as though to clear it, and came to when Frank put his head round the door and said, 'All done, guv. Ready for you to have a look.'

Still rather dazed by his mother's apparent reasonableness, Jamie descended the stairs to the storeroom, which had now become an Aladdin's cave of personal effects. The furniture was mainly French, with one or two English pieces that had clearly been of sentimental value. Jamie had hoped that Lord Bedlington might have hung on to at least one or two gems – a Chippendale sideboard, perhaps, or a Vile and Cobb commode, maybe even a piece or two by George Bullock, whose use of ormolu and brass inlay might have appealed to someone of Lord Bedlington's tastes – but from the most cursory of inspections, it seemed that the late lord had indeed been forced to part with the gems that comprised his inheritance. His legacy was a collection of good but not great furniture.

There were, however, one or two fine pieces of porcelain – a Sèvres part dinner service, several Meissen figurines and some Bow and Derby china.

'Any pictures?' he asked casually.

'Over there against the wall, guv,' offered Len, the shorter and quieter of the two men in overalls.

Jamie wove his way between the furniture to the pictures that were leaning against the end wall. There were a couple of large landscapes of sylvan scenes and half a dozen watercolours that had faded from being left in bright sunlight – the penalty for living in the south of France. One nineteenth-century portrait stood in the centre of the wall: with any luck it might turn out to be a decent one – perhaps by Lawrence or Beechey – but in his heart Jamie felt it was probably a studio copy.

Then he saw the final group of paintings. These Len and Frank had leaned in a pile, since space had almost run out. They were facing the wall and so their subjects could not be seen. Jamie picked up the one on the outside of the pile and turned it round so that it faced him. His heart almost stopped. He had admitted only a few days ago that this sort of painting was not his bag, but in that few days he had learned a lot. Only by being curious did an auctioneer and valuer improve his skills, and Jamie had never been short on curiosity. He had absorbed all that Artemis King had told him since they had met again and had built on it with further research. Whether it was his love for her that had spurred him on or simply a quest to know more he did not really know. What he did know for sure was that the work on which he now gazed had been painted by Sir Alfred Munnings.

It was of the start of a race, with jockeys jostling for position

in their bright silks. The sky was azure blue, and the flanks
of the assorted horses seemed to shine in the sunlight,
reflecting the green of the grass and the iridescent shades of
the silks. He put down the painting and stepped back from
it. There was no doubt. The signature confirmed his suspicions;
the work was by Munnings. Wait until Missy saw it! How
excited she would be. He almost wanted to run up the hill
and tell her now.

There were other paintings to see as well, though. He turned
over the next one and did a double-take. It was another
Munnings, this time of a gypsy encampment. The third
painting was similar – the label on the stretcher indicating
that it had been painted at Epsom Races.

The fourth painting was superb – of a woman on horseback. The label on the back of this one indicated that it was
Lord Bedlington's mother. She was rather a plain woman,
but the composition made the most of her horsemanship –
she looked superb atop the bay horse – and the landscape
around her reflected the heat of a summer's day somewhere
in the Cotswolds. It was as good an example of Munnings's
work as he had seen. He lowered it carefully to the floor and
cast his eye across all four paintings. What a find!

The fifth and final painting lay facing the wall. He hardly
dared turn it round. What could it be? Another Munnings,
or just a boring landscape? For a few moments he stood
quite still, trying to regulate his breathing. If the fifth painting
was also by Munnings, then it did not matter a jot that the
furniture was not up to much. The paintings alone would
make this a sale to end all sales.

He bent down. He grasped the frame in both hands and
slowly revolved it. When he took in the scene that met his
eye, he had to steady himself to avoid dropping it. It was not
possible. How could it be?

He propped the picture against the wall alongside the

others and stood back to take it in. It was most certainly by the same hand. It was even signed by the artist. It was a sumptuous, beautifully executed painting of a woman on a grey horse. The only trouble was, this was not the first time he had seen it. This was exactly the same picture that he had sold to Missy just a few weeks ago.

'King's Fine Art.' She answered the phone in an assured manner, though self-assurance seemed to be conspicuously lacking in her at that moment. She had too many things to think about, too many things of which she was not sure whirling around in her head. Like Jamie. No, she was sure of him. Like her grandfather, and her father. She was not at all sure about them. And the paintings. What were they? What was going on? Was she creating problems where problems did not exist? No, she was sure she was not. If her grandfather had taught her anything during her father's long absence, it was to rely on her instincts. When had they ever let her down? And yet right now she really did not want to believe them.

The voice at the other end of the line invaded her consciousness. 'Missy?'

'Yes?'

'It's Jamie.'

She was so relieved to hear him, so pleased that he should have called and proved himself a constant in a world that seemed suddenly to be on the move in the kind of direction that unnerved her.

'Hi!' Then in her agitated frame of mind she wondered if there was a problem here as well. He did not normally call her at work, certainly not on her land line. 'Is everything all right?' she asked.

'Yes. Well, no. I mean, there's something I need to see you about.'

Her anxiety intensified. 'What is it?'

He read her unease, seemed to realise that she might think he had got cold feet or something and wanted out. 'I mean, not about us. That's fine. It's just . . . there's something I want to ask your advice about.'

Her relief was palpable. 'Fine. Ask away.'

'Not on the phone. Can we talk about it tonight?'

'Yes, of course.'

'Only, perhaps it shouldn't be at your place.'

'Oh?'

She was worried again now, and once more he read her feelings. He wanted to avoid talking to her at the gallery, but was aware that he needed to calm her feelings, remove any sense of disquiet at not wanting to meet her at the Royal Crescent.

'I just thought you might like to come and see the house at the Circus. Gran and Granddad will be out sizing up their new place and they said I could go in and measure up, that sort of thing, though what I'm measuring up for I'm not quite sure.'

He thought it best to give her no idea of what he really wanted to talk to her about until they met face to face. He did not want her to worry for the rest of the day, and he also wanted to be with her when he dropped the bombshell. For better or worse they were both involved in whatever it was, and one or other of them – he was not certain which – was caught up in a situation that was at best embarrassing and at worst . . . Well, he did not want to think about the worst bit. His main concern right now was getting those paintings out of the saleroom and into storage somewhere safe until he had worked out just what was going on.

Frank and Len, the removal men, had seemed unconcerned. To them, they were just pictures. Jamie doubted whether either of them would remember selling *The Laughing Cavalier* twice in one week, let alone some painting of a woman on a horse.

'I'll come and pick you up at seven, if that's OK?' he asked.

'Yes. Seven. Fine. I'll see you then.' She hesitated. 'Everything is all right, isn't it? I mean, between us?'

'Yes. Course it is. Don't sound so worried. I'll see you at seven. I'll wait outside for you.'

He wondered, when he had put the phone down, whether she had detected anything in his tone of voice that would have given any clue as to the nature of his enquiry. He convinced himself that she had not, though he had never been very good at acting. His teacher at school had told him to avoid a stage career simply because he was too honest and easily read to be believable. He had never worked out whether she had meant it as a compliment or whether it implied that he was excessively naïve. Whatever the case, the next few hours would prove to be something of a trial.

At least with Missy he could be perfectly straight. They could share their knowledge and work out the best course of action. At the moment, in his own mind, he had absolutely no idea what to do next.

27

Villa Fabrice, Menton, Côte d'Azur
August 1959 – June 1965

Friendship is a disinterested commerce between equals; love,
an abject intercourse between tyrants and slaves.
The Good-Natured Man (1768), Oliver Goldsmith

Finding John Macready on his doorstep was not a scenario
that Leo Bedlington had ever contemplated, certainly not ten
years after their last meeting, and especially since their final
farewell and muttered goodbyes as Mac carried his bags
towards the station – had been memorable only for its awkward-
ness. Leo had sought to find some common ground between
them, maybe some tacit understanding of their circumstances,
without overstepping the mark and embarrassing his friend,
but Mac had responded gruffly, offering no more than a brief
handshake and a vague indication that they might meet again
one day. He doubted that a doorstep in the south of France
had been regarded as a likely possibility.

At first he was unsure who the apparent stranger was. He
took him for a tramp, this grizzled character with a fox-
coloured beard and threadbare clothing. It was only when he
spoke that Leo recognised his old college friend underneath
the shabby coat, the concertina trousers and the matted hair.

'Hello,' was all that Mac had said. Leo was reaching into
his pocket for a few francs to send the traveller on his way,
but the Glaswegian tones stopped him in his tracks.

'Mac?' he asked, peering as if through thick fog to find the
man he knew beneath the disguise.

'Aye. Here I am, then.'

It was as simple and as straightforward as that. For a few moments neither man said anything more. They stared at one another after the fashion of two tomcats stalking each other on a wall. Then Leo, aware of his temporary lapse in manners, said, 'Come in, come in. You must be exhausted. Where have you come from?'

Mac said but one word in reply. 'Oblivion.'

That night, in the warm Mediterranean air, they dined on the terrace of Villa Fabrice overlooking the bay. The taciturn cook, Madame Farage – birdlike in both appearance and manner – brought them large bowls of homemade bouillabaisse and freshly baked bread. Leo watched as Mac fell upon the meal as if he had not eaten in a year, spooning up the nutritious broth as though his life depended upon it. But then, thought Leo, it probably did.

In the lanterns that were strung along the blue-painted timbers of the villa, Leo could see how his friend had aged over the last ten years. His cheeks were sunken, his eyes seemed haunted, and the once-ruddy countenance was pallid now. Only his nose showed any colour, and that was obviously due to an overfondness for the bottle. That night Mac declined a glass of wine, opting instead for water, as he was to do for the rest of his life.

The serious business of eating over, Mac sat back in his chair, suddenly embarrassed at his apparent lack of manners and gratitude. 'That was very good,' he said. 'And very necessary. Thank you.'

Leo smiled. He was reluctant to lunge into any kind of inquisition. He would wait until Mac was ready to talk. It did not take long. After polite conversation about Madame Farage and her culinary skills, Mac gradually opened up. He had gone back to Glasgow to tell his family that he intended to support himself as an artist. He was not sure where. In the meantime he had rented a flat near the docks and set to on his canvases. The results were, he thought, quite good, but failed to interest what few galleries there were in the city. He began to paint portraits, but the clientele in the early 1950s was almost non-existent in Glasgow. He planned to move to Edinburgh – a city more supportive of the arts – but then, without warning, his father, a strapping postman, had collapsed and died on his round, leaving Mac to support his mother and two sisters. It had not been easy, but he had travelled once a week to Edinburgh with his paintings, trying to make enough money to keep the family together. In the evenings he worked at his canvases with a glass of Scotch at his elbow. It helped keep him going. Feverishly he worked on canvas after canvas, but the money he earned barely kept him supplied with materials and the family supplied with food. If only he could get away, but it was not an option.

The two sisters eventually married, and just when things should have been getting easier Mac's mother was taken into hospital. She died there after a short illness. Now at last he found himself free to pursue his own life, but the glass of Scotch by his elbow of an evening had turned into two bottles a day. Without them it was difficult to keep a steady hand. Gradually his few commissions had dried up. He had no idea what to do until that one day in his grim attic room when he had realised that unless he made a fresh start, his life would not last much longer. The only things he had, apart from his paints and his brushes, and the company of a vagrant cat, were a book given to him by Munnings and a letter that Leo had sent him on his birthday the year after they had parted.

'Good God!' said Leo. 'I'd forgotten about that. I'm afraid I rather gave up on you then. You didn't reply, so I thought it was pointless to carry on corresponding.'

'I'm not surprised. Yours was the only address I had. I've lost touch with the others.'

'Yes.' Leo looked thoughtful. 'We've not done very well at keeping up, have we?'

Mac shrugged. 'It happens.' He was tired of talking about himself. 'So what about you?' he asked.

'Oh, I think they call them "straitened circumstances".'

Mac looked around. 'Everything's relative.'

Leo felt suddenly guilty. 'Quite.'

'The house had to go, then?'

'Bedlington Park? 'Fraid so. And the staff, and all the appurtenances. I felt very bad about it, but there really was nothing I could do – not with death duties at that rate.'

'Why here?'

'A bit like you: I wanted a fresh start, where I had no baggage.' He laughed at the appropriateness of his comment. 'So here we are, the two of us with no baggage between us.'

Mac said nothing, but gazed out towards the sea. Leo endeavoured to fill the silence. 'You can stay as long as you want, you know. There's no one else here.'

Mac turned to face him. 'You didn't find anybody either?'

Leo looked down and shook his head. 'No,' he said softly. 'I didn't find anybody either.' He played with his spoon for a moment or two, as if trying to formulate what he wanted to say, but afraid that once again his words might not have the desired effect. 'I'd be glad of the company, and there really are no obligations.'

Mac did not meet his eye, but said, 'You're very kind. Perhaps just until—'

'No,' said Leo emphatically. 'Don't set any constraints. Just stay for as long or as short a time as you want. I won't ask anything of you. Oh, except that you give me a hand in the garden. There's a man who comes in, but he tends to be overzealous. I like it looking wild, so that it fits in with the view. He has a fondness for bedding plants; I do not.'

A flicker of a smile crossed Mac's face. It was the first

glimmer of humour or ease that Leo had seen since he arrived. Perhaps Mac would find himself here, find his true painting skills, maybe even earn a living at it – there were plenty of little galleries in Cannes and Antibes selling paintings of local scenes to tourists.

'Well,' said Leo, pushing himself up from his chair, 'I tend to go to bed early. Stay up as long as you wish.' He pointed to the doorway; 'Your room's right at the end. Sleep well.' Then he looked up at the sky, studded with stars. 'It should be a nice day tomorrow, the nicest for a long while.'

It was several months before Mac could do anything constructive when it came to painting. It took that long for his hands to stop shaking. Instead he gardened, mindful of Leo's entreaties. He pulled out grass and tangles of bindweed, but allowed the wild flowers and the cultivated ones that Leo enjoyed to flourish. The following spring he planted up large terracotta pots with olives and myrtles and moon daisies, of which Leo approved. He shaved off his beard, and Madame Farage cut his hair once a month. Within a year Leo could hardly remember what life had been like without him, and Mac settled into life at Villa Fabrice with quiet gratitude.

Not that the two always got on. There were moments of taciturnity from Mac, occasions when he could be less than gracious to the man who had rescued him from 'oblivion', but then Leo could be maddeningly pernickety about the colour of the paintwork on the terrace, or the planting of garish bougainvillea. Even so they rubbed along.

They rubbed along for six years – amusing and irritating one another in equal measure, living together yet leading, in their minds, quite separate lives.

Then, one morning in early summer 1965, a letter came that brought unwelcome news. Mac had just climbed up the garden to the terrace. He was an early riser and enjoyed a swim before breakfast. Leo was sitting at the table under the vines and holding the letter in his hands. They were trembling, Mac noticed, and Leo's face was ashen.

'Bad news?' asked Mac, with his usual laconic capacity for understatement.

'Very.'

'Want to share it?'

'I think I'll have to, since it affects you almost as much as me.'

Mac cocked his head on one side, waiting for the response.

'He needs more money.'

'Who does?' asked Mac, assuming that Leo was having to shell out for some earlier indiscretion.

'The taxman.'

Mac was pouring himself a coffee from the silver pot on the breakfast table with one hand and rubbing a towel through his hair with the other. 'After fifteen years? I thought he'd bled you dry already.'

'He has,' said Leo.

Mac detected the quavering note in his voice. 'How much?' he asked.

'Another fifty thousand.'

'And it's taken him all this time to work it out?'

'Apparently.'

'Bloody hell.'

Leo dropped the letter on the table. Mac could see that he was close to tears. 'It's not bloody fair. I mean, where am I meant to live? They've taken the Park; they've taken just about everything it contained. What's left?'

Mac watched as Leo stood up and walked to the edge of the terrace.

'I might as well walk off into the bloody sea and disappear.'

Mac went up to him and laid his hand on Leo's shoulder. 'Not yet.'

'Well, what else can I do? The only thing left is the paint-ings, and there's only half a dozen of them.'

'Are they worth fifty thousand?'

'Oh, quite a lot more, but one of them's of my mother.' The composure that had always been so assiduously main-tained finally failed. The dam burst and Leo's body was convulsed in heaving sobs.

Mac said nothing, but put his arm round Leo as his body shook and the sorrow of the last fifteen years flooded out. He held him silently until the torrent subsided.

'How can I keep giving them what I haven't got? When will they leave me alone? I'm not harming anyone. I'm just a sad old queen who wants to get on with his life.' He reached into his pocket and pulled out a large silk handkerchief, then made a valiant attempt at stemming the flow of tears and his running nose. 'I'm so sorry. Not your problem. Very silly of me. No self-control.'

'Bollocks,' said Mac. 'And it is my problem, just as much as yours. I wouldn't be here if it weren't for you. I probably wouldn't even be alive, so don't start apologising.'

Leo blew his nose again and shook his head in despair.

'How badly do you want to keep those paintings?' asked Mac.

'What do you mean?'

'What I said. How badly do you want them?'

Leo was trying in vain to understand where the conver-sation was going. 'Very badly. They're all I have of Bedlington Park, all I have of a life, of a heritage.'

'OK, then, keep them.'

'But I can't – not if I want to pay this bill.' He held the letter aloft and it fluttered gently in the warm breeze.

'Have they given you a deadline?'

Leo checked the letter. 'Six months.'

'That should be enough.'

'Enough for what?'

'Enough for me to get to work.'

Leo looked bewildered. 'I don't understand.'

'Look, the shakes have gone now, yes?' He held out his hand to show that it was steady.

'Yes.'

'And my paintings are selling – not just down in Antibes, but the few I've sent back to Blighty.'

'Well, yes, but . . .'

'But they're not selling for the sort of money you need, I know.'

'No.' Leo felt bad at having to spurn his companion's efforts. 'Though it was very good of you to offer.'

'A Munnings or two, on the other hand, would bring in far more.'

'Yes, but . . .'

'So we sell a Munnings or two.'

Leo looked bewildered. 'I don't understand.'

'A Munnings or two painted by me.'

Leo stood quite still, trying to take in the significance of what Mac had said and wondering if he had heard correctly. 'You don't mean . . . forgery?'

'Exactly.'

Leo sat down abruptly and the colour drained from his cheeks. 'Oh, I don't think I could let you do that.'

'Why not?'

'Because it's dishonest, and the Bedlingtons are not dishonest.'

'And where has it got them?' asked Mac. 'Right in the shit, that's where.'

'Well, I wouldn't put it quite like that . . .'

'Wouldn't you? I would. So I think it's time you gave the taxman a run for his money. He's had just about all you've got. I reckon you deserve to hang on to what little you have left.'

'But Munnings – he was so good to you.'

'In which case he won't mind continuing to be good to me.'

'Mac, it really is very kind of you, but in spite of your good intentions, and the fact that I think you're a terribly good artist, I don't see how you could manage—'

He got no further. Mac interrupted him with four words: 'Just let me try.'

Three months later Leo found himself standing in front of two paintings by Alfred Munnings, except that they were not by Alfred Munnings, they were by John Macready.

'It's incredible. You've even got the signature right.'

'Ha! The bloody signature. That was the easiest bit. It's the brushwork that's the bugger.'

'Yes, of course.' Leo was bemused, entranced and, if he were honest with himself, rather excited at having two new Munningses in his house, even though they were identical to ones he already possessed.

'But do you think they'll fool the taxman, or, more importantly, the art world?'

'There's only one way to find out, isn't there?'

'Oh, Mac, do you think we should?'

Mac gave Leo a gentle slap on the back. 'Now that I've done them, I think it would be a shame not to, don't you?'

Leo could not pretend that he was happy. 'Well, I suppose so. But where do we sell them?'

Mac looked thoughtful. Then he said, 'There's an art gallery that's just opened in Bath. I think that might be a good place. Out of London, you know – not quite so much attention. Better than sending them to auction, which might cause too much fuss.'

'Yes. Perhaps that would be best.'

'I wonder if Madame Farage would mind handling it for us? Keep our names out of it altogether.'

'Yes, if you think so.'

Leo did not notice the mischievous glint in Mac's eye. He was too busy looking at the new picture of Eleanor on her horse.

'You never know. If they sell well, I could paint one or two more. The others could keep us going into our old age. Maybe even long after "John Macready" has stopped painting.'

28

Bath
December 2007

A man that studieth revenge keeps his own wounds green.
'Of Revenge' (1625), Sir Francis Bacon

By the time six o'clock came, what little concentration Missy had been able to apply to her cataloguing had evaporated. She glanced over to the wall where the mirror-image Munnings leaned, wrapped in innocent-looking brown paper. She would take her father's advice, belatedly, and slip it discreetly into the back of the storeroom before Jamie picked her up.

The store was a strongroom in the basement, climate-controlled and alarmed. At any one time there would be several million pounds worth of pictures in there, all carefully catalogued. Most of them were hung close together on wire grilles that slid from side to side so that a hundred or more pictures could be stored in a relatively small area.

With the mirror-image Munnings under one arm, Missy punched in the alarm code and then turned each of the two keys in turn to open the armour-plated door. Once inside, she shivered a little in the cool, dry air and looked around her at the treasure trove of art works – a potted history of the finest British painting over the last three hundred years. Most were of horses, but there were portraits scattered among them, too. Aristocratic lords in frock coats and tricorne hats gazed imperiously in her direction, as if admonishing her for disturbing their peace. Serene women of varying beauty simpered in clouds of muslin, while the horses grazed and leaped fences and drank from crystal streams.

She could never enter this vault without a frisson of excitement inspired by its astonishing contents. Part of her felt guilty at presiding over such riches, as though she were a miser gloating over her spoils, but that feeling would be quickly replaced by one of awe and wonder and admiration at the skills of the artists who had captured such life and vitality often several centuries previously. They were snapshots of past times, records of lives lived and horses ridden.

She laid down the mirror-image Munnings on the desk beside the ledger and withdrew one of the racks. She came down here perhaps once a day, maybe twice, but always, without fail, she would pull out a different rack and scrutinise its contents, partly to keep up with the changing stock and partly to increase her knowledge. If she came across an artist she did not know, she would read up about him in one of her grandfather's books. They filled almost an entire wall in the office.

On the rack she pulled out today there were several drawings by Edward Lear – misty and mysterious evocations of the banks of the Nile and of Sintra. There was a Henry Edridge pencil drawing of King George III at Frogmore, and a Helen Allingham watercolour of a Surrey cottage. For her, the best picture on this particular rack was of mares and foals in a landscape by the Cumberland painter Sawrey Gilpin. It might have been painted over two hundred years ago, but it seemed to her so fresh and full of life that she could have been looking on the scene from a window of her house.

She sighed. What was it about pictures of horses? Why was she so entranced by them? Time after time she had attempted to analyse her fascination and had finally stopped trying. She loved them. It was as simple as that – as simple as loving Jamie. She smiled to herself. She would be seeing him in under an hour. Her spirits lifted. She would try to put the painting out of her mind, for the time being at least.

She slid the rack back and slowly the pictures disappeared from view once more, but when the rack was two-thirds of the way back, it stopped abruptly. It was jammed.

Normally they worked so efficiently. She assumed that one of the wheels must have come off its runner, so she pulled the rack out again. It seemed to run smoothly in this direction, so she tried to push it back once more. Still it jammed. She leaned sideways and looked along the side of the rack, but in spite of the bright fluorescent light, she could not see what was stopping it from returning. She pulled out two racks on either side of the sticking one, the better to see into the void. Now she had a clear view of the obstruction. It was a large but slender cardboard box, which had presumably been slid between the racks until someone had time to hang up its contents. It had obviously tilted when she had pulled her chosen rack out and would now not let it return. She slid out two more racks until there was room for her to squeeze between them and retrieve the parcel. It was too heavy to lift, so she slid it along the floor and out through the gap.

'Damn!' She was covered in dust now. She would have thought that the package would have been clean if someone had propped it there temporarily, but it was filthy. She rubbed her hands against one another to rid them of the dust and looked more closely at the package. It was sealed up with parcel tape, and there was nothing on it to indicate what it could be.

Missy looked around her for something with which she could slit open the package and examine its contents, the better to decide where they should go. There was a screwdriver on the shelf by the ledger. It was used for adjusting the position of the hooks that hung the pictures. That would do. She ran the sharp edge of the blade along the tape, slicing through it cleanly until the end of the box flipped up. She reached inside. She could feel several framed pictures. She withdrew the first one.

Perhaps she should have realised what it might be, but her mind was, at that moment, on other things – on hiding the picture she had brought down there and on the evening in prospect with Jamie – so the Munnings she withdrew from the package came as a shock. As did the second one, and the third. Would it ever end? There were four in all. She glanced at them just long enough to see what they were, then slid them back into their hiding place. She could feel her heart beating in her chest. Breathing seemed to be more difficult. She steadied herself on the rack and took deep breaths, her mind reeling.

Carefully she slid the parcel alongside the last rack in the vault, hoping that there it would be less likely to snag the mechanism. She pushed it out of sight, but kept hold of the mirror-image Munnings.

She did not check the ledger. She knew that the paintings would not be recorded there. Instead she switched off the light, locked the heavy door, punched in the alarm code and climbed the stairs back to the gallery on the first floor.

'I wondered where you were.'

Missy jumped.

'Sorry. Did I surprise you?' Her grandfather had been looking out of the window towards the town, now resplendent with Christmas lights. He nodded in their direction. 'Must cost a fortune. Never mind the electricity.' Then he noticed that the colour had drained from her cheeks. 'What on earth's the matter? Are you all right? Sit down for a minute – you look as white as a sheet.'

'Yes. No. I mean, I'm fine.'

'No you're not. What is it?'

Missy shook her head. 'I don't know. I'm confused, that's all.'

'What about?'

'Everything.' Missy walked over to the gilded sofa and flopped down among the cushions. Then she rested her head in her hands.

'I'll get you a glass of water,' offered her grandfather. He slipped through the door of the gallery and returned a few moments later, handing her the glass.

'Thank you.' Missy sipped gently at the water, her eyes focusing on the middle distance.

'Are you going to tell me what the matter is, or do I have to guess?'

Missy looked up at him. 'The pictures.'

At first Richard King looked bemused. 'Which pictures?'

'The Munningses.'

He looked more concerned now. 'Which Munningses?'

Missy smiled sardonically. 'All of them – the ones in the picture store, hidden away in the box, the one you've taken away of the woman on horseback and the one that arrived yesterday. That makes six in all.'

'What do you mean, "the one that arrived yesterday"?'

Missy held up the mirror-image painting, which was still under her arm. 'This one. It came with a note.'

She handed the piece of paper to her grandfather, who read the few brief words silently. Then he lowered the paper and said, 'I see.'

'What's going on, Grandpa? What is it? And why were the other pictures hidden?'

'They weren't hidden, they were just stored.'

'They're not catalogued.'

'No.' Richard King's face looked different now. The confident grandfather she was used to seeing had melted away and been replaced by a man who looked increasingly uncomfortable.

'Why not? I know how meticulous you are about logging

every painting. You've drummed it into me since I was little. Why aren't they recorded?'

'Because . . . because I'm not certain what they are.'

'*What* they are, or *whose* they are?' Missy asked with a note of panic in her voice.

'I need to make sure.'

'Are they by John Macready?'

'No, of course not.' Her grandfather hesitated, then added, 'I don't know.'

'But if they're not by Munnings, why have we got them? If you know they're not genuine, you wouldn't have them in the gallery. I mean, we can't sell them, can we? So why have we got them?'

Her grandfather looked flustered. 'It's a long story.'

'Are you going to tell me? I mean, I think I ought to know. If we sold a Munnings as genuine and it's really a fake, then at best we'd be in deep trouble and at worst it would be the end of King's Fine Art. You've built this firm on respectability.' Missy stared at him uncomprehendingly. Her grandfather avoided her eye. She got up and walked towards him, laying her hand on his shoulder. 'Grandpa, please! Share this with me. If we're to sort all this out, I need to know.'

Richard King sighed heavily and seemed simultaneously to diminish in stature. 'Sit down,' he said softly.

Missy did as she was bid and sat down once again on the sofa.

'A long time ago – I suppose it's around sixty years now . . .' Almost immediately he was lost in reverie. He murmured to himself, 'Goodness, where does the time go?' Missy watched as he collected his thoughts, then continued, 'I was at university in Oxford. I had a group of friends. Your grandmother was one of them, and John Macready was another.'

'And Harry Ballantyne?'

'Yes.'

'And Lord Bedlington?'

'Yes. Five of us. Well, after university we all went our own ways. Your grandmother and I never heard from any of them for years and years. And then, in the mid-sixties, a few years after Munnings's death, when we'd just arrived in Bath, I was sent a couple of his pictures to sell.'

'Genuine ones?' asked Missy.

'I thought so. They came from a collector in the south of France, not someone I knew.'

'And you sold them?'

'Yes.'

'For a lot of money?'

'Oh, nothing like as much as they fetch now, but a tidy sum, yes.'

'And that was that?'

'Not quite. Every few years another one would arrive. I thought nothing of it. Collectors do occasionally sell individual paintings, either to keep the wolf away from the door or to reinvest in others. I bought five paintings from this particular collector over, I suppose, about thirty years. They were all by Munnings. Then I came across some work by John Macready. He'd been selling reasonably well in other galleries. I'd never been interested in them myself, but I'd acquired one with a group of other paintings a few years earlier and I had that funny feeling . . .'

'Intuition?'

'Yes. You have it, too, don't you? I can't paint to save my life, but I understand paintings. I have a feel for them. I sense things in them. Maybe not as strongly as I once did, but I do still sort of "feel" them as well as look at them.'

'And you saw similarities with Munnings in Macready's work?'

'More than that. I knew at once that the Munningses I'd sold were by Macready. We'd all met Munnings while we were at Oxford. Mac, your grandmother and Ballantyne even went to watch him paint for a couple of days. Munnings thought quite highly of Mac. Suddenly it all dropped into place: the fact that the paintings had come from the south of France, where Macready was living with Leo Bedlington, that Leo Bedlington's father had owned paintings by Munnings. The alarm bells rang.'

Missy was wide-eyed now. 'So what did you do?'

'I tried to buy them back. I thought the only way I could save the firm would be to take them out of circulation.'

'And did you find them?'

'One or two of them.'

'But not all?'

'No. It took me a long time to locate them all, and of course the prices kept going up.'

'So why not just let them stay out there, in private collections?'

'Because when they came up for sale, the fact that this gallery had sold them as genuine would be a part of their provenance. I couldn't risk someone discovering that they were really fakes when they were originally sold by King's Fine Art. It would have ruined us . . . could still ruin us.'

'So the painting I bought in the auction last week, is that a fake?'

'I think so. The trouble is that I'm not quite so certain as I used to be. I bought that one back for sentimental reasons as much as to preserve the firm's name. It was not one that I should have ever sold. If I'd kept it, I doubt that I'd have been sent another. It was a sort of test, I suppose – a test that I failed. I think it was sent to me to see if love was more powerful than money. '

Missy looked bewildered. 'I don't understand.'

'It's a painting of your grandmother, when she was a

student. It was painted the day they went to see Munnings. Well, the original one was.'

'Oh my goodness,' Missy murmured. 'So that's what it was. Jamie said it reminded him of me . . .'

'Sorry?'

'Nothing. Just remembering.'

'Yes. Remembering. I should have been less concerned with making money and relied more on my intuition. To fly in the face of it can prove an expensive mistake.'

'But if the one you've bought is a fake, it means that you've effectively lost three quarters of a million pounds.'

'Yes.' Richard King lowered himself into the chair by the desk. 'I'm afraid we've lost rather more than that over the last few years.'

'Grandpa, are we in trouble?'

'Well, our finances are not as strong as they might be . . .'

'How much trouble?'

'We have a seven-million-pound overdraft.'

Missy slumped back on the sofa. 'Oh my God!'

'But we have almost enough stock to cover it.'

'And the gallery? And Peel Place?'

'Not quite that much. Mortgaged, I'm afraid.'

'But couldn't you just have come clean and admitted that we'd made a mistake with these paintings?'

'Of course I could. I could say, "Sorry, we're not as good at spotting genuine paintings as we should be." That would be wonderful for market confidence, wouldn't it? People buy from us because of the very fact that we know our stuff, Missy.'

'But paintings are reattributed all the time.'

'Old Masters, yes. There are Holbeins that have been Holbeins, then English School, then Anglo-Italian School and then Holbeins again. That's scholarship, not forgery. There will be no question of attribution over these Munningses –

only over the attribution of blame to the man who sold them.'

Missy got up and walked across the room. She found it difficult to sit still now. Up and down she paced, running over in her mind the possibilities and probabilities that could result from her grandfather's actions. 'So why did John Macready paint fake Munningses?'

'To make money of course, for himself and Leo Bedlington. Leo had lost everything to death duties and Mac was living with him. He obviously saw it as a way of staving off further financial problems. He might even have done it just for Leo.'

'But why did the paintings come to you? Why would you get someone who had been a friend of yours at Oxford to sell them when you knew he'd get into trouble if they were found to be fake?'

'Ah, yes.' Richard King looked uncomfortable.

'Did you fall out?' asked Missy.

'In a manner of speaking, yes.'

She looked at him questioningly, but somehow felt unable to ask any more.

Her grandfather was clearly finding it difficult to explain. He attempted to form words and then did not speak. He lifted his hand and lowered it, then shifted in his chair until finally he said, 'I think John Macready was in love with me.'

Missy looked at him wide-eyed.

'Oh, I know it's difficult to believe, but it happened even then, you know, although we didn't speak about it as much.' He paused before continuing, 'I turned him down, and hell hath no fury.' Richard thought for a moment, then said, 'The painting that arrived yesterday seems to be some kind of apology . . . if it's genuine. It isn't one that I've ever seen. But why would it arrive now? Mac died more than ten years ago.'

'So did he sell you the paintings to get his own back? As revenge?'

'Yes. That and to avenge a friend of his whose true love I stole.'

'Oh, Grandpa, what an unkind thing to do to you.'

'Oh, I don't think I was the kindest of people myself back then.'

'You were young.'

'Yes.'

'And unsure of yourself?'

'Not in that way, no. I knew I wanted your grandmother. It's just that I wasn't the only one.'

'Harry Ballantyne?'

'Yes.'

'Rivals in love?'

Her grandfather nodded.

'And that's why you don't want me going out with Jamie Ballantyne.'

Richard King got up from his desk. 'It's not just that, Artemis.'

Missy felt a shiver go down her spine. He only called her Artemis when he was being serious. She responded firmly, 'Grandpa, it really is my own life. I can't keep your feud going. I *won't* keep your feud going. Just because you and Harry Ballantyne fell out over a girl doesn't mean that this Montague– Capulet thing should be kept going for generations. We're not rivals any more. It's time we got on with our lives.'

'But—' he tried to interrupt.

'No, Grandpa. I'm not giving up Jamie, and certainly not now. I need a friend as well as a lover to help me see my way through all this.'

But Richard King was determined. 'It's not quite as simple as that.'

'What do you mean?'

'Harry Ballantyne was your grandmother's lover at Oxford.' Richard was red in the face now. 'It's something that your grandmother and I have never talked about. Nobody knows it except the two of us, and we've never referred to it in fifty years.'

'What, for goodness' sake?'

'Your father is not my son. Your grandmother and I found we were unable to have children some time after Patrick was born. It was then that your grandmother told me that Patrick is Harry's son, not mine. You and Jamie Ballantyne have the same grandfather. Now do you see why I don't want you going out with him?'

29

Villa Fabrice,
Menton, Côte d'Azur
December 2007

Still to be neat, still to be drest,
As you were going to a feast;
Still to be powdered, still perfumed,
Lady, it is to be presumed,
Though art's hid causes are not found,
All is not sweet, all is not sound.

Epicene (1609), Ben Johnson

The South of France is mild in December. Mild, but not always warm, and the old woman slapped her hands against her sides to improve the circulation in her body; the rough woollen shawl seemed suddenly thin in the chill gust of air that blew up from the sea. The Villa Fabrice was empty now, cleared of its furniture and its draperies, such as they were. The front door was open, and the owner of the local *brocante* had finally left with the last lot of cardboard boxes that had been filled with the things too inconsequential to accompany their more elegant roommates, which had been sent for auction in England.

She should have done the job sooner really, but she had not had the heart. Now she went from room to room with a broom, giving the place a final sweep. It broke her heart to think that they were both gone now. Both her men. Well, both her boys really. She had washed and cleaned and cooked for them for fifty years. Since she had been made a young widow she had no children of her own, just the two of them to mother. But not any more.

Still, perhaps now she could have the holiday she had always promised herself. In Paris, perhaps, or London. Maybe she would go to London.

Pah! A ridiculous dream. Why would she want to go there? What would she find to do there? The Tower? The Palace? There were towers and palaces here, what need had she of more? But she would quite like to go to Oxford. That was where they had both been to college. That was what had made them the way they were. Ach! Now there was a good reason for steering clear of Oxford.

She mused on the last half-century. Was it really that long? Had she really been here for fifty whole years? With a few hiccups, yes. A few rows and arguments. One or two broken pieces of china. But they were all, as Milord would say, '*Tempêtes en tasses*'. Silly man. Nice man. Kind man. Different from the other one. But then he was good in a different way. Dry, like she was. A man of few words in the same way that she was a woman of few words. When he was painting there was no talking to him. She would leave his coffee and his brioche on a stool by the door without saying a word if she wanted a quiet life.

But he looked after Milord, in his own funny way. Acted as a kind of protector. She thought, when she was young, that they might be lovers. But she soon learned that such was not the case. She thought that Monsieur might have a lover down in the town; he occasionally went off for a few days. But she never found out anything for sure, and certainly no gossip came her way.

Then there was the swimming accident. The day their lives changed for ever. It was she who had made Monsieur his breakfast. She who had remonstrated with him about not swimming in the sea on a full stomach. But would he listen? Did he ever? She had watched as he walked down the winding path from the house that one last time, his towel over his shoulder, whistling softly until his whistle was drowned out by the sound of the wind in the mimosa tree.

It was she who found the towel on the tree trunk by the beach two hours later. And his shoes, neatly stowed below it. But there was no sign of Monsieur.

She sat with Milord all that day and through the night, but still Monsieur did not return.

Week after week they combed the beaches, and waited, the two of them, thinking that one day he would walk through the door and rebuke them for thinking anything unusual had happened. But he did not. He did not come back and they gradually learned to live their lives without him.

Milord changed from that day on. He said very little, but looked out to sea a lot. He was angry for a while, and embittered, but then he became accepting. Quiet. It broke her heart to see him like that. For ten years he lived quietly, seeing only the very occasional visitor. The end, when it came, was swift, praise God. He had not suffered long. Not from the disease anyway, though he had suffered in a different way every day since the loss of Monsieur.

When he knew the end was coming he said he wanted to write some letters. She gave him pen and paper, and summoned the notary as he requested so that he could finalise his will. And there it was. Finished and done with.

She brushed the last pile of dust out through the open French windows, where it was seized by the breeze and taken out towards the sea.

Gone. It was all gone now. She bolted the windows, turned the key in the lock and slipped it into her pocket. She would take it down to the notary later in the day. He would know what to do with it. It was he, after all, who had told her what to do with the parcel. She had found it tucked away behind

Monsieur's bed. Milord had insisted that the room was never altered, never tidied, in case Monsieur should return one day. The room was to be kept clean but nothing was to be moved or disturbed – they both knew how Monsieur resented anyone interfering with his 'things'. 'You move them, I lose them!' was his frequent cry.

She had come across the thin parcel when the bed had been carried out. It had been wedged between the bedstead and the wall. It felt like a picture in a frame, and she was curious about it, but she did not open it, as it was properly wrapped and addressed in Monsieur's hand. There was a letter with it. She did not read English well, but the notary had translated. It said that the parcel was to be sent directly to the addressee and that a note for the recipient was already included. The parcel was to be insured and there were even some old franc notes to cover postage. Quite a lot of them.

The notary had looked a little doubtful, but he could see the worried look in Madame Farrage's eyes. Eventually he suggested that she simply take it down to the *bureau de poste* and do as her former employer had asked of her. He would turn a blind eye.

And that was what she had done. It was over a week ago now and there had been no repercussions, so perhaps all was well. Perhaps the parcel had been expected, though why it should be so more than ten years after it had been wrapped she could not understand.

But why should she worry? It was none of her business. She had only done what the Monsieur had instructed her to do. And now her work here was finished. She leaned the broom against the end post of the veranda and began the slow walk back to her cottage at the top of the hill, muttering to herself. Bath. It was a strange name for a place. But then, so was Bains. Maybe she should use the money to go to Bath.

But no. Paris would be more fun. Fun! The very idea. She was rather too old for fun now. The fun was gone from her life, along with Monseur and Milord. They had had fun. Once.

30

Bath
December 2007

Surprises are foolish things. The pleasure is not enhanced, and the inconvenience is often considerable.

Emma (1816), Jane Austen

Jamie sat in the car outside King's Fine Art, tapping the steering wheel. He had so much to tell her, so much to show her. Oh, come on! Why was she so slow? She had told him that she was pathologically punctual, yet it was now a quarter past seven. The paintings were in the boot of the car, his grandparents had given him the key to their house, and he was desperate to share all these things with her.

She emerged from the house at twenty past seven and walked across to the car looking preoccupied.

'I'd almost given up on you,' he said.

Missy made no reply but slipped into the passenger seat. She did not kiss him.

'Oh dear, bad day?' he asked gently.

Missy nodded. 'The worst.'

'Do you still want to see the house?'

She did her best to sound enthusiastic. 'Yes, of course.'

'We could have walked, only I've got some things to show you. They're in the boot.'

Jamie could not work out why she was so down, so uncommunicative. She seemed to be in a different place to him. He told himself that this was real life, that he could not always expect her to be bright and bouncy, but deep down he did feel disappointed – he had not expected the bloom to wear off their love affair quite so quickly. Added to that, he was worried at her reaction to the paintings. What would she say? What would she think of them?

It took only a couple of minutes to drive to the Circus. Jamie parked up and got out of the car. She had hardly spoken during the short journey. Never mind. He would cheer her up when she saw the house. He would wait a while before he showed her the paintings in case they put her in an even darker mood. He went round and opened her door. She got out and looked up at the imposing frontage. 'Impressive,' she said softly, but, he thought, without much feeling.

'Hang on,' he instructed. He went round to the boot of the car and lifted out one of the pictures, wrapped in a blanket. Then he picked up a cool bag and winked at her. She did her best to smile. 'Right, time for the private view.' She walked beside him to the front door and waited while he unlocked it. 'Welcome to my little pad,' he said as she stepped inside.

He took her through the rooms on each of the floors, showing her in cupboards and round strange corners, hoping that she would feel as excited by it all as he did, but she only seemed to get quieter and quieter. Finally they reached the top floor and he put down the painting on an old chest of drawers, took down a couple of stacked chairs and unzipped the cool bag. 'Champagne,' he said. 'To celebrate.'

'Oh,' she said. That was all.

'Look, I'm sorry if it's a bit much,' he offered, thinking that perhaps he was being too self-centred, too intent on showing her his own world and not listening to the reason why she had had a bad day. 'But there is something else, something that I'm rather concerned about.'

Missy heard the words, but her mind was elsewhere.

Jamie picked up the blanket-wrapped painting and slipped it from its cover. 'We're handling the sale of Lord Bedlington's estate and his pictures arrived this week. I thought you ought to see them.'

Missy came out of her reverie. She looked at the painting and let out an involuntary gasp. It was an exact copy of one that she had found in the storeroom at King's Fine Art, except that she knew it could not be a copy: it was the real thing.

'Oh God!' she said.

'What do you think?' asked Jamie. He was worried now, worried at her reaction and worried at the implications. 'Is it real?' he asked.

'Almost certainly,' she murmured. Then she asked softly, 'Are there any more?'

'Yes. If you wait here, I'll go and bring them up.'

Missy nodded. While Jamie went downstairs, she took a large gulp of the champagne. She would need every ounce of courage she had, and a shot of alcohol would help.

A few moments later he returned and leaned the other pictures side by side against the attic wall. They were all there: the start of the race, the gypsies at Epsom, the gypsy encampment, the woman on the bay and even the painting of her grandmother on the grey. Every last one of them she had seen in the last few days, but on different canvases.

'What do you think?' he asked. 'What's it all about?'

Missy took a deep breath. 'It's all about jealousy, really,' she said.

Jamie looked bemused. 'Jealousy?'

'And what it can lead to.' Missy could not take her eyes off the paintings. Her eyes ran from one to another as she explained to Jamie the best she could from what her grandfather had gone on to tell her. 'When our grandparents were at uni together, they had a bit of a thing about Munnings. Well, one of them did, a man called John Macready. He even went to see Munnings – in Dedham, where he lived. Macready was a painter, a good painter. Munnings thought very highly of him.'

Jamie listened attentively, but Missy did not meet his eye.

'My grandmother went with Macready and your grand-father to Dedham and ended up sitting to Munnings. That's her on the grey.'

'The one I sold to you?'

'No, the one you didn't sell to me. Mine is a copy.'

'Oh God!'

'My grandfather didn't go. He was in bed with the flu. Anyway, to cut a long story short, this John Macready char-acter didn't approve of Grandpa and Grandma marrying, so he decided to work a bit of mischief and at the same time help out Lord Bedlington, who he was now living with in the south of France. He painted copies of all Bedlington's Munningses over the space of about thirty years and sent them to Grandpa, who flogged them thinking they were real.'

'Just because he didn't approve of the marriage?'

'And because he and Leo Bedlington needed the money. Once Grandpa realised what had happened, he bought back every painting that he'd sold – often at inflated market prices.'

'That's dreadful. But why did John Macready take it out on your grandfather?'

Missy shrugged. She was reluctant to give away all the secrets that she had been told: about Mac being in love with Richard, about Richard spurning him and about Jamie's own grandfather being in love with her grandmother. She so wanted to tell him, but something inside her could not share it. Least of all, she could not divulge the one secret that had been eating away at her heart from the moment that it had been shared with her.

'It's all a bit of a mess, isn't it?' offered Jamie.

'You can say that again.'

'So what do I do now?' asked Jamie, looking at the paint-ings and scratching his head.

'You sell them, of course. I have all the copies under lock

and key in our strongroom. As far as everyone else in the
world is concerned, they don't exist. Grandpa's bought his
way out of trouble. It's cost him the business. You might as
well enjoy your commission.' Then she added, 'You won't be
able to sell the one of Grandma, of course, since you sold a
copy to me last week. While I have my copies locked away,
you'll have to keep that particular real one locked away for
a year or two. You'll be able to sell it then, when people think
it's just come on the market again, and make even more
money. At least you'll know it's of my grandmother.'

'But this is dreadful. And you think King's Fine Art really
is in trouble?'

'Oh, yes, I know it is – a seven-million-pound overdraft
and every property mortgaged to the hilt. There will be
enough stock to stave off bankruptcy, but that's about all.
We'll have to sell up.'

Jamie slumped down in a chair. 'I can't believe this.'

'Neither can I, but it's absolutely true.'

Jamie brightened. 'It's absolutely bloody awful, but at least
we've still got each other. We'll find a way through somehow.
It's not as if I'm without means now.'

Missy smiled. 'Oh, Jamie, you're so kind, but it's not going
to work, is it? You with all this' – she gestured around her –
'and me living in some grim little basement flat.'

'That's silly . . .'

'It's not silly at all. It's realistic. We won't have a bean.
King's Fine Art is finished. We'll have the fifty-year exhibition
and then we'll close down. Nothing lasts for ever.'

'Except us. It doesn't mean that we're finished. It doesn't
affect what we've got, does it?'

Missy walked towards him. He had never seen her look
so serious, so low. He was standing up now. She put her
hands on his shoulders and looked into his eyes. 'I'd love to
say it doesn't change anything, but it does. I can't be with

you, Jamie – not with all this going on. I can't do it to the family.'

'Bugger the family. Bugger both families. I don't want to keep alive some old feud just to satisfy the pride of a couple of grandfathers. It's our time now, not theirs. They've had their lives. Why should their messing up affect our happiness? Just because they fell out when they were our age doesn't mean that we can't love each other. Does it?'

'I'm sorry.' She could not look at him now. She bowed her head.

Jamie could hardly believe what he was hearing. 'This isn't true! Tell me I'm imagining things. We said it was special. What happened to that "ease" we had with each other? Did it go flying out of the window at the first little difficulty?'

'It's hardly a little difficulty,' said Missy.

'Well, whatever it is, we're not worth much if we let it spoil what we have. It's not insignificant, I know – it's massive – but we can overcome it. Who cares if your firm goes bust? Who cares if my firm goes bust? You're the most important thing to me and I don't want to lose you.'

She heard the desperate note in his voice, listened as the words caught in his throat. She so wanted to say, 'No, you're right,' and to throw herself into his arms so that he could tell her that it would be all right, that he would sort it all out, but how could she, knowing what her grandfather had just told her? How could they be lovers if they were of the same blood? There was no way round the problem.

'Well?' asked Jamie.

She could hear that he was close to tears, but then she could hardly hold them back herself. 'I'm sorry,' was all she could manage as she ran through the door and down the three flights of stairs, imperilling her life with her blurred vision. Out of the front door she ran, along Brock Street and into the Royal Crescent. The tears were flowing freely now, and her body was wracked with sobs. Feverishly she tried to get her key into the lock, finally succeeding, entering the hallway and slamming the door behind her, to collapse in a heap under the uncomprehending stare of Sir Joshua Reynolds.

At the far end of the street, Jamie watched as the love of his life ran away from him, until he, too, could no longer see for the tears.

31

Rose Cottage, Bradford-on-Avon
Christmas 2007

Oh, what can ail thee knight at arms,
Alone and palely loitering?
'La belle dame sans merci' (1820), John Keats

'God rest ye, merry gentlemen,' intoned the carol singers on his mother's doorstep. He was not merry, and even God offered him little rest from his turbulent thoughts, but he gave them a fiver all the same before shutting the door and going back inside. It should have been the best Christmas he had ever known. Instead it was the worst. She had not contacted him in the two weeks since that fateful day when she had told him it was all over. He had not dared call her, did not want to beg her to reconsider, but he had half hoped that she would call him to say that she was sorry, that it had all been a mistake, perhaps that everything was happening too fast and she wanted to slow things down a little. He would have been happy with that, would have gladly taken it at a pace to suit her. That would have been better than no pace at all. The silence from her was deafening.

And now it was Christmas Eve and the only thing in prospect was dinner with his mother and grandparents in Emma's cottage. Just as well, he thought. Better than being stuck alone in his own house. Solitude had never bothered him before. He had always been happy in his own company. Even being alone in a big house did not fill him with dread. It was just that having accustomed himself to the prospect of Missy being around, having come to look forward to it, even, the fact that she had now withdrawn from his life made it unbearable. He wanted more than anything to enjoy his new-found good fortune, but if it was not to be with her, it did not seem like good fortune at all – only deprivation.

They had been together such a short while, but in that time his life had turned round; he had found it easier to get up in the morning knowing that at some point during the day he was likely to see her. And the nights. It made his heart sink to think of them now. His bed seemed the loneliest place in the world.

He knew he should snap himself out of it. He had faced rejection before. He had got over it. He would get over it again. But then something in him did not want to shake it off this time. Why should he? What was the point? The prospect of a relationship with anyone else was not a consideration. If he could not have Missy, then he would have nobody.

'You're very quiet.'

The voice was his mother's. Jamie was suddenly aware of the silence at the dinner table. They had been talking about heaven knows what and it had been easy enough to let the three of them get on with it, but now all eyes were on him.

'Having second thoughts?' asked his grandfather.

'Sorry?' Jamie was unsure what his grandfather meant. Surely he could not know about her?

'About the Circus?'

It was a relief in a way. 'Oh, no, no, I'm very excited.'

'Well, you don't look it, dear,' chipped in Emma.

Jamie's grandmother reached out and took his hand. 'I think Jamie's mind is somewhere else.' She looked at him fondly and Jamie smiled back at her.

Sally had always been the voice of common sense and reason in the Ballantyne household. Jamie put it down to her Yorkshire background. He had never known his great-grandfather, but Sally spoke of him from time to time and

Jamie felt that he would have appreciated Ernie Bowker's no-nonsense approach to life, much of which his daughter had inherited. She, of all of them, thought the family feud a tiresome distraction, but in deference to her husband she studiously avoided social contact with the Kings. It was easier that way.

Harry had never levelled with her about his university days. Why should he? What young man would think it wise to burden his new wife with a list of his previous conquests? And yet he had never really viewed Eleanor Faraday as a conquest. One night of passion did not, after all, constitute a conquest, did it? Well, not much of one, certainly not as far as Eleanor herself was concerned.

Sally put the acrimony between Richard and her husband down to male pride, nothing more. She had never pressed Harry for information on the intricacies of university life, regarding current reality as more important than history. Men at university got up to all kinds of things. In any event, that was nearly sixty years ago and of even less consequence now than it had been when she had got married.

Nevertheless, she was astute enough to know when a man's preoccupation was down to woman trouble rather than accommodation, though she was not about to pry. She left that to her daughter. Emma did not disappoint.

'So what's Artemis King doing over Christmas?'

At the mention of her name, Sally Ballantyne's eyes widened and Harry sat bolt upright.

Jamie shrugged. 'No idea.'

'Ah!' exclaimed Emma. 'So that's it – lovers' tiff.' She seemed pleased that it had come out into the open, relished sharing the news with her parents.

Jamie felt himself colouring up. 'Rather more than a tiff, actually. I've been dumped.' He saw little point in beating about the bush. He might as well admit it and clear the air.

At least that way he would not have to cope with innuendo and sideways glances for the entire Christmas holiday.

His grandmother's tone was sympathetic. 'Oh dear, how sad, and just before Christmas, too,' she said.

Harry was normally content to let the women do the talking when it came to affairs of the heart, but he was not about to sit idly by and watch his grandson being grilled, taunted or fussed over by two women with varied motives, whoever the third party. His daughter was clearly delighted that the affair had been broken off, and his wife evidently hoped that her grandson would pour his heart out to her. He himself had been totally unaware of the liaison. It surprised him and made him a little uneasy, but then he reasoned that if it was all over, there was little point in worrying about it.

'I don't think Jamie's love life has anything to do with the rest of us,' he offered.

'Thank you, Granddad,' was Jamie's heartfelt response.

'Whatever we might think.' He looked at Jamie over the top of the spectacles that he had been using to read a cracker motto. The remark was not lost on the two women, who momentarily fell silent. Harry continued, '"What do you get if you cross a pullover with a kangaroo?"' he asked, examining the small strip of paper.

'Oh, Daddy! That's such an old one,' groaned Emma exasperatedly.

'Well, how about a cup of coffee instead, then?' asked Harry. 'Give Jamie and me a break from female conversation.'

Sally smiled indulgently. 'Come along,' she said in the direction of Emma. 'It won't actually take two of us, but I think we'd better do as he says.'

The two women got up and carried out the plates and cutlery, leaving Jamie and his grandfather alone at the table.

'Do you fancy a cigar?' asked Harry.

'Not for me,' replied Jamie. 'They give me a sore throat,

and even though I'm not working for the next few days, I'd rather not risk it.'

'Well, I'm on my own, then,' said Harry. 'My Christmas treat, though I don't think your grandmother approves, or your mother. Emma probably thinks it'll stunt my growth.' He shot Jamie a jocular glance, but the sentiment was lost on his grandson. Harry went over to the fireplace in search of a box of matches. He found them and made a small hole in the end of the cigar, before lighting it and inhaling the smoke luxuriantly. 'First of the year,' he murmured, 'and the last.'

Whatever else Harry Ballantyne was, he was not unaware of atmosphere and mood. He had been an auctioneer. It was his job to sense these things. He looked at Jamie, who was still sitting at the table. 'I didn't know you were hooked up with Artemis King.'

'Past tense,' shot back Jamie.

His grandfather ignored the reproachful reply. 'I expect you're waiting for me to say, "Just as well," or some such sentiment.'

'Everybody else has.'

'Since when did your mother constitute everybody else?'

'You wouldn't have minded, then?'

'I can't say it thrills me, but then it's not really up to me. I choose not to have much to do with her grandfather. Our business paths cross from time to time and that's enough, but I can't really form a judgement on his granddaughter, if I'm honest.'

'Well, her family weren't too keen on us being together, either. Positively discouraging, so I expect it's relief all round.'

'So that's that, then, is it?'

'Looks like it,' muttered Jamie.

'And you're just going to let it go?'

'I don't have much choice. It was pretty final.'

'Any reason given?'

Jamie thought for a moment, and then said, 'I think the Kings are about to go under.'

His grandfather put down his cigar in an ashtray. 'I must go and get my hearing sorted. Your grandmother tells me it's not what it was. I thought you said they were about to go under.'

'I did.'

Harry Ballantyne dropped down into an easy chair by the fire. 'Good God! Are you sure?'

'That's what Missy says.' Jamie deliberated what to tell his grandfather. Not wanting to betray Missy's trust, he said, 'Something to do with some ill-advised buying. I think it's confidential, Granddad. Don't go telling anybody. I wouldn't want it to get out from us, whatever we think of them.'

'Well, I'll be . . . I thought they were as safe as houses. Established firm and all that. Richard should be resting on his laurels now, not coping with financial difficulties. Did she say how it happened?'

Jamie shrugged, conscious of the fact that he had already said too much.

Harry thought for a few moments and then asked, 'And you think that's why she finished with you?'

Jamie nodded.

'Family pride,' murmured Harry, and then looked thoughtful. After a few moments he said, 'You look pretty cut up about it.'

'You could say that.'

'The one for you, was she?' Harry picked up his cigar again and relit it.

'I thought so. I really thought so.'

'Well, you'd better do something about it, then, hadn't you?'

Jamie looked up, having been intent on studying the pattern of his mother's Rajasthani rug. 'Not up to me, is it?'

'Who else is it up to?'

'Missy. She was the one who broke it off.'

'Mmm. Sounds a bit defeatist to me.'

'Granddad!' Jamie was both surprised and irritated at his grandfather's stance. Normally he did not interfere. Normally he was the one member of the family he would go to when he wanted to talk of things other than his personal life. His mother would intrude unbidden, and his grandmother would always offer a shoulder to cry on, but his grandfather was the one person who would snap him out of any low period by talking of things other than those that preoccupied him. The fact that he appeared to be encouraging him to take up with a King was also totally unexpected.

'Oh, I know it's none of my business. Tell me to shut up if you want, but if you're sure that she's the one – and it seems that you are – then don't let her talk herself out of it. Unless you think she wouldn't be happy with you. That's different. But it sounds to me as though you think that she's keen.'

'I thought she was. I know she was. It's just that circumstances seem to have changed things.'

'Head versus heart, eh?'

'I suppose so.'

Harry drew on his cigar and exhaled deeply. 'So you're just going to wait and see if she comes round?'

Jamie sighed.

His grandfather put down the cigar and murmured thoughtfully, 'Why is it that the second minute of smoking those things is never as good as the first? I think they call it the law of diminishing returns.' He looked across at his grandson and said, 'Don't lose her, not if you know she's the one.'

Jamie looked up. 'Why are you so concerned?'

He watched as Harry got up and walked to the window. He was looking out over the wintry garden of the cottage while he spoke. 'I wouldn't want this to go any further. It was all a long, long time ago, and I've had a lovely life with your grandmother, lovely, but there was somebody before her. Somebody that I really, well . . .' He paused for a few moments, gathering his thoughts. 'I've always wondered . . . if things had been different . . . what it would have been like. It was very . . . strong.' He turned round to face his grandson. 'I wouldn't want you to go through the same – not knowing what might have been. That's all. If it was just very pleasant, a nice way of passing the time until something else came along, fair enough, but if it's more than that, something you've never felt before or think you might never feel again, then fight for it. Don't give in. Don't take it lying down.'

Jamie did not know what to say, not least because his grandfather was encouraging his relationship with a member of a family he so disliked. He tried to find the words, but before any came his mother and grandmother entered the room with the tray of coffee.

'Here we are, then. What have you two been talking about?' asked Emma. 'Put the world to rights, have you?'

'Not quite,' replied Harry. 'Not quite.'

32

Peel Place, Corsham
Christmas 2007

Generations pass while some trees stand, and old families last
not three oaks.

Hydriotaphia, (1658), Sir Thomas Browne

Missy's Christmas was, if anything, even more deadly than
Jamie's. At her grandfather's house in Wiltshire, the atmosphere was funereal. Only Patrick's presence would lift the
gloom. Patrick, the one who had had the toughest time of
them all. Patrick, the one who had lost his wife in childbirth
and gone off the rails. Patrick, who had finally come back
home and joined the family firm, albeit half-heartedly. Missy
could not think why she should regard him as the only bright
light in prospect this Christmas, bearing in mind their history.
She knew she had every right to despise him for his cavalier
attitude to her and his self-centred approach to life, but still
he lifted her spirits whenever they met – exasperated and
amused her in equal measure.

Richard still considered him a liability. Missy was a far
better bet when it came to needing someone he could depend
on, and look what had happened now: the firm he had hoped
to hand on to her was on the brink of ruin. There really
seemed no way out of it, and all because of his own short-
comings, his own stupidity and, from Mac's point of view,
his own greed. If he had kept the painting of Eleanor on the
horse, put his love of the woman in the picture above his
desire to get on in life and make more money, then he never
would have discovered it was a fake and fate might have

smiled on him. As it was, fate, aided and abetted by John Macready, had dealt the final blow so late in life that he wondered if he would ever pick himself up. What was the point?

For most of Christmas Eve he had shut himself away in his study, leaving Missy and her grandmother to prepare the evening meal and wait to see if Patrick turned up at all. He had promised to do so, before going off with his latest amour on a cruise. He had treated the news from his father with his usual equanimity. 'Not to worry,' he had said. So long as there was enough to pay the bills he would find something else to do. Nothing lasts for ever. And, anyway, he had a few deals cooking that should see him through.

There was no word of what Missy would do. It did not seem to have crossed her father's mind that she was now high and dry without a job and with the prospect of not even having a roof over her head. But then, why should she be surprised? He had left her alone for the first twenty-odd years of her life, why should he start caring what happened to her now? She really should hate him more, and yet, for some unfathomable reason, she could not.

Peeling Brussels sprouts with her grandmother was not how she had envisaged spending her Christmas Eve. She wanted to be with Jamie, sitting in front of a log fire with his arms round her, talking of the future, *their* future.

'I know it's sad,' said her grandmother, 'but try not to blame your grandfather.'

'I don't blame him,' replied Missy, tossing another sprout into the saucepan of water on the kitchen table. 'I just can't help thinking that it all seems such a waste.'

'Yes.'

'I mean, what will you do? Where will you live?'

Her grandmother was putting a brave front on it. 'Oh, we'll manage. We'll move into a flat, perhaps a little cottage, with a garden, a small garden. We won't be destitute.' She smiled, but Missy was not being fooled.

'But Grandpa can't live in a small flat, or even a cottage. His whole life has been lived in big houses. That's what's important to him.'

'The first house in Bristol wasn't so big,' mused Eleanor. 'Maybe it's just what we've all got used to.'

'I suppose,' murmured Missy.

'You too,' said her grandmother.

'Yes.'

'Your grandfather told me, you know,' Eleanor confided.

'Told you what?' Missy looked apprehensive.

'About Jamie Ballantyne.'

'I see.' Missy looked embarrassed. Her grandmother knew, then, that her granddaughter had been told that Richard was not Patrick's real father, and that, therefore, he was not her real grandfather, that the elegant seventy-nine-year-old with whom she was at the moment peeling sprouts had had a love affair before she married, an affair with Harry Ballantyne.

'I'm sorry that he told you.'

'You mean you think I should have been kept in the dark?'

'No, of course not. I mean that *I* should have told you, not your grandfather. He's the one who's had to bear all the hurt.'

'Not you?' asked Missy pointedly.

Her grandmother put down the knife she was using to peel the sprouts. 'Shall we have a glass?'

Missy nodded. 'Yes, please. I could do with something.'

'Me too.'

'I'll get it.' Missy went to the fridge in the corner of her grandmother's kitchen and took out a bottle of chilled Chablis. 'This all right?'

'Perfect.'

Missy found two glasses, pulled the cork and poured two

generous measures of the wine, handing one to her grand-mother, who took a small sip.

'I don't think there's any point in disturbing your grand-father. Not for a while. Leave him to brood.'

Missy sipped her wine but said nothing.

'I expect you want to know how it happened?' offered Eleanor.

'Oh, Grandma, I—'

'No. You should know. It was a long time ago, but you ought to know about it. It affects your life, after all.'

'Yes.'

'I'm sorry about that, Missy – about Jamie. I really am. If there was anything at all that I could do . . . But I can't turn back the clock.'

Missy took a large gulp of wine to bolster her courage and asked, 'Was it a quick fling, then?'

Her grandmother tried to contain her surprise at the direct-ness of the question. 'Well, yes, I suppose it was in a way.'

Missy looked at her sideways.

'Oh, don't look like that. It was not quite that straight-forward. We were all at university. Three years we'd been together – me, your grandfather, Leo Bedlington, John Macready and Harry Ballantyne. Leo and Mac, as we called him, were never really interested in girls, but your grand-father and Harry were both quite keen on me, apparently.'

'And you?'

'Well, I married your grandfather.'

'But . . . ?'

Eleanor looked across at the kitchen door, which was firmly closed. There were no sounds of activity in any other part of the house. 'Oh dear, it was all such a long time ago.'

'Grandma!'

'I was very fond of your grandfather.'

'But you were in love with Harry?'

Missy saw the trancelike look in her grandmother's eyes.

Eleanor nodded. 'Yes, yes, I was.' She spoke as though she were far away.

'And he with you?'

'I never realised, not until the other week. When we were at university, we'd been to see an artist.'

'Munnings?'

'Yes.' Eleanor seemed to come back to reality for a moment. 'Oh, of course, your grandfather told you.' Then she slipped back once more into her reverie. 'Well, it was in the hotel. We had to stay over. Your grandfather was back in Oxford with a cold – he said it was flu, but it was a cold.'

Missy smiled at her grandmother's ability to make a joke even when opening her heart.

'Harry finally melted a little. He'd never given me much hope that he had any feelings for me until then. Well, it was just a sort of torrent, I suppose – of emotion, I mean. We had one . . . well . . . glorious night together and I had no reservations at all. It was wonderful.'

Missy saw a gleam in her grandmother's now tear-filled eyes and felt her own welling up.

'Oh, Grandma. So why didn't you carry on, with Harry I mean?'

'Who knows? We had no chance to talk the following day. Mac was having breakfast with Harry when I came down. Then we went to see Munnings again and after that Harry drove us back to Oxford. He dropped me off. It was difficult to say anything, what with Mac being there and the traffic and things. We just had to say goodbye quite briefly.'

'But you thought he knew?'

'I was certain of it.'

'So what happened?'

'Nothing, absolutely nothing. Harry just disappeared. He'd said he wanted to travel about the country – to look for somewhere to start up an auction business – so I suppose he went off and did it.'

'Without even saying goodbye?'

'Apparently. Mac was the same. I never got to say goodbye to him, either.'

'Oh.'

'It's all right. I know why that was now. Your grandfather told me about Mac, about being in love with him, but only when the picture business had got out of hand.'

'So you never saw Harry again?'

'Not until we came to Bath. I needed to buy Patrick a bicycle, so I went to the local auction rooms. You can imagine how I felt when I saw Harry. I thought I'd die.'

'And did he say anything? Like sorry? Or explain why he ran out on you?'

'No. He seemed almost as shocked as me.'

'How dreadful. Well, I think you ended up with the right man.'

'Yes. Your grandfather was very kind, very understanding.'

'And nobody knew? About you and Harry?'

'Oh, I think Leo Bedlington knew, and probably Mac as well. Not about the baby, just about Harry and I being . . . well . . .'

'But what about Grandpa? Did he know?'

'Not at the beginning. He suspected that Harry and I were attracted to one another. Well, he knew we were, I suppose. There was always a rivalry between them. The day after Harry and I had . . . been together . . . I went to see him, to tell him that I wanted to be with Harry, but I couldn't actually tell him before he produced a ring and asked me to marry him.'

'So you just said yes?'

Eleanor saw the look of incredulity on Missy's face. 'No, of course not. I told him as gently as I possibly could that I was fond of him and I didn't want to hurt him, but that I just couldn't marry him.'

'How did he take it?'

'Oh, very much as you'd imagine. He was shocked, and disappointed, and said that if I ever changed my mind, he'd be there for me. I didn't tell him about Harry. Not then.' Eleanor took another sip of wine and put down her glass before continuing. 'I went back to finish packing, expecting Harry to come and find me. Well, he didn't, so I went and looked for him. I found that he'd already packed his bags. They were on the bed. I waited and waited, but he didn't come, so I wrote him a note and went back to my digs. He didn't respond and I went back to see if he'd returned. His bags were gone, and all I could see was my note screwed up in the waste-paper basket.'

'Oh, how dreadful!'

'Yes. It was very hard. I thought that I must have assumed he felt more for me than he did.'

Eleanor seemed to lose herself in her thoughts for a while; then she murmured, 'Though Leo seems to think that Harry really did . . . so why . . . ?'

Missy waited for a few moments before asking, 'And Grandpa?'

'Well, a few weeks later I found out that I was pregnant. I knew it was Harry's. I hadn't been with anyone else. I didn't know what to do. I thought of getting rid of it, but I simply couldn't, and anyway, it had been created out of love. Well, that was my reasoning – not that I had much proof of that, with Harry having gone away.' Eleanor smiled, a stoical sort of smile, the sort of smile that people smile when they are making the best of things. 'And then your grandfather came back into my life, found me and asked me again. He said that he understood that I didn't love him, but he hoped I would in time and that it was a chance he was prepared to take.'

'So you said yes?' asked Missy.

'I did.'

'Without telling him?'

Eleanor looked at her granddaughter with haunted eyes. 'Oh, I wanted to be honest with him, believe me I did. There are some things that I find it very difficult to do, Artemis, and one of them is deceive, at least not for my own ends. I was a young girl who had lost her father in the war. I wanted to prove to myself that I was capable of getting a degree and having a life of my own, but I came to realise that what I wanted more than anything was a family. It may sound odd nowadays, old-fashioned even, but that's how I felt. I wanted to be a mother with a family more than anything else in the world, almost at any price. I should have been honest with your grandfather. At least then I would have known he would be marrying me because of who I really was, rather than because he had put me on a pedestal. But I didn't. I thought at the time that it would have been folly to do so. That he would not have married me. I think now I was wrong. I didn't tell him the truth until we found that we couldn't have children together, but by then, of course, he must have known.'

'And did you tell him that you were in love with Harry?'

'There are some things in life that don't need to be said. I thought that would be rubbing salt in the wound. It was enough that he knew I had borne another man's child and that we could never have children together.'

'And he didn't mind?'

'Of course he minded. It hurt him deeply. He was still prepared to stay with me, though, and that, in my mind, makes him a prince among men.'

'So is kindness more important than love?'

Eleanor shook her head. 'Oh, Artemis, in an ideal world love is worth more than anything, but I wasn't in an ideal world. I was in a nightmare world. I was about to be an unmarried mother at a time when only "trollops", as my

mother would call them, did that sort of thing. I had no father
and a mother who had all but lost her reason on account of
the only man she had ever loved being killed in the war. I
had two choices: break my mother's heart – what was left of
it – and bring up the child on my own or agree to marry a
man of whom I was very fond and who would be its father.
What would you have done?'

Missy looked away. 'I don't know.'

'No. Well, I did the best I could. The thing that seemed
right at the time.'

'And nobody knew?'

'I think Leo Bedlington suspected, bless him. He was always
quite astute. He gave me away, you know.'

'No. Grandpa never said.'

'Well, he doesn't talk about the wedding much. I don't
think it was quite the celebration he had hoped it would be.'

'And does Dad know that Harry Ballantyne is his father?'
She paused for a moment, then added, 'And that Emma is
his half-sister?'

'We told him when we thought he was old enough to understand.' Eleanor looked enquiringly at Missy. 'I presume he
didn't say anything to you when he knew you were going out
with Jamie Ballantyne?'

'I didn't tell him about Jamie, and he never asked.'

'Yes, well, I can't say I'm surprised. Your father's very good
at wrapping himself up in his own world.'

Missy's mind was reeling now, at the possible consequences
of all the knowledge she had so recently acquired. There were
so many questions going round in her head. She asked the
first one that occurred to her: 'So does Harry know that
Patrick is his son?'

'No, certainly not.'

'And you didn't mind deceiving him?'

The accusation stung Eleanor. 'Of course I mind, but I

had to think of what it would do to their family. What good could possibly come of it, other than satisfying myself that Harry knew I had borne his child?'

'But did Dad not want to talk to his real father?'

'We did have a period when we thought he might want to, but to be honest, we discouraged it. Patrick did have the sense to see that such a thing could cause more problems than it solved. It's not as if he doesn't know who his father is. Your grandfather has always been grateful to him for that. I think it's the reason he's been so forgiving of his later activities, and losing your mother and his best friend in such a short space of time was a bitter blow.' Eleanor drained her glass. 'After all that I think I deserve another one. You've hardly touched yours.'

'No,' said Missy distractedly. 'Rather a lot to think about.'

Her grandmother put her hand over Missy's. 'I'm sorry, Artemis. I'm sorry that the mess I made of my life has affected yours. I'd give anything for it not to. I've been in love myself and I know how it feels. I know how all-consuming it is. I wish with all my heart that I could rewrite history, but I can't. Whether you like it or not, Harry Ballantyne is *your* grandfather as well as Jamie's and there's absolutely nothing I can do about that. Believe me, if there was, I would do it.'

'Thank you,' said Missy, but it was hollow gratitude. She stared at her glass of wine. Even the prospect of getting drunk offered her no solace, on this the gloomiest of Christmas Eves. Her life, so recently on the mend, was going nowhere, and she had no idea where the story would end.

'There is one little ray of hope,' offered Eleanor.

Missy raised her eyes.

'Leo Bedlington has been rather kind to us in his will.'

'What do you mean?'

'Well, he has some American relation from what I can make out, and he hasn't left much – he lost almost everything to death duties – but half of the residue of his estate goes to her and the other half to you.'

Missy looked at her grandmother blankly. 'To me?'

Eleanor nodded.

'But why? He never even met me.'

'Oh, various reasons, I would guess. He was very fond of me, but I think he was also fond of your grandfather – your *real* grandfather, Harry – if he did suspect that was the case. Who knows? People's minds work in peculiar ways. Anyway, I don't expect there will be much – perhaps just a few hundred pounds – but I thought you'd like to know.'

Missy could not speak. She had thought that the year had already evinced enough surprises for a lifetime and now here was another one. The implication slowly dawned on her. She could not have Jamie, but she would have, instead, half the proceeds of the sale of the clutch of Munnings paintings that he had shown her.

How cruel was fate. How cold and how bloody cruel, to give with one hand and take away with the other.

33

Bath
January 2008

The unexpected always happens.
                    Late nineteenth-century proverb

As Jamie walked through the abbey churchyard, he noticed that the workmen were clearing away the remains of the Christmas market. The neat little wooden chalets that had offered German nutcrackers and scented candles were now flat sections of timber being stacked on the back of a lorry. A robust girl in navy blue overalls was sweeping up litter and tipping it into a small wheeled truck. The last year was being packed away, all traces of it removed, and the new year was being welcomed in, along with better fortune.

The cold wind whipped mercilessly round the corner by the National Trust shop and Jamie quickened his pace. He thought about her again and half laughed at the lack of novelty: he had thought about nothing else the entire holiday, though 'holiday' was an inappropriate word for the two weeks he had just endured. He had spent Christmas Eve and Christmas Day at his mother's, and Boxing Day with his grandmother and grandfather jammed into their new flat. His familial obligations fulfilled, he had then knuckled down to sorting out the Circus. He was relieved at the respite from their questioning. Good-natured though the enquiries as to his well-being were, he was grateful for his own company, glad of the chance to be miserable alone. Of course, he would rather have been doing this with her, would rather have spent his evenings poring over a Farrow and Ball colour chart with Missy at his side instead of trying to sort it out on his own, but there was some kind of solace in solitude.

And now it was back to work. He had let the electrician and the plumber in at 8 a.m. It had surprised him that they had turned up at all. The events of the last few weeks had dented his confidence in human nature, and although both firms had assured him that they would turn up immediately the Christmas break was over, he had felt sure that they would find some excuse to delay. But turn up they had, and having left them with an electric kettle and enough teabags, milk and sugar to sustain the population of a small town, he had headed off for work.

He was at his laptop in the office now. It was the practice of Ballantyne's to hold an auction in the last week of January. It was something that had been established by his grand-father and which his mother had continued, though there were times when she cursed it. It meant that there was no chance of a winter holiday immediately after Christmas – no skiing or Caribbean cruises. Instead the firm was plunged into industry: lots had to be catalogued and numbered, catalogues had to be printed and mailed, and the rooms had to be readied for the sale. This year Jamie was grateful for the distraction.

From behind his desk he could see the activity within the saleroom – Frank and Len, the removal men, were heaving about large pieces of brown furniture. He glanced across the room to where the five Munnings paintings were propped against the wall. They should not be there, he knew, but for now he wanted to look at them. They seemed to offer him some kind of link with Missy, the only link he had, and in a couple of weeks they would be sold and even that link would disappear.

He leaned back in his chair and reflected on the words of his grandfather. His grandfather, who had so little time for the King family and yet who had asked him to look into his heart and ask himself if she was really worth fighting for. He tapped the edge of his laptop impatiently and reached for the phone. Quickly he dialled the number, before he had time to reconsider. The call was answered almost immediately.

'King's Fine Art.'

'Missy?'

'Yes.'

'It's me.'

For a moment the line went quiet. Then she said softly, 'Hello.'

'I just wondered how you were.'

'Oh, you know, battling on.'

There was a reserved note in her voice. He was unsure how to progress the conversation. Half of him – the head half – wished he had not been so swift to dial her number, but the other half – the heart – was glad simply to hear her breathing at the other end of the line.

Before he had time to think properly, he heard himself asking, 'Do you fancy a coffee? Only, I'm up to my neck in a sale that we're having in a couple of weeks and I could do with a break. It would just be nice to see you, not having seen you over Christmas. Nothing . . . I mean . . . nothing serious. Just—'

'Yes.'

At first he did not hear the word. He was sure she would say no, was sure that she would give him the brush-off.

'Oh. Right. Well . . . the café by the abbey, the one with—'

'Yes. In half an hour? I'll see you there.'

She put down the phone almost immediately and Jamie was left holding the handset in stunned silence. He replaced it gently and sat back in his chair to think. He would have to handle their meeting with great care.

★   ★   ★

Harry Ballantyne was sitting in his armchair in the window of his flat when Tilly came in and gave him the envelope. She called in and 'did' a couple of mornings a week now. There was not nearly so much to attend to as there had been in the Circus, but she was grateful for that, what with her arthritis. It was good not to have to negotiate all those stairs.

Harry looked at his name and address on the front of the envelope. It was executed in the spidery handwriting of Tilly's brother. It had been good of him to help out, but then Tilly was a good sort who would do Harry's bidding without too many questions. Theirs was a relationship based on trust, and Tilly had learnt to have faith in the man who had employed her for thirty years now. He was a good man, she knew that, even if occasionally he was hard to fathom. Sometimes he needed to have things done quietly, and Tilly was the mistress of discretion.

Having delivered the post, Tilly bid her boss a brief farewell and left to do her shopping. Harry slit open the envelope with his finger and withdrew the handwritten note and the cheque. It was a sizeable sum – six figures. Not a fortune, but certainly enough to help keep the wolf from the door.

Dear Mr Ballantyne,
I received the cheque from the auction house this morning. I have banked it and now enclose my own cheque for the same sum less the ten per cent you instructed me to take from it. I have done so very reluctantly. I am always happy to help out, since Tilly thinks so much of you, but it really was very kind of you to be so considerate of my small part in the transaction.
Yours sincerely,
Edward Stephenson

Harry got up and walked to the small bureau that stood against the opposite wall of the flat. From one of the small drawers he took his chequebook and fountain pen, and set about filling in a deposit form from the back of the book. He tore it out and tucked it into his wallet. Then he wrote out a cheque for the same amount and slipped it into a plain envelope, which he carefully addressed with the name of the recipient. He did not write out an address; he would deliver the cheque by hand.

He got up from the bureau and went into the hall, where his overcoat was hanging on a peg. With a look at the sky that decided him against taking an umbrella, he closed the front door behind him and set out on the short walk into town.

34

Villa Fabrice, Menton, Côte d'Azur
August 1995

Who could deceive a lover?
Aeneid, Book IV, Virgil

Madame Farage had gone home, leaving Leo to face the day alone. It mattered not that the sun shone from a cloudless sky, turning the sea into a shimmering sheet of sapphires. Neither did he feel the benefit of the warm breeze that played among the leaves of the acacia trees and whispered through the needles of the pines. Such sensitivities were lost on him now. It was all lost, and he had no one to blame but himself.

He turned away from the view and went indoors to fetch a pen and writing paper, then settled himself in the wicker armchair on the veranda once more and considered his options. He could end it all now. Madame Farage could go to the pharmacy and bring him enough medication to fall into a sleep from which he would never wake. Perhaps that would be the easiest way out, but then it would also be a cowardly one, and supposing he got it wrong and did not take enough? What then? A life of embarrassment and maybe even brain damage. He shuddered at the prospect.

But what were the alternatives? Did he really want to continue out here, on his own? He had been on his own before Mac had arrived, so why could he not go back to being on his own now? It was not as if they were lovers. Well, not physically, anyway. Mac had made it quite clear that that was out of the question. Leo had settled, instead, for an understanding, an understanding of which he was now deprived.

It would not be so bad had he not known what had really happened. If he had believed it was an accident, he could have wallowed in his grief for as long as it took and then recovered and battled on. He was used to that, had done it before. Maybe that was being selfish, though – not an accusation that he could ever have levelled at Mac, except that, in a way, this was the most selfish thing Mac had ever done.

During the weeks after his disappearance, when Leo and Madame Farage had combed the local beaches, asked everywhere about a body being washed up and gone to hell and back several times over, he had been convinced that Mac had had an accident, got out of his depth, refused to heed Madame Farage's advice about not bathing after a heavy meal and been caught out by the tide, or an attack of cramp. That seemed the most rational explanation.

There were other times when jealousy raised its head. When he thought about the youth from the café in Menton, the youth for whom Mac seemed to have developed some kind of fascination. They had argued about it occasionally, when Mac had come home late. In moments of anguish he had fantasised about their relationship, about how Mac preferred the youth's company to his own, about how he might simply have run off with him.

And then he had found the note, the note that made it so hard to bear.

During the weeks before his disappearance their relationship had become strained. Mac had snapped at him more than usual, had gone into himself and been quiet and distant. It had happened before. Leo had put it down to artistic temperament, had told himself that Mac had a good heart – his kindness over the paintings had proved that. He must have loved him in some way, mustn't he, to have done all that? Oh, he did it grudgingly from time to time, muttering to himself that he was betraying Munnings's trust, that hell and damnation must follow, but he had also said that the old man might be laughing up there in heaven at their audacity in fooling the art establishment, the very people that Munnings despised for their folly in raving about the kind of art that he considered worthless. That was what Mac had persuaded Leo to feel, and now he had gone, gone for all the wrong reasons and without ever sharing it all. And here he was, left with no more than a mountain of confused thoughts and a growing sense of bitterness that he had been betrayed by the 'stray' he had taken in.

Leo found his body shaking with tears that suddenly flooded out of him. He could not remember having cried in years, and now he sobbed uncontrollably, the tears falling on to the notepaper on his lap. He put the pen and paper to one side and buried his head in his hands, then got up and shouted at the sea, at the flowers around him, at the gull that flew overhead and at everything that came into view until, exhausted from the outpourings of years of frustration, he slumped down in the chair and tried to breathe more evenly.

He mused on the futility of it all, of love. Who had ever done well out of it? Not him, that was for sure. Maybe Mac had – for a while – but even that had not lasted. Was anyone ever sure of love? Of trust? Of the durability of a relation-ship? Did one simply have to live for today – *carpe diem* and all that? Was it better never to love at all than to risk pouring everything into a relationship with one person only to have it destroyed?

He remembered his college days. Richard, whom Mac had loved and failed to win, Eleanor, who had settled for Richard and not Harry, her true love. He could still remember the day Harry had come to see him at Bedlington Park, the day his father had died. It was indelibly printed on his mind. He saw in Harry, that day, a man who had found the love of his life and who only needed an ounce of courage to make his dreams come true. Where had it all gone wrong? He knew that Eleanor loved Harry and that Harry loved Eleanor, so how could they end up without each other? In his heart he knew the answer: fate. It was all down to fate. The odds could be stacked in your favour, the future could seem assured, but one twist of fate would be all that was needed to bring the world crashing down around you.

He took up his pen and the writing paper and began the letter.

Dear Harry,

I know you have not heard from me for a dreadfully long time, so forgive me for writing to you now, but I am rather in need of a friend at the moment and you are one of the two people who came to mind. I have been living here since I had to give up Bedlington Park after Father died, and I have become used to the French way of life now – and the climate!

A few years after I came here who should turn up on my doorstep but Mac – in need then of the same sort of comfort that I find myself in need of now. We lived together for over thirty-five years (oh, where do they go?!) in perfect disharmony. Anyway, now Mac has gone. You may read in the paper of his death. He went swimming and is presumed drowned.

I cannot go into more details here, and I know that this letter comes completely out of the blue, but it would be so good to see you. If there is any way that you feel you could spend a couple of days with an old (and very poor) friend, then I would be deeply grateful. I have very fond memories of our time together all those years ago, as, I hope, do you.

As ever,

Leo B.

P.S. I will be very happy to put up Mrs Ballantyne, if she chooses to come.

★   ★   ★

Leo hardly expected an answer, so it came as a tremendous relief when Harry not only replied, but also said that he would be happy to pay a brief visit. That September he turned up on Leo's doorstep – the second old college friend to do so, albeit three and a half decades since the first one. He was not accompanied by his wife. She had a concert to organise in Bath, he said, and he could not stay long. He was on his way back from an antiques fair in Nice. As they sat down opposite each other on the veranda of Villa Fabrice, the years fell away and Harry was sorry that he had not been better disposed to Leo's invitation. Now that he was here, he remembered with fondness Leo's kindnesses of nearly fifty years ago, and also the fact that both he and Mac had encouraged him in his pursuit of Eleanor.

After the kind of awkward preliminaries that are necessary when two estranged friends meet after a long period of absence, the two men fell into the sort of conversation they might have had nearly fifty years ago. Conversations about dons and parties and, eventually, about relationships.

'So why did it never happen?' asked Leo eventually, topping up Harry's glass of wine.

'Why did what never happen?'

'You and Eleanor. She was mad about you, and I know how you felt about her. What went wrong?'

'She married Richard.'

'Well, I know that. I was their best man,' Leo said reflectively. 'But why did she marry Richard when she was in love with you?'

'How do you know she was in love with me?'

'Because she told me so.'

Harry stared at him disbelievingly. He had always known that Eleanor liked him – fancied him, even, as their night of passion in Dedham proved – but how could she have loved him if she had married Richard?

Leo watched as Harry tried to find the words to continue. Seeing that it was unlikely, he offered, 'When you left Bedlington Park and went back to Oxford, you said you were going to ask her to marry you. Why didn't you?'

'Because Richard beat me to it,' murmured Harry, gazing into his wine. 'I went to find her and ended up at Richard's digs. I was right outside the door when he proposed. I was too late.'

'You mean, you heard him ask her?'

'Yes, quite clearly. It makes me go cold to remember it.'

'And you heard her say yes?'

'As good as.'

'Oh, Harry!'

'What? What do you mean?'

'I don't think she would have said yes. How could she have? She was probably trying to let him down gently.'

Harry butted in, 'Oh, you're very kind, but . . .'

'No. Not kind. Honest.' Leo shook his head. "Yet 'B' is worthy, I dare say, of more prosperity than 'A'."

'Gilbert and Sullivan?' asked Harry.

Leo nodded.

Harry took a sip of his wine. 'Well, it's too late now, isn't it?'

'Reluctant as I am to admit it, I think you're probably right.'

Harry put down his glass and leaned back in the chair. 'I do think about her. Even now, and about how different it might have been.'

'I thought you might.'

Harry smiled. 'I see her occasionally, walking in the street. They live in Bath, you know. Not far from us.'

'That must be hard.'

'Yes, very.'

'And does she see you?'

'It's difficult for us to avoid each other, moving in the same sort of circles.'

'And does she say anything?'

'No, we don't really communicate. I'm afraid that Richard and I haven't spoken for years.'

'Because he got the girl?'

'I suppose so, but I think I could have learned to live with that. The animosity really came from him. I was ready to bury the hatchet, but he never gave me the chance. Strange, to be honest. He got the girl and I got the cold shoulder.'

'And you don't know why?'

'No, not really.'

Leo looked hard at Harry, who was deep in thought. He considered giving an opinion, but thought the better of it. Instead he stood up and said, 'There's something I want you to see.'

Harry looked up at him.

Leo motioned Harry to follow him indoors. They walked through the cool hallway, into the drawing room of the villa and across to Leo's mahogany desk, which stood against a wall. Above it hung a painting, the sight of which took Harry's breath away. 'Oh my goodness, I haven't seen that for . . .'

'Nearly fifty years?'

'Yes.'

The painting was of a grey horse upon which sat a woman in a riding habit.

'Eleanor, painted by Munnings,' confirmed Leo. 'The genuine article.'

'Yes. She was,' murmured Harry softly.

'I mean the painting,' said Leo.

Harry looked at him quizzically.

'There's something you ought to know,' confided Leo. 'About Munnings's paintings.' He took Harry by the arm and led him out on to the veranda. 'You see, because I ran out of money, Mac had this idea. It was really a way of keeping the wolf from the door. It was a wicked thing to do, but it was the only way we could survive.'

It was half an hour before Harry spoke. It took Leo that long to explain.

'I see,' said Harry at last.

'And you think it was a dreadful thing to do?'

'Well, I can't condone it.'

'But you can understand?'

'Yes, I suppose I can.' Harry considered for a moment. 'So where are these paintings now?'

'Who knows? Scattered to the four corners of the earth, I suppose.'

'And where did they go?'

'I've no idea. Mac arranged to sell them through some gallery in England. Madame Farage did it all, so that our names wouldn't come into it.'

'And you kept the real ones?'

'Yes.'

Harry shook his head in despair.

'And now you know, and you won't want to hear of me ever again,' muttered Leo.

'No. You shouldn't have done it, but then who am I to judge you?'

Leo got up and walked to the edge of the veranda, looking out across the sea. 'It's funny how things turn out, isn't it?'

'You could choose a better word than "funny",' countered Harry.

'Weird, then.'

'Yes, weird will do.'

'He didn't die by accident, you know.'

'What?' said Harry, not following the change of direction in the conversation.

'Mac. His death wasn't an accident.' Leo saw the look of

confusion on Harry's face. He came and sat down in the chair next to him. 'He took his own life.'

'No, not Mac – he wouldn't do that. He's not . . . I mean . . . he wasn't that selfish.'

'He didn't do it for himself. He did it for me.' Leo saw that Harry was not following him. 'He'd discovered that he was ill, terminally ill. What's the one thing that Mac would never have countenanced?'

'Being dependent on someone else,' murmured Harry.

'Exactly. He couldn't cope with being a burden on me, the man that he'd looked after for the past thirty-five years.'

Harry saw the tears building in Leo's eyes.

'What was he thinking, Harry? Why did he think that I'd mind? He spent most of his life making sure that I was all right: why on earth did he think that I wouldn't do the same for him?'

'Oh, Leo, he knew you would. It's just the way that Mac was made – bloody-minded till the end.'

Leo pulled a large white handkerchief from his pocket and blew his nose. 'Stupid bugger,' he muttered.

Harry watched as the tears coursed down Leo's cheeks.

'We were never lovers, you know – just two people who lived together for mutual benefit, though heaven knows I had the lion's share of the benefits. All Mac did was paint to keep us alive, and now . . .'

Harry leaned forward and put his hand on Leo's arm.

Leo looked up at him through the tears. 'But I did love him, Harry. I really did love him.'

Harry could not remember the last time he had hugged a man, except his grandson, which he did only rarely. He and Leo sat side by side with their arms round each other while Leo allowed years of pent-up love to spill out, his aged body shaking uncontrollably.

Finally he eased away and blew his nose loudly. 'Thank

you, Harry. It seems a long time since you poured your heart out to me. I had to wait nearly fifty years for my turn!' He wiped his eyes on the handkerchief and pushed it back into his pocket.

Harry smiled at him. 'At least you had a long time together – you and Mac.' Then he said wistfully, 'More than me and Eleanor.'

'Yes.' Leo got to his feet and looked out over the sea once more. Late-afternoon shafts of sunlight slanted on to the water like spotlights, glinting on the crests of rank after rank of shimmering waves. He turned to face Harry. 'That's why I want you to have the painting, the painting of Eleanor, the Munnings. You might have lost the real girl, but at least I can make sure you have the next best thing.'

35

Bath
January 2008

The life you lead sets all your nerves a jangle,
Your love affairs are in a hopeless tangle . . .
Poor little rich girl, don't drop a stitch too soon.
On With the Dance (1925), Sir Noël Coward

If asked why she had said yes when he had asked her out for coffee, her reply would have been brief and to the point. 'Because I wanted to see him.' She knew that. It was the only certainty in her life at the moment. She knew it was inadvisable, knew it would only lead to more heartache, but she so wanted to be in his company, even knowing that in the long term it was not possible for them to be together. She had tried staying away from him, keeping her distance, doing her best to get on. She had tried it for three weeks now and she felt not one jot better than she had at the beginning. If anything, she felt worse.

What harm could come of talking to him over a cup of coffee, provided she stayed on an even keel and didn't say anything that would give him cause to hope? She would be pleasant; she must avoid being too offhand, but still strike a balance. She desperately wanted to keep him as a friend. No, she still *needed* him as a friend. Had she not been away in the States for so long, she might have had others she could turn to, but they now had their own lives. She had remained in touch with them, but irregularly, so the level of intimacy they could offer was not enough. She needed him, in so many ways.

As she walked down Gay Street towards the abbey, her doubts began to surface. Was this really a good idea? Would he not expect more than pleasant conversation? There was simply no way she could tell him what the real reason was behind her ending their relationship. What if he probed more deeply? Outside the café, she had been on the verge of turning back, her confidence had evaporated and she knew she was vulnerable, but by then it was too late: he had seen her through the window and waved. She walked through the doorway and across to where he sat. He stood up and leaned forward. Before she could make a decision whether or not to kiss him, he had already lightly brushed her cheek. It seemed as though her chest was thumping. She took a deep breath, sat down opposite him and said, 'Hi.'

'I've ordered you a hot chocolate. They said they'd bring it over when you came. Was that all right?'

She nodded. It was nice he had remembered.

Jamie, for his part, was so overwhelmed at her turning up that he had no idea how to begin the conversation. The result was a few seconds of silence while he busied himself catching the eye of the barista, who had already seen that his companion had arrived. Companion, date, friend? What was she now? What did it matter? She was here, that was the main thing.

'How was Christmas?' he asked.

'Oh, not very good.' Missy smiled bravely. 'Grandpa wasn't himself. Hardly surprising, really.'

'So what . . . ? I mean . . . is anything happening? With the business?'

'I'm not sure. I haven't really felt that I could ask, not just yet, what with Dad being away.'

Jamie looked at her incredulously.

'He went on a cruise on Boxing Day.'

'What? You mean in spite of . . . ?'

'Oh, yes. That's Dad. Never lets anything get in the way of his social life.'

The barista came over with her drink. 'Hot chocolate for the *signorina*?'

Missy nodded and tried to change the subject. 'How about your house? How's it coming on?'

'Oh, nothing much has happened yet, really. The plumbers and electricians moved in this morning, so with any luck I might manage to get them out by next Christmas.'

Missy smiled. 'It'll be lovely when it's finished. You wait.'

'Yes, "wait" is probably the operative word.'

There were so many things he wanted to say – important things like 'Won't you change your mind?' and pathetic, mundane things like 'I want your opinion about paint and wallpaper' – but he thought she might simply get up and go if he asked too much. Instead he heard himself ask, 'And is the exhibition going ahead?'

'Yes. A last hurrah, I suppose. One final fling for King's Fine Art.'

'It might do better than you think,' he said encouragingly, 'might net you enough to carry on.'

'I doubt it somehow.' She felt guilty at being so negative, aware that she was countering each and every comment he made with a defeatist remark. 'There is one little light at the end of the tunnel.'

He felt hopeful suddenly, wondering if she were beginning to come round, if she had realised that in spite of the Kings' heavy losses, he really would be there for her and that perhaps they could make a go of it. He looked at her expectantly.

'The Munnings pictures from Lord Bedlington.'

'Yes?'

'Grandma told me that I'm due half the proceeds.'

Jamie sat back in his chair.

'I think he was rather fond of Grandma, and I think also

maybe he hoped it might make up for all that business with the copies. I guess he felt rather guilty about that.'

'So why didn't he leave them to her?'

'Oh, he said that he thought she had enough money already. He clearly had no idea how badly the firm had been hit. He imagined Grandpa would have sold them on, I suppose, but obviously had no idea that he had bought them back and how much it had cost him. As far as I'm concerned, it doesn't really matter. I'll just use the proceeds to help reduce the overdraft.' She saw the hopeful look on Jamie's face. 'Don't get too excited – it won't be enough to cover our debts, but it should go some way towards keeping the bank happy for a while.'

'But that's brilliant. If I can get enough for them at auction, then you'll be OK.'

'It's not really that simple, Jamie.'

'But it is, don't you see? That's wonderful. The catalogues go out this week – the sale is at the end of the month – and I'll make absolutely certain that they go to every single Munnings collector in the country. I'll mail every London art dealer, and the provincial ones. You watch – by the end of the week there will be no one who's ever seen a horse on canvas who doesn't know that the finest set of Munnings paintings are about to go on the market.'

'Yes, but . . .'

Jamie motored on, 'What do you need? Seven million was the overdraft, wasn't it? Well, the five paintings won't get you that – and you only have a half-share – but we can reduce our commission and—'

'Oh, Jamie, I don't think your grandfather, or your mother, would be very happy with that . . .'

'You leave them to me. If you do well with your exhibition and I do well on the platform, then at least we can drastically reduce your overdraft and you needn't go out of business. After all, most art galleries have an overdraft, and if you can reduce yours by half, then the bank is hardly likely to foreclose.'

She watched his face as he enthused about the prospect of getting her out of the red and back into the black. She found his enthusiasm and his passion so overwhelming that it was hard not to break down. Oh, why could she not have this man? Clearly they were made for one another. It was all so desperately unfair.

'If we can get between three and four million . . . Well, I suppose four is pushing it, but if we can get three, then you'll get the best part of one and a half million, and with your exhibition as well, which is bound to do well because it's your fiftieth anniversary, we can hopefully halve your overdraft.'

'We?'

'Between us – me in the auction and you in your exhibition.'

She could not deny it; she liked nothing more than hearing him say 'we'. She could not encourage him to think that there was any more to their relationship than that of good friends, but to his credit, he did not appear to be pressing for more. Not at the moment, anyway.

He seemed to read her mind. 'Just let me try, that's all,' he said gently, aware that he might have sounded over-enthusiastic, proprietorial even.

'You're very kind. I don't really think I deserve your help, though.'

'I think that's for me to decide. Now drink your hot chocolate and tell me what are the most exciting paintings in your exhibition. Then I'll work out the sums.'

She could not help but smile. He was, without a shadow of a doubt, the most special man she had ever met in her whole life.

Harry had taken a taxi. He did not know the way, having never been there before, but he did know the address. The taxi dropped him off at the bottom of the tree-lined drive and he began to walk up the crunching gravel towards the imposing Georgian house.

He had come unannounced. He saw little point in doing otherwise, but he reasoned that if it were early enough in the morning, the man he wanted to see would not yet have left for work, if indeed he still went to work.

The house was as imposing as he had imagined – with five bays and a central door, probably around 1700, Queen Anne, really, rather than Georgian. Supremely elegant, its mellow brickwork seemed to glow gently in the weak January sunshine. It was the sort of house people dream of, but then he had expected no less. The sweeping lawns that flanked the drive were beautifully cut, in spite of the fact that it was winter, and arched over by the bare, sweeping branches of majestic beech trees. It was all a far cry from the centre of Bath. Here, just a few miles out, you were in the heart of the country. He heard a horse whinny and it made him start. He could not deny that he was nervous, but he hoped that the enmities of the past sixty years could finally be laid to rest. He was too old and too tired to keep up the silent feud. Things should be settled, for all of them.

He climbed the four wide stone steps to the pillared portico that encased the front door and rang the bell. At that moment he knew it was too late to change his mind. There was no going back. It seemed like an age before there was any response. Eventually he heard a door close somewhere in the house and then heard a key turn in the lock on the other side of the door. It was opened quite smartly by a middle-aged man in a black jacket and tie and pinstriped trousers.

'Hello, Mr Ballantyne,' said the man. 'Please come in. Mr King is expecting you.'

This took Harry rather by surprise. He had certainly not said that he was coming. In fact he had assumed that if he had done so, then Richard King would have made sure he was unavailable. He stepped, as bidden, into the hallway and the man closed the front door behind him.

'Would you care to come this way, sir?' The butler, for that is clearly what he was, led the way towards the back of the hall – a light and airy space with small, lozenge-shaped black tiles set geometrically amid the larger white flagstones. The walls were a warm shade of buttermilk, and several well-chosen pictures of horses were hung between the four white doorways that led off to other rooms. A white marble bust of Charles James Fox stood to one side of the pair of double doors at the back of the hall, and a bust of Nelson on the other. Harry could not help but be impressed, though there was little time to take in the finer points of decoration, for the butler was now opening the double doors and saying, 'Mr Ballantyne, sir.'

Harry stepped forward into the book-lined room and saw the figure of Richard King with his back to him, gazing out of the French windows across the wintry garden. At the sound of his name, Richard swivelled round and the two men faced each other for the first time in nearly sixty years.

'Hello, Harry,' said Richard.

'Hello, Richard,' said Harry.

'Well, here you are, then.' Richard motioned Harry to a chair in front of the large walnut desk that stood in the centre of what was clearly his study-cum-library. He did not attempt to shake hands, considering that perhaps a move too far.

'Your butler said you were expecting me,' said Harry questioningly.

'Yes. I was in the drawing room when you were coming up the drive. I saw you from there. I didn't want him to think your visit was a surprise.'

'Oh.'

'Which of course it is.'

'Yes.' Harry cleared his throat. 'I thought it was about time we called a halt to all this.'

Richard remained standing behind the desk, while Harry sat in front of it. 'All what?'

'Oh, you know – the so-called family feud. It seems to me that it's got out of hand. It was all so long ago and I really don't see why we should burden future generations with our differences, Richard, do you?'

Richard sat down in his chair and leaned forward on the desk. 'Why now? Why have you left it so long?'

Harry shrugged. 'Who knows? Why have either of us left it so long?'

Richard looked implacable. 'Maybe some of us prefer it that way.'

Harry was taken aback. He had hoped that Richard would be as eager as he was to put aside the animosity that had smouldered for so many years. It seemed that this was not the case. Harry continued, 'I know that my grandson and your granddaughter are . . .' he paused to choose his words carefully '. . . fond of one another, and I don't think that what happened with us all those years ago should get in their way, do you?'

Richard looked uncomfortable.

Harry continued, 'Whatever we felt all that time ago – and we were friends for three years before . . . well . . . before . . .'

'Before I married Eleanor.'

'Yes.'

'And you think we should go back to being friends?' asked Richard sardonically.

'No, I don't think we could ever be friends again, but I think we should develop some kind of . . . well, in politics I suppose they would call it détente.'

Richard said nothing.

Harry persevered, 'If not for us, then for their sake. It simply isn't fair, Richard, that we expect them to continue our grievances.'

'It isn't fair,' said Richard slowly and softly. 'It isn't fair.' He was not looking at Harry now, but his eyes were focused on the middle distance. 'It isn't fair that I got Eleanor and you didn't. It isn't fair that your business is prospering and mine is about to go under. It isn't fair that your grandson and my granddaughter are probably in love with each other. It isn't fair.' He looked at Harry now. 'Life isn't fair, Harry. None of it's fair. You and I burying the hatchet now won't solve anything. It's all too late. It's too late for me and it's too late for you.'

'But it's not too late for Artemis and Jamie,' interrupted Harry.

'On the contrary, it's far too late. It was too late when they were born, for reasons you'll never understand.'

'What reasons? What reason can there possibly be why they should not be together, except for the pride of their aged grandparents?'

Richard got up from his chair and walked round the desk. As he did so, the door of his study opened. Harry heard the click of the catch and looked round to see Eleanor walking towards him. For a moment they just stared at each other. Harry might have expected to encounter Eleanor, but she had most certainly not expected to find him in her house.

'Harry,' she said absently.

Harry nodded. 'Hello, Eleanor.'

'Harry is just leaving,' said Richard.

'Oh, but—'

Richard interrupted his wife. 'We've had a brief meeting, but I think we've said everything we need to say.'

Eleanor looked troubled. Her eyes darted between the two men and lighted on Harry as he spoke.

'Well, if that's how you feel,' said Harry.

'Yes, yes, it is. Thank you for coming. I'm sorry we can't do business.'

Eleanor looked confused. 'Would you at least like a cup of coffee?' she offered.

Richard was about to interrupt, but Harry got in first. 'No, thank you, I don't think so. I must be going.' He walked towards the double doors through which he had entered. As he reached them, they opened as if by magic and the butler was waiting on the other side. Harry turned in the doorway. 'Thank you for seeing me,' he said. 'I'm sorry things have turned out the way they have.' Then he turned to Eleanor. 'Goodbye, Eleanor. I'm sorry we didn't meet for longer. It would have been nice, but . . .'

Eleanor watched as he walked from the room and disappeared from view. Then she turned to Richard. 'What was all that about?'

Richard stood quite still for a moment and then said, 'Too little too late.'

Harry waited at the bottom of the drive, stamping his feet and pulling up the collar of his coat to keep out the bitter wind. It was half an hour before his taxi came. By the time he got home he was chilled to the marrow. Sally was out so he had a hot bath and then sat by the radiator, but still did not seem to be able to get warm. All the time he could see Eleanor standing in front of him in Richard's study. She looked wonderful. Funny how after all these years she could still make his heart beat faster.

When Sally got home, she found Harry sitting in the chair by the radiator. He was so very cold. She held his hand for half an hour, but it never got any warmer. History, it seemed, was repeating itself. She lay her hand on his head and gently stroked his hair; then she called the ambulance.

36

Bolton Abbey, Yorkshire
January 2008

You can take the man out of Yorkshire, but you can't take
Yorkshire out of the man.

Proverb

They laid Harry Ballantyne to rest in his beloved Wharfedale,
a reminder of the times when he and Sally had started out
with nothing more than high hopes and a leg-up from her
father. There were not many at the funeral. Well, Harry was
nearly eighty after all, and Yorkshire is a long way from Bath.
Sally didn't seem to mind, or to notice, even. Her heart was
back with Harry in those early days when they would come
up here in the Morris on a Sunday afternoon and paddle in
the river.

'We sent 'im off with a good 'am tea,' was what they always
said at funerals in those days, so Sally arranged that they
should do just that – at Betty's café in Ilkley. There were just
the four of them: Sally and Emma, Jamie and his sister, Fran,
who had come over from Argentina especially. The rest of
the mourners had dispersed by then – just a few locals who
came out of respect for a man who loved this part of Yorkshire enough to be buried here. Among them was a man in
his fifties who stood behind a pillar at the back of the church.
Nobody seemed to notice him, but then he took care to make
sure of that. Patrick King had come to say farewell to the
father who never knew he had a son. When the coffin had
been carried out into the churchyard, he slipped quietly away
and melted into the moorland mist.

Fran was tearful, Sally rather out of it, and Emma as matter-of-fact as ever. Jamie did his best to hold himself together, losing control only once, when the coffin was lowered into the Yorkshire soil and the vicar intoned the words that Harry had loved from Housman's *A Shropshire Lad*:

> Clay lies still, but blood's a rover,
> Breath's a ware that will not keep.
> Up, lad: when the journey's over,
> There'll be time enough to sleep.

The journey home was a quiet and sorrowful one. Harry had enjoyed a long and fulfilling life, but the fact that he had died so suddenly had left them all in a state of shock. Emma travelled with Fran to Heathrow Airport – her visit was a brief one since she had to get back to the stud, where the breeding programme was at its height – and Jamie took Sally back home to Bath.

He worried about her, not because she was so devastated, but because she seemed to be almost anaesthetised from it all. They got back to the flat quite late in the afternoon and Jamie elected to stay with her rather than leave her alone in the now silent rooms. It might have been a small flat, but it felt quite large and empty now that they were there alone.

He sat her down with a cup of tea, and the conversation turned to happier times: of Wharfedale, not surprisingly, and Ernie Bowker, and the early days in Bath. She told of how she had met Harry and said, quite simply, 'I don't think I was his first love.'

Jamie was surprised at her candour, that on this day, of all days, she should want to think of such a thing.

'But I know I was his last,' she said, with a smile. 'He was such a good man, such a fair man.' Then she turned to Jamie. 'Like you,' she said.

Jamie crouched at her feet and took her hand. 'Oh, not all that good,' he said, holding back the tears.

'Oh, yes,' continued Sally softly. 'I can see him in you so clearly. He was very fond of you, had high hopes. I know he won't be disappointed.'

Jamie could no longer speak. Instead he rested his head in his grandmother's lap and let the tears flow on to her tweed skirt. There seemed no point in holding them back. His hero had gone. He was on his own now.

Jamie left his grandmother when Emma returned later that night, and went back to the Circus, which seemed, more than ever, to be filled with the spirit of his grandfather. He could see him in every room, standing by the windows in the drawing room, sitting on the club fender by the fire, reading a book in his armchair, but the thoughts were happy ones. At least here he would feel that his grandfather was always with him, that his spirit lived on in the old stones of the house.

It was late the following morning when his grandmother called him at Ballantyne's and asked if he could come over. 'Of course,' he said. 'I'll come now. Is everything all right?'

She assured him it was and said, simply, that she had a few things she wanted him to sort out. He would rather have done so in the evening – the auction was the following day and the saleroom was awash with those who had come to view – but he reasoned that she would not have asked had it not been important, so he went straight over.

He found his grandmother sitting at his grandfather's bureau going through his papers.

'I know what to do with most of what's here,' she said, 'but I can't understand what this is.'

She handed Jamie an envelope addressed to Harry Ballantyne in rather spidery handwriting. Jamie pulled out the letter. As he did so, a cheque fluttered to the floor. He read the letter, which was apparently from Edward, the brother of his grandparents' cleaner. Then he stooped and picked up the cheque. It was for the sum of five hundred thousand pounds. That alone would have made him gasp, but what really took his breath away was that it had been made out by his grandfather in favour of Richard King.

'What on earth?' exclaimed Jamie.

'That's what I said to myself,' said his grandmother. 'And there's this.' She picked up a bank statement and put on her glasses. 'There's an entry here for a week ago – a deposit in our bank account of exactly the same amount of money. I've rung the bank and asked about it. The cheque was made out by Tilly's brother. All quite above board, apparently.'

'So why did Tilly's brother pay Granddad so much money? And why did Granddad make out a cheque for half a million pounds to Richard King? I mean, they weren't even on speaking terms.'

'I was right to call you, wasn't I? I mean, it is important, isn't it?'

'Well, yes. I mean, I suppose it obviously was. The thing is that now he's died, I wouldn't have thought this cheque could be cashed, anyway.' Jamie looked baffled, then asked, 'When is Tilly due?'

Sally squinted at her watch. 'In about half an hour.'

'Have you been through the rest of Granddad's stuff?'

'Well, all except the bureau. I don't know if there's anything else in here that might shed light on it. I thought I knew about everything.' Sally began to look tearful. 'Perhaps I didn't after all.'

Jamie made to comfort her. 'Oh, come on, Gran, I'm sure there's some perfectly simple explanation. Do you want me to look through the rest for you? I know it's private, but . . .'

'Oh, I've no secrets from you,' she said, wiping her eyes with a tissue pulled from the sleeve of her cardigan. 'You go through it all and I'll make some tea. If you're sure you have the time?'

'Yes, of course. You make the tea and I'll have a look.'

While Sally busied herself with the pot and the tea, the cups and saucers and the milk, Jamie turned out every drawer and every pigeonhole in search of anything that might offer a clue as to the reason for the cheque. There were the usual things – rubber bands carefully preserved in envelopes and hoards of paperclips. There were bank statements going back several years, but in spite of poring over them, Jamie found no further clue as to the reason for the cheque.

There was only one place he had not looked: in the centre of the bureau, in between the pigeonholes, was a tiny door. It was locked. 'Do you have a key for this?' Jamie asked his grandmother.

'Oh, yes. It's in a leather purse in the bottom drawer.'

'So that's what it was for.' He located the key, slipped it into the lock and turned it. The tiny door popped open and Jamie felt inside and pulled out a bundle of letters tied together with a piece of faded blue ribbon. 'Do you know what these are?' he asked.

Sally came closer and took the bundle from him. 'Yes. I think they are the letters I wrote to your grandfather when we were going out.' She smiled as she remembered. Slipping off the ribbon, she sifted through them. 'Yes. Oh goodness, what a lot, and we weren't far away.' Then she stopped and turned one envelope over. 'No, this one isn't mine – not my handwriting.'

Jamie worried that his grandmother had discovered something that would upset her. 'Let me see . . .' He held out his hand and she passed it to him. If he were quick-witted, he could think of some excuse if it was a letter she would be better off not seeing. He looked at the postmark and the stamp. 'This letter is from France, and the postmark is much later than your courting days. 1995, I think.' He looked up at his grandmother. 'Shall I open it?'

She nodded, and Jamie, his mind racing over what he might say if it proved to be unfortunate, slipped back the flap and withdrew the letter it contained. Nervously he unfolded the paper and read the contents. He had barely finished when there was a brief knock at the door and Tilly bustled in. She was her usual matter-of-fact and jovial self, until she saw Jamie and his grandmother exchanging sideways glances.

'What is it?' she asked. 'What's the matter?'

Jamie got up. 'Tilly, sit down for a minute.'

Tilly looked apprehensive. 'I'm not sure I should. I never sits down – too much to do.'

'No, really, sit down. There's something I need to ask you. It's about this.' Jamie handed her the letter that her brother had written to his grandfather.

'Oh, I see,' said Tilly in a low voice.

'We just want to know what it was about, that's all,' said Jamie gently.

'Well, it was between the master and me, or the master and my brother, Edward.' Tilly looked up and saw that Sally was distressed. 'It was all perfectly legal,' she exclaimed. 'Nothing underhand, nothing dishonest, I promise.'

'Just tell us, Tilly,' pleaded Jamie.

Tilly began to look tearful, then made a visible attempt to pull herself together. 'It was the picture.'

'What picture?'

'The picture of the woman on the horse, the grey horse, the one that the master had.'

Jamie looked at his grandmother. 'I didn't think we had a

picture of a woman on a horse,' she said. 'Lots of ships, but no horses.'

'Master kept it in his dressing room at the Circus, wrapped in brown paper, behind his suits.'

'Oh.' Sally steadied herself and then sat down. The colour had drained from her cheeks.

Tilly continued, 'Master had it for a few years, ten years p'r'aps. That's how long it was at the back of his dressing room. I should know, I Hoovered around it often enough.' She looked apologetic at appearing to complain and continued, 'Well, he decided he wanted to sell it, quietly, like. He explained to me that the mistress knew nothing of its existence, that it had been his investment, so to speak, and that he now wanted to part with it. He knew he couldn't sell it through Ballantyne's himself, not without everyone knowing it was his, so he asked if my brother would put it in the sale for him. He very kindly said he would make it worth his while.'

'I see,' said Jamie softly.

'Edward didn't really want the money. He would happily have done it just for the master, but the master insisted, so . . .' She shrugged.

'So the painting was sold in the auction house,' said Jamie. 'By me, as it happens.'

'And then Edward sent the master the proceeds, less the ten per cent that the master had insisted he take.'

'Five hundred thousand pounds.'

Tilly's voice began to crack. 'Oh, it's such an awful lot of money, I know, but . . .'

'Tilly, you mustn't get upset,' consoled Jamie. 'You only did what was asked of you.' He looked across at his grand-mother and asked, 'Can I hang on to this letter, the one we've just found? I just need to think things through, but I've an idea that I might be able to make some sense of all this.'

Sally nodded. Then she asked in a quavering voice, 'Who was it from?'

Jamie smiled at her reassuringly. 'It was from Lord Bedlington.'

37

Bath
January 2008

Like other parties of the kind, it was first silent, then talky,
then argumentative, then disputatious, then unintelligible, then
altogethery, then inarticulate, then drunk.
            Letter to Thomas Moore from Lord Byron (1815)

That evening in the quiet of his attic room, where he had
made up a bed to be out of the way of the workmen on the
floors below, Jamie pored over the letter and pieced together
what he could from the information he had acquired over
the last few weeks. There were still some things he could just
not get clear in his head, certain pieces of the jigsaw that did
not seem to fit. There was only one person he could call
upon for help. The question was, would she come?

He called the number of her apartment in the Royal Crescent, but it rang and rang. She was not there, either that or
she was not answering. He rang her mobile and got the answer-
phone. 'Hello, you've reached Artemis King – or, rather, not
reached her. I'm afraid I'm unavailable at the moment, but
please leave a message and I'll make contact as soon as
I can.'

He dropped the phone into the pocket of his jacket and
reread the letter:

Dear Harry
It was so good of you to come, especially at a time when I
needed some solace from a true friend. As you suggested,
I am sending the painting by courier. How I wish I had been
there when it was painted. Hopefully it will bring back

memories of your happy, if brief, affair with Eleanor at Oxford. I know that she loved you deeply. Oh, it may be pointless and even mischievous saying all this now, but you should not doubt it.

It occurs to me that it might be difficult for you to explain the arrival of the picture, and of its subject, but what you do with it is up to you. Should it embarrass you too much, then you must feel free to sell it. The last thing I want to do is to embarrass you. I simply want it to go to what I feel is its rightful home.

As to Mac, I have come to terms with his actions. If I continue in my well of despondency, then his life really will have been wasted. He wanted to spare me pain and so, apart from the pain that his loss has engendered, I cannot feel anything but a lasting love for him and a respect for his wishes. I like to think that is what he wanted.

It really is no business of mine, but I do hope that you will make your peace with Richard, and he with you. That he landed Eleanor and you did not will be a lifelong regret for both of us, but in my experience, it is better to let the past stay at a distance and to get on with the here and now. I would hate to think that you both left this life without making peace with one another.

Anyway, the picture comes with much love. Do not feel that you need to keep in contact if you do not wish to. It has been so lovely seeing you again and, in a funny sort of way, I feel I have laid to rest the ghosts of the past, getting all this off my chest. Neither should you worry about my well-being. I have just enough to see me out comfortably, and when the time comes, I shall know where to send what few goods and chattels that remain. The scandalous commission exacted by auction houses should help keep the wolf from your door! (This is meant as a joke, which I hope you will take in good spirits.)

There is a relative in America who is due part of my estate. I don't know her, but family ties and all that . . . I have a mind to leave the rest to another old friend.

Hopefully that day is a while off yet, and I shall be able to find some peace before then.

Goodness, what a colourful life I have led, and how different from that which I thought I was going to lead that day when you came to Bedlington Park! I hear it is a retirement home now. I only hope they can afford the heating bills. We never could.

Enough. I have said all I need to, except that I shall always look upon you as a staunch and trusted friend who was there in my hour of need.

With fondest good wishes,

Leo

There was so much to take in. His grandfather had been Eleanor King's lover at Oxford, for a start. Well, the letter said *she* loved *him*, but did *he* love *her*? He must have done. Leo would not have given the painting to someone who had simply been a friend, and yet she had married Richard King. That must have been when the estrangement between the two men began.

Then there was the fact that the Munnings Jamie had sold to Missy that day back in November had actually been put up for sale by his grandfather. At least that was another plus for Missy. Her painting was, by the sound of it, genuine: Leo Bedlington had not given Harry Ballantyne a fake – that much was clear.

Then there was John Macready, who had clearly not died accidentally but had taken his own life. The mirror-image picture that had been sent to Richard King was presumably some kind of posthumous apology. Did that mean that it, too, was real and not a fake? And the cheque made out to Richard King. Why would his grandfather do that? Unless . . .

Jamie's head swam. He folded up the letter, slipped it into his jacket pocket, went down the stairs and out into the night. It is a short walk from the Circus to the Royal Crescent along

Brock Street. Jamie simply wanted to walk past Missy's house to feel her presence in some way. He so wanted to talk it over with her. It was not long before he saw the lights blazing at King's Fine Art. He thought at first that something must be wrong, but then he remembered: it was the evening of the exhibition. The great and the good of Bath – the patrons of the arts and the attenders of soirées – would be there in the gallery, knocking back the Laurent Perrier and wolfing down the canapés. Some of them might look at the paintings. A few might even ask for a red dot to be placed on the ticket. He hoped so, for Missy's sake.

He walked along the pavement opposite, keeping close to the iron railings. He was in the shadows here and could see through the generously proportioned sash windows into the rooms beyond, from where the hum of a party in progress spilled out on to the streets. The cold wind caught him and he zipped up his leather jacket and raised the collar, the better to keep warm. One or two latecomers ambled from their cars, through the open doorway and into the brightly lit hall. The crystals of the chandelier shone like diamonds, their opulence belying the likely outcome of this last hurrah for King's Fine Art.

Jamie caught sight of Richard King through a window on the first floor, chatting amiably with a well-dressed man and woman. He appeared relaxed and at ease. Jamie imagined what must be going on inside his head. He had no idea that Richard King was the last man to have seen his grandfather alive.

Missy had seen most of the guests in. Dressed in a smart honey-coloured two-piece and a white cashmere polo-neck sweater, her hair held back in a tight bun, she had greeted them effusively, as one did, and directed them towards the waiters holding silver salvers laden with champagne.

She had stayed for an hour before she felt the need to escape. Her grandfather seemed as relaxed as she could hope, and Patrick had turned up, surprisingly, only half an hour late. She left the two of them holding court, knowing that she could not be gone for more than a few minutes, but desperately in need of a breath of air. She slipped on her coat, mentioning to the girl on the door that she would be back very soon.

Pulling up her collar, she had strolled along to the end of the Crescent to look out over the city for a few minutes and reflect that this would, in all probability, be her last exhibition.

It was not the only sadness she felt. There was, if anything, a deeper sorrow within her: sorrow at the loss of the grandfather she had never known, the grandfather who had not known her. She had sent Jamie a note, expressing her sympathy, but she knew that she could never tell him the truth, that a piece of history that was the fault of neither of them would always stand in their way. Oh, what a mess it all was.

She turned to look back at the gallery, shining like a jewel on the cold winter night. Below her, the golden lights of the city glinted and winked in the gloom, and then, without warning, the air was suddenly filled with large white flakes. The street lights, a moment ago casting their rays into the blackness, now illuminated a million tumbling stars. It was snowing. Missy turned her head to the sky and felt the ice-cold snowflakes falling on to her face. They caught in her eyelashes and settled on her nose. Almost instinctively she reached behind her head and pulled her hair from the neat bun, shaking it out around her. The snow eddied about her, and the freshness of the air was exhilarating – it seemed to hold a promise of freedom. She sighed at the ridiculous thought, took a deep breath and headed back towards the gallery.

In the denseness of the blizzard she almost fell over the figure huddled against the railings. 'I'm so sorry,' she exclaimed, putting out her hand to steady herself. Then she saw who it was. 'Jamie!'

'Hi.' He felt embarrassed, embarrassed at her finding him there like some stalker, embarrassed that he had got in her way and she had fallen over him.

'I'm so sorry,' she said.

'No, I'm sorry,' he replied.

'About your grandfather, I mean. So very sorry.'

Jamie smiled weakly. 'Yes.'

Missy looked around her. 'What are you doing? I mean, what are you doing here?'

'Oh, just out for a breath of fresh air.' He hoped the excuse sounded plausible.

'Me too.'

'And then it started to snow. Caught me by surprise, really.'

'Yes.'

Jamie looked at her standing in front of him with her collar pulled up, the flakes of snow swirling around her, and he could not ever remember seeing anything quite so beautiful. 'You look stunning,' he murmured.

Missy was caught unawares by the compliment and struggled to reply. 'Come inside,' she said.

'What?'

'Come inside for a drink.'

'But I can't. I mean, your grandfather . . .'

'And my father. They're both in there. And Grandma. The whole family. Who cares? We're just friends, aren't we? They have their friends and I have mine. If I can't invite *you* to the last exhibition at King's Fine Art, then who can I invite? Come on.' She took him by the arm and led him up to the front door of the gallery. 'Just don't say a word about this being our last show, that's all.'

'Yes. I mean, no. I mean . . . I'm not really dressed for this, am I?'

She looked down at the well-worn jeans and trainers, and then at the leather jacket. 'This is the art world – full of eccentrics. The ones in the suits are probably not the ones spending the money.'

In the doorway he watched as she slipped off her coat and handed it to a waiter, and then she took him by the hand and led him over to where the champagne was being served.

'Two glasses, please,' she said to the svelte youth carrying the silver salver. She took one for herself and handed the other one to Jamie. 'Cheers!'

'Cheers!' They clinked glasses and each took a rather larger sip than normal.

Missy smiled bravely and said, 'Dutch courage.'

'Do you need it?' Jamie asked.

'Oh, yes. Tonight more than ever.' Then she took him by the arm and said, 'Come and look at this. There's one painting I especially want you to see.'

Missy wove between the chattering guests and up the stairs to the first floor, where even more patrons were packed into the rooms. She negotiated her way past the canapés to the far wall, where a painting of gypsies around a campfire was hanging in splendid isolation.

'You remember the mirror-image painting I was worried about?'

Jamie nodded.

'This is it. But there's good news. We've had it verified. It's the real thing. The one in the catalogue that I found – the one that was sold in the States – that was the forgery. This is the real McCoy.'

Jamie gazed at the painting and then said quietly, 'I thought it might be.'

Missy regarded him quizzically. 'What do you mean?'

'I need to talk to you. Not here, not now, but tomorrow, after the auction.'

'Oh God!' she said. 'I'd forgotten, what with the exhibition and everything. It's tomorrow, isn't it? When you sell the stuff from Lord Bedlington.'

'Yes, but I need to see you. I think you might be able to help me sort something out.'

'Me?'

'"Fraid so. No one else will do.'

Missy looked anxious.

'Don't worry. I'm not going to give you any trouble. I just need your help.'

'OK.' Missy looked apprehensive. 'What time?'

'Around four o'clock? Can you come to the Circus? The workmen will have gone by then – they're always back at the yard by four – and we'll be alone.'

'If you're sure . . .'

'Trust me. It's about the paintings, that's all.'

Missy's expression changed. She had looked worried and preoccupied, but now she looked determined. 'I'm sorry. You must think I'm really ungrateful. Come on, I want you to meet my father.'

'What?'

'And my grandfather. I've had enough of all this pussy-footing.' Missy took Jamie by the arm and propelled him across the room to where a man in a navy blue blazer and open-necked pink shirt was standing talking to three women who appeared to be hanging on his every word. 'Dad, this is Jamie, a very good friend of mine. Jamie Ballantyne.'

At first Patrick King did not speak. He turned towards Jamie, but it appeared that he had not registered the name. 'Yes, of course,' he said absently. Then, 'Jamie? Jamie . . . Ballantyne?'

Jamie took a deep breath and held out his hand. 'Hello,' he said.

Patrick's face broke into a beaming smile. 'I'm delighted to meet you, Jamie. Thank you for coming.' He gesticulated around him. 'Bit full, I'm afraid. Sorry it's so packed. Seen anything that takes your fancy? Apart from these ladies, I mean!' The clutch of well-coiffed ladies dissolved into fits of giggles at their host's witticism. Jamie smiled politely and, to his surprise, Patrick King gave him a knowing wink and then said softly, 'Brave of you to come. Glad you did. Missy will be relieved to have your support.'

Before Jamie could reply, he felt Missy's hand on his elbow and heard her voice speak softly in his ear: 'One down, one to go . . . the big one.'

Jamie experienced a churning sensation in the pit of his stomach. It did not subside. Instead it grew to epic proportions when Missy led him up to a short, dapper man dressed in a dark grey pinstriped suit with a blue shirt and primrose-yellow tie. Jamie looked down and noticed the shiny black handmade shoes, a sharp contrast to his own battered trainers. He had seen him from a distance from time to time – you could not live in Bath and be unaware of the presence of Richard King for long – but he had never met him, or even been this close. He could detect the faint aroma of citrus as the owner of King's Fine Art turned to face him.

'Grandpa, this is Jamie Ballantyne.'

Richard King stared at Jamie for what seemed like an age. 'Is it, now?' was all he said.

Jamie, doing his best impersonation of a Harvard freshman, said, 'Good to meet you, sir,' and held out his hand.

For a moment it looked as though Richard King would ignore the gesture, but then, aware that he was surrounded by clients, and that he would appear ill-mannered were he not to respond, he shook Jamie's hand firmly and said, 'I was sorry to hear about your grandfather.'

'Thank you,' responded Jamie.

'We were at university together, you know.'

'Yes.'

And then Richard King turned back to the couple with whom he had been in conversation and it was clear to Jamie that his audience had ended.

He felt a hand on his side and heard a voice whisper in his ear, 'Well done. That's the hardest one out of the way.'

'You mean there's more?' he asked.

'Only Grandma.' Missy's words were intended to reassure, even though her own heart was now beating rapidly in her chest. She wanted Jamie to meet the woman who had been his grandfather's lover and borne his child, even though she could not tell Jamie that was so, or that it was the reason why she and he could never be together. Half of her knew it was a rash thing to do, but something deep inside impelled her to effect the meeting. Emboldened by the fact that she had already introduced him to both Patrick and Richard, she felt that meeting Eleanor would somehow lay a ghost to rest. It would clear the air, if nothing else. No more might come of her relationship with Jamie, but at least she would feel that all the parties had met one another by the end of this fateful evening, that the strands of her life were at least drawn more closely together. She was unaware that Jamie already knew that Eleanor and Harry had been lovers and, therefore, of the magnitude of this encounter.

The sweet old lady sitting on the Louis Quinze sofa between the windows looked for all the world as though she had always been a sweet old lady. Her thick, grey hair was swept back off her face, and a triple row of pearls graced her neck. She had a poise and elegance that shone through her fragile frame, and her eyes glowed. On seeing Missy coming towards her, she rose to her feet and Jamie was surprised to discover that she was almost as tall as he was. Suddenly he felt an overwhelming sense of her presence, as though he were being introduced to royalty.

'Grandma, I want you to meet someone you haven't seen since he was very small, when we used to go to school together.'

'Goodness, that's a long time ago,' said Eleanor.

'Hello,' said Jamie, this time not offering his hand, for fear of further embarrassment.

'Good heavens! Harry!' murmured Eleanor. 'I mean . . .'

'Jamie,' corrected Missy.

'Yes, of course,' agreed Eleanor. 'I'm so sorry. Just for a moment . . . Oh dear . . . how very strange.' With practised ease the old lady brushed aside her solecism and continued, 'Memory . . . silly tricks. Jamie. Of course.'

Jamie watched as Eleanor retrieved the situation, but saw, in that brief glance, the truth that shone in her eyes. For a split second she had looked at him as she must have looked at his grandfather, and he knew without a shadow of a doubt that they had indeed been lovers. Something within the old woman burned like fire. For one fleeting moment the years had fallen away and Jamie had seen that this was no 'sweet old lady' but a pretty young woman perfectly capable of sweeping a man off his feet. There was, in Eleanor's eyes, the same fire that he had seen in her granddaughter, the same fire that had captivated his grandfather all those years ago.

'Eleanor!' called a voice from across the room.

It was Richard King.

'The Bayntons are going.'

Eleanor replied almost without drawing breath, 'Coming, dear.'

'Do excuse me . . . er . . . Jamie. I must go and say goodbye to our guests. Book people, fine bindings, very skilful. It's been lovely to see you after all these years.'

Eleanor held out her hand. Jamie took it and felt a strange tingling sensation, and then she was gone, sweeping across the floor in a wonderfully diaphanous dress that had clearly not come off a peg. Eleanor King was perhaps the most elegant older woman he had ever encountered. He wondered if he would ever speak to her again.

The waiter was at his elbow. 'Another glass of champagne, sir?'

He glanced sideways at Missy, but saw that she seemed distracted. He shook his head at the waiter, kissed her lightly on the cheek and with an aching heart quietly headed for home. He had begun the day looking for answers. He had ended the day with even more questions.

38

Bath
January 2008

Not till the fire is dying in the grate,
Look we for any kinship with the stars.
'Modern Love' (1862), George Meredith

Before any auction Jamie would always get a bit of a lift. The heart rate would climb slightly, the muscles tauten and the nerves sharpen. It should really have been Peter Cathcart on the podium this particular morning, but yet again he had cried off, citing the ailment of another distant relation. The excuses were wearing thin. But then again, Jamie was glad to be in the driving seat today. From somewhere deep within him a rare seam of confidence had been mined. He would give it his best shot.

There were untold lots of brown furniture and assorted porcelain to get through before he arrived at the pictures – the star lots of this particular sale. As a result the room was only moderately full at 10.30 a.m., when the sale began. Reasonable if unspectacular prices seemed to be the order of the day. That would do. As long as there were no real embarrassments he would be happy. Leo Bedlington's furniture made a respectable amount of money, but nothing that would assure the beneficiaries of early retirement.

Around noon the room began to fill up, and at a quarter to one Jamie took a sip of water, cleared his throat and announced the first of the paintings. 'Lot two hundred and ten, the first Munnings of the day, ladies and gentlemen. The property of the late Lord Bedlington. This is the first of two paintings of gypsies that I'll be auctioning this afternoon and I have a lot of interest already, many commission bids. I'm starting the bidding at a hundred thousand pounds. Any advance on one hundred?'

'One ten, one twenty, one thirty, one forty . . .'

From behind a pillar, where she had been the last time she attended an auction at Ballantyne's, Missy watched silently as rival bidders raised their paddles or their eyebrows. On this occasion she was not bidding, but the tightening knot in her stomach was, if anything, even more acute than normal. She stared first at the floor and then at the ceiling, doing her best to keep out of Jamie's eyeline and hardly daring to breathe.

'All done, then?' Jamie raised his gavel and scanned the room to make sure he had not missed any bids. Then he looked across at the girls manning the telephones. Two had already replaced their handsets; the third was shaking her head.

'If you're all finished, then, I'm selling at eight hundred and fifty thousand pounds . . .' Jamie brought down the hammer smartly on the desk. 'Number fifty-three. Thank you sir,' he said, noting down the bidder number and the amount in his ledger.

The adrenaline was pumping now. Jamie felt buoyed up by the success of the first major lot. Swiftly he moved on to the second of the gypsy pictures. Interest was slightly less fervent here and the painting went to a telephone bidder for six hundred thousand pounds. These were still huge amounts for a provincial saleroom.

'Thank you, ladies and gentlemen, thank you.' Jamie had the novel experience of having to quieten the room in between lots. This was not a normal occurrence, but then, this was not a normal sale.

Missy found her hands were shaking. She steadied herself by putting her back to the pillar. It did not really help.

The painting of the start of the race went for seven hundred and thirty thousand pounds.

'And so, ladies and gentlemen, to our final lot: the painting of Lord Bedlington's mother on horseback and the star item in today's auction. This is one of Munnings's finest paintings and I have several commission bids. I'll start this one at five hundred thousand pounds.'

Missy's heart beat loudly in her chest. So did Jamie's, though he struggled manfully to keep his voice steady and authoritative. He caught the eye of his mother at the back of the room, staring at him over her glasses, catalogue in one hand and pen in the other. No pressure, then.

On and on went the bidding. It seemed that the world and his wife wanted this painting. Jamie took his time, savouring the moment and conducting the auction as though it were a symphony. First he would bring in this bidder and then that one; then he would glance at the girls on the telephones.

Finally all the bidders in the room had fallen out and the competition was between two telephone bids. Hawklike, Jamie darted between the two – to the left, then to the right and back again. The room was silent now, except for the sound of Jamie's voice and of a lone pigeon cooing on the glazed roof of the saleroom, as though expressing surprise at the continually rising price.

Eventually the right-hand telephone bidder dropped out and Jamie stared, gimlet-eyed, at the girl holding the handset. 'It's against you, then . . . and I'm selling . . .' He scanned the room once more to make sure that the final bid had been received. 'If you're all done, I'm selling at one million eight hundred thousand pounds . . .'

Bang! The hammer came down and the room erupted as though a winning goal had been scored in a cup final. A spontaneous round of applause followed, and Jamie could not resist a little bow. 'And that, ladies and gentlemen, concludes today's sale.'

Even the grumpy dealer, Mr Blunt, in his usual place on the front row, could not suppress a grin. 'You did well there, lad,' he muttered as Jamie left the dais and made his way through the thronging crowd to the office at the back of the saleroom. He was patted on the back at regular intervals, like a cricketer who had just scored a century, and acknowledged the approbation with an embarrassed smile and muttered thanks.

Once inside the office, he closed the door behind him and leaned against it, sighing with relief. He heard a loud 'pop', which made him jump, and turned to find his mother opening a bottle of champagne.

'I think we'll tell Peter Cathcart not to bother coming back,' she said. 'I can't believe he could have done any better.'

'Bloody lucky!' murmured Jamie.

'A bit, but well handled, too.'

Neither of them had noticed Missy behind her pillar, and she was glad of that. She slipped out of the saleroom, making a mental note of the likely total and doing her best to work out its implications.

Only one thing puzzled her: what would he do with the fifth painting, the one of her grandmother on the grey horse?

Jamie could hardly wait to see her, though at the same time he told himself not to expect too much. The sale of Lord Bedlington's effects had totalled almost four and a half million pounds. Not bad for someone who had been thought all but penniless. Missy would get around two million. Surely, with the proceeds from the exhibition, that would be enough to save King's Fine Art?

She arrived on his doorstep at four-fifteen, she who was

normally never late. He kissed her lightly on the cheek and again felt that rise in his heart rate that he always did when she was around. He closed the door behind her and said, 'It's all pretty chaotic, I'm afraid.'

'Yes,' she replied. 'It all is. But thank you so much for what you did this afternoon. You made such a difference.'

'Oh, I think they would have sold well, anyway.'

'No, I mean you made such a difference by being there. I'd rather have listened to you handling it than anyone else. It made it more . . . meaningful, I suppose.'

Jamie led the way to the attic, where he'd done his best to create some sort of order out of the mess that was domestic-life-with-the-builders-in. He'd rigged up a lamp in one corner and tossed a couple of throws over the sofa and armchair. Several piles of books were arranged to make a table, and on them stood a tray carrying a bottle of champagne and two glasses.

He motioned her to sit down on the sofa as he uncorked the champagne.

'I shouldn't really,' she said. 'I have to drive over to Dad's to give him the good news.'

Jamie handed her a glass. 'Have you told your grandfather?' he asked.

Missy nodded.

'And?' asked Jamie expectantly.

'He didn't say much – just that the money was mine and I must do with it as I see fit. He's so bloody proud. Sometimes I want to shout at him.'

'I know the feeling.'

Missy brightened. 'But thank you for this.' She raised her glass.

'My pleasure. Happy to help.'

They both drank silently, allowing the bubbles to hit the backs of their throats and seal the day's proceedings. Then

Missy asked, 'What will you do with the other painting, the one of Grandma on the horse?'

'I'll hang onto it if you don't mind. It's the one painting that isn't genuine.'

He explained about the bureau, about his grandfather and the cheque, about the letter from Leo Bedlington, and did his best to piece things together for her.

'So, you see, Granddad was given the real painting – the one you bought. The one I have is the fake. I'm sure of that – from Leo's letter. That means you have another real Munnings to sell.'

'An *embarras de richesse*,' murmured Missy.

'Well, hopefully not an *embarras*,' chided Jamie.

Missy looked apprehensive. 'So now you know about my grandmother and your grandfather.'

'Yes. They were obviously lovers before your grandmother married Richard, and that was the start of the family feud.'

'Yes,' said Missy softly. It was the closest he had come to knowing the secret she would have to keep to herself. She felt her heart beating faster, felt the beads of perspiration beginning to form on her brow. 'Can we open a window?' she asked. 'It's awfully warm up here at the top of the house.'

Jamie walked over and struggled with the latch on the attic window, finally freeing it and letting in a blast of icy air.

'And the mirror-image painting?' asked Missy, changing the subject. 'The one that we found was real . . .'

'Well, I should think John Macready sent that to your grandfather to say that he was sorry.'

'But he died in 1995. Why has it only just arrived?'

Jamie shrugged. 'Maybe they only found it when Leo Bedlington died, maybe Leo Bedlington sent it on Macready's behalf. I don't expect we'll ever know for sure, but it looks as though it was some kind of peace offering.'

'Yes, and a way of telling Grandpa that in spite of it all he still loved him.'

'Loved him?'

'When they were at college, Mac told Grandpa that he loved him. Grandpa was horrified and just sort of cut himself off from Mac. I think Mac's actions in copying the Munningses were a way of getting back at Grandpa for turning him down, as much as to make money.'

'And then there's this,' said Jamie, pulling a cheque out of another envelope. 'It's made out for half a million pounds – in favour of your grandfather.'

Missy took the cheque and looked at it. 'But it's from *your* grandfather.'

'Yes. It's the money he made from selling the painting of Eleanor. I think he felt that the money really belonged to your grandfather. Leo wanted my grandfather to have the painting for sentimental reasons, but he simply couldn't hang on to the money knowing that your grandfather was in financial difficulties, even after all these years of disliking one another.'

'But he never delivered it?' asked Missy.

Jamie shrugged. 'Apparently not.'

'And now it won't be valid anyway.'

'I've checked,' said Jamie evenly. 'Gran hasn't yet informed the bank of Granddad's death. I don't know why. I think she just forgot in the confusion of it all. If your grandfather presents it within the next few days, it should be honoured.'

'He won't do that,' countered Missy.

'It's what Granddad wanted,' said Jamie. 'Otherwise he wouldn't have gone to all the trouble of selling the painting. He never told Gran it had arrived. He kept it hidden for ten years and only took it out to sell it and help an old friend.'

'A friend who had married the girl he loved,' whispered Missy.

'Yes.'

Missy gazed into the middle distance. 'As long as I live I don't think I'll ever understand love,' she said.

'No,' agreed Jamie. 'Nor me.'

He saw her down the stairs, then kissed her softly on the cheek at the front door. He so wanted to take her in his arms and kiss her properly, and he thought he detected something in her look that wanted it, too, but she was careful to keep him at arm's length after the kiss on the cheek and he did not want to spoil whatever it was that was left.

39

Bath
January 2008

O what a tangled web we weave,
When first we practise to deceive!
'Marmion' (1808), Sir Walter Scott

The kind of sadness she felt in her heart as she left him was of a depth she had never encountered. She had not thought it possible that she could feel more distressed, but the elation she felt at the results of the sale and the relief at knowing now why all these things had happened only served to emphasise the profoundness of her sorrow.

She gripped the steering wheel of her car fiercely as she drove to her father's to tell him the day's news. His flat was in a tall block in the centre of Bath, not particularly handsome, but functional. Anyway, he seldom used it, preferring to visit the homes of his conquests and disport himself on their territory rather than his. Maybe the complexities of his parentage went some way to explaining why he felt the need to put the City of Bath behind him as often as possible.

He had better be in. He had said he would be. She rang one of the bells by the front door. After a few seconds the intercom crackled and she heard Patrick's voice. 'Hello?'

'It's me.'

'Who's me?'

'Oh, don't be stupid, Dad. Let me in.' She really had little time for his silly games tonight. With a heavy heart she climbed the stairs to his floor.

'You should have taken the lift,' he scolded as he greeted her at the door.

'It's only four flights of stairs,' she countered.

'Four too many for me,' he replied. 'Fancy a drink?'

'No, I'd better not. I've already had a glass of champagne and I've got to drive home.'

'Oh? Have we cause to celebrate, then?'

'Who knows. I think we'll have made about two million all told.'

'*You'll* have made about two million, you mean.'

'It's not mine,' said Missy. 'Not really. I can't keep it; I never knew the man.'

'No, but he knew your family – or a couple of members at any rate.'

Yes, I suppose so.' She wanted to get up and go, having given him the news, but instead, to Patrick's surprise, her knees buckled underneath her and she collapsed on to the sofa.

'Hey! What the dickens . . . ? What's all this for? You should be pleased to have done so well. You can save the firm if it means so much to you, or you can call it quits and start again on your own. Who cares? It's not that important.'

For several minutes he could get no sense out of her at all. She sat on the sofa with her head in her hands and sobbed.

Patrick came over, sat next to her and put a comforting arm round her shoulder. 'What is it?' he asked softly.

She could not recall him ever being so solicitous as to her welfare. She shook her head, unwilling to share her own woes with the man who had hardly been worth calling a father. 'Just . . . stuff,' was all she could say.

He still had his arm round her. 'What sort of stuff?'

She did not speak.

'Love stuff?' he asked.

She nodded.

'Anything to do with that man I met last night? Jamie Ballantyne?'

Again she nodded through the tears.

'I see.'

'But you don't see,' she said angrily, looking up now and scattering the tears from her cheeks. 'He's the loveliest, most gentle man I've ever met – will ever meet – and I can't have him because of . . .' Again she dissolved into tears.

'Because *his* grandfather is also *your* grandfather.'

'Y-e-s,' she wailed. 'And I don't think . . . I want to . . . live without him.' The words came out stertorously between the sobs. 'I tried hard not to want him. I went to America not just because Grandpa sent me, but because I wanted to get away, to make a fresh start, to meet other people, other men. And I did, but there was no one.'

'No one who measured up?'

'No.'

'And certainly not me.'

Missy did not like to speak. Instead she began to dry the tears with the back of her hand. 'I'm sorry. You don't want to hear all this. What is it to do with you?'

'Nothing really,' said Patrick calmly, 'but maybe that's an advantage.'

Missy looked at him questioningly.

'You never really forgave me for leaving you, did you?'

Missy made to object.

'No, don't say it. I've been a lousy dad and you have every right to treat me like the shit I've always been when it came to bringing you up.'

Missy began to fill up once more. 'But it was because of Mum. You couldn't help it. Why should you love me when she died having me? The woman you loved. What was I except the thing that caused you to lose her?'

Patrick's eyes also began to fill with tears. 'It wasn't just that. It wasn't just you.'

'What, then? What else was there?'

'I had a friend, Charlie Dunblane. He died in a car crash two weeks before your mum gave birth.' Patrick stabbed at his eyes with his fist, to knock the tears from them.

'Which made it even worse,' said Missy, who already knew about Charlie.

Patrick shook his head. 'Not for the reasons you think.'

'What do you mean?'

Patrick put his other arm round her and cradled her head in his hand. 'The reason I went away, the reason I couldn't cope here any more, the reason I didn't want to know you . . . was because you weren't my daughter. You were Charlie Dunblane's.'

The shock of hearing the words was enough to stop Missy's tears. She began to shake.

'He and your mum had a fling. He'd been drinking, so had she. I was away buying paintings for Dad. Simple as that.'

'How did you find out?' she asked, trancelike.

'Your mother confessed, out of remorse. I don't think she loved him. It was just her way of getting me to take more notice of her. I always thought I had. I adored her . . .' He could not go on. Missy held on to him as they both wept. Finally Patrick took a deep breath and found the words to continue. 'And then when she had you, she lost a lot of blood and . . . well . . . It came as a double shock, you see, and then it struck me that history was repeating itself. exactly the same had happened with Mum and Dad – Richard and Eleanor. I'm not really his son, and you're not really my daughter. What a bloody mess, eh?'

'Yes,' she murmured through the tears. 'What a bloody mess.'

'So I'm sorry. I know it must be just another shock in a

long list of them, but when you can come to terms with it, and when you stop hating me, maybe in a way you'll see it was all for the best. You'll want to know all about Charlie. I can tell you that. He wasn't a bad man; he was a good friend to me, in spite of the fact that he let me down in the worst way possible. I can't hate him; God knows I tried. You needn't worry about discovering a whole new family; there isn't one. Charlie was an orphan. He went through life not knowing who he was and then died crashing into a tree. He never did find out. I think that's why he was the hedonist he was – he felt he had nothing to lose.'

Missy tried to dry her eyes with her hands as best she could. She sat up and looked at the man she had thought was her father.

'You look quite dreadful,' he said.

'You don't look so good yourself,' she replied.

'Don't hold it against me, Missy. Don't hate me for what I did. I might be a mixed-up old sod, but I do have some feelings. Too many for my own good, I think.'

Missy smiled through the tears. 'How could I hate you? You've just told me the best thing you possibly could: that Jamie and I aren't related and there's no reason . . .'

Patrick finished the sentence for her: 'Why you can't be together?'

There were tears of joy now. She hugged him so hard that the very breath seemed to be squeezed out of him.

'You've no idea,' he said, 'how long I've had to wait to make you this happy.'

Missy considered for a moment. 'Why did you never tell Harry he was your father?'

'Oh, I nearly did, several times. I wanted the bastard to know, for revenge as much as anything, but then I reasoned that I'd be more of a bastard if I did that, and it would have upset Eleanor and Richard. I learned to live with it, as you'll have to, except that I hope it doesn't ruin your life like it did mine. Anyway,' he said, 'there's no reason to let it now, is there?'

'No,' said Missy. 'I suppose not. But I've lots of thinking to do.'

'It's a lot to take in, I know,' said Patrick. 'But you'll cope. You always have.'

40

Bath
January 2008

I don't do happy endings. I don't like to patronise my readers.

Joanna Trollope (2008)

She did not ring Jamie until the following morning. It was a Saturday. He was sitting in the attic room wondering whether to bother getting up when the call came.

'I wondered if you fancied a walk in the snow?' she asked. 'I've got something to tell you. Well, quite a lot of things, actually. Some of them might surprise you, but it's a risk I've got to take. Only, the thing is, I don't want to have any secrets from you any more. I've decided I don't like secrets.'

He was not sure how to read her tone, or her words. He met her, as she had instructed, at the foot of Beckford's Tower, high up on Lansdown Hill. The city seemed to glisten way down in the distance as he waited in the silence that only snowfall can bring. In the deep, icy stillness he saw her climbing the slope below him, saw her smile and wave as she spotted his solitary figure at the top of the hill. Then the sound of her crunching footsteps came to his ears, and the clouds of her breath were borne away on the chill air.

By the time she reached him she was panting, but her eyes were shining more than he could ever remember and her ice-cold cheeks were glowing as he bent to kiss her.

'Why this place?' he asked.

'Because you can see clearly from here,' she said.

'See what?'

Missy slipped her arms round his waist and looked over the city towards the hills. 'Out into the future.'

'Do you want to?' Jamie asked.

She turned to face him and looked searchingly into his eyes. 'Only if it's with you,' she said.

He bent to kiss her, and in that moment felt more sure of himself and more certain of anything than he had ever done before. 'Do you believe in happy endings?' he asked.

'I'll start with a happy beginning,' she said.

Author's Note

The endpapers are of a painting by Sir Alfred Munnings that exists in several versions. It is entitled 'My Wife, my Horse and Myself' and this particular example was painted in 1932–3. It shows the back of Castle House, Dedham. The horse, in this version, is Master Munn.

Extracts

An extract from *Far From the Madding Crowd* by Thomas Hardy
An extract from *Henry VI* by William Shakespeare
An extract from *Water Poetry* by Lady Wortley Montagu
An extract from *Oxford*: With 8 plates in colour from paintings by Jack
    Merriott (Our beautiful homeland) by D.Erskine Muir' with permission
    of Springer Publishing
An extract from *Wit & Mirth or Pills to Purge Melancholy* by Thomas D'Urfey
An extract by Ben Marshall
An extract from an article in *The New York Times* by Jan Morris
The poem *An Artist's Life* by Sir Alfred Munnings with permission of The
    Castle House Trust
An extract from the poem 'In a Bath Tea Shop' by Sir John Betjeman
The poem 'Shadows in the Grass' by Sir Alfred Munnings with permission
    of The Castle House Trust
The poem 'A Ballad of Bath' by Algernon Swinburne
A quote from John Ruskin
A quote by Fanny Burney
An extract from *Writers at Work* by John Updike
An extract from the Bible
An extract from the poem 'Stately Homes of England' by Noel Coward
    with permission of A&C Black
An extract from 'Sotheby's Guide for Prospective Buyers'
An extract from 'The Corsair' by Lord Byron
An extract from 'Lettre du Provincial' by Charles Peguy
An extract from *The Adventures of Sally* by P.G. Wodehouse with permission
    of Random House
An extract from 'Odes, Book 4' by Horace
An extract from 'Historia Naturalis' by Pliny the Elder
An extract from 'Pagett, MP' by Rudyard Kipling
An extract from a letter to the Daily Telegraph by Sir Alfred Munnings
An extract from *Othello* by William Shakespeare
An extract from a letter to the Sunday Telegraph by Lord Franks
An extract from *The Good-Natured Man* by Oliver Goldsmith
An extract from *Of Revenge* by Francis Bacon
The poem 'Epicene' by Ben Johnson
An extract from *Emma* by Jane Austen
An extract from 'La Belle Dame Sans Merci' by John Keats
An extract from *Hydriotaphia* by Sir Thomas Browne
19th Century Proverb
An extract from *Aenid, Book 4* by Virgil
The poem 'On with the Dance' by Noel Coward with permission of A&C
    Black
Yorkshire Proverb
An extract from a letter to Thomas Moore by Lord Byron
An extract from *Modern Love* by George Meredith
An extract from 'Marmion' by Sir Walter Scott
Extract by Joanna Trollope. Used with kind permission of United Agents